Praise for "Lady,

"*The Tudors, but not as we think we k*
which speak to us down the centuries, an
dilemmas and trials are timeless
—Annie Whitehead, author of The Sins of the Father

"*[A] delightful read that continues with Heenan's idea of having characters who would traditionally have been seen as side characters in other historical fiction novels as the heroes of their own stories. A story full of love, heartache, and intrigue that fans of historical fiction will adore.*"
—Heidi Malagisi, Adventures of a Tudor Nerd

"*This is a beautiful and timeless novel of a marriage unfolding and growing in love.*"
—Laury Silvers, author of The Sufi Mysteries Quartet

"*A nuanced portrait of a young woman finding her way within both the dangerous world of Tudor politics and a far-from-conventional marriage.*"
—Marian L Thorpe, author of Empire's Heir

"*To read this book is like watcing it all being acted out in front of you.*"
—Discovering Diamonds Historical Fiction Review Blog

"*A love story that beautifully exhibits how true love is neither instant nor static, but a growing together of two hearts over time.*"
—Eva Seyler, author of This Great Wilderness

This is a work of fiction. Names, characters, incidents, and dialogues are products of the author's imagination and are not to be construed as real. Any resemblance to actual events or persons, living or dead, is entirely coincidental.

©2022 Karen Heenan

All rights reserved. No part of this publication may be reproduced in any form without prior written permission from the publisher, except for use in brief quotations as permitted by United States copyright law.

E-book ISBN: 978-1-957081-04-5
Paperback ISBN: 978-1-957081-05-2
Audiobook ISBN: 978-1-957081-07-6

Cover design and illustration ©2021 Anthony O'Brien. Image used under license from Shutterstock. All rights reserved

Interior layout ©2022 Eva Seyler.
Typeset in Adobe Garamond Pro and Gondola.

Lady, in Waiting

KAREN HEENAN

Table of Contents

All shall be well, and all shall be well,
and all manner of things shall be well…

For there is a force of love
moving through the universe
that holds us fast and will never let us go.

~Julian of Norwich

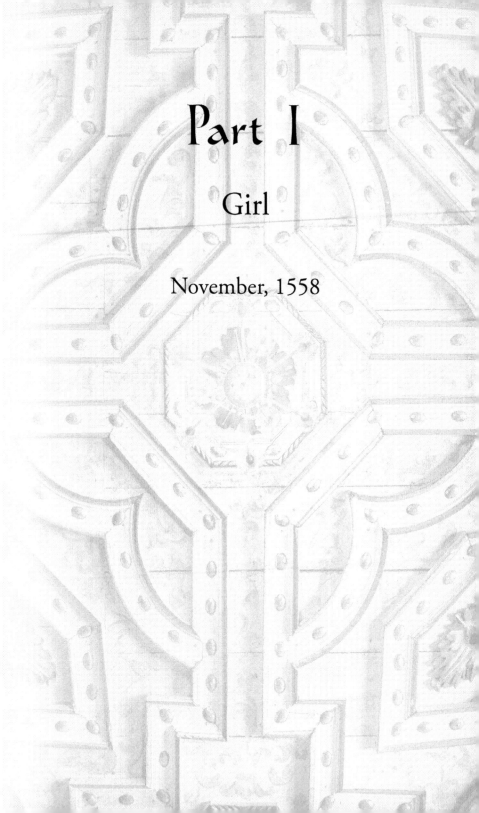

Part I

Girl

November, 1558

Chapter 1

IF MY FATHER HADN'T lost his head, my life would be very different. In point of fact, he did not *lose* his head; it was severed from his body with three strokes of an ax.

I should know. I was there.

One day I was a happy child, the center of a loving family, and the next my father was dragged from the house, accused of treason, and executed. My family left England, and I grew to womanhood far from home.

With such uncertain beginnings, a young woman might find herself capable of anything. She might wish to escape her situation so badly that she proposes marriage to a man she's just met, thinking it will give her some measure of control over her life.

Less than a week after our wedding, my husband left for England. My grandmother and I followed on the next ship.

We had been out of England eighteen years, during which time Winterset had become Robin Lewis's home. It was one of the reasons I married him. When he first appeared at our isolated home in Normandy, I resented his presence, but I quickly realized he was a solution, not another problem: he was more acceptable than the men put forward by my mother and her husband, and if I married him, my grandmother could return to her beloved estate.

Tall and bony, with red hair gone thin in the back and a decided way about him, Robin was not my dream husband, but then I'd never dreamed of marriage. I knew only the sort of man I did not want, and if Mama had her way, those men would soon be lining up in the lane, eager to claim my inheritance.

Family money aside, most men wouldn't consider me a prize. While I was young, and looked well enough, I had been raised away from society and my manners showed it. I read books that young ladies did not read. My opinions were strong, and I had been known to raise my voice in company and interrupt my betters.

Such behavior was not cherished by my mother, and my stepfather found me troublesome in the extreme. He tried various methods to break my will, and I ran away to my grandparents after one incident, having forced a stable lad to swap clothes so I could travel unnoticed. After close questioning, my grandfather declined to return me to their care. With my grandfather, I could live as I pleased—within reason. After his death, Grand-mère deflected my mother's marital plans until I made one of my own. Then she fell in with my scheme, deeming it no worse than theirs, and possibly—when she realized we would return to England—far better.

Robin was the one who balked. He claimed to be too old and set in his ways, and that I would not be happy. I bribed him with Winterset, and a promise not to disturb the peaceful life he'd built there. I was an heiress, I blithely assured him, and could make a new marriage when he died of old age.

But I didn't want that. I didn't know Robin well—he did not allow himself to be easily known—but I liked him. In time, I thought we could learn to care for each other.

When the coach stopped, Grand-mère peered through the window, a gloved hand at her throat. "Do you remember any of it, Margaery?"

I remembered the tall limestone gate through which we had just passed, the gate where I had been playing the day my father was taken. "I think so. A bit."

"Hmm." She sounded doubtful.

The cart with our belongings stopped behind us, and Leon climbed down, glancing around the empty courtyard. "Should I knock, *madame?*"

Before he could raise the knocker, the round-topped door swung open and a young maidservant appeared. Her mouth fell open when Grand-mère informed her we had come to stay, but she ushered us inside, seating us at the hall table and bringing cups of ale. "The master is away from home." She twisted her apron in reddened hands. "I will send a boy for Fowler. He'll know what is to be done."

Grand-mère inspected the pewter cup—for quality or cleanliness? "Fowler is still here?"

"He's been here since before I was born, m'lady."

"Fowler was my husband's steward," she said. "This was my house."

She sat with a cushion at her back while I paced the floor. The fire thawed the chill from my flesh but did nothing for the icy sliver of worry in my heart. Why was Robin not here to welcome us?

Nearly an hour passed before Fowler burst into the hall, tearing off his cap at the sight of my grandmother. "Welcome back, my lady."

"Thank you, Fowler. It is good to be home." She put a hand on my shoulder. "Do you not recognize my granddaughter?"

A hasty bow in my direction. "Little Mistress Margaery, welcome."

"The girl said Master Lewis is away." Grand-mère was never one to hide her displeasure. "When will he return?"

Fowler's face, weathered by decades of outdoor work, grew pale at her question. "I'm not certain," he muttered. "He was called to London."

I'd never been to London. Couldn't he have waited a few more days?

"Well, that is a shame. He promised to be here." She glanced at me. *Stop fidgeting, child.*

He rocked on his heels. "As I said, it was unexpected."

I looked around and saw little evidence my husband had ever been here. "How long has he been gone?"

"Nine days. We hope to hear something soon."

"I would hope so," Grand-mère said crisply. "I have come all this way to deliver his bride."

Fowler choked. "Master Lewis has taken a wife?"

"He has." I nearly curtsied, remembering just in time that he was a servant. "Little Mistress Margaery is now Mistress Lewis."

As Leon and the Winterset servants emptied the cart, the hall filled with our things: chests of clothes; small furnishings; crates of silver and pewter plate; wall hangings; the great bed Grand-mère brought from Winterset to France and back again.

When we found our possessions in her old room and not one of the smaller chambers, the maid explained simply, "The master sleeps in the corner chamber. They say he likes to hear the sea."

"He will soon change," Grand-mère told her. "That chamber is too small for a married couple, but it will suit me well enough."

While she rested, I explored the rest of the house and found it surprisingly familiar. Wandering its rooms, I recalled the carved overmantel in the hall and the triple mullioned windows in the room which had been my grandfather's office and was now Robin's library. I lingered there, trying to get a sense of my husband from his books. There were volumes in English, French, German, and Latin. Histories and religious texts abounded, but there was also philosophy, literature, and even some verse. My fingers hovered over a slim book of Wyatt's poems, but it was not my place to borrow his books without asking.

Much was the same, and yet much was different, because when we left, the furnishings went with us, and Grand-mère had returned with only the best pieces, on the assumption that Robin had furnished the house.

He had, but it was an odd assortment. A few carved chests, an exceptional convex mirror in the hall, some painted wall hangings. Most of the furniture was plain, serviceable stuff. It apparently suited him, but my grandmother's disappointment was palpable.

"Will you send for more of your things?"

"It would cost too much," she said. "But I did think, as an officer of the court, that Master Lewis would have more refined tastes."

Robin hadn't been an officer of the court when he took the house, and he didn't strike me as the sort who cared about his surroundings so long as his basic needs were met.

I peeked into his bedchamber, remembering it as the room where I'd slept between my parents. The maid was right: the murmur of the sea was audible through the closed shutters. I sat on the edge of the green-curtained bed and imagined my possessions fitted in with his, and smiled.

I would not mind starting my married life in this room

Chapter 2

ROBIN DID NOT ARRIVE for four days, during which my grandmother began to set the house to rights. He had been absent for some years, and though the place had been cared for, it showed, to her eyes, a lack of attention. I watched her marshal the servants and did what I was told, but even when occupied, my thoughts returned to the missing master of the house.

"I'm not sure about this." She gestured at the painted hanging on the wall opposite the hall fireplace. "It's a bit gaudy."

"I like it." The bright colors and leafy pattern were pleasing, and I thought it could only be improved by adding a repetition of the design to the plastered areas between the ceiling beams.

Grand-mère indulged my fancies but this was her home. "Definitely gaudy." She directed Fowler's men to carry the pieces of her great bed upstairs. "Leave them in the hall until the master returns. Then we shall sort out the sleeping arrangements."

Alice brought breakfast to our bedchamber each morning, and while we ate, Grand-mère lectured me on what to expect in my new situation. "Marriage," she said, "benefits the man more than the woman."

Most things did. Why should marriage be any different?

My finger crept to my mouth as I thought about my husband, and where he might be. The longer he stayed away, the more I wondered if he'd had a change of heart.

"Margaery." Her voice was imperious. "Hands."

I looked surreptitiously at my nails, which had grown ragged in the last few days. "I'd better fetch my work basket." Embroidery was how I kept worry at bay. Riding was better, but stitching was more ladylike and less damaging to the complexion, according to Grand-mère.

"Let me see." She peered across the table and sighed. "I hope Master Lewis doesn't mind a wife who chews her fingers like a child."

She didn't mean to be harsh; she hadn't rested since the wedding, supervising the packing as well as trying to turn her headstrong granddaughter into a satisfactory wife. It was enough to turn the kindest woman sharp, and while I loved her dearly, I understood she wasn't always the kindest of women.

"Please go on." I rummaged in my basket.

"A man needs someone to keep his house and raise his children," she told me, as if she hadn't herself taken over the keeping of the house.

"Surely there is more to marriage?"

Her gray eyebrows drew together. "You'll find those are the important things. A man may say he wants intelligent conversation, but what he really wants is a full belly, a warm body, and children who don't cry when he's trying to work."

"I don't think he's like that." I cut a length of pink silk to continue working on the gloves I'd begun aboard ship.

"He is not all higher things, that husband of yours." She looked at me beneath lowered lids. "He did consummate the marriage."

The problem was, of course, that he had not. Wanting to give me time to accustom myself to the idea of intimacy—but knowing proof would be required—Robin cut his arm and bloodied the sheet himself. As far as my grandmother was concerned, I was a properly bedded wife.

What would happen when he returned? Would he bed me then? Despite my grandmother's morning lectures, I still had no idea what to expect. When my mother remarried, I moved out of her bed and into a trundle, but that lasted only one night because I thought, behind the closed bed curtains, that my new stepfather was trying to kill her. I was given my own chamber the next day, but their mysterious carryings-on could be heard through the door.

A woman's body belonged to her husband. Having observed Robin, I thought he would not be rough or uncaring, as my stepfather seemed to be, but I could not be sure. He treated me with utmost politeness, and his speech varied from the avuncular to a directness that disregarded my gender, neither of which seemed the usual way to address a wife.

Yet I had spoken more of physical relations with him than either of the women who should have enlightened me. Bed sport did not appear to interest him greatly, but according to my grandmother, that was a ruse to make me more pliable.

"Men have urges," she said. "If you are lucky, the act becomes pleasant over time. Even if you do not enjoy it, the children make it worthwhile."

I hadn't thought about children. They were certainly a consequence of marriage but some couples were not blessed. My parents had no more after me, and my mother's second marriage was childless.

Grand-mère advised me to become pregnant as soon as possible, and that Robin should keep trying until I fell; then he could rest. "Don't expect him to be faithful while you're breeding, either. Men have—"

"Urges." It occurred to me that my grandparents had four children. "Was Grandfather faithful to you?"

"Your grandfather was a paragon." She folded her hands, the gold marriage band glinting in the light from the narrow window. "And Winterset was quite isolated."

"It still is."

I stayed at my stitching while she napped, wondering how to let Robin know I was ready for marriage. I wasn't certain I was, but he was a kind man—and he'd waited weeks already. His patience, if Grand-mère was to be believed, would not last forever.

I did not know if her advice could be trusted, and my small knowledge of my husband did not help. The one thing I was relatively certain of was Robin's fidelity. A man who had been alone for fifty years was not likely to seek out a mistress once he had a wife, no matter how disappointing I turned out to be.

Grand-mère suggested that I take the small room behind Robin's library as my parlor. It had been used for storage during his absence, and after Leon moved the great cheeses and sacks of roots to the larder, it was very nearly empty. Fowler said there was little in the attics, but I ventured up with the maid to see for myself.

After diligently inspecting the items stored in the dim, slant-ceilinged space, I found nothing worth carrying downstairs. I wandered to the unglazed window at the front of the house, my eye caught by the dust dancing in the small square of light. It was from there I saw, far along the coast road, three figures on horseback.

My throat constricted. "I believe that is my husband."

The maid left what she was doing and joined me. "I've never met the master, but that is surely Brother Anselm."

"Who is Brother Anselm?" I stepped back as she latched the shutter.

The girl looked at me, as if wondering at my ignorance. "Brother Anselm lives here, mistress." She fled to warn the other servants of the master's imminent arrival.

I followed more slowly, rubbing my neck. Who else lived in this house that I did not know about?

Word had spread by the time I reached the hall. Grand-mère stood by the fire, clad as always in a dark gown and an old-fashioned gabled headdress. "Hurry, Margaery, they're almost here." Her lips compressed into a thin line as she inspected me. "What a shame you haven't time to change."

At the first sound of hooves on cobbles, Fowler strode forward and flung open the door. "Welcome back, Master Lewis!"

I followed, but Grand-mère caught my arm. "Stay here," she said. "That is what he expects of you."

Was it? I checked that my coif was straight, and smoothed the skirt of my gray kirtle. Voices drifted in from the courtyard—Robin; his manservant, Sebastian; and a third, the mysterious Anselm.

As they entered, Robin was speaking intently to the older man. When he removed his cloak, he saw us for the first time. His face registered a variety of emotions, but his words were simple. "You've arrived."

"Welcome, Master Lewis." Grand-mère's curtsy was exquisite.

He raised her up, kissing her hands. "Thank you, Lady Margaret. It is good to be home. I'm sure you feel the same."

"I did not think I would ever see this place again." Her cheeks flushed; something about him turned her girlish.

I watched their interaction, torn between wanting his attention and appreciating a moment to observe him. This was my husband.

Robin looked at me then, his pale eyes wary. "Hello, wife."

I curtsied, as submissive as Grand-mère could want. "Hello, husband. I am thankful for your safe return."

He smiled unevenly. "No more than I am." He kissed me on both cheeks, then took my hand. "Margaery, you remember Sebastian."

"Of course." I smiled, and Seb broke into a shy grin, his teeth bright in his dark face. It had not taken much to win him over.

"And this," Robin said, "is Anselm."

The man shuffled forward, his movements stiff. He appeared to be Grand-mère's age; I couldn't imagine the ride from London had been easy for a man of his years.

My reverence was deeper than the one I made to my husband. "I'm very pleased to meet you, sir."

He bowed over my hand. "And I you, Mistress Margaery. I have waited a long time to see Robin wed."

"Anselm has known me since I was a boy." He guided the older man to a bench. "So he has had quite a wait."

At Grand-mère's whispered direction, I excused myself and ran upstairs to change into something more suitable for a celebratory feast, leaving her to speak with the men.

When I returned, she and Anselm were alone by the fire, silent, and apparently content. I ducked into the kitchen to help Mistress Dunham with her preparations, and found her giving orders to the two maids, as well as Fowler and Sebastian. Caught short, she would nevertheless produce a supper to Grand-mère's exacting standards.

The day's pottage had been improved with bacon and spices, scenting the air. A joint of beef was brought forth beautifully crusted from the flames and settled on a platter. Stewed turnips and a fresh-baked loaf joined the meat, all served on our recently-unpacked pewter plate.

Fowler and Leon carried wine, beer, and ale from the buttery and set them upon the table. Dried fruit and raisins brought from France were heaped in bowls, all to welcome the master of the house.

"All is ready, mistress." The maid looked from my grandmother to me, confused as to who bore the title.

Grand-mère sat at the foot of the table, opposite the master's chair. By right of marriage, that position was mine, but I was content to sit beside Robin—except his seat was empty. "Where is he?"

Anselm inclined his head. "Getting reacquainted with his library." The door was closed. "Should I...?"

Seb slung a leg over the bench. "I'll get him."

"Let me do it." I might as well learn how he responded to interruption.

My knock garnered no reply, and I opened the door. Robin stood before the cold hearth, one arm on the mantel, his face hidden in the crook of his elbow.

"Robin?"

He gathered himself quickly. "Yes?"

Foolishly, I curtsied again. "Will you join us for supper?"

"Ah." He straightened and shook himself, oblivious to the fact that I was now clad in the blue gown I had worn for our wedding. "Yes, of course."

"Would you rather have a plate in here?"

"Part of me would," he said, smiling faintly, "but I now live in a civilized household. I will adapt."

After the meal was over, I went to my parlor to ignore my embroidery. Sitting on a stool borrowed from upstairs, I rested my elbows on the deep sill and stared out the window. It was snowing, flakes drifting lazily from a slate-colored sky.

My husband was on the other side of the wall. He had returned to his lair as soon as manners allowed, after imparting the shocking news that we would not live at Winterset, but instead travel to London.

"London," I said into the silence that followed his announcement. "I thought you wanted peace."

He looked up, but his eyes saw none of us. "I do. And we will work toward that end."

I was to be one of the queen's ladies-in-waiting, he informed me. My grandmother clasped her hands; Robin was already over-performing his husbandly duties with this unexpected elevation. I was happy to hear we would not leave until after Christmas.

Before I became a lady-in-waiting, I needed to learn to be a wife.

We retired early. I hoped for conversation—an explanation of his absence—but my hopes were dashed. Robin undressed behind the screen, said his prayers, and was asleep before Alice had taken my hair down.

After I was changed into my nightdress, I got into bed and stretched my toes toward the warm brick Alice had placed there, nudging Robin in the process. He did not wake.

His quiet breathing made me realize there was nothing worse than listening to someone else sleep when I could not. Closing my eyes, I tried to quiet my thoughts, but questions bubbled like a pot left too long over the fire. In France, Robin had spoken of his desire to never leave Yorkshire again, yet the life he outlined tonight would be far from that peaceful prospect.

And where had he been all this time? He'd promised to have the house made ready, and instead, all was in shambles, giving Grandmère the opportunity to sweep in and arrange everything to her liking.

Winterset was hers again. We might as well go to London. If we stayed on, we would only be her tenants.

Chapter 3

NOTHING CHANGED IN THE week after Robin's return. I saw him at meals and briefly before bed. He was distant and polite, speaking to me as if I were a cat who'd wandered into the room. The warmth I'd felt in France—had I imagined it?

He plowed through his breakfast like one starved, tipping back a cup of ale to wash it down. "Well," he said, and pushed back his chair, "I'm off."

His destination was obvious. "Wouldn't you rather do something together?"

Robin looked over his shoulder; in his mind, he was already in his library. "I'm sure you can find something to occupy yourself."

The door closed behind him.

Not for the first time, I wondered what I'd gotten myself into. The odd conversation we'd had the night before he left for England came back to me.

"What do you want from this marriage, Margaery?"

I was not accustomed to being asked what I wanted. After some thought, I told him the truth.

"I want to feel safe."

The moment the words left my lips, I also wanted to disappear, mortified to have revealed such weakness to a man I barely knew.

He seemed unbothered. "Ours may not be the most conventional marriage, but I can guarantee your safety."

It surprised me that I wanted more than security. My grandparents were my exemplar, and there was an element of partnership in their marriage—they got through the difficult months after my father's death by drawing strength from each other. "I would like the kind of union my grandparents had."

Robin was still, listening. "And what kind of union was that?"

How to put it into words? When I thought of them, it was as allies, holding fast against the world. Even after his death, my grandfather's spirit was with her; unlike my mother, while she was saddened by the loss of her husband, she was not broken.

"They were one," I said vaguely. "In their thoughts, their decisions. I believe they always knew, no matter what, that their spouse would support them." My voice shook. "That is what I want."

"Darling girl, you have my support," he said. "I may not be capable of the kind of affection you want, but what I have to give is yours."

The question was, what did he have to give—and what did I want from him?

The previous night I instructed Alice to bring wine to our room, a reminder of our wedding night. I thought sharing a drink might lead to something other than sleep, but when he finished, he spiked his fingers through his hair and declared he was too tired even for prayers, and went to bed.

I spent another hour lying awake, wondering what I'd done wrong—why he lay beside me each night, still as a tomb effigy. After this much time, he no longer had the excuse of being exhausted by his journey.

It had to be me.

The snow had blown away overnight, but the sky—pearl gray and smooth as the inside of a bowl—gave the promise of more later. The moors spread before us in shades of brown and gray, streaks of white in the deepest hollows where the sun had yet to reach.

Robin had rolled out of bed in the morning and shaken himself like a dog. "Ride with me," he said. "I cannot see England from my library, and I've been too long in other countries."

"I wouldn't know anything about that," I returned, making him laugh.

It was pure pleasure to be on horseback again, although I dared not risk a gallop on Anselm's gelding, which was not accustomed to the sidesaddle. A sedate ride was unsatisfying; I would ask Robin to purchase a mare for my use. Surely I would need a riding horse in London.

We passed a pleasant hour exploring the manor lands, familiar to me as the edges of a dream after waking. Below the house, behind the stone barn, was a cluster of shabby cottages for the estate workers.

Sheep rambled on the far hillsides; the rye fields were brown stubble that crunched beneath our horses' hooves.

I led him to Bowman's Hill, my favorite spot—not so much to share it as from a desire to see it again myself. It was the highest point on the estate, a slow-rising hill topped with a circle of fallen stones that had once been a watch tower. Now it was a pile of rubble no higher than my waist, but from there, you could see across the moors on one side and the pastures on the other.

"Where were you?" I'd been waiting for Robin to tell me on his own, but he seemed content not to discuss anything of substance.

"When?" He squinted at the cottages. Smoke from their roof-openings drifted straight up in the still air.

"When we arrived." Perhaps it wasn't the best time—Grand-mère had warned me never to question a man before he'd eaten.

"Did you not get my letter?"

I squeezed back on the reins and brought my horse to a standstill. "I received no letter. And the servants would say no more than that you were away."

"They didn't know where I was." He brought his horse close to mine and the gelding ducked its head, nickering softly. "I'm sorry you were concerned."

I exhaled; he wasn't angry, at least. "What about the letter?"

Robin shrugged. "I suppose it was lost. Sebastian gave it to the cook for safekeeping."

"If she had it, I'm certain she would have given it over."

"It's of no consequence." He reached across and put his hand over mine on the pommel. "All is well now."

I was glad to hear it, but I wondered what had been wrong before that prompted his assurance.

I had debated with myself all morning; Robin's words should have been enough, but if the letter had not been lost, I wanted to read it. After dinner was done and Grand-mère safely upstairs, I made my way to the kitchen.

Many happy hours of my childhood had been spent there getting under Mistress Dunham's feet. It was a warm and fragrant place, with crockery piled on a tall dresser and a broad hearth over which a chimney crane and pot swung. In front of the fire was a rack with a cradle spit, and the table held several limp grouse which would soon be roasting there.

"It is good to be home, Mistress Dunham." I ran my hand along the tabletop, polished smooth by generations of use.

"It is good to have you back, Mistress Margaery." She took up one of the grouse, correcting herself immediately. "Mistress Lewis."

A small pottery bowl held a few speckled eggs. I picked one up, turned it in my fingers. "Master Lewis left a letter for me when he went away. Do you know what happened to it?"

She began to pluck, her fingers moving rapidly over the small bird. "Sebastian said not to give it to you."

"Why?" I kept my voice level, though I wanted to scream the question.

"I don't know." Her gaze was on the planked floor. "He said I should give it over only if we received word of the master's death."

"His death!" A white pinfeather clung to the egg. I scraped it loose and watched as it floated to join the grouse's gray-brown feathers on the floor.

One of the maids entered with a basket, and the rush of cold air from outside made me yank my shawl up around my neck. She saw us and ducked into the buttery.

"He said I should wait." She plucked the bird so energetically that the flesh tore.

"But it makes no difference now." I was not accustomed to exercising authority, and hid my clenched fists in my skirts so she would not see my discomfort.

She hesitated. "He said, only if the master was dead."

My face grew hot. "Is Sebastian the master here? Or the mistress?" It was unkind to threaten her; she'd been with my family for decades—yet apparently, her loyalty was now to Sebastian.

Clearly unwilling, Mistress Dunham put the bird aside and wiped her hands on her apron. She slid her fingertips along the top of the dresser until she found the letter, offered it wordlessly, and returned to the grouse.

I retreated to my parlor, which had acquired more furniture when Robin realized I had taken it over. Settling myself in the small chair near the brazier, I broke the seal and cast my eyes over a page written in Robin's close, slanted writing.

My dearest wife,

Please accept my apologies for being absent upon your long-awaited return to your home. It was, alas, unavoidable, but I feel no better for that fact.

I discovered, upon my own return to Winterset, that it would have been better had I lingered a few days more in your very pleasant company, for I have been arrested. Only the weather has delayed our departure for London. The charge is heresy, which is punishable by death— unless I recant. Possibly even if I recant.

If you are reading this, I am either in the Tower or have already met my fate at Smithfield, no more than a breath of smoke on the wintry air.

It pains me that we will not meet again. While the making of our marriage was unusual, I would have you know that its brief span was a time of peace and happiness for me. I have lived alone by choice, but in our short acquaintance, I came to see that I could easily learn to care for you.

You are an interesting, challenging young woman, and the plan you stated will be achieved, somewhat earlier than expected. You will be a widow of some standing, especially when the new queen comes to the throne. Prospective husbands will flock to Winterset, and you may interview them and turn them away at will. I hope the process proves enjoyable.

I have asked Sebastian to return to you upon my death. If his service does not comport with your own desires, send him to my friend, Sir Edward Pickering, who will give him a place and all that he deserves, for

his love and care of me.

Also in the house you will find Anselm, who has these twenty years been known as my uncle. He is not; he was a brother at Hatton Priory, and an important part of my childhood. I owe him a very great debt, and I hope you will permit him to spend his remaining years at Winterset.

I will close now, else I will go on writing until morning, and I do not wish my captor to read this.

You will be in my prayers until my last breath.

Your husband,
Robert Gideon Lewis

The pottage roiled in my stomach, and I pressed my fingers to my lips. Tales of the burnings had reached us in France, and Robin mentioned he fled England because of such a charge. Why had he not told me?

Voices intruded. I moved to the window, the letter dropping from my fingers. Sebastian was in the yard with Fowler, the reins of the horse I'd ridden earlier looped around his hand. Until this moment, I had liked Seb, but he had deprived me of Robin's words—possibly his last words—for some caprice of his own, and turned Mistress Dunham against me. I could not allow such behavior to stand.

How had Robin escaped? And had he literally escaped, or did the queen die before the sentence could be carried out? Had he been in the Tower? He obviously didn't want to talk about it, and I could not ask Sebastian; he wouldn't speak unless Robin gave him leave, anyway. This filled me with respect and irritation in equal measure.

I shoved the letter into my embroidery basket, under the soft, multi-colored silks, and sank back before the brazier, marveling that while we were being tossed by the North Sea, Robin was being carried off to London to face execution.

Chapter 4

SOUNDS FROM THE HALL recalled me to myself. Putting thoughts of the letter aside, I assumed my seat at the table with a muttered apology, and Anselm said the grace. Tainted by my conversation with Mistress Dunham, the grouse held no interest, but the platter of roast meat made my mouth water.

"It's not the season for mutton, is it?" In addition to the meat, there was a silver bowl of mustard sauce alongside.

"Fowler found her on the hill," Robin told me. "She was down, one of her legs broken." He cut the beast's throat and dragged her back to the barn, where he and Seb did the butchering.

I made a mental note to avoid the area until all evidence of the bloody deed was washed away. I liked mutton, but I also liked sheep, and the sight of too much blood made me see spots.

"When do you expect to leave for London, Rob?" Anselm served himself with turnips and a large hunk of bread; he ate little meat.

"In a few weeks." Robin put several slices of mutton on my plate. "It will depend on the weather."

The Yorkshire roads were treacherous in winter, more often bogged with mud than frozen, and he had already made the journey twice. I could understand his reluctance.

Grand-mère gave him a dimpled smile. "I cannot believe my granddaughter is to be lady-in-waiting to the new queen."

"Neither can your granddaughter." I speared a bit of mustard-covered meat with my knife.

Robin leaned to one side so Seb could pour the ale. His shoulder brushed mine, and he moved quickly away. "It was not my plan."

"I thought you were done with the court, after Cromwell?" Anselm's tone was even but there was another meaning behind his question.

"It is difficult to refuse a royal request." His eyes closed briefly. "I believe Elizabeth will be a just queen."

"And I believed that of her sister." Anselm's knife clattered to the table. "You'll excuse me?"

"What did he mean?" I watched as he disappeared into the chapel.

"Nothing for you to worry about." He sounded calm, but I heard the control behind his words. Robin showed nothing unless he meant to.

Robin often removed his own clothes, to save Seb the embarrassment of ministering to him in my presence. I waited at the table, my eyes closed, listening to his progress.

"Shall I pour?" My hand hovered over the pitcher.

He put his things on the bench and stood before the dying fire wearing only his shirt. Away from its heat, the room was frigid. If we were to talk this night, it would either be there, or in the warmed bed.

"I'd prefer to sleep, if you don't mind."

He did look tired. Sebastian had shaved him upon his return, having promised me in France that I would have a beardless husband, and his bare face showed his weariness. "May I ask a question?"

"Of course."

"What did Anselm mean?"

"Nothing," he said. "We disagree on many things."

They might disagree but it did not stop the older man from caring deeply for Robin. It was clear Anselm considered my husband as a son.

"Are they things you cannot tell a wife?" His expression showed my coaxing tone was the wrong approach.

"They are things of which I choose not to speak." He blew out the candle.

We said our separate prayers and got into bed, and I knelt on the shifting feather mattress to close the curtains. The warming-stone had done its work: with the thick coverlet and the curtains, we would be snug until morning.

He crossed his hands on his chest. "Good night, wife."

"Good night." I settled myself, and immediately sat up again. "Ouch."

"What is it?" Robin raised himself on one elbow.

"My hair." I pulled it from beneath me. "Alice forgot to braid it."

Robin had braided my hair on our wedding night, and every night after until he left for England, but he hadn't offered since his return. I had asked Alice to leave it loose in the hopes he would notice.

"Nonsense." He ducked out of bed and returned with a ribbon. "Let's see if I can manage this without making a light." Taking the thick mass into his hands, he divided it into parts and commenced to work. I closed my eyes, enjoying the feeling of being tended to.

"There." He flipped the braid over my shoulder. "Better?"

"Better." I leaned back against his chest, testing his reaction. I didn't expect him to fall in love with me, but if men had needs, as I had been assured by both my mother and grandmother that they did, why did he not take advantage of my presence in his bed? Even if I was not appealing, I was there.

He shifted away from me. "Sleep now, Margaery."

"Why do you call me wife without being a husband?" It was easier, in the dark, to say words that made me blush. Men could say whatever they wished, but a female had limits on her speech. If my elders were to be trusted, I should deal with him in roundabout fashion, but that seemed the wrong approach for a man like Robin, who, if nothing else, had dealt fairly with me.

"I would not have this conversation now."

"You never talk to me," I said, "not about anything important. I thought I married a man of letters."

"Of letters," he said. "Not of words."

"Nonsense." I used his own word against him. "You talk to Sebastian."

With a great thrashing, he turned over onto his stomach. "That is different."

"Why?" I could feel his breath on my cheek; it was strangely intimate. "He's your servant. I'm your wife."

"Seb has been with me for twenty years."

"Whereas I am new, and unworthy of your trust." A tear slipped down my nose and was absorbed into the pillow. "Will it take twenty years to trust me?"

He was so still I thought he slept, but then he spoke. "I did not think you desired that sort of marriage."

"What woman speaks of such matters? I was far enough from comfort when I asked you to marry me." I turned over again, to stare at the invisible ceiler, tears leaking from the corners of my eyes. "How freakish do you think I am?"

"Not freakish." He sat up against the carved headboard. "Very special and unusual, else I would not have accepted your proposal."

"Why did you accept it, sir?"

He found my hand. "Do not call me sir. I am your husband."

"And don't wives often call their husbands thus?" I retorted. "I am trying to be such a wife as you would expect."

"I expect no such formality," he said, "but I would have my wife expect no light behavior from me."

My brow wrinkled as I parsed his meaning. "What lightness? Treating me as a husband treats a wife is in the Bible, even your English Bible. We are commanded to bring children into the world."

His sigh was enough to stir the bed curtains. "I have seen more of the world than you, and it is not fit for children."

My hand was still in his. "Our parents likely felt the same."

"Not mine."

"You don't know that."

"You're right." Releasing my fingers, he swung his legs out of bed. I thought I had driven him away, but he came back carrying the wine he had earlier refused. "Here."

I took the cup. "I thought you were tired?"

"That was when I thought I would be permitted to sleep." There was a smile in his voice. "Drink deep, wife."

I drank, wondering what I had started. "I did not mean to keep you from your rest."

"And yet you have." He touched the rim of his cup to mine. "It's all right, Margaery. You are entitled to know some things."

"What things?" The wine slowed the fluttering in my chest. "You've made it clear I cannot ask where you were, or what there is between you and Anselm, or why you trust Sebastian more than me, or why you haven't consummated our marriage." I finished my drink quickly. "And those are just this evening's questions."

He dropped his cup over the side, and it rolled beneath the bed with a hollow clank. "I was doing my best not to be burned alive," he said. "Forgive me if I choose not to dwell on it. I can't forgive Anselm because I betrayed him, and he forgave me. I trust Sebastian because he's risked his life for me, more than once." He inhaled sharply. "And I have not consummated our marriage because it would be an obscenity."

"Am I so unattractive to you?" Hot shame washed over me, and I ducked under the covers.

"No!" He cupped my shoulder with his hand. "It's because you're young and lovely and I am...not."

I sniffed. "Were you lovely when you were young?"

Robin snugged me in against him. "I was never lovely enough for you, but now I could be your father. There is the same number of years between us as there was between King Henry and little Kat Howard." His tone was bitter. "He was nearly fifty when he married her, and she but seventeen."

"It is not the same." I swallowed my frustration. "I am a full seven years older than the child the king married."

"It feels the same from where I stand."

He was very warm, and I burrowed against him. "Many men are older than their wives and the world has not ended because of it." I paused. "Not yet, anyway."

He shook with laughter. "You are an exceptional girl."

"I'm not a girl."

"You are to me." He moved to his side of the bed. "And this is all the conversation I can bear tonight."

I lay back, defeated. "Good night, husband."

He took my hand beneath the covers. "Good night, wife."

Chapter 5

I OPENED THE SHUTTER and rested my forehead against the glass, letting the cold dispel the last vestiges of the dream.

Robin found me gazing into the still-dark morning. "Is something wrong?"

"No." I turned away; what I sought was not outside. He was fully dressed and appeared to have been up for hours. "Just a dream."

He held out his hand. "Come, tell me about it."

"There's not much to tell." I settled on the edge of the unmade bed. "It was about my father."

"Do you dream of him often?"

"Not since I was small." Not since I'd stopped the nightmares, the dreams that clawed me awake with vivid images of the day I would never forget. "He spoke to me—I heard his voice. And it was *his* voice." My eyes brimmed. "I didn't think I remembered how he sounded."

Robin stroked my hand. "What did he say?"

"I don't know." I sobbed. "When he spoke, it woke me up. I heard his voice, but I don't know what he was trying to tell me." Robin gathered me against his bony shoulder, rubbing the center of my back and making soothing noises.

It had been so real. He was wearing his brown coat, the same one he was wearing when they took him. One side of the collar was turned under, and I was reaching up to fix it when the shock of his voice woke me up.

"How well do you remember him?" Robin's palm circled between my shoulder blades, a most comforting feeling.

"Not very well," I lied. "I remember his eyes and his smile, and the coat he wore when we went riding." I remembered the last time I saw him, but I would not speak of that.

"That's a fair amount for a four-year-old." He dropped his hand. "I went to my foster parents at four. I don't remember anything before that."

His words reminded me that he had no family at all, other than

Anselm. "I think I dreamed of him because of you."

"Because I'm his age?" His smile was wry.

Instead of teasing, I told him the truth. "Because I feel safe."

Within days of our first ride, a new mare had appeared in the stables. Artemis, Robin called her, after the Greek goddess of the hunt. She was a beautiful, fine-boned chestnut, already trained to the sidesaddle. On that first morning, I could sense her eagerness to run and let her have her head. We took off across the fields, leaving Robin far behind.

It was like flying. My leg hugged the pommel, the reins tight in my gloved hands. The buffeting wind made my eyes stream, and my cap tore loose from its pins. When we finally stopped, Winterset was almost out of sight, just the tiled roof and chimney pots visible beyond the hill.

It had been a long time since I'd ridden to escape myself, letting speed take me to a place where there was no thought. I slid down, tossing the reins over a branch, and leaned against Artemis's side, both of us breathing hard, both of us—I believe—exhilarated. She nosed at my hair and I stepped back and stroked her damp neck, admiring her intelligent black eyes. I'd never gotten up the nerve to ask for a horse, but Robin saw my need.

Hoof beats jarred the ground, and my husband slowed his gelding just short of us. My cap dangled from his fingers. "Are you this careless with all your belongings?"

"Not always." I attempted to replace it, but my hair had also come loose. "I don't imagine I'll have much opportunity to ride like this in London."

"Probably not." He looked at me closely. "It agrees with you."

"Artemis agrees with me." Riding was another thread connecting me to my father; my first experience of horses had been on the saddle in front of him, long before I could walk.

"There are royal parks aplenty," Robin said. "If Elizabeth doesn't ride, perhaps we could find a way for you to go out for a bit."

Life at court sounded painfully structured, but I could not object to the path he had chosen for us. For himself, really—I would be the queen's lady because he was her gentleman. My wishes did not enter into it.

"You cannot be a lady of the court without a maid."

Grand-mère and I had shared Alice for years, but this pronouncement, much as I disliked it, was sensible. "Do I hire one here," I asked, "who might not know court fashion, or should I wait until we reach London?"

The thought of finding a maid in London made my head spin. I would need help, and I was not prepared to ask Sebastian.

"A Yorkshire maid is fine for a Yorkshire mistress," Grand-mere said. "I'll take on a new girl, and you take Alice with you. If you find someone who suits you better, you can send her back."

It was a solution, but Alice was my grandmother's maid, not mine. Would she be willing to change?

"I might want someone younger." I fiddled with my knife. Thinking about London made me lose my appetite.

"Don't be ridiculous." She gave me a hooded glance. "You make her sound as decrepit as me."

"Of course she's not—you're not—I meant no insult, Grand-mère. I'm sorry." I reached for her hand. "If you think Alice will suit, I will take her, and gladly."

She waved her napkin. "Then it is decided. You will need her, being in the queen's presence every day."

At the mention of the queen, my heart lurched in my chest. I looked at my dinner and swallowed; the meat was greasy, and it wouldn't sit well.

"You're not getting sickly, are you? Or perhaps...?" Her voice trailed off.

"You needn't worry in that regard." I put a piece of beef in my mouth and forced myself to chew.

"It would please me greatly," she said, "to see a child of yours brought into the world. I would die a happy woman."

The room was warm; my woolen gown felt like a blanket. "Well, I don't want you to die," I said, a touch too brightly. "So perhaps we'll hold off on making you happy so soon."

I was darning stockings by the window when Alice knocked. "Lady Margaret told me I'm to accompany you to London." She looked more excited by the prospect than I was. "I wasn't certain you'd want to come." I put my work aside and flexed my stiffened fingers over the brazier. "You spent half your life out of England already."

"More than half," she said. "I was fourteen when we went to France."

Alice was thirty-two; not so old, after all. "Why did you come with us?"

She blushed, something I'd never seen in all the years I'd known her. "Master Walter asked me to."

Walter had been seventeen, a bright, laughter-filled boy who had my father's looks without his seriousness. He would have been very attractive to young Alice.

"Did Lady Margaret know?" I smiled to let her know I was jesting.

"Not right away." She looked at the floor. "But she found us together, in his chamber."

My eyes widened, as I saw her in a whole new light. "Do you mean you were actually…involved with Walter?"

Her color deepened. "He wouldn't have married me, but he loved me."

Walter caught a fever when I was sixteen, and Grand-mère and Alice had nursed him. I'd wondered at her devotion, but once he was dead, my attention turned to my grandparents and our maid's unusual behavior was forgotten.

"Did my grandfather know?" I asked stupidly.

"Of course. Lady Margaret wanted to dismiss me, but Sir Ralph would not abandon me in a foreign country." She smiled faintly. "But he did speak to Walter, and that was the end of it."

Her loyalty wasn't to my grandmother, but to my family. "I'm glad you're willing to come," I said, my worries dissipating. "I will be lost at court. Having someone familiar—especially someone with your ability to make me look better—will be a great help."

"You worry too much," she said with a return to her usual brisk attitude. "You will outshine everyone but the queen."

The thought of being looked at by so many people made me cold all over. "This was not the future Master Lewis and I discussed."

"Begging your pardon, mistress, but we don't often get much say in the matter."

On the evenings that Grand-mère supped in her chamber, Robin and I ate on a small table in the library. Sometimes Anselm joined us, but the habits of monastic life were hard to break, and he rarely ate a third meal. Sebastian kept his distance; he seemed to understand my feelings for him had changed.

After we finished, Robin would read and I would stitch or peruse his books. We talked only occasionally, but it was a friendly silence.

"Will Queen Elizabeth's court be anything like King Henry's?" I was curled on the window seat, a bit of blackwork on my lap. Rain pelted the glass; soon I would close the shutters and move closer to the fire, and take advantage of the candles on his desk.

He looked up. "All courts are much the same," he said. "I worked only for King Henry, but my friend, Ned Pickering—you'll meet him—was there through Edward and part of Mary's reign."

"What is she like?"

"A handsome woman," he said after a moment. "Exceptionally intelligent. Canny."

"Will she marry?" An unmarried princess was one thing, but could she rule without a husband? Her sister married Philip of Spain the year after her accession, though their union had produced no heir.

"She must," Robin said, "but I don't think she will like it. Too many of the Catholic countries still consider the queen to be illegitimate. England needs protection."

"Why do you think she won't like it?" Was he simply giving his own feelings about marriage to the queen?

His lip curled. "Elizabeth has waited years to rule. She will not willingly subordinate herself to a man—any man—whether he be from France, Spain, or darkest Africa."

I stitched another row before speaking again. "What of the other parts of marriage? There is more than just being subordinate."

Robin turned a page. "She may not be eager to experience that, either, with the examples she has been given."

I sucked in a breath. I was as comfortable with him as I was ever likely to become, given that my mind was constantly taken up with the unknowable topic of marital relations, and the question of why my husband refused to touch me.

"Not all women fear marriage." I closed the shutter; my arm was nearly frozen from leaning on the glass.

"Margaery…"

"I don't understand." I fiddled with the latch. "You knew my age when you agreed to the match."

His expression was strained. "It did not seem, at the time, that you wished for the physical side of marriage."

"But we are married." I gathered my courage. "I understand men have needs, and if I am fortunate, I will not find the act distasteful."

Robin turned his laugh into a tactful cough. "Not all men have the same needs."

I thought about this while he went back to his book. "Is it that I'm female?" I settled myself on a low stool beside his chair. "You said you had been attracted to both men and women." I wasn't sure what that actually entailed, but I would rather know an unpleasant truth than live in ignorance.

"I have been." He turned another page. "But it has been a long time. Since before I came to Winterset."

Almost my entire life. How did anyone live without touch for so long? He meant it in terms of physical relations, but I had observed him closely; Robin kept an emotional distance as well.

"But you have been intimate before?" It would be terrible if it was the first time for both of us.

His ears turned red. "I have."

One question answered, at least. "With women? Or with men?"

He put a slip of paper in the book and closed it. "Both, if you must know."

I wasn't certain of the mechanics of the act for men and women, so the thought of a man with a man, while it did not disgust me, made no sense. "Why then, if you've had both, have you been alone for so long?"

Robin sighed. "You did warn me about your propensity for questions, didn't you?"

"I did." I leaned against his leg, and he tensed. "And I have seen how you avoid answering them."

He straightened some papers and put them carefully to one side. "I've always found relationships difficult," he said. "There are few people whom I have not, at some point, upset or angered or disappointed.

"Aside from that, there's my work. Without connections, I've had to work harder, and relationships are a distraction."

"Am I a distraction?" I tried to sound cheerful; his self-isolation saddened me.

"You're trying to be." He picked up the book again.

The words on the leather cover were in Latin, and I tried to puzzle them out. I could read English and French, but my Latin studies had been cut short.

"Tell me about them," I said. "The people you've been with. I'm curious about your life."

He closed his eyes, whether in defeat or to avoid looking at me, I could not be sure. "There were a few casual…encounters." He rubbed the back of his neck. "One relationship of long standing, a woman I knew in London."

"She was your mistress?" I wanted to know all about the woman who could tempt Robin Lewis into such unlikely behavior.

His lips thinned. "I prefer to say we were lovers. I was no more than a boy—having a mistress would have been ridiculous."

"How long did it last?"

"Several years," he said. "It faded over time, though our friendship did not. I stayed with her in Venice earlier this year, before I came to France."

"Were you lovers then?" I peered into his face. "Robin?"

"That ended decades ago," he said. "Please, allow some privacy."

Chapter 6

THE SEASON OF ADVENT was upon us, and my virginity lingered like a bad cough. I rolled against Robin in bed and he feigned sleep or, worse, put me off. "It is the season of fasting," he said the second time it happened. "Fasting and austerity."

"Do all married people keep apart during December?"

"Many do." He sounded as though his patience were exhausted before breakfast.

"Just Catholics?" I persisted. "Or people like you?"

"Most people."

My parents must not have been good Catholics, for I was born on the nineteenth of September, and thus likely conceived during Advent. Yet they were devout—my father had died for his faith.

Robin was a mystery. Animated when the conversation interested him, he would shut down completely if uncomfortable. His thoughts on marriage were something which could be explored only so far. One thing he would talk about was England: its history, both past and present, and his hopes for the new queen. I found this fascinating, but he could not tell me what I most wanted to know—what my life would be like at court.

"I'm sorry," he said. "I can't tell you much about the ladies of Henry's queens, other than that they had them. And Elizabeth is young—she will have different ways."

It amazed me he'd known more than one queen, but, as he often reminded me, he was old and Henry had been king for a long time.

"I was at court for his first three." He rubbed his chin, still missing his beard. "I left before the German princess, and I never met Kat Howard, though I knew her family. His last queen I knew when she was Lady Latimer."

"What about Mary?" Perhaps I could deduce from his tales why she wanted him burned. "Did you ever meet her?"

"Only as a child, the same as Elizabeth. I met *her* when she was but fourteen." He smiled at the memory. "Her tutor introduced us."

"Is that how you got your new position?" If he didn't know my duties, perhaps he could tell me about his.

"Possibly. She remembered me when we met, the day after she was proclaimed queen. Ned worked with William Cecil, her principal secretary. I'll be working with them."

"Doing what?"

He shrugged. "The same as you—whatever is required of me."

In Grand-mère's opinion, none of my clothes were suitable for London. She summoned a sewing woman from Whitby to rectify the problem. While the idea of new things was exciting, I worried a Yorkshire seamstress could not produce garments fine enough for court. I kept these frets to myself; my grandmother's decisions were not open to discussion.

As we met with Mistress Pearson in the hall, Sebastian came through with Robin's freshly polished boots. "Good afternoon, Lady Margaret. Mistress."

"Good afternoon." I looked from him to the seamstress. "Is my husband about?"

Seb's bashful smile blossomed; it was difficult to stay angry with him, but I continued to try. "He's in the library."

Grand-mère glared at me. "Margaery, do not bother Master Lewis over women's business."

That nearly stopped me; I didn't want to be a nuisance, but I also didn't want to rely on the fashion sense of a woman who had been out of society longer than I had been alive. "Could you ask him to join us, Sebastian? Tell him I will be brief."

When Robin emerged and saw the table covered in cloth samples, it was clear he wanted to turn around and bolt the door behind him. Good manners won out. "How can I help?"

"Mistress Pearson has been called to make my court clothes, and she was kind enough to bring samples from the mercer." Some of the fabrics were very fine, but I was too unsure of my taste to choose on my own. "I do not wish to spend your money unwisely."

His face puckered. "I am no expert on ladies' finery."

"I do not need expertise, only your opinion. Should my gowns be made here, or should I wait until London?" Grand-mère and I had quarreled about it earlier; she wanted it done now, because it would cost less, but I feared the results would be unsuitable.

Robin exhaled. "We do not yet know what will be required— some of Henry's queens put their ladies in livery. It would be a shame to have new gowns made and not wear them." He turned to the seamstress. "There is yet work for you, mistress. I would suggest a black kirtle, of the best quality. And so my wife is not deprived of pretty things, something to go with her blue gown. One or two petticoats, as well. Palaces are much colder than you'd think."

A new kirtle was no small work, and its color could be hidden beneath my gowns. I disliked black; who would wear mourning unnecessarily?

"What about sleeves, sir?" Mistress Pearson asked. "If I could see the young mistress's blue gown, I could work up a pair of sleeves to give her a change, and perhaps a forepart to match."

He held up his hands. "This is now beyond me. My wife will look lovely in whatever is made for her." He bowed to Grand-mère and the seamstress, and kissed my hand. "With your permission, I will return to my books."

We picked out a black sarcenet for my kirtle and, after Alice fetched my gown, a pretty primrose yellow for my sleeves and forepart. My petticoats, for reasons of warmth and health, were of good Bristol red, and my farthingale was white.

Robin's suggestions satisfied Grand-mère, although she did order an extra pair of sleeves in blue bombazine, and enough fine lawn for several neck and wrist ruffs. "I think one set plain, and one with blackwork." She pleated the thin stuff with her fingers. "Do you have enough black thread, child?"

"I think so." I chafed at the endearment; I was a married woman, if only in the technical sense. "What about my shifts? They're a bit worn."

She nodded. "Mistress Pearson, add enough lawn for two more shifts."

"And a nightdress." I looked at the ceiling. "Something I can embroider myself."

The two older women shared a glance. Ignoring their smiles, I asked Mistress Pearson to bring an assortment of embroidery silks when she returned. "For I do not know my husband's favorite colors, and I will want to ornament it to his taste."

Their laughter set my teeth on edge, but I was sincere: I wanted a nightdress with which to tempt my husband, and I needed occupation for my hands on the days when it was too cold or wet to ride. Needlework was calming when my brain whirled, and I was training myself not to need the release of riding in anticipation of courtly captivity.

"He has a beautiful stride." I leaned against Robin's gray gelding. The scent of horse took me straight back to childhood. "I'd love to try him."

"We'll trade horses tomorrow," he said easily.

I gave him a sideways glance. "Or I could ride him now."

His brows raised. "You want to swap saddles?"

Robin had called me an interesting creature. "I can ride astride," I told him. "That's how I learned. Grand-mère forced me to take up the sidesaddle when I was twelve, to turn me into a lady."

"Then go ahead." Robin came over to Plato's left side and made a step for me with his hands. I hauled up my skirts, stepped from his palm into the stirrup, and swung my leg over the horse's rump. It had been years since I'd ridden this way, and I landed a little harder than anticipated, making Plato paw the ground. I spoke softly to him, and he calmed.

I smiled down at my husband. "We'll be right back." Touching my heels to Plato's flanks, we leaped away as if shot from a cannon. My hat came off again, taking my pins with it, and my hair flew out like a banner.

Riding was different when I could feel the horse with both legs. On a sidesaddle, with one leg hooked around the pommel, riding was more about balance. This was the smooth movement intended by God when He created horses. I laughed with pleasure and urged Plato onward.

We reached the top of the hill, and I circled the tumbled remains of the tower before heading back. Robin was a small figure in the distance, standing beside Artemis with her reins in his hand. I waved, and he raised his free hand in return.

Plato kept up the same speed on the way back, thundering smoothly beneath me. I slowed when I saw my hat suspended on a bit of blackthorn, and trotted back to Robin's side.

"That was lovely!" I trembled with something very like joy.

He raised his arms to help me dismount, but instead I jumped into them. "Thank you," I said into his ear. "It was like flying."

Robin staggered and drew back, without letting go. "You ride as though you were born to it."

I wanted to tell him about riding with my father, but I was so wordlessly happy that I couldn't, and only hugged him again. "May we ride again tomorrow, please?"

"Of course. I'll make sure there's a saddle for you."

Up close, I could see the faint freckles that spattered his face, and the rusty stubble along his jaw. Seb did not shave him every day.

"Thank you," I said inadequately. "This is the best I've felt since I've come home."

"I'm glad." He helped me back onto Artemis, seeming glad to have separation between our bodies. "I wouldn't have gone to all the trouble finding a horse trained to the sidesaddle had I known I married a centaur."

"I'm sure they'll expect me to ride sidesaddle at court," I said. "Grand-mère knows best."

He vaulted awkwardly onto Plato, who shifted from foot to foot and swung his head around to look at Robin. "Lady Margaret is quite a strong character. Do you not mind?"

"Mind what?" I enjoyed our conversations, except when I didn't understand him.

He raised a shoulder. "That she has taken it upon herself to be mistress of Winterset."

I stared at him, the chill settling into my fingers. "She is."

"No," he corrected gently. "You are. The house was your dowry, was it not? To convince me to accept you."

"Yes." My voice was barely audible. Put like that, it sounded as though I'd sold myself to the highest bidder. "Yes."

"Well, then." He spread his hands, as if it were the simplest thing in the world. "If I am the master, you are the mistress. If you are unhappy with any of the changes she has made, you should say so."

I imagined telling my grandmother I disapproved of her management of the house. "I couldn't."

Robin gathered his reins, shaking his head. "You're her granddaughter, but you aren't a child. You need to realize that."

We awoke the next day to gray skies and sleet. Even I did not wish to ride in such weather, and instead worked at finishing my nightdress. My court wardrobe had been delivered, and it was difficult to contain my excitement. The silk nightdress had been made up to my specifications, but I worked out its decoration myself and did the embroidery when I was alone.

The parlor became my refuge, a place where even my husband knocked before entering. Only Grand-mère did not observe this convention, but she was preoccupied in returning Winterset to its former glory and only visited me before dinner.

As she rearranged and refurbished and drove the servants mad, my parlor grew crowded. Some were pieces deemed too plain for the hall, while others came from her chamber, made redundant by the superior things she'd brought from France. She attempted to give me the wall hanging she so disliked, but Robin refused to have it moved.

"If you're certain." She looked from him to the colorful canvas.

"I am."

It was shocking to see him stand up to her. I didn't think he cared about the house, or who ran it, so long as his precious library was left untouched. My grandmother subsided, but I knew when we next returned, the hanging would be in my parlor. Her opinion would be known, without saying another word.

A light tap roused me from my musings, and I tucked the gown into my basket. "Come."

Sebastian entered, a small carved chest in his arms. "Good afternoon, mistress."

I was still wary of him. "Is there something you require?"

Placing the chest on the floor, he said, "The master went into

Whitby this morning, after the weather cleared. He thought you would like this."

First a horse, and now a random piece of furniture. For a man who treated me like a sister, he was very open-handed with his gifts.

"Thank you." I wondered why the giver had not presented it himself. "You may go."

He lingered at the door. "If I may…"

I glanced up, wanting to get back to my stitching. "Yes?"

"Have I done something to offend?" He rubbed his thumb over the knuckles of his other hand.

"How could you offend?" There was something endearing about him, but I refused to smile. Sebastian needed to understand I could not be easily charmed.

"I don't know." His hazel eyes were earnest. "I thought we were friends, once."

"We are not friends," I said. "You are my husband's servant."

He flinched. "I know that, mistress."

"Then why would you assume we are friends?" I rose and came toward him. "A friend would not have told Mistress Dunham to conceal a letter that was rightfully mine."

Seb hung his head. "I feel bad about that."

"And so you should." Anger was an indulgence, one I rarely permitted myself. "Do you frequently disobey Master Lewis's orders? Or did you so resent me that you wished me to feel unwelcome?"

He knelt, turning his face up to mine. "That is the last thing I wanted, mistress. I was afraid of what was ahead, and there was little time to act with them in the house. I didn't want you to be frightened before the worst was known."

I opened my mouth, then stopped, remembering the violence of my reaction when I read Robin's letter. How much worse would it have been to believe him dead, and then read those sorrowful, caring words? I would have been in mourning when he walked through the door.

Wife, widow, and wife again, in a matter of weeks.

"It's all right." I sighed. "I understand."

Seb passed a hand over his eyes. "It was never my intention to frighten you. He wanted you prepared for whatever you might face on your arrival."

I extended my hand. "Get up. I'm not the queen, you don't have to kneel before me."

He moved to adjust the shutter, stopping the draft that reached me even across the room. "I am glad things are better between us."

I sank into the chair again. "And I am glad you will be with us in London. Master Lewis will need you."

He nodded. "I have listened to his stories for many years," he said. "He will go, Mistress Margaery, but only because the queen asks it." He risked a smile. "Any contentment he finds in London will be because of you."

Chapter 7

THE THOUGHT OF KEEPING Christmas at Winterset had Grand-mère as excited as a child. While we observed the strictures of the Advent fast, she plotted and planned with Fowler and Mistress Dunham to make the holiday a perfect send-off to our new life. Every day more festive greenery was added to the house, and appetizing smells emanated from the kitchen, though nothing could be tasted until the feast.

The holiday began with a dawn ride, so we would be back in time for church. It was more adventurous than usual, because of Robin's gift. "I'm sorry if you don't like them." He handed over a cloth-wrapped parcel. "I couldn't resist."

I beheld a pair of brown woolen slops, below-the-knee breeches such as sailors or young boys wore. Mystified, I looked at Robin.

"So you can stop sitting on your petticoats." He watched my face, as if afraid of my reaction. "Do you like them?"

I laughed with delight. "Grand-mère had me whipped for wearing breeches once—I've never dared since. Wherever did you get them?" I stroked the sturdy fabric, imagining what it would feel like to ride without a wad of skirts folded under my seat.

"Your sewing woman made them," he admitted. "I thought the longer length would be best, since you could use your own stockings."

"They should suit." I raised my skirts. "I'm wearing my heaviest ones today. St. Mary's is always cold."

"Will you try them this morning?"

I was already in my kirtle, but I took the breeches and ducked behind the screen, rucking up my skirts and removing my petticoats. Not knowing what to do with my shift, I tied the tails between my legs, then worked the unfamiliar breeches up past my stockings. "Oh! Do yours close with ties like this?"

"No," came his amused voice. "I told her to construct them like a female garment, rather than with points and an unnecessary codpiece."

Blood rushed to my face. "That makes sense," I said when my

voice could be trusted.

With my skirts lowered, my new breeches were invisible. I wished for the courage to wear them with just a shirt and jacket, but Grand-mère would expire at the impropriety.

The stable boy was waiting with our horses, walking around the courtyard to keep himself—and them—warm. "Thank you, Dickon." It was bitterly cold, and he had been up long before dawn to accommodate us. "Run up to the house. Mayhap Mistress Dunham will turn her back and you can snatch breakfast."

He handed over the reins and sprinted across the cobbles. When he was gone, I reached beneath my kirtle and loosened my under-skirt.

"What do you think?" I twirled before Robin, the skirts of my gray kirtle flying out, the long breeches ending just below my garters, a brief slice of stocking visible above my leather boots.

"Very nice." He grinned like a boy and boosted me into the saddle, then mounted Plato.

We trotted out of the stable yard and past the cottages. All was quiet, the workers readying themselves for church, followed by feast-ing and twelve days of well-deserved rest from their labors.

They would come to the house for dinner. Grand-mère had orga-nized a proper feast, the kind I remembered from childhood, with music and games and food, and someone elected Lord of Misrule. I was looking forward to it, although I wondered how Robin would react to such an invasion.

On most estates, tenants and workers came for the Feast of Stephen, the day after Christmas, but Winterset had always com-bined the celebrations. The custom started under my great-grand-father; I didn't know why, any more than I knew the identity of the bowman for whom the hill had been named.

"Up to the tower?" he asked unnecessarily.

"I'll race you!" Artemis took off at the touch of my heels, and Plato followed. Each time Robin caught up, I coaxed more speed from the mare, gripping her with my thighs and bending low over her neck, her mane blowing against my face.

Riding in breeches was a new kind of freedom. I didn't have

to worry about exposing my anatomy to the cold air or offending Robin's eyes with a glimpse of flesh. I concentrated on the feeling of the horse between my legs, the grip of my unaccustomed muscles, and the sensation of having nothing but my knotted shift and a layer of wool between me and the saddle.

Robin drew close when we neared the top of the hill, but I kept on, reaching the tower just ahead of him, and wheeling Artemis around with a whoop.

He laughed with me, delighted by the success of his gift.

My heart pounded and there was a fluttering in my stomach. Dizzy with exhilaration and tingling from the cloth between my legs, I asked, "Do you think women are forbidden to ride astride because it feels good?"

"I don't know." He considered my question seriously. "It's probably something more mundane, like propriety."

My kirtle had fallen forward, only my boot visible now. "That's probably it," I said. "The fact that it feels good just makes it worse."

Back at the stables, I ducked into a stall to tidy my costume, emerging to walk back to the house on Robin's arm, a properly-clad wife once more.

The door opened at our approach, and Grand-mère cried, "Stop right there!"

We halted, confused. "What is it, Lady Margaret?"

She pointed, cackling. "You've stopped under the kissing bough."

Her latest bit of decoration was an arch of woven branches above the door: pine and holly and a clutch of mistletoe.

Robin froze. I kept my hand on his arm, waiting to see what he would do, the joy of the ride draining away.

He turned to me. "It is Christmas, after all."

"Indeed it is." Grand-mère was not the only witness: Fowler was there, as were Sebastian, Alice, and the maids. Only Mistress Dunham and Leon would miss my humiliation as my husband kissed my cheek.

The touch of his lips on mine—the first time he'd kissed me since our wedding—was shocking. They were cold; they exerted a friendly pressure, then retreated, to general applause.

I risked a glance; his face was flaming. It could be the cold, but I knew he was embarrassed at being forced to kiss me in front of everyone.

The feast began after we returned from church, over forty people crowding into the hall to seat themselves at the extra benches and tables constructed by Fowler and his men. There was scarcely room for Mistress Dunham and the maids to pass through with their steaming platters of brawn and Christmas pie. A haunch of venison, sent by a neighbor as a welcome gift to Grand-mère, was the highlight of the meal.

Ale flowed, with never a cup being completely empty before it was refilled. There was music, several of the farm workers having come with pipes and a drum, and Fowler produced a battered lute which was enthusiastically seized upon by one of the young men.

As master of the house, Robin was at the head of the table, but it was Grand-mère's day. When the meal was over and the tables littered with cups and bits of bread, she rose and addressed the gathering, looking like a relic from another age in her stiff black gown and a headdress which had not been fashionable for two decades.

"Many of you were not here when Sir Ralph and I left this place almost twenty years ago." As she spoke, the other voices quieted. "I came to Winterset as a bride, and now it belongs to Master Lewis and his wife, my granddaughter. They will away to London soon, to serve the queen, but I will remain here, to keep watch over Winterset until their return."

Her cheeks were rosy with ale and emotion. "I have been touched by your care for this place I love so much. I wish to thank Jasper Fowler for his stewardship while we were gone, and for the assistance you have rendered him. I find Winterset as good, or better, than when I left."

As her speech went on, Robin glanced repeatedly toward his sanctuary. I'd never seen him at anything larger than our wedding party, and his discomfort was obvious. When the singing began, he excused himself and took his cup into the library. The sound of the door closing was audible only to me.

The celebration reminded me of childhood Christmases, but for one thing: as a child, I could just clap my hands and enjoy myself. But now, I was a wife. A wife with a husband who was hiding because his house had been taken over without his ever having been consulted.

I was certain my grandmother hadn't asked his approval; why would she? Even had I thought to tell her Robin wouldn't care for such a gathering, she would have asked his permission in such a way he would have felt compelled to grant it.

There was nothing I could do. I drank and sang along with the carols, my irritation simmering. It was soon joined by anger at Robin. It was one day—it was Christmas! Could he not put aside his selfish need for solitude and pretend to enjoy himself?

It was disrespectful, not just to me, but to the whole of Winterset. Those who crowded the hall worked hard all year, and looked forward to a proper celebration as their reward—especially since our return. Hiding away with a book showed disregard for the rest of us.

"Where is he?" Grand-mère asked, under cover of the music. "I thought he had just gone—" Her head jerked in the direction of the privy.

I pressed my lips together. "He's in his library."

"His library!"

Across the room, Sebastian looked up, more sensitive to criticism of his master than I could ever be.

"You told me to respect his wishes," I said. "Should I drag him out?"

She subsided, and Mistress Dunham refilled her cup.

I looked at Seb, who had not moved from his position outside the library door. He gave me a tiny shrug—*what can we do?*—and went back to watching the musicians.

The more I thought, the angrier I became, and the more I forced myself to enjoy the party. When the tables were pushed back, I danced with everyone who asked: Fowler, Sebastian, even Dickon the stable lad, who had never questioned why I no longer required a sidesaddle.

Anselm and Grand-mère had a sedate dance off to one side, and I smiled to see the former monk leading my elderly grandmother out. This was even less his milieu than Robin's, but he made an effort, and seemed to enjoy himself.

The gathering broke up after ten, people stumbling with exhaustion and drink. When Fowler opened the door, there were cries of amazement at the snow that had fallen while we were at our revels. Dickon and the other boys ran clumsily toward the stables, and returned with shovels and brooms.

The cold set my teeth on edge and I waved everyone off and went back inside. The library door was still closed. I stood before it, my hand raised, but instead I turned away and wearily climbed the stairs.

My embroidered nightdress was laid out on the coverlet. I snatched it up and threw it across the chamber.

Robin came to bed at some point. Early the next morning, I heard him moving around, humming softly. I checked: I was still angry, a faint pounding in my temples when I thought of his disappearance from the party.

The green curtains parted. "Margaery? It's past seven, and the weather has cleared. Are you riding this morning?"

I rolled over. "I'm tired."

He pulled the curtain further, sitting on the edge of the bed. "I'm not surprised. It sounded like quite the celebration."

"I'm sorry if we disturbed you." I put the pillow over my face.

Undeterred, he came around to the other side. "It's all right. When I'm lost in a book, I can ignore anything."

"Hmm." Could he not go away until I decided how to be both a good wife and murderously angry at the same time?

"Did you drop this?" He tossed something weightless onto the bed. "It was on the floor."

I opened my eyes, saw the crumpled wreck of my silk nightdress with its hours and hours of pointless embroidery. "That was where I left it."

Robin ran his fingertips over the delicate stitching at the neck with our entwined initials. The way I thought marriage would be, before I realized. "You do such beautiful work. Why didn't you wear it?"

I sat up. "Because it was *your* Christmas present." My jaw ached from holding back the words. "And you decided not to observe Christmas."

He took a step back. "I didn't think I was required," he said. "Lady Margaret had everything under control, and I neither dance nor play music."

"Nor do you allow yourself to be seen with your wife at the high point of Winterset's year." I twisted the silk in my hands, resisting the urge to shred it. "Fowler, the farm workers, even Dickon—everyone asked where you were."

"I'll apologize," he said with an easy smile. "Are you sure you don't want to ride? Where are your breeches?"

They were stuffed in a chest, out of sight. When Alice saw them, she dissolved into laughter and asked what sort of man wanted his wife to dress as a boy. Her reaction had taken away my pleasure in them.

"I'll not wear them again," I said stiffly. "You shouldn't encourage me to behave in such a fashion."

Robin dragged a hand over his face. "I neither encouraged nor discouraged you." He sounded irritated. "You wanted to ride Plato, remember?"

"You shouldn't have permitted it." Seeing I was not going to be allowed to linger in bed, I got up and ducked behind the screen.

"You haven't been yourself lately."

I threw off my very ordinary nightdress and reached for a clean shift. How did he know whether I was myself? Even I wasn't certain. "Could you call for Alice? There's no water."

He brought the bowl from across the room and placed it within reach of the screen. "You seem...quieter than you were in France."

"You did not know me then." I snaked out an arm and wetted a cloth. The water was still warm.

"And now?" I watched him from between the panels.

"If I'm quiet," I said, rubbing the cloth over my face, "it is because I'm trying to figure out what you expect. How you wish me to behave."

I had always been good at giving people what they wanted: Grand-mère wanted a loving, well-behaved granddaughter; my grandfather needed someone to talk to about estate matters, to be a replacement son; Walter wanted a little sister. I rarely had to search for clues, but Robin was more opaque than most.

I continued washing, passing the cloth under my arms and between my legs. The sensation reminded me of my breeched ride, and then of my husband.

What did he need? He was the most self-contained man I had ever met. If I didn't watch him eat, it would have surprised me to learn that he required food. He was an island, and I was on shore with no means of reaching him.

"I have no expectations," he said. "I did not marry you to shape you to my will. Just behave naturally."

Behaving naturally did not come naturally. He had no idea how difficult an instruction that was for someone like me.

I threw the cloth into the basin and pulled my shift over my head. "But what do you need?"

"Nothing." He appeared genuinely confused. "I just want you to be happy."

What made me happy was not only clarity, but to feel needed. *'I want you to be happy'* meant I would plaster a smile on my face, and let him believe I was whatever he wished me to be. Inside was a maelstrom of fears: that I would embarrass myself at court; that I would make no friends; that the queen would not like me. Worst of all, that Robin would continue to withhold himself and prove he'd never wanted to marry me in the first place.

I wasn't certain what I wanted from him, but relations were a part of marriage, and I was happiest when rules were followed and expectations met. His flouting of this most basic tenet made me doubt everything else.

Edging past, I sat at the dressing stool, deliberately pulling on my stockings in front of him. He looked away, folding his arms, his fingers digging into his dark wool sleeves.

I undid my braid and reached for my wooden comb. It was gone, replaced by a smooth curve of ivory with delicate flowers carved on the shaft. I touched the raised design. "Robin?"

His hand dropped lightly on my shoulder. "It's your other

Christmas gift. I bought it on the way back from Hatfield."

"It's beautiful." I could see only a portion of his face in the small mirror; he looked as uncertain as I felt.

My anger drained away. I could not begrudge him his beloved library. He wanted nothing more than the peace of Winterset, and we would soon be going off to a place which I suspected would offer him little peace.

I lifted the comb to my shoulder. "Why don't you try it?"

As he drew it through my hair, I tilted my head back and closed my eyes. Robin was opaque, but one thing was obvious, if I but wished to see it: he had not meant to hurt me. He retreated from his own discomfort, and being solitary, had not thought what his absence would mean.

"You were missed," I said softly, hoping he understood. He continued to comb my hair, long strokes, both stimulating and soothing. If this was the only form of touching he was capable of, I would learn to accept it.

"I am not accustomed to being missed." He placed the comb precisely on the chest and kissed the top of my head. "I'm going down. I'll send Alice up to help you dress."

Chapter 8

IT WAS UNNATURALLY SILENT. Not even the birds sang. The headsman's footsteps echoed like thunder as he walked across the platform. He picked up the long-handled ax and dragged it over the splintered boards toward the block—

I sat bolt upright, my heart pounding, the nightmare evaporating into the rumbling from outside. Scrubbing my eyes with my fists, I found my cheeks wet. Had I screamed? No—Robin was still sleeping peacefully beside me.

I slipped between the woolen curtains and crept to my chair. It was still dark, and the embers had burned down to ash, leaving the room frigid. The thunder rolled, long and low, and in that herald of approaching cold, I again heard footsteps. I brought my knees up and tucked my nightdress around my bare feet, shivering.

How long since I'd last had that dream? Ten years, at least, and they were scattered by then, not like the ones that tore me from sleep every night after my father's death. Those lasted for years after we left Winterset.

I wore out my mother with screaming. She had her own grief; having a child who howled but refused to speak was too much for her to bear.

"It's all right, love," my grandmother said. "You speak when you're ready. For now, cry on me."

And I had, soaking her broad bosom with wordless tears, and soon I could speak again—though not to my mother.

I shook my head. Where had all this come from? The memories were with me always, but I avoided them, letting my mind glide past as easily as a trout slips through the swaying reeds in a river. Tipping my head back, I listened to the storm, doing my best to stay present and not fall back into that dangerous darkness.

When Sebastian came to light the fire, he found me asleep in the chair. He helped me up and ordered me back to bed. "It's not fit to ride this morning," he said, his voice low. "Did you hear the storm?"

"That was what woke me." It was only a small lie.

"A tree came down and took some tiles from the stable roof." He lifted the covers and I scooted in. "I won't let the master help, but he can supervise. You go back to sleep."

I burrowed deep into the warm bed as Sebastian shook Robin awake. Their voices were the last thing I heard for several hours, and when I woke again, the shutters were open and the sky was clear and blue all the way to the horizon.

The banging of the front door startled us. It was followed by loud voices and the sound of something heavy being dragged across the hall floor.

"What in heaven?" Grand-mère's view was blocked by the parlor door. "Go and look, Margaery."

I darted into the hall to see Sebastian and Fowler, with Robin slung between them. All three men were wet and covered in mud. Beneath the dirt, Robin's face was quite gray.

"What happened?" I reached for him.

"Nothing." He pulled away. "I'm fine."

"He is not," Fowler said. "His knee buckled, and he went right down, he did."

They hauled him into the library, and I followed. "What can I do?"

"Sebastian will manage." Robin's mouth was tight with pain.

Once he was settled, Seb began to remove his wet clothes. He looked up at me. "You could get some wine, mistress, and ask Anselm if he has any poppy."

Robin made a sound of dissent. "I don't need poppy. If I can just put my leg up—"

I left them arguing and ran to the buttery for wine. Anselm appeared, drawn by the uproar, and I told him what had happened. "Seb is asking for poppy syrup."

"The first time he hurt it, he didn't walk for a week."

"But we're leaving in two days," I said, thinking of all the packing we'd done.

Anselm shook his head. "Not likely."

Sebastian barred my way and relieved me of the wine. "I can pour, mistress."

"I'd like to do something."

"Not now." He leaned against the door frame. "Let me get him cleaned up. He's embarrassed to be seen like this."

Despite Robin's repeated assurances that he was fine, it was clear he was not. His knee was swollen and painful, but he would only allow Anselm to treat it with hot and cold compresses and willow bark infusions.

Ordered to stay off his feet for fear of making it worse, Robin lived in his library for the next ten days, bedding down on a pallet with Sebastian to watch over him. I was excluded from his care entirely. I stitched late into the night and chewed my fingernails until they bled.

We would miss the coronation. Robin sent a courier with a letter explaining our delay, and I hoped the queen and Cecil would understand. I was both disappointed and relieved. I wanted to witness the pageantry of Elizabeth's crowning at Westminster Abbey, but I was petrified that my clothes would be wrong and I would be marked as an outsider from the first.

To add insult to injury, it rained nearly every day, causing the ditches to fill and the roads to disappear in a welter of muck. One night, when Robin insisted he was able to travel, Sebastian responded, "It's going to be mud up to the axles. If the coach gets stuck, are you telling me you're capable of helping to push it free?"

"No." It was the tone of a small, sullen boy.

I was glad of my parlor, as it kept me away from the other bad-tempered inhabitants of Winterset. Grand-mère stayed in her chamber; Robin in his library; Anselm in the chapel or his small room upstairs. He and Sebastian took turns making Robin bend his leg and walk up and down, but I was excluded even from these exercises.

I missed our morning rides and evening conversations. I might not have his love, but I liked having his attention. Until his injury, I had thought we could form some kind of unconventional partnership.

Now, I wasn't so sure.

The weather broke and Anselm suggested we take advantage of it. "I made that ride in a storm," he said. "I wouldn't wish it on Thomas Cromwell."

Robin had graduated from two sticks to one, and then to moving slowly and deliberately without it. Sebastian rode into Whitby to hire a coach, and we left the next morning before dawn.

"Where will we stay?" I put the last of my personal items into a small casket that would travel in the coach: Grand-mère's jewelry, now mine; my grandfather's rosary; my ivory comb. My embroidery basket would also stay with me, in the hope that the roads would be smooth enough for me to stitch while Robin read.

He glanced at Seb, who was hefting one of the trunks containing my new wardrobe. "We could duplicate some of our recent journey," he said. "What do you think, Seb?"

His manservant stumbled, from the weight of my gowns or Robin's suggestion. "There are a number of inns between York and London. I suggest we try those instead."

My grandmother embraced me, her eyes bright with tears. "Be a good girl, Margaery. Listen to your husband."

"Yes, Grand-mère." I hugged her, wiping my eyes so she did not see my weakness. We'd never been apart for more than a few weeks since I was born.

Robin bowed. "Lady Margaret, Winterset is yours. I trust you will do naught but improve it in our absence."

"No doubt, you impertinent man." She offered her hand. "Take good care of my granddaughter."

He looked around the hall. "Thank you for entrusting her to me."

A floorboard creaked, and Anselm emerged from the chapel. "I was offering prayers for an easy journey." He put his arms around Robin. "Go with God, my boy, and carry my blessings to the queen."

"I thank you, brother." Robin's face was very white. Pain or emotion? "What about your prayers that she does not become a Protestant version of her sister?"

Anselm drew back. "I pray for that without ceasing. Do your best. Keep England safe."

The coach waited out front, Artemis and Plato standing patiently alongside Seb's horse. He would ride and lead our mounts, and I could choose to ride if being closed in became unbearable. It had been made clear to Robin that he would not ride.

Seb helped me in, and I looked back at Winterset, tears pricking again. Mimicking Anselm, I said a quick prayer that we would reach London without incident.

Chapter 9

THOUGH WE GOT STUCK several times the first day, the roads cleared as we traveled south. Still, we missed the coronation by two days.

We stopped frequently—for meals, for changes of horse, to sleep—and I listened to Robin and Seb talk. Seb made comparisons to their recent journey, but Robin said little except in the most general terms. I had hoped prolonged time away from his library would make him more forthcoming.

When the coach finally bumped its way into London, banners and flags still hung at the crossings, and workers were busy dismantling barriers and stages set up along the route of the procession. We traveled down a wide street, which Robin said was the Strand, and through the gates to Whitehall, where we were met by a liveried servant.

An apartment awaited us inside the palace, he said, and Sir Edward Pickering had taken care of acquiring its basic appointments. We were to be housed by the court, along with our servants, and we would be fed by the court, if we chose to take our meals in the hall. Our horses would be stabled, and our lodgings supplied with firewood.

The servant looked across Robin to me. "Sir Edward apologizes for any offense, mistress—he wished you to have some comforts on your arrival."

Robin was pleased. "I lived here, when I worked for Wolsey," he said. "It was called York Place then."

"Has it changed?" I looked at the enormous structure with trepidation. How would I ever find my way around?

"When Henry took it over, he spent a fortune enlarging it. By then, I was with Cromwell, and Ned and I took lodgings nearby."

"Would you rather be here than in lodgings?" I shifted on the padded seat. After a week, the coach was no more comfortable than my sidesaddle, and only slightly warmer.

"A court apartment will be easier," he explained. "You'll be with the queen well into the evening, and Cecil will undoubtedly keep late hours, as we sort out the damage done by Mary and her council."

The court gave much, but at a cost. If we were as busy as Robin anticipated, when would we find time to set about starting our marriage?

Whitehall encompassed more than two thousand rooms—great galleries and halls and chambers for council meetings; the queen's privy apartments; spacious rooms set aside for nobles, councilors, diplomats, and the like; and upstairs, modest spaces for people of our status.

A door off a side corridor opened into an anteroom, which led to a larger chamber with a fire, and, finally, to a snug bedchamber with a window overlooking an interior courtyard. There was a withdrawing room for Alice, and Sebastian insisted he would sleep in the anteroom, to guard the door. The furnishings secured by Sir Edward were sparse, but adequate: a tester bed with curtains, several chests, a table and two chairs before the fire. I thought it very pleasant, with little room for Robin to hide.

Sir Edward soon found us, and tried to lure Robin away to the principal secretary's offices. "Cecil needs you, Rob." He shifted from foot to foot like an anxious child. "It will take weeks to even know how much there is to be done, and Her Majesty wants a parliament before the end of the month."

Robin had warned me about Ned, and I watched with good humor. He was like a large, over-excited dog in his enthusiasm. I half-expected him to put his hands on Robin's shoulders and lick his chin before he finished speaking.

When we were introduced, he looked at me with frank admiration. "Mistress Margaery is much the same age as my own sweet wife when we wed," he said. "You two will have much in common when she comes to court."

"She is not here?" It would have been nice to have a ready-made acquaintance.

"Alas, no." He made a sad face. "She lives in Surrey with our girls. We have hopes of another babe."

When asked, he described his children with great enthusiasm. "Young Ned is fifteen. I wanted Rob to guide his education, but he was away, so my uncle took him on. He's off to Oxford in the spring. My second boy is thirteen—he's with my wife's brother's household." There were two daughters, nine and six. I wondered at his energy with that many younglings, but understood his wife bore the brunt of their raising.

"Mistress Ashley will wish to know that you've come," he said. "You're the last of the women to arrive."

When I presented myself at the doors of the presence chamber, I was given over to Katherine Ashley. She was a woman of Robin's age, with a pleasant, worried face. "You were expected weeks ago."

I bit my lip. "My husband was injured."

"It's no matter. You're here now." She led me into a small chamber which was set up as a library, and explained my duties. I was not to be a lady-in-waiting, but something less: a chamberer—not as important as a lady of the bedchamber, nor as decorative as the maids of honor who were there chiefly to find husbands.

"What am I to do?"

"Whatever you are asked," she said. "The ladies of the bedchamber have specific duties in dressing and undressing Her Majesty, serving her food, and many other tasks. You will do what they require of you." My confusion must have shown. "You'll not be bored, if that's your worry. I've known the queen since she was three years old. Much will be asked of you."

I hoped so. I did not wish to become a glorified lady's maid, even if the lady happened to be the queen. I'd barely gotten used to having a maid of my own; providing those services to someone else would require skills I did not possess.

"Do you have any particular talents, Mistress Lewis?" She reviewed a column of figures as we spoke, her finger traveling slowly down the page.

"Talents?" My chest grew tight with the anticipation of being found wanting.

"Do you sing, or play an instrument? Do you ride? Can you shoot a bow?" She looked at me expectantly. "Her Majesty likes active people."

"I can ride," I said with relief. "And I embroider very well." I removed the gloves which were tucked into my girdle and showed her the elaborate cuffs. "I've enjoyed handwork since I was a girl."

She examined the stitching, her mouth pursed. "Her Majesty loves pretty things. If you have no other duties, there will always be work for you."

As the first lady of the bedchamber, Mistress Ashley administered my oath of service. Perhaps I was naïve, but I hadn't expected to swear an oath to be a waiting-woman; I understood it, in Robin's case, but was my job so important?

"I was told you were French," she said. "Your English is very good. Were you given much of an education?"

"I am English," I said, my cheeks hot. "I lived in France until recently and speak both languages—equally well, I hope." To mask any rudeness, I continued, "My grandfather had me educated until I was fourteen, and I've kept up my reading since then."

"Very good." She nodded. "Her Majesty is highly educated, and prefers the same from her women."

She continued checking her figures, and I wondered what sort of records were required for an enterprise as sprawling as the court. "What was the coronation like?"

A proud smile spread across Mistress Ashley's face, at odds with her serious demeanor. "Glorious." She described the river progress, with its multitude of barges, its music, the abundance of fireworks. Two days later, there was a procession through the city, with the queen carried on a golden litter, and her ladies following behind.

"The ladies wore scarlet velvet." She looked down her nose. "A warrant had been written for five yards for Mistress Lewis, but it was given over in your absence."

"Do the queen's ladies always wear scarlet?" I was glad Mistress Pearson had not made my entire wardrobe.

"The royal livery is scarlet." In a twinkling, her pride was put away and she was all business. "The queen's ladies wear black, and the maids of honor white." She stroked her brocade skirt; the fabric was rich, but it was dark as a crow's wing. "Her Majesty likes her women to be soberly dressed."

It was silly to be disappointed, but I did not want to spend my days dressed as a crow, or a mourning woman.

"It's not so bad." She smiled at my crestfallen expression. "For some evening events, you may wear your own gowns, so long as they are appropriate to the occasion."

I took a deep breath. It was what it was; I was a chamberer; I would wear black; I would learn to like it.

"There is something else." Mistress Ashley looked at me squarely. "The queen comes first."

"Yes, Mistress Ashley." She was the queen, after all.

"Mark me," she said. "Anything you overhear in these chambers is confidential. Unless the queen speaks publicly, her words are not to be repeated, even to your husband."

"But he works for the queen." Being unable to speak of my day beyond the most mundane events—when I might finally have something interesting to say—would make our evening conversations rather one-sided.

"Master Lewis works for *William Cecil*." It was a distinction I hadn't known existed. "Master Cecil works for the queen, but even he does not know what is said in Her Majesty's apartments, unless he is with her." Looking over her shoulder at the women clustered nearby, she said more quietly, "My own husband, who has served the queen these many years, knows nothing of my daily life. That is how it must be for you."

"You were wrong."

Robin looked up from the papers spread across our table. "About what?"

I waited until I had his full attention. "I'm not a lady-in-waiting."

His brow creased. "The queen said—"

"I'm a gentlewoman of the privy chamber," I explained hastily. "The important roles are all filled by the queen's relatives or women who have served her since girlhood." On further consideration, the unimportance of my role pleased me. I hadn't yet been presented to Elizabeth, but I was already frightened of her.

Robin let out a breath. "That's all right, then."

"What do you mean?"

"I was afraid she'd changed her mind," he said. "I wouldn't want to send you back at this time of year. It would be difficult to be without Seb for so long."

Seb entered, picked up Robin's discarded doublet and disappeared again. *It would be difficult to be without Seb for so long.*

I rummaged through my work basket, searching for my black silk, but looked up at that. "What about me?"

"There would be no point in your staying without some occupation."

Drawing the silk over the stub of candle I kept in the basket, I threaded my needle, and thought of stabbing my husband with it. "I don't want to see you once a year, when you get leave to come north."

He shuffled his papers, an indication that he wished to return to work. "Many couples live thus, when one is in royal service." Robin smiled briefly. "I imagine this isn't what you had in mind when you asked me to marry you, is it?"

Chapter 10

THE NEXT MORNING, I returned to the presence chamber, clad in the gown I'd worn for my grandfather's mourning. Mistress Ashley was nowhere to be seen. Fixing on another black-garbed woman with an air of authority, I presented myself. "I was told to come at nine, when the queen awoke."

The woman introduced herself as Lady Mary Sidney. "You are early, Mistress Lewis. The queen is still abed." Smiling affectionately, she said, "She is not a morning woman."

Why was I here, if there was nothing for me to do? Seeing my distress, Lady Mary led me past the yeomen of the guard and into the privy chamber, dominated by an empty throne under a cloth-of-gold canopy. The room swarmed with people—mostly women, but some men—all waiting for the queen to show herself. While they waited, they amused themselves with conversation or cards, and a girl in white picked out a tune on the lute.

My gaze was drawn to a young woman across the room: red-haired and beautiful, she stood before the banked windows with two attentive gentlemen. "Is that not the queen?"

"Fie, that you would think it!" Lady Mary's expression let me know the extent of my error. "She is the queen's cousin, Katherine Grey." Her voice dropped. "She is not much in favor."

Even standing still, Katherine Grey appeared to be dancing, her white hands, liberally jeweled, gracefully punctuating her conversation. "Why then is she here?"

"Her Majesty keeps her family close, whether or not she likes them."

There was a shout from the inner chamber, and Mistress Ashley appeared at the door. She saw me and beckoned, then changed her mind. "You will meet Her Majesty," she said, "but we will wait until she is dressed."

Several women, including Lady Mary, followed Mistress Ashley into the bedchamber. I fell back, not knowing what to do with myself.

"Her Majesty likes new faces." It was another woman in black, this one not as frighteningly pretty as the queen's cousin. I was glad to hear it, until she added, "It gives her a wider range of targets."

Before I could respond, she burst into laughter. "Don't be alarmed," she said. "You must be the missing chamberer. I'm Cressida Doulton."

Cressida was of middling height, with red-brown hair crimped into tight curls, and a strong Cornish accent. Sensitive as I was to my own French-accented English, I liked her immediately, especially when her next words were a complaint about our monotonous wardrobe.

There was a shout of laughter from the knot of men around Katherine Grey, and Cressida made a face. "That one always has her admirers."

"Lady Mary says she's the queen's cousin."

"She is," Cressida confirmed. "She's also always in a temper."

I knew how to placate, to cheer, to do a hundred different things to lighten a mood, but a woman in a permanent bad temper was a challenge—and the queen would likely be challenge enough. I looked at Katherine Grey again, noting the sulky mouth in an otherwise lovely face, and thought she must be like my mother, a woman permanently aggrieved.

While we waited, Cressida filled me in on our duties, and the women with whom we shared them. There were two other chamberers: Dorothy Bradbelt, fast friends with Mistress Ashley, and Grace Phillips, who had previously served Queen Mary, but whose husband supported Elizabeth.

By the time Her Majesty was dressed, I had grown to like Cressida very much. At last the bedchamber doors were flung open. Mary Sidney peered out. "Mistress Lewis," she called. "Her Majesty wishes to meet you."

I passed through the doors, at first not noticing the queen in the excess of her surroundings. Everything was draped and swagged and tasseled, covered in spangles, or heavily carved. If there was a surface, it was ornamented. In the center of all this was the jewel herself, Elizabeth Tudor, a woman almost subsumed by the glory of her dress.

At Mistress Ashley's nod, I approached and sank into what I

hoped was an acceptably deep curtsy.

"Your Majesty," she said, "allow me to present Mistress Margaery Lewis, your newest chamberer."

"You may rise, Mistress Lewis." The queen's voice was light, surprisingly girlish, considering the shouts I had heard earlier.

I risked a glance before directing my gaze elsewhere; I had been warned the queen did not like to be looked at directly. A handsome woman, as Robin had said. Her skin was clear and very white, a startling contrast with her dark eyes. Her hair was more red than gold, and elaborately dressed with a pearl set into each ringlet.

"It is an honor to serve you, Your Majesty," I said, managing not to stammer. "Thank you for allowing me a place in the royal household."

"We are surprised at your youth. When Master Lewis told us of his recent marriage, we assumed he had married a widow of some years." She smiled archly. "Instead, we discover the reason for his tardy arrival."

Apparently, Robin was not the only one unsettled by my age. Not knowing what to say, I ventured something extemporaneous. "My husband is grateful Your Majesty asked him to assist Master Cecil."

"They shall have much to do." She looked past me then, at someone in the doorway. "Has he arrived?"

"Not yet, Your Majesty," said Mary Sidney. "I'm sure my brother will be here soon."

"We would hope so," she said, an edge to her voice. "We thought to go riding this morning."

Her women looked at each other in dismay. Riding would require an entirely different costume.

Mistress Ashley caught my eye, and jerked her head toward the door. I curtsied again, and backed slowly from the chamber.

"You will return to your apartments after the queen retires," Mistress Ashley told me when she next emerged. "If Master Lewis is elsewhere with the principal secretary, you may sleep with the queen's women if you choose."

"I would not wish to crowd anyone." Cressida said she shared quarters near the privy apartments with several others, and that the maids of honor were crammed together like figs in a crock.

"There is always space," Mistress Ashley said. "One of us sleeps in the royal bedchamber each night."

"Why?"

"Elizabeth is not just the queen." Her gently lecturing tone reminded me of Robin. "She is England, and her body must be protected at all times—from slander, as well as from physical harm. When she rests, the doors are locked and watched all night by four esquires of the body, in addition to the yeomen guards." She looked narrowly at Elizabeth, who was speaking fondly to a dark-haired gentleman. "The queen does not sleep well. If she wakes in the night, she wants someone there to talk with her."

That seemed a great responsibility, to calm the queen's terrors and talk her back to sleep. It made me glad I was an unimportant northern gentlewoman, married to a slightly more important northern gentleman.

I served the queen five days a week, with Wednesdays and Sundays off. Robin was with Cecil every day, barring attendance at church on Sunday, the only time I saw him during daylight hours. Afterward, he kissed my cheek and disappeared until nightfall, when he frequently returned with Ned Pickering. I could only bear so much solitude, and often went to the presence chamber during my time off, to observe the courtiers, so I might learn how to become one of them.

It was a youthful court. Men like Robin, of fifty or more, were less common than the graceful and athletic young men who dominated the presence chamber. But courts were run by older men, whose heads could not be easily turned by pretty women.

The gentlemen who spent their days in the privy chambers flirted with us at every opportunity, and each word and glance was scrutinized upon their departure. Games of flirtation were new to me, and I tried to play along, but when it became known I had been married only a short time, their next pursuit was to see if they could make me blush.

Cressida stepped in when I grew flustered, but she frequently let me flounder, saying, "You must learn to handle yourself. You're a grown woman."

But the world into which I had been thrust was a constant puzzle; my sheltered upbringing had not prepared me for this.

There were two pairs of sisters in the royal household. Philadelphia and Katherine Carey were cousins to the queen on her mother's side, while Katherine and Mary Grey were related through King Henry. They were also sisters to Jane, the executed usurper queen.

The Careys were maids of honor, bright and charming girls, secure in their place in the queen's affections. The Greys were not so fortunate. Under Queen Mary, they had been ladies of the privy chamber, but Elizabeth demoted them to maids of the presence chamber. Their status required they be there; their closeness to Mary—and the queen's dislike—required they not be too close.

The Tudor blood was strong in Katherine Grey. She had the same ivory skin and red-gold hair as every royal relation, but in her case, it was a particularly happy mix. When I mentioned her to Robin, his brief history explained at least one reason for her unpleasant attitude. "Her father married her off to the Earl of Pembroke's son," he said, "on the same day Jane married Guildford Dudley."

"I didn't know maids of honor could be married."

He flexed his fingers, stiff from a long day of writing. "When Jane fell, her father-in-law sent her back to her family and applied for an annulment."

"Poor Katherine!" I could not like that she took out her unhappiness on the rest of us, but I understood her a little better. "What was the ground?"

"Non-consummation," he said blandly. "She was but thirteen."

How humiliating, to be returned like an unwanted gift.

"Her father was imprisoned by that point, so she was sent home to her mother and young sister Mary." Robin shook his head, remembering. "And a few weeks after Jane and Henry Grey were executed, the mother married her steward, who was nearer her daughters' age than her own."

"Goodness." I sat back and considered the complicated lives of courtiers, and the amount of space it took in Robin's brain to keep all those relationships straight. But keeping them straight, knowing who was rising and who was falling, and their relations to others, was his job.

It was also mine. I returned to the privy chambers armed with new knowledge—and some sympathy—for the Grey sisters.

Other than Cressida, I had no friends among the queen's women. Most of them had known each other all their lives, and a late-arriving northerner was a short-lived novelty. They weren't unkind, but neither were they welcoming. They dressed in fashions far beyond Robin's purse, despite the unpaid nature of our positions, and spoke in a near-impenetrable code. I was surrounded by people, yet I had never been lonelier.

I turned to Alice for comfort. Grand-mère had been right: I did need her.

We explored the public areas of the palace, making frequent reference to Sebastian's map, and walked the gardens when the weather was fair. Growing bolder, we ventured through the gates and walked the Strand, admiring the great houses that stretched along its length toward the city proper. I felt like a fine lady, escorted by my maid, but spoiled the effect by conversing with her as though we were friends.

"The queen suggested I learn the lute," I grumbled. "So as to be more useful." We paused to admire the gaily-painted barges tied up beyond the water stairs. "Does every other family in England give their daughters music lessons?"

"The only family I've known beside yours was mine," Alice said, "and they could barely feed us."

My complaints were petty in comparison to what other people suffered. "We can afford lessons, at least."

Alice stepped aside as several young men in scarlet livery sped past on some errand. "Do you think Master Lewis would like that?"

Her words were innocent; Alice wasn't like the women with whom I spent my days, full of probing questions. "I don't know," I said. "I have no idea what he likes."

She touched my cloaked shoulder. "I think he would like anything you do. He dotes on you."

I stopped walking to stare at her. "Are you mocking me?"

Her mouth dropped open. "No, mistress. It is obvious."

"Not to me." We resumed our stroll, and I focused on the wherries skimming over the water. It was difficult to fathom that inside each small boat was a person whose life was as interesting or overwhelming to them as mine was to me.

"He may not speak his feelings," Alice said, "but I am dismissed early each night, so you can be alone."

I closed my eyes, stunned by this vivid, incorrect impression of my marriage. "He does not touch me," I said wearily. "He never has."

"But mistress…" Alice's brow wrinkled. "I saw the sheet, the morning after you were wed. I helped Madame Dupree with the laundry."

If I had a personal coat of arms, it would be that stained sheet, gules on argent. "It was his blood, not mine. He thought to give me time to accustom myself to marriage."

"That was kind." Alice pulled her hood forward to block the wind. "It is often a shock to young girls."

"Were you shocked?"

"Walter was seventeen." Her cheeks reddened, but not from the cold. "He knew how to make it good for me."

There was a world of knowledge of which I was completely ignorant. My maid could not read, and yet she knew more than me on this most important topic.

"I don't know if that was the intention." I pulled my gloved hands into my sleeves. "I believed so then, but what reason could he have to leave me untouched since?"

Alice was silent for a long time. "I know not," she said at last. "But he does care." She narrowed her eyes. "He is…older. Perhaps he cannot? Or he is afraid he cannot, and does not wish your pity." Arriving at a conclusion which fit her image of Robin, she nodded. "That must be it. He fears being unable to satisfy you, and would rather not attempt the challenge."

I was skeptical. Robin was not a man to shy away from a challenge, and he was direct enough that if he were physically incapable, he would have said so, instead of putting me off with platitudes.

"Let's go in," I said. "I'm freezing, and I want to finish my partlet so I can wear it to church on Sunday."

Chapter 11

"Just because he's known her since childhood doesn't give him rights over her." Ned Pickering yawned and stretched his legs toward the fire, the very picture of a man at home. "Master of Horse, indeed."

Ned had a house in London, but I wondered if he would recognize it, so rarely was he anywhere but at Robin's side. They were together all day, eating supper in the hall while I waited upon the queen, and then he spent at least an hour in our rooms, still talking, after my return. I liked him well enough—Ned was alarmingly likeable—but his constant presence made it impossible to be alone with Robin. There were many nights when the murmur of their voices lulled me to sleep.

They were in deep discussion when I came in, and did not look up. Sebastian offered me a glass of wine, which I accepted gratefully. At least someone acknowledged my weariness and thirst.

Sinking into my chair—Ned having thoughtfully procured a third, so I would have a place to sit—I eased off my slippers and curled my toes, trying to work the soreness out of feet which had been stood upon for the better part of twelve hours.

My seat had started out between theirs, but I couldn't bear it: they talked around and over me, passing papers across the table as if I were invisible. After a few days, I moved to Robin's other side. They didn't notice.

"It gives him leave to touch her as no other man in England is permitted." Robin looked grim. "As no other man would dare."

"Who are you talking about?" The wine went down easily; I hadn't managed any with my quick, standing supper in the privy chamber.

"Dudley." Robin refilled my glass, then his own.

I thought I knew who he meant. "Is he quite tall, with dark hair? Very blue eyes?"

Robin's own eyes narrowed. "I can't say as they're blue," he said, "but the rest of the description is apt. Is he with the queen often?"

As soon as the queen was dressed, Robert Dudley was in the bedchamber, getting in our way. After that, they walked in the privy gardens or rode together in the park, and when Elizabeth finally got down to the business of governing, he retreated no further than the presence chamber—in case she required a smile or a wink.

"I've seen him," I said, my answer limited by my oath. "Occasionally."

Ned huffed, and reached for the wine. Robin moved it out of range. "He's too free with Her Majesty. It's going to drive Cecil to drink."

"He is no more free with her than you are with me." They were criticizing someone Elizabeth had known since girlhood. "Can the queen not have friends?"

They laughed, but sobered quickly. "The queen must be above reproach." Robin echoed Mistress Ashley. "No man should ever think to lay hands on her unless he is her husband."

I pursed my lips. "Could she marry him?"

"Lord, no!" This from Ned, whose face turned red at the very thought. "He's a commoner, whose family has been accused of treason more than once. Justly, I might add. More important from the standpoint of your question, Mistress Margaery, he has a wife already."

There were so many women I hadn't learned all their names. "Which one is she?"

"Amy Robsart," Robin said. "She does not come to court."

I reconsidered my opinion of Robert Dudley. He was very attractive, with his brilliant eyes and charming manners, but I did not like that he left his wife to pay court to Elizabeth. I couldn't imagine she would want his wife among her ladies, either, to watch her husband behave like a greensick boy.

The queen had gone to Eltham, and those of us left behind were free to take dinner in the hall. Cressida and I finished tidying the detritus of Elizabeth's last-minute change of gown, and found space at a table near the doors, away from the other women. It was loud in the hall, a different sort of noise than the controlled chaos of the privy apartments.

I glimpsed Robin and Ned at a far table with a few other

gentlemen. Unable to catch his eye, I continued the conversation begun with Cressida on our way from the privy chambers. "Why did you not mention you were married?"

"Geoffrey is with his family," she said, "in Penryn. His father is a shipbuilder."

A Cornish shipbuilder's wife did not seem an obvious choice for a queen's gentlewoman. I wondered at her path to Whitehall; was it as convoluted as my own?

"My husband works with the principal secretary." I thought to point him out, but decided not to.

"You're lucky." She reached for the ale. "You have conjugal lodgings."

"They're quite small." I didn't want her to think we lived in any luxury.

She snorted. "They're better than where I sleep." Her mouth turned up, unable to resist poking fun. "Women snore as loudly as men, and fart nearly as much."

I giggled at the thought of the queen's fine ladies, piled three to a bed, lying in their own reek while Her Majesty slept under scented linens and fur-lined velvet covers.

"Do you miss your husband?" What would court be like without Robin? Even with the restrictions placed on my conversation, I enjoyed his company at the end of the day.

"I miss my daughter more," she said. "Ebrel is with my parents, being raised with my youngest sister."

I could not bear to have someone else raise my child. "How old is she?"

Cressida's gaze was distant. "Five. My sister is six, so they're good companions."

I hadn't thought her old enough to have a child that age. "Ebrel is a pretty name."

"It means April." She popped a bit of bread into her mouth. "She was born five months after we were wed."

I couldn't get my husband to touch me, and hers wouldn't keep away long enough for her to marry as a virgin. I was more impressed than judging.

"We were impatient." She turned penetrating hazel eyes on me. "You've no children?"

Shaking my head, I said, "We've only been married four months."

"That's plenty of time to catch a baby. But it wouldn't be convenient now, just as you're trying to get into the queen's good graces."

It would not. Nor, I thought, would it be convenient when I was still trying to get into my husband's good graces. He had already lost the quiet life he craved; a squalling babe would be the death knell of his peace.

It took hundreds of pins to assemble the queen's daily costume, and because she was too impatient to stand still, they scattered everywhere as she was undressed. My chief task as chamberer was to collect them in a small jeweled box, searching for their bright heads glinting between the floorboards; it would be worth my life if the royal foot trod on one. I counted them in the morning, and tried mightily to have the same number at night.

After Elizabeth retired, her women departed or moved to the presence chamber, because the queen required silence. Her window overlooking the Thames was shut tight against river sounds—much less the noxious night air and the disturbing influences of the moon.

Many things could disturb an unmarried woman, I learned: the moon; the air; music; dancing; the presence of gentlemen. We were—apparently—so full of ungovernable lusts that we could not be trusted to manage our own behavior. No wonder the queen slept with a companion; if her chastity meant so much to England, it could not be questioned.

It was questioned, however, by my own husband, who asked with increasing frequency about Robert Dudley, and was surprised by my reticence.

I assumed he and Ned had sworn their own oaths, but they gossiped each night like old women. While I would never repeat their conversations, I held the information in my head and used it to interpret what I saw: the glances, the caresses, and once, a quick touching of lips as Dudley bid her good night. There was a yearning in his behavior; if they were lovers, I thought I would be able to tell.

There was no opportunity, besides, for Elizabeth was never alone. As much as Mistress Ashley caved to the queen's wishes, she would throw Robert Dudley into the Thames if he harmed her mistress. And harm it would be, not just to her reputation, but to a small, guarded portion of Elizabeth that few people—possibly only Robert Dudley and Katherine Ashley—knew existed.

A normal woman might have risked herself, but Elizabeth had never been normal. Growing up with the awareness of her mother's disgrace, delegitimized by the father she adored, she watched as her stepmothers were disposed of by death or by law, one meeting the same fate as her mother.

All this, before considering the everyday risks run by women to bear children. Sexual love must have been as tempting—and as terrifying—as playing with a razor.

Chapter 12

Because the queen was an enthusiastic horsewoman, I was frequently able to ride Artemis. At least three times a week, we galloped across the royal parks, the queen's Master of Horse at her heels. Hunting was exhilarating and eased the tension of being so frequently indoors. My ability to keep up went some way toward excusing my lack of musical ability.

As we pounded across the grass in pursuit of deer and excitement, I thought regretfully of my breeches, folded away in a chest at Winterset. After hours in the saddle, I longed for them. Riding astride wasn't ladylike, but there were times when being a lady was more trouble than it was worth.

Her Majesty had a variety of elaborate riding costumes: good English wool trimmed with sable for cold days, and rich purple velvet with embroidery for finer weather. Her extravagantly plumed hats rarely made it back intact because she was such an intrepid rider. The feather merchants must have loved her.

"You ride very well, Mistress Margaery," the queen said one afternoon as we trailed her back into the palace. "Do they grow centaurs in the North?"

I remembered when Robin had called me a centaur. This was the third day in a row we had been out, and I was beginning to feel that Artemis and I were one. "I spent my girlhood on horseback, Your Majesty," I said. "It is where I am happiest."

Her dark eyes focused on me. "Until you met your most excellent husband." Despite her flirting and fondling of Robert Dudley, her remarks about husbands always had a mocking tone.

I risked a jest in return. "Perhaps even then."

The queen was silent for a long second before bursting into raucous, inelegant laughter. The rest of her ladies followed suit, some dutifully, and others with genuine mirth.

My mouth fell open. I had made the queen laugh, even if it was at Robin's expense. Her amusement was worth the slight to my husband, who in any case would never hear of it.

While the queen was being changed, I hurried back to our rooms to resume my black gown. I was shocked to find Robin at the table with an unfamiliar young man, his pen scratching away at a sheet of paper.

"Good morrow." I tossed my cap, with its short, practical feathers, onto a chest. "Husband."

He wrote another line, then looked up. "Ah, Margaery. This is William Hawkins. Will, my wife, Mistress Lewis."

William Hawkins—medium-tall, brown-haired, unspecial—bounded up at my entrance and bowed over my hand, murmuring pleasantries. "Shall I take this back to Cecil for you?"

Robin handed over the sheet. "Careful, the ink's still wet."

I rested my palm on the table, waiting until the door closed. "What are you doing here?"

"I often come back after dinner to work in peace."

Alice had never mentioned this, and I felt deprived in a way I didn't quite understand. "Is it just Ned," I asked, "or are there more like him?"

Robin's smile wasn't as satisfying as the queen's laughter, but it mattered more. "There is no one quite like Ned, but when there are a dozen men, all vying to make the same point, it is sometimes easier to disappear for a while."

I understood that well enough, for the privy apartments, especially in the mornings, sounded remarkably like a cage of exotic birds.

"I don't often get away for dinner," I said, "but if I am able, should I send a page?" The only time we ate dinner together was after church.

Robin cleaned his quill. "I generally eat with Ned. You would be bored."

As it sounded like an extension of our evenings together, he was correct, but couldn't he—just occasionally—choose me over his friend? I might as well give my loyalty to Elizabeth; there was not much call for it at home.

William Cecil's duties as principal secretary were many, but chief among them seemed to be convincing the queen to marry. It was necessary, he said, to provide an heir to the throne and stability for England. Elizabeth understood this well enough, but she did not like it, and her opinions on his candidates were expressed in colorful language quite unbefitting a queen—but very entertaining nonetheless.

"God's blood," she muttered, pacing the chamber, a sheet of paper crumpled in her fist. "Are we to be tied to one such as this, simply because a woman must marry and bear sons? The Prince of Sweden! Is Sweden the best our council can offer?"

No one ventured a response; it was not our place, and the queen was not actually speaking to us. She was rehearsing her next conversation with Cecil before a captive audience.

She threw down the list and stamped on it with her velvet-shod foot. "And Philip—we are living proof of our father's break with Rome. Why would we ever agree to such a match?"

I knew nothing of Sweden, but France and Spain, the only countries powerful enough to be useful allies, would not marry a heretic and were indeed the countries England needed protecting from. Philip's politic offer would be rejected: in addition to conversion, such a marriage would also require a papal dispensation because he had been married to her sister.

Robin and Ned's endless conversations were educational, at least; because of them, I knew the Tudors had a bad history with papal dispensations for marriage.

Despite pressure from Cecil, Elizabeth had named no heir, and was unlikely to do so, as her two closest relations were the young Scottish queen, now in France, and Lady Katherine Grey—geographically closer, but whose very presence was enough to bring out the rough side of the queen's tongue.

Katherine did herself no favors, being as imperious as the queen without the position to back it up. In the beginning, I thought to find some kinship with her, but she could not bring herself to be civil to someone so far beneath her, no matter that both our fathers had been executed. She alternated between pretending I did not exist and aiming barbed comments when I least expected them.

"It's not every woman who can wear the same gown day after day and still look fresh, Mistress Margaery," she said with a coy smile. "It must be your upbringing."

My upbringing had taught me how to hide my feelings, so she didn't know how much her words hurt. To Katherine, I was a raw girl from the country, more likely to smell of horse dung than flowers. While it was true I had fewer changes than the other women, I did not wear the same gown, and my body linen was always fresh, scented with the lavender Alice folded in with my clothes.

My husband's position in Cecil's retinue did nothing to improve my status with Katherine; she acknowledged Cecil's rank, but a man such as Robin, self-made and sprung from nothing, did not impress. If anything, his hard work made her look down on him.

Cressida fit in no better, but cared far less. I envied her ability to snub Katherine Grey and make the maids blush and titter with her ribald jokes. They were drawn to her, for all that she mortified them daily.

She was lecturing them about their prospects when Robert Dudley strode across the chamber. "None of that," she said as their heads turned in unison. "He is not for the likes of you, children, no matter that you are here to find husbands."

For all their fluttering, they smiled with the confidence of girls who knew their faces and fortunes would earn them an appropriate match, if not on the level of the queen's favorite.

Katherine raised her pointed chin. "Not all of us."

A smile spread, cat-like, across Cressida's face. "I forgot, we have a married woman among us."

This could go badly wrong for my friend; Katherine was not beloved by the queen, but she still had power. "There are several married women among us," I said. "And there is more to life than catching a husband."

Instead of appreciating my defense, Katherine turned on me. "How did you catch yours, Mistress Margaery? With a bow, or does a snare work better with the intellectual sort?"

My jaw clenched. "I did something unconventional," I told her, smiling with a calm I did not feel. "I talked to him."

Her sharp laugh showed her disbelief, but the door opened

before she could continue, and all eyes were drawn to the queen, who entered the presence chamber on Dudley's arm.

The maids looked at him the way a cat would look at a bird on the other side of a window—hungrily, and completely incapable of achieving their goal. Dudley, a cat himself, was focused only on the royal bird so nearly within his grasp.

In the matter of bedtimes, Elizabeth had no more self-control than a child; if she was having fun, she did not wish to sleep. This evening had been particularly lively, with music and dancing until even the maids drooped with exhaustion.

When I at last escaped, Sebastian waited in the hall. Unless Robin needed him, he often came to escort me home. He was a peaceful presence after the fuss of putting the queen to bed and emptying the privy chamber, and we often walked without speaking until I could hear my own thoughts again.

As we turned toward the stairs that led to the upstairs apartments, I saw a movement in a side corridor. "Wait." I turned, dropping Seb's arm.

The torch had been extinguished, but I could see a blur of white skirts, pinned to the wall, and white sleeves wrapped around a dark doublet. The man's back was to me, but I recognized the glinting jewel on his hat and knew him to be Edward Seymour. The woman with him was Katherine Grey, behaving in a most unmaidenly manner. Her small sister, who had left with her, was nowhere to be seen.

The maids were secured in their chamber when the queen went to rest, but the Grey sisters, and a few others with family at Whitehall, had their own lodgings. Although their mother was not at court, Katherine and Mary had an apartment near the privy chambers, with their own servants to wait upon them.

I should have walked on, but I stood for a moment. The icy demeanor Katherine presented in the privy chambers was nowhere in evidence. Her head was thrown back, her white throat visible as Seymour lowered his head to her breasts.

The sounds of their passion were audible, and I thought how inappropriate it was to watch them, and with my husband's servant.

I tugged at his arm. "Let us go."

As we continued to my comfortable apartment and my sterile marriage, I tried to puzzle out why I was so shaken by the abandon Katherine displayed and understood that it was control. Loss of control was a fearful thing; I could not imagine behaving like that, not with Robin or with any other man.

Chapter 13

GRACE PHILIPS, ONE OF the other chamberers, had fallen pregnant. This was seen as a great inconvenience, considering we had all just settled into our positions. When Mistress Ashley informed her she was expected to continue with her duties until the month before her confinement, barring any ill health, she appeared grateful not to have been dismissed for having been impregnated by her husband.

"I'm shocked he managed it," Katherine Grey said, not quietly enough. "The man is nearly decrepit." She glanced in my direction. "Look at Mistress Margaery. Her husband is of similar age, and she is still slender as a reed."

Robin was at least fifteen years younger than George Phillips. "A man is never too old to sire a child," I said. "It is only we who grow too old to bear them."

"Since that is not your case, should we place the blame on your husband?" The other women tittered, willing to be led by Katherine unless her spite turned in their direction.

"Must there be blame?" Cressida spoke up. "Margaery is fortunate not to be burdened with a child so soon after her marriage. It gives her time to grow closer to her husband."

"I'm not so sure," I said. "I only see him for about twenty minutes a night. He often gets in later than I do."

Cressida sidled closer. "I do hope he gets in," she said softly. "Even for twenty minutes."

The blood mounted inexorably to my cheeks, and I busied myself with the queen's books, so the others would not see my red face.

One morning, Grace Phillips failed to appear. Several hours later, a page arrived and spoke with Mistress Ashley. She gathered us together, her expression solemn. "Mistress Grace has lost her child," she said. "She will spend the next week resting. When she returns to service, I would have you treat her as if nothing untoward had happened."

"But Mistress Ashley," Philadelphia Carey said, "it's a terrible thing to lose a child. Why can't we tell her we're sorry?"

"It is sad," she agreed, "but it is a matter between husband and wife."

In due time, though slightly longer than the expected week, Grace returned. Tentative and as easily startled as a rabbit, it was too soon for her to be back amongst the foxes. Even Mistress Ashley understood when, after a sharp word from the queen, Grace folded at the waist and sobbed into her skirts.

Mistress Ashley spied me nearby. "Margaery, please take Grace back to her apartments."

She continued to weep as we walked the empty corridors. When I saw that her lodgings were near ours, I said, "They will not expect me back for a bit. Would you take a glass of wine?"

Grace stared at me. "Why?" she asked. "We've barely spoken since your arrival, and no one has had a kind word for me since...the baby."

"We were told not to mention it, for fear of upsetting you." I bit my lip. "I have every sympathy for your loss."

Sebastian was tidying the room, and sprung to attention at our entrance. Greeting him, I said, "Could you bring wine, please?"

"Of course." He ducked out.

"I've seen that blackamoor before," Grace said. "Walking around with a tall, thin man. Is that your husband?"

Robin and Sebastian made an eye-catching pair, so pale and so dark, and so obviously devoted.

"Younger than my George," she said, "but I'm sure they've made remarks."

"They have. And I believe your husband is higher-born than mine, so perhaps in their eyes, that makes up for his years."

Sebastian returned with a bottle and two glasses, then disappeared tactfully into the antechamber.

Grace sighed. "This is the first conversation I've had since my arrival where I haven't been judged or mocked or laughed at."

It was a relief to hear my own thoughts spoken aloud. "I was raised away from society," I told her. "This is different from anything I've ever experienced."

She took a sip of wine. "Some adjust better than others. And some are at their best in a place where they have inexperienced women to prey upon."

Seb had brought a small plate of suckets and I popped one in my mouth and considered her words. "There are a few kind women," I said. "I know Cressida Doulton, and now you."

"I am leaving." A smile spread across her face. "I will not spend my life surrounded by basilisks."

I could have had another friend, if I hadn't been afraid to speak. Perhaps she would have made it through this difficult time and stayed in the queen's service if she'd had friends.

"Would you reconsider?"

"That is very sweet, Margaery, but this place is not for me." She tilted her head. "I am not sure if it's for you, either."

By the spring, Ned's constant presence had begun to grate. When I came in and found him sprawled in his usual seat, with Robin nowhere to be seen, the blood rushed to my head.

"Where is my husband?" I could not be bothered to observe the pleasantries.

"God give you good evening, Mistress Margaery." There was a glass at his elbow, and one of Robin's books was open on his knee. "He'll be along soon. A few last minute details."

The queen had been short-tempered all day, and I wanted nothing more than silence. "Couldn't you have done them, and sent him home?"

"I can't do everything." His smile was indulgent. "Rob's a useful fellow. That's why I wanted him so badly."

So it was his fault we were here. "You couldn't have found someone else to do the job?"

Ned tossed the book aside. "Of course, but I like working with Rob. After I encountered him on his way to the Tower—well, after I relieved his captor of his responsibility and took Rob to the queen, there was no way he could say no."

Where was Sebastian? It wasn't proper for me to be alone with Ned, but his easy chat made me realize just how indiscreet he could be; Seb might spoil it.

"Robin mentioned you took him to the queen," I said carefully. "But I didn't know *you* were the one who rescued him, Sir Edward. I must thank you."

His round face flushed. "Please, call me Ned when we're here. I like everything that comes with Sir Edward except the formality."

"Ned." It was the first time I'd used his name, but it would not be the last, if I could also make use of him to learn the things my husband did not think to tell me. "How did it come about?"

"Well, I knew they'd taken him," he said. "A courier came with the news, and Anselm reached me a few days later. That ride nearly killed Rob—I can't conceive how the old man managed it."

Knowing Anselm only a short time, and still not completely understanding his relationship with Robin, I knew he'd managed it from love. "How fortunate he got word to you in time."

"Once the old queen was dead, we intercepted them outside Cambridge." Ned offered me a glass and refilled his own. "I don't think young Hawkins's heart was truly in his task."

I choked on my drink. "Hawkins?"

"William Hawkins," Ned said. "You've met him, haven't you?"

"Yes." We'd met a few times now, but Robin never mentioned he'd been the one to storm into Winterset and arrest him.

"He's not a bad sort—" Ned broke off as the door opened.

Robin leaned heavily on Sebastian's arm. After shedding his doublet and cap, he eased himself into his chair.

"That damned knee." Ned looked around for an empty glass and, realizing he'd given it to me, pushed his own toward Robin. "What a day, eh?"

"You escaped promptly enough." He raised the glass, his Adam's apple bobbing with each swallow.

"Seniority, my dear man." His smile was ingratiating, but Robin wasn't having it this evening. "No?"

"Not tonight, Ned," he said. "I'm tired, and my head aches nearly as bad as my knee. You have a bed waiting for you, do you not?"

I smiled into my wine and watched his departure with satisfaction.

Robin tipped his head back. "I hope you didn't have to put up with him for long."

"Not too long." I reached for my embroidery, then stopped. "He's very talkative."

"Ned can talk the ears off a statue." There was a smile in his voice. "What was he on about this evening?"

I leaned over and picked up the book Ned had cast aside, placing it carefully on the table. If the binding was damaged, I wanted Robin to know who had been responsible. "He was telling me about how he rescued you from William Hawkins."

He froze. "Mary's death rescued me," he said slowly. "But Ned helped, I'll grant him that."

"How can you even look at him?"

"Ned?"

"Hawkins. He tried to kill you."

Robin pressed at his temples. "He did no more than I would have done in his place, and when the wind changed, he went with it."

Talk of changing winds was all well and good, but I was not about to forgive the man who had nearly widowed me. "But you see him every day—you work with him." A thought occurred to me. "You want to keep an eye on him, don't you?"

"I don't need to." He turned his head so his neck cracked. "I trust him."

I moved behind him and began to rub his shoulders. They relaxed slowly under my hands. "Is that better?"

"Much." He raised his glass, then stopped as my hand slipped inside the neck of his shirt. "What are you doing?"

Elizabeth had done this to Dudley, just the other day. I remembered the way her fingers dipped inside his collar, and how his face changed when she touched his flesh. There was nothing of Dudley in Robin's response.

He nodded toward my chair. "Sit with me."

"Yes, husband." I took a long draught of wine, hoping he would credit my embarrassed flush to the grape.

"What are you trying to accomplish?" He looked at me steadily.

I stared back. "I'm trying to accomplish marriage, and making a fool of myself. How you must laugh at me!"

"I would never do that." Moving his glass aside, he took my

hands. "And we are married."

"Barely." His hands were warm and kind, like him, and insufficient, like our marriage. "We are not married in the eyes of God, nor in the eyes of the church."

A log popped and split, showering sparks on the hearth. Robin leaned forward to deal with it. "We are married in my eyes, Margaery."

"But not in mine." I took another mouthful of wine.

"You knew when we married that I was not an overly physical man." He watched the fire, failing to see the explosion building inside his wife.

"I didn't know you would lie beside me each night like a corpse," I burst out, clutching the glass so tightly it should have shattered. "Think how I feel, knowing you are so repulsed you cannot bring yourself to touch me."

He blinked at me. "Repulsed?" He reached for me again, and I pulled away. "Why would you think that?"

"Let me count the ways," I said, then stopped. "No. I am done with begging." I called for Alice. "When you have something new to say, feel free to wake me."

Chapter 14

THREE HOURS INTO THE sermon, Robin twitched beside me like a bored child. I closed my eyes and tried to look reverent as I worked out a new embroidery design in my head. Had Catholicism ever been this tiresome?

After several days of rain, the weak sun was more of a benediction than anything that occurred beneath the godly ceiling of Westminster, and we walked slowly back toward Whitehall.

"Rob!" Someone jogged up on his left. "I thought it was you."

"Good morrow, Will," my husband said. "You remember my wife?"

William Hawkins swept off his cap and bowed. "Mistress Lewis."

I bobbed a curtsy, looking at him guardedly. This was the first time I'd seen him up close since I learned of his role in Robin's arrest. He appeared unremarkable to have been given such a foul assignment.

Robin glanced from me to him. "Was there something you wanted, Will?"

"Just a question, if you have a moment."

I ignored their conversation, trying to work out the connection between them. It was all well and good for Robin to trust him; he had the backing of William Cecil, and Sebastian and Ned constantly at his shoulder, whereas I—

What was I thinking? I was at no risk from this innocuous young man. If he hadn't hurt Robin when he was under orders, it wasn't likely to happen now, when my husband was ingratiated with those in power.

"You weren't very pleasant." Robin said as Hawkins sprinted away toward the river. "It's not like you."

I picked up the pace as I walked through the gate, knowing it would pain him to chase me. "I will not be pleasant to such a man." If Robin was not keeping an eye on him, perhaps Will Hawkins followed Robin to keep himself safe.

He groaned. "If I don't hold it against him, why must you?"

The door opened; Sebastian always knew when he was needed.

He took my cloak and Robin's hat, and, looking between us, backed into the anteroom and shut the door.

"Perhaps I'm more attached to your life than you are."

He lowered himself into his chair. "I doubt that." His tone was wry.

I met his eyes, and spoke plainly. "He would have made me a widow before you have made me a wife."

He put his hands over his face. "Margaery, we agreed our relations would not necessarily be those of a married couple."

"I believe you said"—and I glanced at him—"that if there was another bloody sheet, it would be when we agreed to it."

"When *we* agreed," he said precisely.

I took a deep breath. Any serenity I had achieved during the endless service dissipated. "It is too much." My heart pounded; though Robin encouraged me to speak my mind, it still felt unnatural. "You expect me to be pleasant to a man who wished you dead—in addition to Ned, who must have a home of his own, though he never seems to go there. Forgive me if I find it all a little difficult."

Robin pushed himself up, bending to rub his knee. "Is there anything you like about me today? Certainly it is not my friends and associates, nor my treatment of you." He caught up his short cloak, and paused at the door. "I will hunt down my unsuitable friends, and spend the afternoon elsewhere. I hope my absence is more agreeable than my presence."

It was agreeable, at first, as I paced the chamber and rehearsed the unkind words I could not speak, because he was kind, and logical, and generally correct. And there was nothing wrong with Ned, other than that he intruded on my time with Robin. William Hawkins was likely no different, but I was not yet ready to accept him.

The time came for supper, and I called for Sebastian to bring me a tray, but he did not respond. When I checked, the anteroom was deserted; of course, he would be with Robin.

I ate in the hall with the queen's women, and watched Katherine Grey and Edward Seymour's sister with their heads together. It was late when I returned, and I stitched and talked to Alice, marking the bells.

It was after midnight when I snuffed the candle. Perhaps something was wrong. If he had gone to a tavern, or was on the streets after curfew, anything could have happened. He could be injured, or dead in a ditch, for all I knew.

Not long after the bells chimed one, the door to the outer chamber opened. Robin bumped into something and swore softly, then paused, waiting for me to call out. A sigh, followed by quiet sounds of undressing. The bedchamber door edged open, and he slid in beside me, his breathing deliberately shallow.

"I thought you weren't coming back."

He started. "I wasn't certain you wanted me to."

"I'm not angry with you." He smelled of ale and smoke; he and Ned had been revisiting their youth at some tavern. "Just with the situation. I don't have a place in your life."

"We could have figured this out at Winterset." He sounded tired, as he often did since we'd come here. "Bringing you to London was a mistake."

When had it become so important that he want me—not just because of our vows, but as a woman? When had I begun to desire my own husband? "I want to be here. With you."

"I cannot bear the thought of disappointing you." He sounded almost afraid.

"What about that other woman…the lover you told me about?" I wanted to say *mistress*, but he hadn't liked the word. "Did you disappoint her?"

"I'm sure I did," he said. "You deserve better."

"Then why did you marry me?" I wanted to see his face as he said these things. "Did you pity me so much?"

His hand found mine. "I assure you, it was not pity." His tone was rueful. "I'm not enough for you, Margaery. I'm too old, I'm too—"

"You're too busy deciding what's wrong to look at what's right." I sat up. "What if you are older? I'm not a child, for all that you treat me like one."

"Our day starts early." Robin pulled the covers up around me. "You should rest."

"I'm not tired." My bones ached for sleep, but in some areas I could be as stubborn as Elizabeth Tudor. "Talk to me."

Sitting up against the pillows, he said with his particular weary patience, "What would you have me say?"

There was only one question. "Why do you not treat me like a wife?"

He took a deep breath and held it for an endless moment. "I do treat you like my wife. How would you have me behave?"

"Words matter," I said, using his own against him. "I said 'like a wife,' not 'like your wife.'"

"And the difference is?"

I thought of my French kitten, given to the cook when we left for England. I was no more than that to him, something to be petted and given treats. But I'd had enough. Robin Lewis would find out his kitten had claws.

"The difference is a wife is due more affection than a kiss on the cheek or a pat on the head." Cressida and the other ladies were quite blunt about the physical aspects of marriage, and ascribed my blushes to my newlywed status.

"Margaery…"

"You were different when we met." I struggled to put it into words, knowing only that I wanted what he freely gave to Sebastian and Ned. "I thought you trusted me."

"I do."

"I am glad of it." I put my hand on his thigh, so close to mine. "But why don't you trust me to be your wife?"

His muscles tensed, and he carefully removed my hand. "Perhaps I do not trust myself to be your husband."

The headsman's footsteps boomed like thunder. I opened my eyes as his scuffed boots passed before me. Another pair of boots followed: black this time, buffed to a shine. Despite their gloss, they moved slowly, one leg dragging a bit.

The hose above the boots were also black. I raised my eyes past the inky doublet to the shockingly pale throat of the condemned, a throat I knew well. My husband knelt in the straw, looking straight at me, his lips moving. I strained to hear him over the roar of the crowd.

I couldn't make out his words, but the hollow step of the headsman, returning with his axe, was unmistakable.

I jerked awake, pouring sweat, my midsection in familiar knots. Scrambling from the bed, I made it to the chamber pot before I released the contents of my stomach. I stayed on my knees until my head cleared.

The nightmare had come with increasing frequency ever since we'd arrived in London, but this was the first to feature Robin in my father's place. I pressed my hand to my mouth as I thought about what I'd escaped seeing by waking up.

Moving to the window, I unlatched the shutter and shoved the casement open to the gray dawn. If we were at Winterset, the rhythm of the sea would lull me back to sleep, but here, my ears were assailed by the early-morning sounds of the palace: servants calling, clopping hooves, and rumbling wheels on the cobbles below. The sounds of a normal day.

I turned to see if I'd disturbed Robin. The bed was empty, his shirt folded neatly on the chest. It was barely light—where had he gone so early, and why?

My years in France had not prepared me for any of this. Robin was supposed to save me, to carry me away from my dull life. Which he had done. It could be worse, I reminded myself: he could have passed us by, and eventually I would have married my mother's choice of husband, and been miserable.

I wasn't miserable, but I was unhappy in a way I couldn't explain. If I could, Robin would attempt to make it better, but it wasn't his job to make my life easy. If I wanted to be treated as an adult, I had to become one, and stop being cowed by every new experience.

I also needed to stop biting my nails and depriving myself of food because my stomach failed me when I was anxious. I had lost weight since coming to London; Alice mentioned it just the other day.

"I thought you'd have filled out," she said, "but I'm going to have to take your gowns in if you keep shrinking."

She meant, of course, that she'd expected me to be pregnant by now.

"Good morrow, mistress." She pushed aside the curtain separating her space from ours. "I heard them leave a while ago. I'm surprised, considering how late they were. Was it all right, when he came in?"

"We spoke." I did not tell her I'd begged my husband to deflower me, and been refused—again. "It is the same."

She folded my nightdress and handed me a cloth. "Good things take time, mistress."

Another platitude! I washed, spattering water everywhere in my haste to be finished. It gave me no pleasure to see or touch my body, as I was likely the only person—other than Alice—who would ever see it.

Katherine Grey lingered near the doors of the presence chamber, apparently with the sole purpose of greeting me. "Here is Mistress Margaery, fresh as a spring breeze from the byre!" Her hangers-on laughed, even as some showed sympathy. "No sunny smile today?"

My throat closed. Cressida was not there to defend me. I looked into her cool blue eyes and said, "Not today, Lady Katherine. At least, not in present company."

She was shocked into silence, and I continued to the privy chamber, where she was not yet welcome; the queen could only look at her after noon.

"I wish I had your nerve," Philadelphia Carey whispered. "She needs to be taken down a peg."

I took the basket of fine mending to the window where the light was strong. Elizabeth was careless of her things, and they needed constant upkeep, much of which had fallen to me. I selected a glove whose embroidered cuff had been damaged when she'd caught it on a branch while riding. The queen had peeled it off and flung it aside without a second thought.

It was fiddly work, not fit for my state of mind, but if I did not make a start, it would be guaranteed that she would demand those same gloves because they best matched her Lincoln blue riding dress. I brought out a tiny blade and picked at the stitches that attached the cuff to the leather.

"Mistress Lewis!" From her tone, it was not the first time Mistress Ashley had said my name.

"I'm sorry." I looked up from my work. "This makes my mind drift."

"You've been cloud-brained for days, don't use your stitching as an excuse." She looked at the glove. "This isn't your usual quality." Pointing out a few nicks in the leather, she said, "These aren't worth repairing. Pull off the cuffs and attach them to a new pair."

"Yes, mistress." If I'd looked more closely, I would have noticed and asked Blanche Parry to send for the glover. Instead I'd wasted an hour.

"You're less capable now than when you arrived. How is that?"

"I don't know."

Her expression softened. "I forget that despite your age, you're less experienced than the maids. Coming to court has been quite a change for you."

I grasped the proffered excuse. "My grandparents kept a very quiet household."

"It will become more natural, in time," she said. "Come to me, if you have questions."

What advice could Mistress Ashley give me? She would be kind—of that I had no doubt—but I could not bring myself to explain that after six months of marriage, I was as virgin as the queen.

"I am sorry for my shortcomings," I said. "I will do better."

Chapter 15

DESPITE THE LATENESS OF the hour, Sebastian lingered outside the presence chamber. I rested my hand on his arm, wishing I could lean on him as Robin did. "Is my husband in our rooms?"

"The gentlemen are waiting for you," he confirmed.

It was expected, now, that Ned would be there. "They are not," I corrected him. "They are drinking and putting the world to rights, and wouldn't notice my absence unless you called their attention to it."

His expression said more than words. "The master enjoys your company. He is just not good at showing it."

I resisted rolling my eyes. "That is the most truthful thing you've ever said."

There was a mess of plates and glasses on the table, but no food remained. After Seb took my things, he went in search of bread and cheese to settle my stomach before bed.

Seeing the space before him fill with my black skirts, Robin looked up. "Good evening, wife," he said. "How is Her Majesty?"

I bent down so he could kiss my cheek. "In her bed, I hope," I said. "She appeared ready to dance all night."

"With Dudley, no doubt?" Ned's face shone pink as a ham in the firelight.

"And many others." I did not like how free Dudley was with the queen, but I continued to defend her honor.

Not receiving the hoped-for answer, they resumed their conversation, while I closed my eyes and waited for my supper. One reason I misliked Ned's constant presence was I either had to stay trussed in my gown until he departed or retreat to the bedchamber. If it was just us, or even Sebastian, I could have changed into a loose gown for my supper.

Seb returned, and I ate quickly, listening to what Robin was saying.

"They take it as a matter of course—Feria and the others—that she will step into her dead sister's shoes, rule as Mary did, with her policies, her advisors, and a husband to direct her actions."

"That she will not," I said, startling them both.

"I think not either," Robin said, "but what is your reasoning, Margaery?"

I chewed my lip, discomfited by their abrupt attention. "Because she is her own woman." I wiped my palms on my skirt, uncertain how to explain what I knew of the young queen without violating my oath. "She is not her sister, and I believe if she is treated like Mary, she will do the opposite simply to rid you of the thought that all women can be managed in the same way."

"She couldn't be so stupid." Ned reached for the wine, and Robin slid it out of range. "What of the other, Rob? Hasn't she been in enough trouble?"

"I don't think she's part of it." He looked at me, then at Ned, and moved the bottle to the chest behind him. "It's time for you to make the arduous journey back to Lothbury Street."

Ned looked stricken. "But I'm so comfortable." He appealed to me. "Mistress Margaery, what say you?"

I smiled. "Only that my feet hurt, and I can't do anything about it while you are here, Sir Edward."

He sighed theatrically. "Then I shall see you on the morrow. Good rest to you both." Sebastian was there with his things before he was on his feet. "God's blood, Seb, must you be so efficient?"

"I'm only thinking of the lady."

Once Ned left, Robin turned to me. "Are you tired, or did you simply want him gone?"

I shrugged. "A bit of both, to be honest."

"Would you sit with me for a while?" He looked down at his hands. "Unless you'd rather sleep."

Hope surged; it wasn't often he chose my company over Ned's. "Let me change, so Alice can go to bed."

When I returned, Sebastian had smothered the fire, and Robin was turning his glass in long fingers, watching the embers through the deep red liquid. I said his name and he started, the wine sloshing. "I didn't hear you."

I raised my gown a few inches, revealing my bare feet. "I'm

stealthy." Sinking into my chair, I reached for my glass, which Seb had thoughtfully refilled. "Was there something you wanted to discuss?"

The glass continued its turning, but Robin's attention was on me. "Yes...though you may not wish to speak of it."

If his questions were about the queen, he should know I would not answer. "What is it?"

"You are acquainted with Lady Katherine Grey?"

"Acquainted is the extent of it. She does not like anyone but Jane Seymour."

"But you see her?"

"Nearly every day." If there was a purpose to his questions, I could not divine it. "Why?"

He sobered. "Has she ever mentioned Count Feria in your hearing? Have you ever seen her with him?"

Feria was the Spanish ambassador; I knew him by sight, but had not seen him recently. Since the queen turned down King Philip's offer of marriage, he was no more in favor than Katherine, and showed himself less often.

"No," I said. "What would they have to speak about?"

"There is nothing definite," he said slowly, "but Cecil is convinced—through some channel of which the rest of us are ignorant—that Spain is interested in Katherine."

I could not have heard him correctly. "Philip would marry Katherine Grey?"

One shoulder raised. "Why not? She is as legitimate as the Scottish queen, and less trouble than Elizabeth."

"But she is not Catholic." The maids attended church with Elizabeth; if Katherine did not, I would have heard.

"Are you sure?" he asked. "Other than Jane, the family was always flexible in matters of religion. Mary would not have treated Katherine so well if she'd had Jane's conviction."

Robin knew the religious inclinations of everyone at court; in his position, I supposed I would be sensitive to such matters.

"She is...attached to someone," I said carefully. The behavior I'd witnessed was not that of a woman who believed herself intended for a royal marriage. "I think she would not accept."

"It might not be put to her in the form of a question." He yawned, and pushed his glass away. "Say nothing of this, Margaery, but let me know if anything happens that leads you to believe she is in conversation with Feria or his men."

"Mistress Margaery, is that your husband?"

Certain Frances Newton was wrong, I glanced up from my embroidery. I'd never seen Robin in the presence chamber during the day; he could scarcely be tempted there for an evening's entertainment.

But it was him, with Cecil and several other men. The scarlet-clad esquires of the body stood at attention; the queen had not yet emerged from the privy chamber. They were announced: Feria, the Spanish ambassador; William Cecil, principal secretary; Robert Lewis, assistant secretary; Thomas Blyden, assistant secretary.

The presence of the Spanish ambassador intrigued me, having just been questioned about him. Was he calling on the queen, or had he been summoned? Thinking of my conversation with Robin, I turned, and caught Katherine Grey watching them.

No more than a quarter hour had passed before the men filed out again. Robin and Blyden departed immediately, but Cecil and the ambassador lingered, speaking with gentlemen on opposite sides of the chamber.

I kept an eye on Katherine, knowing Robin would ask. Sitting alone in the cushioned window seat, her attention on her lute, she nevertheless appeared very aware of her surroundings. When the ambassador approached and bowed to her, I shifted closer to the window, using my stitching as an excuse. Their conversation was inaudible, but Katherine's face was turned up to his like a flower, wearing her brilliant, infrequent smile.

What then of Edward Seymour? Was she being polite to Feria, or was there some other purpose?

Everyone fell silent as the queen swept into the presence chamber and seated herself under the canopy of state. I chanced a look in her direction; she had observed the unlikely couple at the window, and her expression was ominous.

"Excuse me." I passed between several maids. "Lady Katherine, do you have time to give me a lesson?"

The ambassador's expression darkened at my intrusion. "*Con permiso, Doña Katarina.*" He kissed her hand and turned on his heel.

"Look as if you're explaining something to me." At her confused glance, I said, "Just do it."

"What right have you to break up a confidential conversation?" She questioned me while giving every appearance of explaining the intricacies of lute fingering.

I tilted my head, as if greatly interested in her words. "I am trying to save you from yourself. If you don't know the rumors about Spain, you may be assured Her Majesty does."

Katherine tightened a peg until I thought the string would snap. "I fear I am in your debt, however odd that may be for both of us."

It was a tone I'd never heard from her. This was more than nerves at being caught speaking to a man other than her already-illicit lover.

"I ask nothing but civility," I said. "I'm not your enemy, no matter what you may think."

Her mouth twisted. "In my position, it is easier to assume everyone is against me."

"Mistress Margaery, how are your lute lessons coming along?" Elizabeth's voice cut through the general conversation.

I curtsied. "Poorly, Your Majesty. Lady Katherine is a good tutor, but I am a sad student."

"You must work harder." Ignoring her cousin, the queen lectured me for some minutes on the importance of musical ability in women before being distracted by Robert Dudley.

That evening, as I made ready to leave, Katherine appeared beside me in a rustle of white silk. "Thank you again. You took her attention from me."

"You should not do things that draw her attention in the first place."

"I should not." She smiled, and it was a shocking difference from her usual sulky expression. "I shall have to watch you closely, and see how you manage it."

"I am not much of a defender." Her sudden affability was disquieting, for all that I had asked for it. "I am no one, as you have so often told me."

"At least you have a place." She looked at the floor. "The queen would send us away if she dared."

"Because of your sister?"

"According to our cousin Edward's will, I was to be Jane's heir, if she died without issue." She played with a sapphire that hung from a long strand of pearls. "Mary was the true queen, of course—our father and Northumberland should never have tried to put Jane on the throne—but according to King Henry's wishes, I am Elizabeth's rightful heir." Katherine met my eyes, looking for a reaction. "If he *was* her father."

It was treason to say such things. It was treason even to listen to them. "You are here," I said, "which is more than can be said for your sister. Have a care."

She took the reprimand and slipped through the door. "Good rest to you, Mistress Margaery."

As I waited for Sebastian, I mulled her words. I would never completely trust Katherine, but in the brief time we'd spoken, I'd begun to like her—if only she did not speak so unwisely! I had no wish to end up in the Tower for listening to her seditious talk.

Ned withdrew himself upon my arrival, and I had no sooner emerged from the bedchamber in a loose gown than Robin said, "Why did you warn her off from speaking to Feria, after what I asked of you?"

Did he have spies in the privy apartments? Did Cecil? "I warned her because the queen saw them together, and appeared ready to make a scene." I looked pointedly at my empty glass. "I also thought it might be useful—to you—if Katherine Grey saw me as a friend."

His gaze, when he held out the wine, was one of measured approbation. I took a sip, and allowed the complex flavor to flood my mouth. I should eat, but it was late. My husband's approval would have to be enough.

Now that I knew how Will Hawkins had entered Robin's life, he seemed to be everywhere. Several times he had even been in our rooms when I returned in the evening, though he always departed, smiling and bowing, before I could make him feel unwelcome.

When he appeared beside me in the hall, on one of the rare days when I was able to eat with the women, I closed my eyes in annoyance. "How pleasant to see you again, Master Hawkins."

He greeted everyone, and the maids giggled and fluttered as if he were far more handsome than he actually was. "Could I beg a moment of your time, Mistress Lewis?"

"What is it?" I asked, as Katherine Carey slid over to make room for him beside me.

"I would ask a favor." He looked uncomfortable, as he so often did; he would not get far in Robin's world if he could not hide his emotions. Holding his cap to his chest, as if I were Elizabeth herself, he said, "My sister comes to court next week to join the maids of honor. I would ask you—"

"To keep an eye on her?" I might help, but I would not make it easy on him. He'd nearly cost me my husband, after all. "Make sure she settles in? Make sure the other ladies are kind to her?"

He flushed unbecomingly. "I would ask you be her friend," he said. "She is young, and has little experience of places like this."

"I've little experience myself." I imagined a female version of Will, earnest and awkward, and wondered what I had agreed to. "I will do what I can."

A few days later, Elinor Hawkins was presented in the late afternoon. At first glance, I could see her brother's worries were groundless. Instead of being plain and brown, Mistress Hawkins had an oval face and blue eyes that could have adorned a painting of the Virgin. She was the sort of girl who fit in everywhere, able to charm and please in equal measure. Her brother would have to beat her admirers away with a stick.

Nonetheless, when the audience ended, I joined her as she stood with the maids. "Welcome, Mistress Hawkins. Your brother asked me to introduce myself."

"Are you Mistress Lewis?" When she smiled, dimples appeared in both cheeks. "Please, call me Nell."

I smiled in spite of myself; her good humor was infectious. "Then you must call me Margaery." She took my arm, and we walked to a window overlooking the privy gardens. They were in glorious bloom, colorful flowers contained in neat geometric hedges of box and privet, littered with statuary. "I've not been here long myself, but it's not difficult, once you learn all the names."

"Will worries," she said confidentially. "But that's what brothers do, isn't it?"

"My parents had no other children." I thought of Walter, who played the role of brother while he lived.

She clasped her pretty hands beneath her chin. "You must have been so lonely! I'm the youngest of seven. My father resisted my coming to court, but Will promised I would be well looked after."

Later, I repeated the conversation to Robin, and he burst into uncharacteristic laughter. "I'm sure her father wants her protected," he said when he got control of himself. "She looks exactly like her mother."

"Does Will look like his father, then?"

Robin wiped his eyes. "Will is a changeling," he said. "Lord Kelton is as dark as his wife was fair, and he no doubt remembers the reaction when he brought her to court."

This was another story from Robin's early life which I would never know. "Was it a love match?"

A corner of his mouth turned up. "Belatedly. King Henry arranged it, but Hawkins was lucky enough to fall in love with her."

"How fortunate." I leaned across him for my needle book, brushing his shoulder with my sleeve. "Nell said she was one of seven children. That would be difficult, if a woman didn't love her husband."

My words garnered no response but a raised eyebrow, and Robin soon absented himself for a late meeting, leaving me with my embroidery. I thought of Nell, housed with the maids of honor in their cramped quarters. It might be nice to have another friend—even if she was Will Hawkins's sister.

Chapter 16

WILL HAWKINS'S FEARS WERE unwarranted. Nell's manners were as pretty as her face, and she possessed every skill to make her valued among Elizabeth's maids: she danced and sang and could accompany herself ably on the lute. Within weeks she was at the center of every performance, and had been complimented many times by the queen.

Despite her popularity, Nell chose to spend much of her free time with me. She was cheerful and uncomplicated, as bright and wondering as a baby bird, and I thoroughly enjoyed her company.

While the queen was at her dinner, her women took air in the garden, breaking into smaller groups for conversation. I stayed with Cressida, and Nell darted between us and the maids, trying to keep everyone happy.

"She's like a puppy," my friend said as Nell spun back across the grass, her skirts brushing the rose border on the side of the gravel path.

"A sweet puppy." It was impossible not to like her. "Have you heard from your mother?"

"Just yesterday," Cressida said, relief evident in her voice. "Ebrel's fever has broken and she is much improved." She licked her lips. "I must ask leave to go home."

In addition to our two days off each week, the queen's ladies were entitled to time away, but few had availed themselves of the privilege, not wishing to miss anything.

"It is good traveling weather." At this time of year, I could be at Winterset within days.

She nodded once, decidedly. "I will ask Mistress Ashley now, before I lose my nerve."

Cressida went in, and Nell returned to my side. "You cannot be alone on such a beautiful day."

I gestured widely. "We are never alone."

"You know what I mean."

The gravel crunched beneath our feet as we drifted toward the river. The Thames was crowded with wherries and barges, as bustling as the Strand on the other side of Whitehall. The inevitable kites circled overhead, scanning the banks for food.

"Do you ever regret your marriage?"

"Why would I?" What had she heard?

"There are so many handsome gentlemen." Nell nodded discreetly at a group of men putting on a show of play-fighting. "I can't wait to fall in love." She clapped a hand to her mouth. "I mean no disrespect to Master Lewis."

"They wouldn't be lining up to court me, anyway."

"Why not?" she asked, brushing a butter-colored curl from her eyes. "Just because you're dark doesn't mean you aren't pretty. Your skin is beautiful, and I'd love to have a dimple in my chin. It's too sweet."

No one had ever called my chin sweet; Grand-mère said it made me appear strong-willed, and Walter jested God poked me there when I was formed, to mark me complete. When I said that, Nell's laugh rang out like a carillon of bells. "Your grandmother already thinks you strong-willed, and your uncle was teasing."

"Perhaps." I rubbed the offending dent. "I'd still rather look like you."

"Well, I'd rather look like Lady Katherine," she said, proving even the prettiest woman could be unsatisfied with her looks. "Edward Seymour watches her with calf's eyes, have you noticed? What do you think, Margaery—is he serious about her, or is he just looking for a tumble in the gardens?"

My mouth dropped open. "Nell, where do you learn such words?"

Her expression was impish. "You would be shocked at the conversation in the maids' rooms."

"I probably would."

She glanced up at me. "You won't tell my brother?"

I shook my head. "Just mind your tongue—if you speak like that in front of him, he'll send you home."

Nell shook her head with such vehemence that her curls sprung loose from their restraints. "I'm never going back to Hawkmoor," she declared. "I love it here. I'll marry a fine gentleman and stay at court forever."

No doubt she would; there were several already who eyed her the way Elizabeth Tudor looked at a plate of pastries. Her brother's vigilance kept them at bay, but he would slip, eventually—he had become intimate with Dudley, and it was not as easy for him to watch his sister and his lord at the same time.

Frances Newton appeared at the head of the path, calling to us. "The leavings are being brought out, if you will come to the table."

The queen preferred to eat alone, and what did not tempt her was brought out for our consumption when she was done. It was often cold, but we didn't care. No matter how quickly we ate, the queen was faster, calling for company or entertainment before we had finished.

We filled our plates as the trays of food were carried out—a tasty selection, which meant the queen had eaten nothing but sweets. There was a burst of laughter from the other end of the table, and in the silence that followed, Katherine Grey said, "She must have had no offers at all, to marry such a queer man."

My throat closed around the bite of quail I had swallowed. Since I rescued her from the queen's attentions, Katherine had been easier with me, but her friendship was inconsistent.

Nell put a hand on my wrist. "She could mean anyone."

Frances, seated on Nell's other side, said, "But William Cecil thinks highly of him."

"As if *his* opinion carries weight in choosing a bedfellow." Her tone was cutting. "She must get no pleasure at all."

I turned away, my eyes filling with tears. Robin *was* a queer sort, when compared to the court favorites. He wasn't handsome; his clothes were plain, and his manner more so; he had little in the way of gallant conversation. But he was a good man, kind and patient, and he wasn't capable of the casual cruelty of Lady Katherine Grey.

"What can I do?"

"About Katherine?" Nell dug into a slice of meat pie. "Why do you care?"

"It's difficult not to." I ran my finger along my lip.

"Don't let her bother you." She removed my hand from my mouth before I could start in on my fingernails. "Anyway, you've got a husband, while she does not—and isn't likely to, no matter how many longing glances she casts at Edward Seymour."

As we left, Nell paused at Katherine's shoulder. "Why must you be so unkind?"

"It's no more than the truth." Katherine's ice-blue eyes were guileless. "Your bravery is laudable, Margaery, but not caring how you look isn't the best way to recommend yourself to the queen."

I bit the inside of my cheek until I tasted blood. "I care."

Her brows, golden and nearly-invisible, raised toward her hairline. "You have a strange way of showing it." She waved a hand at my face. "A woman who cared would use powder, or a light coating of ceruse."

The queen had commented that I always looked as if I had just come in from outdoors. I'd thought nothing of it, but was it a criticism?

"Your brows are too thick," she continued, "and your hair too plain. I imagine you don't want to change the color—"

"No!" Both my parents were dark, and although my hair made me stand out like a duck among swans, I would not consider changing it.

She pursed rosebud lips. "You could curl it, or style it more fashionably. That hood makes you look like someone's grandmother."

"You're talking nonsense." Nell squeezed my hand. "Come to us at the end of the day, if you like. We'll do your face and hair, so you can see you're better off as you are."

Grand-mère had nothing nice to say about women who used cosmetics, so I had never attempted them, but current fashion dictated a more artificial effect. The queen had very good skin, but Mary Sidney painted her face every morning.

That evening, once Elizabeth was undressed and the others were putting her to bed, I paused before the doors and instead followed the maids to their chamber. Despite its small size, they had a fine mirror and a chest below spread with an assortment of cosmetics.

"This is such fun!" Philadelphia squealed and handed a jar to Nell. "Give her a good layer of white, her cheeks are very bright."

I was pushed onto a low stool and someone removed my hood and coif. Frances Vaughn took my hair down, dragging a comb through it. "You've such thick hair," she said. "Have you ever tried curling it?"

Curls were the fashion, but I had no interest in being tortured daily to achieve them. "It's fine the way it is."

"Let me try something." She continued to comb and I closed my eyes, giving myself over to the sensation of being worked upon by multiple hands. It was soothing, if I didn't think about what they were doing.

Frances tugged at my hair, and I could smell the Careys' damask rose scent as they added flourishes to the white mask Nell spread on my face. I blinked wildly when they tried to draw lines above my lashes and was told sternly to keep still.

What was wrong with me? While I hated being teased, I liked fuss and paint little more; if that was the price of fitting in, I would remain outside.

"There!" Nell poked me. "Look at yourself!"

I opened my eyes. The woman in the mirror was a stranger. Her dark hair was caught up in a net caul, with padded rolls on either side of a central part. Her pale face was dusted with powder, her cheeks and lips artificially reddened. New, thin brows were drawn on with the same kohl that ringed unfamiliar brown eyes.

"I look like a poppet." My voice sounded wrong, coming from this unfamiliar face.

The maids were of a different opinion, saying how pretty I looked, and how fashionable, promising my life would be easier if I appeared thus every day. "Lady Katherine won't tease you anymore," Frances giggled. "She'll be too afraid you'll steal Edward Seymour!"

When I finally got free of them, Seb was still waiting. "You're late," he said. "Is everything all right?

"Fine." I looked away, unwilling to let him see me. "I spent some time with the maids."

"Sir Edward has already left." Passing under a torch, he stopped abruptly and peered into my face. "What have you done, mistress?"

"Nothing." My fingers curled into fists.

When we reached the apartment, Sebastian opened the door. "I'll take myself off so you and the master can be alone." His hand lingered on the latch. "Though I regret not being there when he sees you."

Robin was reading, a glass of wine close at hand. "Good evening."

"You must do something about Sebastian."

"Why? What has he done?" He put a marker in his book and stood. "Good God!"

I stepped back. "What's wrong?"

"Nothing." He kissed my whitened cheek. "You startled me."

Seb's words rankled more than my husband's reaction. "He said he regretted not being here when you got a look at me."

"He gets a bit above himself," he said apologetically. "Neither of us are accustomed to feminine sensibilities."

"It's not my feminine sensibilities that are outraged." I ignored the glass he held out. "You've let him have his head for so long he just speaks his mind."

Robin placed the glass on my side of the table. "He should speak his mind. So should you."

"Oh, I intend to." I paced the narrow space between the door and his chair. "I don't understand how you can defend him, after what he's done."

"What are you talking about?"

With one final turn, I sat. "He's never made me feel welcome."

"That's not true." Robin tried to take my hand, but I pulled away. "Seb is fond of you, as am I."

"Fond! What am I, a kitten?" I took a deep swallow of wine. It burned all the way down but did not douse the rage that simmered inside—for how long? "The letter you left, he told Mistress Dunham not to give it to me."

He refilled my glass. "How do you know that?"

"Because I forced her to hand it over. She was more worried about his reaction than mine." I picked up the glass and put it down again; I wanted a clear head. "Your precious Sebastian undermines my position, not only with the other servants, but with Ned, and with you."

I'd never been this angry before without crying. Tears were acceptable behavior for a woman; yelling was not.

"He's done no such thing." Robin's voice was even. "He shouldn't have kept the letter from you, but I imagine he didn't want you to be frightened."

"He treats me like a child," I said through gritted teeth. "It's bad enough when you do it."

"I do not treat you like a child."

I laughed in his face. "You've even called me 'child' in front of him." I gulped the second glass. "Why should the servant respect when the master does not? You can't even look at me without saying 'good God.'"

Slamming the bedchamber door behind me, I stared into the mirror. My face was doubly unfamiliar because of my anger. I wanted to get undressed, but Alice could not see me in such a state.

The door opened. "Are we arguing because I didn't compliment you for being painted like a Christmas mummer?"

I threw my cuffs on the chest, wondering how he thought this was still about rouge. "No," I said. "We're arguing—or at least I am—because I'm tired of everyone from the queen down to the servants seeing me as a stupid girl, only worth mocking."

Now the tears came in floods, as I addressed the true cause of my unhappiness. "I hate it here. The other women make fun of me. They make fun of you. I do nothing all day but smile and pick up pins and pretend I don't want to push people's heads in the queen's close stool. Then I come home to someone who has no better understanding of me than a cat."

I cast myself down on the bed, crying for everything I thought my life would be, and was not. How stupid I had been, to tie myself to this man and follow him blindly into a viper's nest.

The bed creaked. After a moment, his hand came to rest on my back. "I'm sorry," he said. "I didn't know how bad it was. You should have—"

"Told you?" I wiped my face on my sleeve and flinched at the mess I'd made. "Would that have been when you and Ned were discussing policy, or when you and Ned were trying to get me to talk about the queen, or maybe when you're talking to Seb about whatever it is you talk about with him?" I twisted away. "I have no place in your life. Tell me I'm wrong."

The silence stretched. "You're not...completely wrong," he said at last. "And it's been somewhat deliberate on my part."

I pushed myself up so I could look at him. "Why would you do that?"

"Self-protection." His mouth quirked. "If you must know."

"What do you need protecting from?" Since it appeared I was not going to explode, I got up and went back to the mirror. "Robin?"

"Closeness," he said. "I can just about manage Ned and Seb. You terrify me."

There were tear tracks through the white paint, all the way to my chin. I snatched up a cloth and began to scrub at my face until the stuff was gone and all that remained was my familiar reflection, but with my eyes redder than usual. It occurred to me that I liked my hair the way they'd done it.

Robin came behind me and untied my ruff. I couldn't look at him. "Am I so frightening?"

His hands rested on my shoulders. "Marriage is something I'm ill-equipped to handle. I've spent my life like a turtle, content to retreat into my shell at the least discomfort. My shell has taken quite a battering over the last year."

"You look more or less intact." I slowly removed the caul and shook out my hair.

"More or less." Robin picked up the ivory comb. When I did not stop him, he drew it through my hair. "But it protects an interior which hasn't often been exposed to intimacy."

I tipped my head back to make it easier for him. "And you do not like intimacy."

The comb stopped. "I cannot tell, Margaery—are you speaking seriously or mocking me for our lack of congress?"

"I've always known you don't like being touched. I thought that might change."

He began to braid my hair, reaching over my shoulder for a green ribbon. "I am more comfortable with you than I've been with any woman," he admitted. "And I have given you everything I am capable of giving." Robin met my eyes in the glass. "If there is something you need that is offered elsewhere, you would face no recriminations from me."

"Are you saying I should take a lover?"

"I would not have put it so straightly," he said, a hint of color touching his cheeks, "but I could hardly be angry if you did."

"I don't want a lover." I spat the words at him. "I want a husband who would not hand me off to some other man without feeling the loss to himself."

He looked down. "I didn't say I would not feel the loss."

I gave up. What I wanted, and what Robin thought I wanted were on two sides of a widening chasm. I had never imagined marriage would entail building a bridge toward my husband, and watching as his own bridge grew in a direction different than my own.

The quarrel changed something between us. There was another chink in Robin's armor. We did not speak of it, but we both knew it.

He had words with Sebastian the next day. When Seb met me in the evening, we had gone only a few steps when he said, "I am very sorry for yesterday, mistress." His eyes were bright. "I was disrespectful."

The fault was not all his. I was too sensitive, and Seb's years with Robin led him into over-familiarity. "You have a different relationship with Master Lewis." I forced the words out. "When you speak to me as you do him, it is not easy."

"I am too familiar."

"It is like this." I took his arm. "In this place, I have only him, but his smiles, his attention—they are for you and Ned. It leaves me alone."

"You are not alone," Seb said fiercely. "The master does not show affection easily, but it is there."

"He shows me no affection at all." My tone made clear what I meant. "Can you explain that?"

"In all the years I've known him, he's had no relationships of the sort you mean." Seb looked at me frankly. "It is why I did not favor your marriage, at first. I did not think he would be happy."

His face blurred before me. "I don't know if he is happy, but I am not."

Seb pulled a kerchief from his sleeve and handed it to me, showing none of a man's typical aversion to tears. "He is happy, mistress, as happy as he ever is." His forehead creased. "He lives in his mind most of the time."

I wiped my eyes. "Is there something that interests him beyond books?" The raucous assembly in the queen's chambers flashed before my eyes. "Does he like music?"

"He does," Seb acknowledged. "He's not one for dancing, as I'm sure you've noticed, but he pays close attention when it's just musicians. He was a chorister for the old king, you know that?"

"Yes." Thankfully, I did. How embarrassing it would be to learn my husband's past from his servant. "He said he was glad when it was over."

"Because he wanted an education. Sir Edward told me he sought out friends among the minstrels when he came back to work for Cromwell."

It was surprising to know Robin had friends beyond Ned and Sebastian. "Where are they now?"

Seb shook his head. "I've never heard him speak of them."

I could hear voices through the door, and I blotted my face to erase all signs of tears. Ned was there, and I greeted him along with my husband. "Good evening, gentlemen. Have you solved all the problems of the world today?"

"Not quite," Robin said. "It may take another glass of wine."

Seb put my things down and looked at Ned. "Perhaps the problems of the day need to be solved with less people."

Ned blinked, looking from me to Robin. "Perhaps I do spend too much time availing myself of your hospitality, Rob."

"That's because my wine is better."

"That is exactly why."

Seb made much of brushing off Ned's seat and offering it to me as Robin watched. "Have you gone from being rude to Margaery to being rude to Ned?"

"He is more equipped to deal with it," Seb said, "having a hide like an elephant. I am going to work on my map now. A good rest to you both."

Robin and I settled in our chairs, the quarrel sitting between us as surely as Ned.

"I nearly forgot." He pulled a small, paper-wrapped parcel from atop the chest. "I got this for you today in London."

Since we were in London, I understood he had left the palace and gone into the city. I undid the paper and beheld a small book of embroidery emblems.

I skimmed the pages; many of the designs were ones I had never seen. It excited me to have something new, even if it was meant as a peace offering. "It's lovely."

"You've worked most of the designs in your old book," he said. "I thought you needed something new to occupy you as Ned and I solve the problems of the world." He looked at the empty chair. "Or as we solve our own."

Chapter 17

THERE HAD BEEN NO time to plan a summer progress for the first year of Elizabeth's reign, but in mid-June, it was announced that we would remove to Hampton Court until the autumn.

Though only twenty miles upriver from London, Hampton seemed a world away. We had moved before, to Greenwich and Richmond, but only for short periods, and our situation had always been the same. This time, Robin was made to stay behind with Cecil, and I would live with the queen's women. I wondered if, after this, I would feel like one of them.

Losing my solitude was a high price to pay for fitting in. Without a quiet place to retreat at the end of the day, I threw myself into the whirl of court life; I had always gone back to our apartments in the evenings unless required to attend an event, and now I saw what I'd missed.

There were late suppers and walks in the garden, fireworks by the water, and dancing—always dancing. Elizabeth was the center of attention, partnered by her beloved Dudley or one of her other favorites, but she wanted us to dance, as well. There was a master available during the day to teach us the latest steps and variations, and I showed far more aptitude with dance than I ever had with music.

Though I'd been in the royal household for seven months, I was still enough of a novelty as a dancing partner that for the first few nights I was passed from hand to hand, exchanging pleasantries with gentlemen who had never before noticed me.

I danced with every man who asked, even with Robert Dudley when I was spun in his direction. I kept my eyes lowered, for fear of the queen's jealousy, but his charisma was unmistakable.

The bells rung midnight before we returned to our chamber, stumbling with exhaustion and wine. My head ached, and I yearned for sleep, but several hours later, I would wake, my demons finding me even at Hampton. Without Robin's soothing presence, the dreams returned with increasing frequency. After I'd disturbed my bedmates a few times, they suggested I sleep on a trundle.

Staring into the darkness, sweat trickling down my back, I closed my eyes and conjured up Winterset.

Hampton vanished: I was at the casement in our bedchamber, and the sounds I heard were not the river but the rush of the waves, far below the house. The astringent scent of rosemary reached me, carried from the garden on a soft sea breeze.

When I finally opened my eyes, jarred by the unmistakable sounds of civilization, there was a faint glow on the horizon; the sun would be up soon. I yawned and lay down on the trundle, wishing for my own home, my own bed. Wishing for Robin.

A courier arrived with word that the king of France was dead. It was shocking news: Henri was still young—only forty—and a known quantity in diplomatic circles. The dauphin was proclaimed king, and his queen was Elizabeth's young cousin, Mary. The new king and queen were just fifteen and sixteen years old, but were advised, as were all monarchs, by men older and hopefully wiser.

Elizabeth was circumspect in her reaction. It was always a sorry day when an anointed king died; jousts and tourneys, while entertaining, could be lethal, and participation should be avoided by those whose untimely deaths might throw Europe into chaos.

Within a fortnight, we learned Mary was not content to be queen of France and Scotland; she proclaimed herself queen of England, as well. While paying a condolence call, our ambassador was made to eat off plate quartered with the English arms. If it upset his digestion, it ruined Elizabeth for any nourishment short of the Scottish queen's bones boiled into a broth.

"That little upstart!" She flung her cup across the chamber. Being made of silver, it did not shatter, but bounced, spraying wine everywhere. "How dare she call herself queen of England?"

It was strange to hear Scottish Mary openly spoken of as a threat. Robin and Ned had spoken thus of her since the beginning. For the first time, I missed their nightly discussions, and wondered what they thought of this development.

"Calm yourself, Your Majesty." Mistress Ashley deftly removed all other missiles from the queen's reach. "She is no more than a child. France will be enough for her."

Her tone was soothing, but the words were a mistake.

Elizabeth's eyes flashed. "Send for Master Cecil, Kat, and do not speak on that of which you know nothing."

Being before noon, the Paradise Chamber—the name for the presence chamber at Hampton—was full of courtiers, chatting and playing cards, waiting for their moment to approach the queen. A murmur ran through the crowd, most commenting on Mary's nerve. The queen calmed as her outrage was reinforced. With any luck, when Cecil arrived, he would be able to restore her equilibrium.

A low laugh undercut the buzz of conversation, and heads turned.

Mary Grey shushed her, but Katherine, her doe eyes wide with feigned innocence, took a breath and said, "Though Mary comes through Margaret, her claim is legitimate."

Into the immense silence that followed dripped the queen's icy voice. "Do you believe your own claim to be legitimate, Lady Katherine?"

"No, Your Majesty." Her face turned ashen. "I only meant to say—"

"You are fortunate we allow you in our presence." Elizabeth drew herself up, the diamonds in her hair sparkling like fire. "Your family are condemned traitors, and you show yourself no better."

Mary began to cry, and tugged at her sister's arm.

Katherine sunk into a deep curtsy. "I am sorry, Your Majesty. I spoke without thinking."

The queen reached out, but found nothing to throw, thanks to Mistress Ashley's foresight. "You may go. I care not where, so long as you are out of our sight."

Cecil arrived in the late afternoon. To my surprise, Robin was with him and sought my company. "Can you spare an hour? It's a fine day."

I accepted gladly, placing my hand on his black sleeve. "The queen will not need me for some time."

He smiled. "Not until she's done shouting at Cecil, in any case."

We passed through the great hall and out into the bright summer day. "I haven't seen Hampton in years." Robin had been a child chorister in this place, before returning as an adult to work for King Henry. "Have you had much opportunity to see the grounds?"

"Not without a crowd." I reveled in the peace of being with just one person. "Will you show me?"

He led me through the manicured perfection of the gardens, turning occasionally to point out something about the palace. Set against the rolling Richmond hills, the mellow red brick glowed in the slanting sun, and its golden weathervanes glittered like Elizabeth's jewels.

"Are you enjoying the change from London?"

"It is a change." I turned from the gravel path into the trees; the dappled shade was better suited to conversation. "I never thought to miss my quiet evenings with you, Ned, and Sebastian."

He laughed. "Has Nell found true love yet?"

"No, but she has several candidates in mind." I wanted to ask if he missed me, but knew better than to ask a question whose answer might hurt my feelings.

"What of Katherine Grey?"

"She is much out of favor." I repeated Katherine's remark and the queen's reaction. "What else do you want to know?"

"The same," he said. "Have you seen her with de Quadra?"

I'd been watching for the new Spanish ambassador, knowing Robin would ask. "Never. If she speaks to him, she is circumspect."

"Cecil has an informant in de Quadra's household. There is talk of smuggling her out of England."

The Grey sisters kept away for the better part of a week. When they returned, their punishment was to be more under the queen's eye than ever. They suffered constant summonses to the privy chamber, where they were made to stand and watch while others served the queen.

Douglas Howard tuned a lute, and Katherine flinched at the discordant sound; her own tuning sounded like music. "I cannot bear this."

"Be patient," I said. "She was very angry."

"Can you not see the injustice?" Anger crossed her face, quickly mastered. "I have as much Tudor blood as the queen."

Her voice was low—she'd learned that much—but still I shielded her from view. "Your blood does not flow from King Henry."

"Perhaps hers does not either." Her eyes narrowed. "Everyone knows Anne Boleyn was an adulteress."

I wanted to shake her. "Tudor blood is strong, Katherine. You and Mary, and even Lettice Knollys, are obviously related to Elizabeth." I cast a glance over my shoulder; Nell was watching, but the other women were occupied with listening to Douglas. "I've seen litters of puppies with less likeness."

My words served their purpose and made her laugh, driving away the resentment that spoiled her beauty. "I will practice restraint," she said. "If you will only stop looking at me with those fearsome eyebrows."

"Leave my eyebrows alone."

"Keep them, if you will." She shrugged. "They add to the fierceness of your glare."

As the dancing got underway, I was watching a more intimate performance. Across the room, Will and Nell Hawkins stood with their heads together. He appeared to be lecturing his sister. Her nails were sunk into his wrist, just shy of drawing blood.

Curious, I made my way over. Nell saw me and let go of him. "He's threatening to send me home!" she wailed. "I can't leave— make him understand, Margaery."

I looked from one to the other. "Why should she leave?"

"I don't like the way men look at her," he said stiffly.

They'd have to be blind not to look at Nell; was he incapable of seeing her as anything but a little sister? "She is perfectly safe," I said. "Mistress Morice, the mistress of the maids, is very watchful."

Will shook his head. "It's not enough." Peering earnestly at her, he said, "Do you not see, Nell? All you have is your honor. It takes no more than a word to bring about a scandal that could ruin a girl, or her family."

"Ho! Are you concerned for me, or yourself? If I flirt with the wrong man, does it harm your prospects?" Her small fists clenched. "Is there someone who might change her feelings for you because of my behavior?"

"There is no one, as well you know." He appealed to me, "Mistress Lewis, make her understand. A woman is judged by her virtue."

"It is as you say," I agreed, "but do you think the queen would risk the honor of a girl who has been entrusted to her care?"

The other maids, in their distinctive white gowns, were clustered together, giggling in a manner guaranteed to make Will Hawkins uneasy.

"I think you're wanted," I said. Nell sped away to join them without a backward glance.

"You encourage her." Will wedged a finger inside his ruff and attempted to scratch. "She must listen."

The minstrels struck up a new tune, and the maids—with Nell at their center—took their places in the middle of the floor.

"She does listen," I said. "A little silliness hurts nothing."

He regarded me skeptically. "You're a married woman. No one worries about the chastity of a wife."

When the dance ended, three young men rushed to Nell's side, jostling to claim her hand. She smiled with genuine pleasure, and the knowledge that her brother was watching.

The next dance was a galliard, my favorite because of its fast, skipping steps and multiple changes of partner. I caught Will's sleeve as he turned away. "If you're going to embarrass her, don't go alone."

He took my meaning. "I'm sorry. May I have the honor?"

"I would like that very much." He found a place near Nell, to try to listen to her conversation. We did our first cinq pas. "If you keep on like this, she'll hate you," I murmured.

Next was the cadence, which showed off the men's athleticism, as well as their legs. Will acquitted himself ably; I had expected him to land like a sack of grain.

"She'll hate being sent home even more." He took a quick breath; it was difficult to argue while jumping. "I asked you to be her friend."

Another cinq pas, and this time I withdrew as he leaped, a move requiring pursuit, recently practiced with the dancing master. "I'm her friend, not her nursemaid," I said when he rejoined me.

"She's sixteen."

"You'll look bad if she weds first." My skirts spun out, brushing his blue hose. "Have you thought of that?"

He moved quickly to one side. "Why is Master Lewis not here to dance with you?"

"Because he is in London this whole long summer," I said, "and anyway, he has no love of dancing. He knows there will be such as you here to amuse me."

Another man would have preened. "Then I am glad I am here to fill the need." The music ended, and he bowed stiffly. "Now I must collect my sister, to continue our discussion without witnesses."

"Don't be too harsh with her," I called after him. Nell, in love with love, was more than capable of doing something stupid to thwart her brother, and there were plenty of men who would gladly join in her stupidity.

Chapter 18

WHILE HER WOMEN WERE made to dress in somber colors so as not to outshine the queen, the men had no such worries. The crowd around Robert Dudley glittered and shone; well born and attractive, like him, they made much of the queen and her ladies.

Edmund Morven was a recent addition to Dudley's coterie. His appearance caused a stir among the maids, and no sooner had Nell danced her first galliard than she declared herself in love—again.

"His eyes," she moaned, sprawling across the bed the next morning. "Did you see his eyes, Margaery?"

I had also been partnered by him, and felt the warming effect of those hazel eyes and the easy smile that accompanied his meaningless, courtly words.

"He is very handsome." He was also the second true love she'd found since our arrival. "Will your brother approve this latest choice?"

Nell sat up, her curls tumbling from beneath her nightcap. "He is of better birth than Father, so he can have no objection there. His family has Scots roots—that explains his name—but their main estates are in Northumberland. He is the only son, so he will inherit."

I was impressed by the breadth of her knowledge. "I hope you didn't ask him straight out."

She pouted prettily. "I can be subtle when the need arises. And people do like to talk about themselves." Twisting a curl around her finger, she asked, "How long do you think it will take for him to fall in love with me?"

The stables were more conveniently located than those at Whitehall, and once I understood the pattern of our days, I was able to ride in the mornings before Elizabeth was up. Nell often accompanied me, as did her brother. Small as she was, Nell was a fearless rider, and gave Will palpitations by racing with me across the hunting park.

His constant presence was exhausting, even when he lagged behind to give us privacy. "Can't you make him stay indoors?"

"He wouldn't listen." Nell giggled. "He fears only two things: our father, and our father blaming him for the loss of my virtue."

The lush park was, at this hour, quite empty. "Your virtue is safe here." I reined in Artemis at the top of a rise, looking at the silver ribbon of the Thames as it curved in front of the palace. Small boats darted like water insects but the larger vessels were as yet moored; like the queen, much of the nobility still slept. "Perhaps you should try to find him a wife, Nell. If he's occupied, you will be free."

"He will never marry." Nell looked at me from under her lashes. "The lady he wants is already wed."

It was not surprising to learn that Will chose to make his life more difficult. "I hope she is kind to him." I leaned forward, stroking Artemis's neck. "Walk on."

"You are *never* kind to him," she said. "Don't you see how sad he is?"

I looked over my shoulder at Will, then back at his sister, pretty as a painting in her blue velvet riding costume. "Don't be ridiculous."

"Do you think he shadows us everywhere just because of me?" she countered.

Nell had no idea how difficult it was for me, even now, to look at him without thinking of his past actions. I recalled all the times he was with us for no reason; his reaction during our dance, when I teased him about his sister marrying first. His lack of artifice when I said Robin knew I would find my own amusements.

Robin! Did he know about this?

Will trotted up behind us. "It's time to go back."

I ignored him, wanting suddenly to be far away from them both. Nudging Artemis with my left heel, I turned from the river toward the distant woods. She needed little encouragement. With a touch of my whip to her flank, she lunged forward, streaming toward the trees. We quickly left the Hawkins siblings behind.

It was a mistake; I knew it immediately. We often galloped while hunting with the queen, but there were so many horses surging together, it was hard to feel out of control. This time, though the reins were firmly in my grasp, I was uncertain of my seat. We flew across the park, Artemis's hooves tearing up clods of earth. Unable to find a rhythm, my rump hit the saddle so hard my teeth jarred together.

What was I doing? I was a better rider than this, and Artemis a more deserving mount. I shouldn't encourage bad habits because I was angry and needed flight. I drew back on the reins, and she slowed unwillingly, dancing and fighting my guidance in a way most unlike her.

"Mistress Lewis?" Will pounded toward me, waving his cap. He stopped short, and his horse reared. Companionably, Artemis stretched her neck, bunched her haunches and did likewise. Not expecting it, I fell off.

The sky was pale blue with just the barest streaks of cloud, and I thought I would like to lie there, peacefully, and look at it while I regained my breath, but Will Hawkins threw himself down on the grass beside me. "Mistress Lewis, are you all right?"

I raised myself on one elbow. "I was fine before you spooked my horse, you damned fool."

He flinched. From my language, or the realization that I could have been seriously injured and he would have had to explain his role in it to Robin?

"Help me up," I said crankily.

"Shall I lead the horses?"

"I can ride," I said, glaring. "Can you?"

A tight-lipped nod. Boosting me into the saddle, he swung onto his black gelding and cantered off without a backward glance.

I followed, alternating between annoyance and contrition. If Will had feelings for me, as Nell intimated, he would be wounded. On the other hand, his careless horsemanship caused Artemis to rear, something she had never done before. I came down on the side of annoyance, and when we reached the stables I handed Artemis off to a groom with curt instructions for her care, and left brother and sister in the stables.

Rain caused the queen to be thwarted of a much anticipated hunt, but as the weather could not be shouted at, she took her frustration out on us. My turn came in the mid-afternoon, after she drove both

Kat Ashley and Mary Sidney from her presence.

Dorothy Bradbelt followed, the twisted kerchief in her hands the only clue to her inner turmoil. "Her Majesty wishes to play cards," she said. "Who here plays a strong game of piquet?"

Her question was met with silence, as everyone chose to forget the rules of a common card game.

She would likely pitch me out, the same as the others, but I had never been alone with Her Majesty, and I was curious. "I will play, Mistress Dorothy."

She smiled in relief, and ushered me to one side. "She will wish you to speak with her."

I had spoken with Elizabeth before, but only on the most innocuous of subjects. "What do I talk about?"

Dorothy looked down her nose—a nose almost as impressive as my own. "Whatever Her Majesty wishes." She did not say 'you foolish girl,' but I heard it anyway.

I passed through the doors and into the royal bedchamber. It was a grand and pleasant room, with more light—even on this rainy day—than Whitehall, and certainly more than Richmond, which the queen called her "warm box." The chamber was dominated by the enormous painted wooden bed that traveled with the queen. Large enough to sleep a half-dozen people, it had a padded red velvet headboard and ostrich plumes at each corner. The feathers hung limp in the languid air.

Elizabeth sat at a small inlaid table, her restless hands shuffling a deck of French playing cards. "Mistress Margaery, have you volunteered to be sacrificed on the altar of my bad temper?"

Hiding a smile, I dropped into a curtsy and said, "It is as Your Majesty wishes—though I would prefer to play cards."

She laughed sharply, spilling the cards onto the table. "You play piquet?"

"My husband and I often play in the evenings."

"You may deal."

I shuffled and dealt two hands, leaving the eight card *talon* in the center of the table. How did one play piquet with the queen? Was I permitted to win? If not, how did one go about losing? I looked at my cards, rearranging them and deciding how many to discard. "You exchange first, Your Majesty."

Her eyes bored into mine. "I know the rules."

"I am sorry, Your Majesty." My stomach tightened, and I regretted my morning pottage.

Elizabeth considered her hand, and eventually put four cards on the table, removing one from the *talon*.

I did the same with three cards, glad I was dealer and she the elder hand; she would have to declare first, and I could follow her lead.

"Point of four." She fanned her cards.

"Good." I had one less card in the same suit, so I was behind without trying. We went through the sequence, and the queen again had the upper hand.

Elizabeth scooped the cards from the table and shuffled. "You need not play in silence."

I bit my lip. "I have not been entirely silent, Your Majesty."

"*Good,*" she mimicked. "You may converse, if you will. I am bored today."

Her words immobilized me, even as she dealt another hand of cards. Did I tell her about my childhood, or my opinions of the court, or my difficult yet somehow pleasing relationship with my husband?

"Have you fallen asleep?"

"No, Your Majesty." My voice quivered, and I reached for my cards.

She leaned back with a laugh. "I don't bite, girl," she said. "You married in France, is that correct?"

"It is." I looked at my cards. Another losing hand.

"Master Lewis came to Hatfield after the death of our sister." She discarded two cards, her long fingers hesitating over the *talon*. "We asked him then to join our court, and he requested leave to return home to welcome you."

"We traveled separately," I explained, remembering my worry over his absence, and realizing he might have been with the queen at that very moment.

"You are not French yourself?"

"My family is English, but I was raised there." I relaxed my shoulders and tried to breathe normally. "We were in France eighteen years."

"Was it business that took them from England?" Her moodiness had faded, distracted by cards and her questioning.

I risked the truth. "My father was executed for his part in the Pilgrimage of Grace. My grandparents decided to leave, to keep my young uncle from the same fate."

She was silent. Considering her cards, or my loyalty? "Is your family still Catholic?"

"My grandmother is," I said. "I share my husband's faith." I thought Robin's faith was centered mostly in what he and men like him could accomplish on earth, not what might happen in an afterlife imagined by any church.

"Your grandmother lives with you?"

"She lives in Yorkshire," I said. "In my husband's house, which was hers prior to our marriage. She is elderly, and has no desire to travel." I told her about Grand-mère, and how much I missed her. "She is the only family I have left."

"I am sorry for your losses." Elizabeth's voice was unexpectedly tender. "It is difficult to lose family."

It would not be appropriate to comment upon the queen's losses, and so I remained silent.

Elizabeth rearranged her cards, eventually throwing them all on the table. "I am tired of this game."

My own hand was exceptionally good, and I threw it away with relief. "Is there another game Your Majesty wishes to play?"

Her gaze was on the window, rain running in sheets down the glass. "No."

"What about noddy?"

She turned, a smile spreading across her face. "I haven't played that since my nursery days. First player to sixty-one wins, do I recall it right?"

Nell had set her giddy heart on Edmund Morven, but in the days that followed, as we rode and walked and danced, it was not to her side he was drawn, but to mine. I rose from my seat at supper and found him behind my chair; when I turned from my partner in the dance, it was to him I was passed; when I dismounted Artemis, his were the hands that took my reins.

It was flattering, but I lived with a constant quivering of nerves in the pit of my stomach. Why would such a man look at me, when the maids of honor—and even the older women—were panting for a word from him?

Morven claimed the first dance of the evening, striding across the chamber and shouldering Will Hawkins out of the way. He was an excellent dancer, graceful and athletic, but the way his eyes lingered made my mouth dry. I wanted to run from the room, but instead I took a deep breath and asked, "Why do you pay such attentions to me?"

He had not expected the question and laughed aloud, causing heads to turn all over the chamber. "Because I live in terror of beautiful, well-born girls who want me to marry them," he said with a glance that caused my heart to jump in my chest. "Also, you do not have a hulking older brother who wants nothing more than an excuse to call me out for slighting your honor."

Will Hawkins, hulking? I searched for Nell, and saw her gaze was fixed on us. Will stood close by, talking in her ear with his usual solemn expression.

"And what of *my* husband?" I looked past Morven's beautiful eyes and focused instead on the black curls at the nape of his neck. "Do you not fear his reaction if you slight my honor?"

His finely-cut lips curled with amusement. "Your husband is neglectful."

"His duties with the principal secretary keep him in London." How did he know I felt neglected?

Morven stood still as I circled him. "His duties cause him to neglect you, then."

"I feel no neglect." Was the room stifling, or had the air between us suddenly grown thick?

"I am glad to hear it." His hand met mine. "May I call you

Mistress Margaery?"

"You may not." I turned away again, glad to have a moment to compose myself. "I do not need to be in my husband's company to consider myself married, sir—nor do I need anyone's protection."

The music ceased and Morven bowed, brushing his lips over my wrist. "Are you sure?"

The imprint of his mouth still burned an hour later, when I came face to face with Nell in our chamber.

"Margaery, how could you?" Her lower lip trembled. "You *know* he is mine."

Sitting on the edge of the bed, I stripped off my ruff, putting it aside for Alice to launder and starch. "He does not appear to be aware of your claim," I said. "It was only a dance, Nell."

She stood still as her maid removed the diamonds from her hair. "He also spoke to you when we rode with the queen earlier today."

"A passing comment on the weather." It was only somewhat untrue—he'd commented on the breeze, and its effect on my cheeks, which caused me to blush and him to laugh.

"I thought you were my friend." Her eyes brimmed with tears. "You've already got a husband."

Alice got between us and started on my laces, giving me a sympathetic wink. "Nell, really—"

The rest of the maids arrived, and Katherine put her arm around Nell's stiff shoulders. "Perhaps Margaery regrets her hasty marriage," she said. "Who wouldn't trade their spouse for a man like Edmund Morven?"

Reduced to my shift, I faced down a half-dozen sulky girls, deprived of their pretty toy. "Would you trade Edward Seymour for him, Katherine?"

She went white. The relationship was not spoken of, even in our private chambers, although all the maids knew and covered for her. "I don't know what you mean."

I met her eyes. "I think you do," I said. "And it will go no further than this chamber, so long as you mind your tongue."

Chapter 19

FOR THE NEXT TWO weeks, Nell avoided me, staying indoors with the maids or strolling the gardens with the Carey sisters. Unless we were both included in a party with the queen, she did not ride. I missed her lighthearted presence, but could not believe Morven meant so much to her, when she was in love with a different man each week. The stubborn pride which Grand-mère deplored would not permit me to apologize for a wrong I hadn't committed.

Cut off from my friends, riding became my only outlet. I slipped out to the stables before the others were even dressed. A group of riders lingered in the courtyard, their horses jostling and snorting with impatience. Morven was among them, on a chestnut gelding with a white blaze on its forehead. "We are riding through the hunting park, Mistress Lewis. Will you come?"

Whether it was annoyance at Nell or a simple response to the darkly handsome man smiling down at me, I said I would, and waited impatiently for Artemis to be saddled and brought around.

I knew the other men—they were part of Dudley's entourage—but the women were unfamiliar. Visiting wives or sisters, perhaps; the queen kept the number of women in her presence to a faithful few.

When we started off, Morven maneuvered his way through the pack until we were together. I tried not to notice how splendidly he rode, remembering the queen's remark about centaurs. He was a fine example of the breed, riding as simply as he drew breath.

"You are lovely this morning," he said with a wolfish grin.

I ducked my chin, knowing the fitted jacket of my dark green riding costume suited me. "And you are impertinent, as always."

He laughed. "We have not known each other long enough for you to be so certain of my temperament."

Sensing my disquiet, Artemis danced and I leaned forward, quieting her with a soft word. "I do not think it takes much time to know you."

Nell was right. I had no reason to flirt with this man. No reason at all, except his eyes, which made me warm all over, and his smile, which raised the hairs on the back of my neck. Being admired by such a man made me feel alive, and I would not deny myself.

Our course took us across the park, along the river, and toward a distant village. When the sun's angle showed me the time, I slowed regretfully. "I must go back," I said. "The queen will soon require my presence."

I had ridden only a short distance toward the palace when a rider approached from behind. I did not need to look to know it was Morven.

"You shouldn't ride alone." He eased his horse into a walk. "It's not proper."

"Nor is it proper for you to accompany me." I gave Artemis a touch of my heel.

He matched my pace. "And yet, here we are."

I fixed my gaze on my horse's ears, but his presence could not be ignored. My skin prickled, aware of his closeness in a way that was new to me.

"People are talking, you know. About how you behave." I risked a sideways glance. "The way you watch me."

His teeth were bright in his tanned face. "And how do I watch you, little bird?"

The reins trembled in my fingers. "Like one of Her Majesty's hunting dogs."

We reached the wide expanse of the park, visible from the palace windows. If anyone was looking, they would see us together.

Morven reached across and looped Artemis's reins over the pommel of his saddle. "Walk with me."

There were consequences for lateness, but these worries were overtaken by a desire for a few moments alone with him. Nothing could happen in such a short time, and anyway, Robin had given his permission—should Morven offer anything that I needed.

When Artemis was settled, I brought my leg over the pommel. Before I could dismount, he grasped my waist and swung me down. My hands came up, and he took them in his, bringing them to his chest.

"Isn't this better than riding?"

"I think I was safer on my horse." He was not as tall as Robin, but

I still had to raise my eyes to look at him.

Morven removed my gloves and tucked them inside his doublet. "Do not fear, little bird, I'll return them."

"Why do you call me that?"

"Because you struggle like a lark caught in a net," he said. "And you have not given me permission to use your name." He raised my hand to his lips, lingering over each knuckle. The softness of his mouth brought a flutter deep inside, and I steeled myself so my knees didn't buckle. "Should I stop?"

I snatched my hand away, but his touch was still there. "My gloves, please?"

He held them out. When I reached for them, he pulled me against him, one arm coming hard around my waist. "Are you sure you want them so soon?"

Another woman might have been frightened, but Morven was only playing a game, trying to stir me up. He didn't need to know he'd won. "You are making my life very difficult."

"I don't want that." His breath was warm on my cheek. "I want to make your life pleasant, little bird. Very pleasant."

"I am a married woman." I shoved against his chest.

His lips brushed my neck. "Unhappily, I think."

I pushed harder. "Not unhappily."

"As you say." He let me go, and I stumbled. "I am close by, should you change your mind."

There was no mounting block, or even a fence. I needed his assistance to get back on Artemis. I gestured at the saddle. "Could you...?"

He laced his fingers into a step and I mounted with less grace than usual. As I arranged my knee around the pommel, his hand came to rest on my other leg, beneath my skirt. I held my breath until he removed it.

When the stables came into sight, I said, "If you want to make my life more pleasant, you could pay court to the maids—to Nell Hawkins or one of the Carey girls. To stop the gossip."

He shook his head. "I think not."

A groom appeared and helped me down. "Thank you for the

escort," I said, already working out an explanation for my lateness. "Perhaps you can still catch the others."

Morven swept off his hat. "Their company would pale after yours, little bird. I shall seek amusement elsewhere." He stalked off toward the gardens, godlike in his hauteur, and I watched him go, wondering what it would be like to give in to his blatant invitation.

The weather outside was beautiful, but there had been a storm in the privy chamber during my absence. Nell and Katherine caught me as I entered, their anger forgotten by the magnitude of the gossip they had to share.

"You've missed a great drama!" Nell cried. "Where were you?"

I raised my hands to fend them off. "What happened?"

"We'll tell you while you change." Katherine linked her arm through mine. "You will not be needed for some time."

I listened while Alice removed my riding clothes, letting their chatter drive the last thoughts of Morven from my mind.

The queen had quarreled with Cecil before she was even dressed, and after he left, her bad mood lingered.

"She was very hard with Mistress Ashley." Nell tucked her legs beneath her on the bed. "We were in the privy chamber and I heard her cry, 'We will not have this, Kat, not even from you!'"

Elizabeth frequently lost her temper with her former governess, but never for long; her moods, though violent, dissipated quickly, and she would be sunny again while those around her were still licking their wounds.

Katherine pitched her words so Alice would not hear. "The door was open just enough that I could see her, Margaery. Mistress Ashley was on her knees, clasping her hands like a beggar woman."

"Don't be unkind." Nell did not dispute the description.

"'But Your Majesty *must* marry,'" Katherine mimicked, her voice warbling as Mistress Ashley's did when she was upset. "'It is the only way to stop these disreputable rumors.'"

Elizabeth paced as Mistress Ashley related what everyone else was afraid to tell her, the ugly rumors about Robert Dudley which made the foreign ambassadors rub their hands with glee at the thought of a tainted queen.

"She howled," Nell said. "That is the only word to describe it. And she struck Mistress Ashley, and two women had to catch her and help her to her feet."

"Goodness." I sat on the bed, considering what I'd missed. "Did she send her away?"

Katherine shook her head. "Not immediately. Mistress Ashley asked if she—the queen—could not see where it would lead, that if she continued on, it could come to bloodshed, if her subjects withdrew their affections. She could be determined unworthy of the throne."

Her voice was even; the queen's disgrace would benefit her, though with the red marks of Edward Seymour's passion barely hidden by her ruff, Katherine was no better.

Nell took up the story, giddy with excitement and fright. "Mistress Ashley said rather than this, she should have strangled Her Majesty in her cradle." She ran a hand over her hair. "And the queen laughed. Can you imagine?"

I could, and it chilled me through. When the queen laughed in response to an insult or contradiction, everyone involved should beware. "What then?"

They both spoke at once, and Katherine cut a glance at Nell. "She would marry to set dear Kat's mind at ease, and to console her people, but marriage is a weighty matter." She grimaced. "Elizabeth speaks and says nothing."

"Will she forgive Mistress Ashley, do you think?" Nell's eyes were enormous.

"The better question is whether she will take instruction from Mistress Ashley." Katherine admired the perfect half-moons of her nails, and the pretty rings that adorned her fingers. "What good is it to serve a queen who cannot look to her own reputation?"

"The queen is virtuous," I said. "You cannot believe otherwise, Katherine. Even you."

She continued to look at her hands, turning them so her jewels caught the light. "Appearances are as important as facts. We should all be mindful of that."

The chamber had gone quiet, but Nell and I were still awake. "I'm glad we're friends again."

"So am I." She reached down to the trundle and patted my shoulder.

"I knew how you felt about him," I said. "I shouldn't have allowed it to happen."

Nell swallowed. "It was a fantasy, really. I was upset when he didn't behave like the other men."

I sat up. "My husband is the first man I have known."

She laughed softly. "I have known no men at all."

"Your brother would never allow it." I stifled a yawn; the day had been overlong. "But you have suitors, and a father, and brothers. I've had none of that." Morven's attentions, so thoroughly male, had given me something I hadn't known I craved.

"Your husband is a good man."

"He is." He was, and I knew it. "But he doesn't have it in him to make such a fuss."

"Margaery?" She rolled toward me with a creaking of ropes. "The queen said one other thing. I don't know if Katherine heard, and I dared not repeat it in front of her—she needs no more arrows in her quiver."

I sat up. "What did she say?"

"Right before she dismissed Mistress Ashley, she said, 'In this world we have had so much sorrow and tribulation, and so little joy.' I felt sorry for her."

As did I. Who could fault the queen for snatching a bit of joy in a life which, for all its grandeur, was often joyless and lonely?

Mistress Ashley's punishment was to be forced to watch the queen with Robert Dudley more than ever. He was invited into the bedchamber while she breakfasted; he rode with her in the afternoons; they played cards and danced late into the evening—and they frequently danced the volta, a form of the galliard where the woman's partner had to grasp her about the waist and leap into the air.

"You're looking at my brother." Mary Sidney was two years older than Dudley, and the overreach of the male members of her family was beginning to show.

I could hardly deny it. "I'm sorry."

"There are no secrets in this place." She sighed heavily. "I suppose you heard what happened?"

"Mistress Ashley thinks only of the queen's wellbeing."

"As do we all." Her lovely mouth thinned. "I do not say she is wrong. The rumors are untenable."

I put my embroidery aside, wishing for Robin's wise counsel. "Could you not convince him to withdraw for a while?" It was dangerous to even suggest such a separation. "A visit to his wife, perhaps?"

Elizabeth might exaggerate her feelings for Mistress Ashley's benefit, but I had witnessed too many caresses to believe they were play-acting. Only the night before, they had embraced in the shadow of the bedchamber door and Dudley's lips had been on the queen's throat, eliciting a whimper her ladies did their best to ignore.

Mary rubbed her temples, as if her brother's foibles pained her. "She would not allow it, and he would not go." Straightening her skirts, she added, "He has loved her since they were children. They could not marry, and so he married Amy."

I had never seen Mary Sidney so distressed, or so confiding. "Does he love her—his wife?"

"It seemed so when they were married. You know how women are drawn to him."

I did indeed, and there were many women who would gladly offer him what the queen could not. If he would not go home to his wife, why could he not choose one of them and be done with it? Disappoint the queen and still pay court to her, as did all men but Cecil?

Elizabeth would undoubtedly banish him, but he could use those weeks or months to rebuild his marriage to the unknown Amy and eventually return triumphant, secure in his place in the queen's heart.

What would Robin think of this commotion? I wanted to hear his opinions on the queen's chief gentlewoman speaking her mind, but he had not come to Hampton after that first visit. I received regular, unsatisfying letters in which he made no mention of his own activities, nor his state of mind. It was too much to hope I was missed.

But I missed him. Despite the stimulating diversion of Edmund Morven, I missed my husband. I wanted to spend time with him again, even in the infuriatingly incomplete state in which our marriage existed.

"Do you travel to Whitehall soon?" I asked Will, as we lingered in the hall, watching Nell dance with Hugh Bacton, her newest conquest.

"I go on Saturday." Nell's partner whispered to her, and Will's fists clenched. "Is there something I can bring you?"

"Not as such," I said, "but if you would tell Master Lewis I wish to speak to him, I would appreciate it. He has been much occupied, and we have not seen each other in weeks."

Will moved to one side, the better to see Bacton did not overstep. "I would have thought you had more than adequate companionship."

"A husband is not so easily replaced," I said curtly. No man at court—not even Morven, with his obvious attractions—caught my eye in the way that dear, odd Robin had caught my mind, and somehow, my heart. "No matter what you might think."

"If he has not come on his own," Will said, "what makes you think I can convince him the journey is worth his while?"

Chapter 20

ROBIN DID NOT COME. His next letter said only that he was too busy to leave London, and looked forward to my return.

Had I truly thought my company would be more important than his work? That was not who he was. With a sigh, I put my absent husband, and Will's suspicions about my fidelity, out of my mind. Hampton offered abundant occupation, and there was no reason not to enjoy myself.

Nell's heart being otherwise occupied, flirting with Morven could do no harm. I flung myself into it headlong: morning rides; playful conversations in the presence chamber; dining with him in the hall. He partnered me almost exclusively in the evenings, and I went to bed with my heart pounding—from dancing, and from the increasingly intimate touch of his hands.

It was foolishness. I was married, and I respected the vows we had exchanged. I cared for Robin, more than a little. But I was lonely, and untouched, and here was a man who said and did all the things I craved from my husband. Edmund was difficult to resist, and I resisted less and less.

I'd never felt desirable before. Attractive, yes—in my best gown, with my hair dressed, and Grand-mère's diamonds sparkling at my throat, I could hold my own in a crowded chamber.

But no one had ever looked at me with hunger, and it made a difference.

I flew like a crow over the emerald grass; there had been no time to change into something prettier. Morven would be in his usual brilliant plumage; like all men favored by the queen, he was a bit of a peacock.

The day was unexpectedly bright, and as a trickle of sweat made its way down my back, I regretted we had not chosen a closer meeting place. It would be warmer in the garden, and being close to Edmund only raised my temperature. My shift would be stuck to me before I could get away from him.

He was already there, leaning nonchalantly against the marble plinth of a statue, his doublet the same azure as the sky. When he saw me, he waved his hat in a lazy arc above his head.

I wanted to run to him, but deliberately slowed my pace. The hot words he'd said in my ear the night before came back in a rush, and I was glad my embroidered partlet concealed any flush to my chest.

His eyes frequently lingered on that narrow opening. If his eyes made me feel that way, what would his hands feel like?

"You're late," he called. "I thought myself abandoned."

"The queen kept me." It was the only excuse he would accept. "She is translating a poem into Latin and wanted me to read her the original French."

Edmund raised an eyebrow. Like everything else about him, it was sleek and graceful, almost too beautiful for masculinity. "What purpose does that serve?"

"Does it have to serve a purpose?" Seeing the queen's joy in her contest with three languages reminded me of Robin—but I had decided not to think of him in Edmund's company; it was too confusing. "Do you not do things just for pleasure?"

"I do indeed." The words were simple, but they brought a clenched fist of desire to my belly. "I would like to show you what I do for pleasure, little bird, and have you join me in it."

Each time we were together, he was more daring. If his speech didn't dizzy me so, I would be better able to defend myself.

"You mustn't say such things," I murmured. I hadn't known a few well-placed words could be felt in every fiber of my body.

Edmund chuckled. "I believe you enjoy it." He drew a finger along my cheek. "I believe you have waited your entire life for someone to speak to you as I do."

The gardens were deserted. On such a hot day, people would either be on the river or sheltering inside. As I contemplated that fact, another bead of sweat started its slow journey to my lower back.

"You know very little of my life, or what I have waited for." The shrubbery was high, blocking all view of the river. Blocking all view of us, from anywhere.

Taking my wrist, he led me along a path between two walls of roses. The blooms were mostly spent, blown and faded by the sun, but the scent was strong. A handily placed bench awaited us, and Edmund drew me down beside him.

"That may be true." He brought my wrist to his lips. "But I know the look of an unsatisfied woman." He trailed kisses over the back of my hand, then onto my palm.

I grew hot all over, and a strange tingling began in my fingers. "Edmund, stop." I stood then sat again, suddenly lightheaded.

Edmund took my movement as assent, and this time his mouth touched mine, a soft brushing that made me gasp. As my lips parted, he kissed me again, loosening that clenched fist and causing a warmth that culminated between my legs.

The buzzing in my ears grew louder. I pulled away. "Stop, Edmund. I mean it." My heart was beating too fast, and my fingertips were numb. What was wrong with me?

He moved away, placing his palms on his thighs. "As you please." There was a smile in his voice; he understood my reaction better than I did. "I suppose it was too much to hope you would lay with me in the grass and let me show you what a man can do to give you pleasure."

I took a few deep, steadying breaths, and my pulse slowed. The air was thick with roses; I would never be able to smell them and not think of this man.

"Can we speak of something other than pleasure?"

"Can you recall the queen's poem?"

His question surprised me, but I battled the haze in my brain, and recited,

> "Dans ce tombeau, qui est une cellule dure et verrouillée,
> Lies l'amant vert, l'esclave très digne
> Dont le cœur noble, ivre d'un amour vrai et pur,
> Perdre sa dame, ne peut pas supporter de vivre."

"Your French is quite good," he said. "You'd improve with practice, but women are overeducated these days, it seems to me."

I took a breath, and found I suddenly *could* breathe. "You think my French is good?"

"More than passable." He ran the back of his finger along my cheek to my throat, dipping—briefly—into the opening in my partlet. "But you weren't born to waste yourself on books, little bird. You were made for other things."

"*Vous êtes beau, mais vous êtes un très grand imbécile.*" I watched as he worked out my words and realized I had called him a great, handsome fool.

"Your pretty friends would never say such things to me." He straightened his doublet, his vanity wounded.

I smiled sadly, knowing I had spoiled my little flirtation, but unable to care. "Perhaps you should court one of them," I suggested. "You'd find them far more amenable."

The barge rocked as more passengers climbed aboard. I settled myself on the cushioned seat and looked back at the palace, understanding how much had changed in the past three months. The woman who was returning to Whitehall—and to Robin—was not the girl who had left. I had experienced desire at Hampton, and sacrificed it for the sake of my marriage vows. In refusing Edmund Morven, I committed myself fully to my husband, but to make it work, I would need that same commitment from him.

It was not a topic I could broach immediately; Robin did not respond well to direct assaults, and his walls were well-defended and higher than most. It would require a cunning siege.

Chapter 21

OUR ROOMS SMELLED FAINTLY of the linseed and beeswax preparation Sebastian used to polish the furniture. I shut the door and leaned against it, drinking in the unfamiliar silence.

The river journey was as crowded and convivial as the summer, and it had been difficult to find a moment of peace to plan what I wanted to say to Robin. When we tied up at Whitehall, I left Alice to deal with our things and came straight home.

Whitehall wasn't Winterset, but these rooms, where we had begun to make a life together, were home.

In the main room, books and papers covered the table, and a stack of books teetered before the cold fire. Another volume lay open on my chair, evidence Robin had expanded to fill the space in my absence.

The bedchamber door was ajar. I barely noticed the faint sounds drifting through the casement, so quiet did it seem after the long summer. Careful not to soil the coverlet with my shoes, I lay down on the bed and stared up at the ceiler.

Desire was a heady thing, I now knew. If Edmund hadn't hurt my pride, I might have given in to his sustained campaign. I was afraid Robin would know what I had very nearly done just by looking at my face.

The speech I planned on the barge seemed all wrong. Before I uttered a word, I needed to know how he felt, if he'd missed me at all. Why he had never come to see me after that first visit.

There was a great thumping outside, and I slid off the bed, not wanting the servants to catch me resting. Sebastian entered with the first of my boxes and Alice followed, her arms full of small goods. When everything had been brought in, I called to Seb.

"Is Master Lewis with the principal secretary?"

"He is," he said. "Is there something you need?"

"I'm not sure." I let out a breath. "Could you sit for a moment?"

"I would rather fetch you some wine."

My smile faltered. "I don't want wine."

"What is it, mistress?" He perched on the edge of Robin's chair.

"Can I help?"

"He is hard to know." I dug my nails into my palms. "I fear being separated for so long means we will have to start over."

Seb nodded, understanding. "There are parts of him which are still a mystery to me. I'm certain he has missed you—he sent Sir Edward home early many nights and sat alone with his books."

"Well, I didn't expect him to start going to brothels," I said, drawing a startled laugh from Seb. "A man can't change that much in three months."

In the hours before Robin returned, the chaos of my unpacking vanished and Sebastian returned the room to order, laying a small fire. The table was bare except for two Venetian glasses and a pewter bowl of small, fragrant apples.

Robin pushed the door open and saw me. "You're here."

"I'm here." I offered my cheek.

"It hasn't been the same without you."

"Ned is no longer an adequate companion?" I tried not to compare his chaste kiss to Edmund's.

"Not in the same way." He draped his doublet over the back of the chair. "Did you enjoy the summer?"

"Yes, but I missed you." I wanted to embrace him, but if he backed away, I would be undone. "I hoped you would come again."

Robin ran his hand over his books, relocated to their proper place on the chest. "My work kept me here." He selected an apple, bouncing it in his palm. "You had more than enough company."

"What do you mean?" My heart rose to my throat.

He bit into the apple, and I waited while he chewed and swallowed. "With so many people, I did not feel my presence was required."

I took the fruit from him. "You're my husband."

"I am your husband whether I am in London or Richmond," he said. "You were well-partnered in my absence, if Will is to be believed."

"What did he tell you?"

Robin retrieved his apple and took another bite, not looking at me. "Court gossip," he said. "Nothing of importance."

Court gossip could mean anything. I kept my voice calm, asking, "Did he give you my message on his last trip to London?"

"No, but I'm not surprised." Tossing the core into the fire, he reached for my hand. "Will's as protective as Seb, in his way."

"There was nothing to protect you from," I said, understanding Will had related some description of my activities. "Other than his jealous fancies. Robin, I—there is—has been—no one."

"If there was, I could not complain." There was a rough edge of tiredness to his voice. "But I am glad there was not."

Relief flooded me—that he was glad, and he did not believe Will's tales. I would have preferred my near-guilt to be buried, but perhaps it was best out in the open, obliquely discussed and forgotten.

Sebastian brought a late supper of cold meat and savory pottage, no less delicious for being plainer than I was accustomed to. I ate and listened to Robin's summary of the last three months.

"One thing I heard," he said, "that did not come from Will, though it apparently happened at Hampton."

My spoon stopped halfway to my lips. "What?"

"Did Katherine Ashley truly reprimand the queen in front of everyone?"

There were times when obeying my oath was pointless; Robin's information was better than anything I had. "She did, and was sent away for her pains, but it lasted only a day. Elizabeth cannot manage without her."

"She is right." He cut another slice of bread. "Mistress Ashley, I mean. De Quadra swears Dudley visits Elizabeth's bedchamber. The rumors are everywhere."

And so he did, though he never stayed long enough to accomplish anything of which they were accused. He simply sat on the end of her bed and chatted while her women waited for him to leave.

"Are there other rumors?"

Robin's eyes darted toward the wine bottle. "Nothing to concern yourself about," he said. "If they are false, they are unimportant."

"And if they are true? If I do not know what they say, how do I know if they are false?" I enjoyed his discomfort; in some small part, it made up for my own.

"Does Dudley spend much time in the privy chamber at the end of the day?"

"Every day, as I am sure your spies tell you." His expression was all the confirmation I needed. "They are in love, Robin."

"They cannot be in love." He balled his napkin in his fist. "His marriage cannot be put aside, not even for the queen. Especially for the queen."

Talking to Robin brought back the unfairness of Kat Ashley's treatment. She had been banished for caring, she who would never act against Elizabeth's interests.

I leaned forward, an idea forming. "Is there a candidate Mistress Ashley would promote, in Dudley's place?"

Robin looked at me narrowly. "What have you heard?"

"Nothing." I wiped my knife on the last of the bread. "But if she is so against Dudley, there might be someone whom she favors."

"Would that matter?" he asked. "The queen takes marriage advice from no one, as we all know."

She did not take advice, but she listened to the opinions of those she trusted, evaluating them before forming her own response. When Kat Ashley returned to favor, her voice was heard, as it had always been.

"There is a suspicion that the Swedes are in contact with her." Robin looked somber. "Independent of their contact with us."

I tried to remember what I'd heard about Prince Erik, and if any of it could be repeated. "I know little beyond what you and Ned talked about before I left, but…" I remembered a scrap of conversation, and a door shut in my face when I was seen.

"But?" he prompted.

"I don't know, precisely," I said. "Mistress Ashley was speaking to Dorothy—Dorothy Bradbelt—and I heard his name. It is no more than that."

"That is not insignificant. We need to know if the queen's women are loyal."

No one would ever accuse Katherine Ashley of disloyalty; she had been imprisoned three times because of her closeness to Elizabeth.

"She would never betray the queen."

"That is my thought." Robin topped up our glasses. "She would not, nor would she permit disloyalty to occur among the ladies, if it came to her attention."

I thought I knew where he was going. "She could be acting on her mistress's behalf." Falling silent, I wondered if those present had witnessed an elaborate masque of Elizabeth's devising. I believed the queen entirely capable of such manipulation.

"How can you be certain," I asked, "if you've seen the truth, or if it was a performance put on for your benefit?"

Robin looked at me the way he had the day I had taken Plato and ridden pell-mell to the top of Bowman's Hill: with admiration and respect. "That, my dear girl, is the question."

Black thread danced its way across the thin white cloth, and the design danced itself, in reverse, across the insides of my eyelids. Another partlet to vary my boring wardrobe, this time with scrolling vines. Once the vines were complete, I would add tiny leaves. Perhaps strawberries, as well.

"Margaery?" Robin called from the outer chamber. "Have you seen my book?"

I stood, my hand going to my back; I had been too long in one position. "Which one?"

He appeared in the doorway. "I'm sorry," he said. "Asking if you've seen my book is like me inquiring as to your embroidery things. *The First Blast of the Trumpet.* I wanted to lend it to Blyden."

I fished it from my embroidery basket, where I had stuffed it when Sebastian came in. "It's here."

"Why do you have it?" He leaned over to admire my vines.

"I was reading over your shoulder the other night, and it interested me. I thought I'd read more before you got in, but I decided to work on this before I lost the light." These complicated pieces felt endless if I didn't work on them every day. "I'm sorry."

Robin put his hand on my shoulder. "Never apologize for reading," he said. "I'd like to hear your opinion on the monstrous regiment of women. Come sit with me."

Even without a fire, it felt right to be there with our glasses of wine, the proper end to our day. Still embarrassed at having taken his book, I tried to ask about his work, but his attention was fixed on me.

"Lady Margaret told me you'd been over-educated." His expression showed he didn't believe such a thing was possible. "I wasn't comfortable asking you then, and I've never gotten round to it since."

Grand-mère's opinions on education differed from mine. "She meant I read things most girls my age wouldn't have found interesting."

"Did she not favor the education of girls?"

"Not really," I said. "My grandfather felt differently. He had a book by a Spaniard—"

"Juan Luis Vives?" Robin interrupted, with a smile of recognition.

"Yes. Our neighbor, Monsieur Allard, had a tutor for his daughters, and I went to them each day." The happy hours I'd spent in the bosom of the Allard family made me wistful: two parents, three daughters, two sons. I had wanted them to adopt me.

"What were you taught?" He was genuinely interested.

"History. Philosophy. Some Latin."

"And French, of course." He rubbed his eyes. "You speak like a native."

"*Merci, mon cher mari.* Grand-mère did not want me to sound like an English girl." She had decreed all mealtime conversation be in French, until I was fluent. "Sometimes I fear I'll lose it, for lack of use."

Robin took a sip of wine. "*Je vais vous parler en français, si tu voulais.*"

He would speak to me in French, if I wished. "I would like that."

"What was your favorite area of study?" He spoke to me as if I were a person, not just a female.

"Rhetoric and philosophy." I twirled the stem of my glass. "And accountancy, so I could help Grandfather with the estate books."

"Numbers were my weak point," he said. "Did you read any literature?"

"Some poetry, not as much as I would have liked." I explained my truncated studies: the Allard girls pleaded for a different master, as they prepared for a life at court.

"Dancing lessons?" Robin was appalled. "Instead of poetry?"

I glanced over at him. "Well, I *was* a girl," I said. "Meant to be decorative, not intelligent."

Shaking his head, he pulled a volume down from the chest and pushed it across the table. "I'm thankful every day you are both. You might like this."

"What is it?"

"Vives." He turned it around so I could see the cover. "I have a copy of his *De institutione feminae christianae* at Winterset, if you would like to read it instead of just benefiting from its tenets."

Was I to be fully admitted to the wonders of Robin's sanctuary? "Do you miss it?"

"My library?" He rubbed his temples, a sign his head ached. "Every day."

I nudged his half-empty glass toward him. "This wasn't the life you had planned."

"Not at all." He closed his eyes. "But the queen asked, and after what nearly happened, I wanted to make certain it did not happen again, to me or anyone else."

I had just dealt a hand of cards when Ned barged in. "Are you free tonight?"

Robin raised a brow. "So free we were thinking of changing into our night robes and going to bed early."

"You cannot!" Ned jigged from foot to foot like a boy. "I want to take you somewhere."

I covered my face with my hands. Not tonight! It was so rare that we saw each other before nine, or before we were both exhausted. I did not want my much-anticipated evening disrupted by Ned Pickering.

"Not tonight." Robin gathered the cards and shuffled them. "Shall I deal you in?"

"Piquet is a two-person game." Ned snatched the deck away. "It must be tonight, Rob. Leave off your court clothes and come out with me."

I waited, hoping Robin would throw him into the corridor, knowing he would not and I would spend the night alone.

My husband pushed back his chair. "Margaery and I are having a quiet evening."

"This will not be quiet," Ned declared, "but it will be enjoyable. And you should come, too, Mistress Margaery. In fact, you must come with us."

His expression was pleading, and I understood how he got around Robin so easily.

Robin met my eyes. "What say you, wife? We've not been outside the palace together for any reason save church."

I wanted to stay in, but I'd seen so little of London that Ned's invitation was tempting. "Must I change my gown?"

Ned's face split into a grin. "Wear something plain, if you have it. We go out among the common folk tonight."

I retreated to the bedchamber and called for Alice to assist me. It was easier for Robin, dressing in black or gray all the time. "Alice," I said as she hurried in, "Master Lewis and I are going into the city with Sir Edward. What do I have that isn't too showy?"

Her forehead creased. "Your plain gowns are all at Winterset, mistress. Couldn't you just wear your black kirtle?"

"It's too fine."

If the evening's endeavors failed, it would not be because of me— perhaps if Ned's plans were not as exciting as he promised, Robin would spend less time with him.

I looked at Alice. "I have an idea."

Chapter 22

SEB REFUSED TO ALLOW us to go into London with only Ned's inadequate protection, and climbed up beside the driver of the hired coach as Robin helped me in.

"You look very pretty," he said. "Is that a new gown?"

I patted my green woolen skirts, shapeless without the support of a farthingale. "It's Alice's," I confessed. "She's wearing my second best nightdress in exchange."

He laughed so loudly Ned leaned in to discover the joke. "It's not far," he said. "We're only going to Cheapside."

Once inside, he and Robin began wrangling about something which happened with Cecil earlier in the day. I looked out the window as we traveled along the Strand, the extent of my explorations with Alice, and turned onto Fleet Street, lurching and stopping frequently to avoid obstructions in the busy road. Soon we passed through Ludgate to St. Paul's, where Robin and I had worshiped a few weeks past. The church yard was busy, and it was slow going to get around it. The driver shouted; Seb shouted; we moved on through milling crowds.

The driver stopped again. "We're at the conduit. Where are you wanting?"

"Just past the market cross," Ned called. "Turn down Bread Street."

Cheapside was a grand and bustling street, the goldsmiths and glovers busy even at this hour. I peered through the coach window, my eyes greedy for the shop windows. Too soon we turned from packed gravel into a smaller street, and abruptly stopped.

Seb opened the door. "The driver can go no further," he said. "It's not far."

I looked down in dismay. The street was churned mud; my shoes would never recover from such abuse.

"Let me carry you, mistress."

"Why are you carrying my wife?" Robin looked up from his conversation for the first time.

"Because the street is a bog," he said, "and you haven't had the lady long enough to lose her in the mud."

He lifted me out of the coach, and we watched with amusement as my husband navigated the muck in his good boots. Ned splashed like a child in a tub, spattering both of them.

"Where are we bound?" Robin asked.

Ned pointed down the street. "Just there, at the sign."

Our destination was an inn, a small place of three stories, its upper levels overhanging the street. The sign, illuminated by torches, read *The Minstrel's Arms.*

"This had better be worth it," my husband grumbled. "It's going to take ages to clean my boots."

"You won't be the one doing the cleaning." Seb hoisted me higher and set out for the door, with Ned trotting alongside. Robin brought up the rear, still muttering.

The door swung open as we reached it, spilling light into the street, along with several cheerful, drunken young men. They doffed their caps and bowed as Seb deposited me on the boards inside.

I looked around, my disappointment at the loss of my quiet evening forgotten. The main room was snug, with crowded trestle tables arranged in a tight semicircle. A fire flared on the hearth, with a basket of split logs nearby. To one side was a small stage, with a man seated on a low stool, his head bent over a lute.

Drawn by the promise of music, I moved toward the nearest empty seat. Seb reached the table first and people shifted to accommodate our party, looking curiously at him. Brushing off the bench, he gestured for me to sit, and took the spot at my side, so no one would bump me. Still squabbling, Robin and Ned sat across from us.

"Would you two be quiet?" I asked. "I want to hear the music."

"What a canny girl." Ned raised a beckoning hand to the serving maid. "That's why I've brought you here."

"Do we not get enough music at…" Robin's voice trailed off.

I had never seen him look like that before. When the maid deposited cups and a pitcher of ale on the table, Robin caught her arm. "Who is that?"

She followed his gaze. "That's the landlord," she said. "He plays most nights. If you're lucky, his wife will sing later."

My husband's lips parted. "Could you ask her to come out?"

The girl looked doubtful. "She sings when she chooses."

"Leave it, Rob." Ned raised his cup. "Here's to a night of music."

The lutenist finished his tuning and began to play. In moments, I understood the queen had no musician on par with this man. Listening to him made me feel as if I had been dropped into another world. After several songs, I turned to Robin. His face was pale, and he looked unaccountably disturbed. "What is it?"

"Nothing."

After another song, and rousing applause, the man stood, leaning the lute carefully against the stool. Jeers erupted from the onlookers, and he held up his hands. "Allow me a drink," he said. "Have I not earned it?"

Robin stood as he passed our table. "Tom."

The man stopped short, breaking into a transfiguring smile. "Rob! I did not know you were in London."

"The last I heard, you were in Wales." Robin's voice was uneven.

Calling for another pitcher, the lutenist slid onto the bench beside Ned. "We were, until King Henry's death," he said. "But we missed England, and we wanted the children to know their country."

He turned to me. His hair was silver-gilt; he must have once been very fair. "I'm sorry for interrupting," he said. "Master Lewis is an old friend."

I raised my brows at Robin, hoping they were as fearsome as Katherine Grey claimed.

"Margaery," he said, "this is Tom, whom I've known since I was a chorister." He waved a hand in my direction. "Tom, this is my wife, Margaery Lewis."

Squeezed onto the bench, I could not rise and curtsy, so I inclined my head in what I hoped was polite fashion. "Did you really know Robin as a boy?"

He kissed my hand, and smiled at me. "I certainly did. He had the second most beautiful voice at court."

Robin snorted. "You would mention that."

"Only because I married the most beautiful voice."

The sound of conversation rose around us, so unlovely after the music. "The maid says your wife might sing?" If she was as good as her husband, I would forgive Ned his next several trespasses upon my good will.

"She will indeed, when she sees who is here." Tom excused himself and disappeared through a door.

"I never thought to see them again." Robin studied his hands. "How did you find them, Ned?"

"Heard a rumor about a pair of former minstrels," he responded. "Thought it might be them. They disappeared around the time of Anne Boleyn's fall, didn't they?"

Robin nodded, looking into his cup. "I believe that's when it was."

"You believe." Ned laughed shortly. "As if you had nothing to do with it."

Tom reappeared, holding a woman by the arm. When she saw Robin, she let out a whoop and ran at him. He got up hastily, stepping back at the impact of her embrace, but his hands came up and he hugged her.

I nudged Seb. "Let me up. I'm missing everything."

He shifted obligingly, and I joined Robin. The woman was sobbing against his shoulder, stopping frequently to kiss him, and then breaking down again. I looked quizzically at Tom.

"She's very fond of Robin," he said.

I didn't think *I* was that fond of Robin. "Why is she crying?"

"He did us a great favor once," Tom explained.

I had many questions, none of which could be asked in such a crowd, or of a complete stranger. "That doesn't sound like him."

The woman finally let go of Robin, kissing his cheek one last time, and allowed herself to be led over to me. She appeared to be my husband's age, with a youthful expression despite the abundant silver threading her dark hair.

She held out her hands. "I apologize for my display, Mistress Lewis. It's been a long time since I've seen him."

Robin squirmed like a boy. "And you've not yet learned to behave like an adult."

"You're such a stick," she said. "Since our husbands both lack manners, let me introduce myself. I'm Bess Llewelyn, married to that handsome and talented musician there." Tom bowed in her direction, and she blew him a kiss.

"My name is Margaery," I said. "Robin and I have been married since November."

"Why, she's just a bride!" Bess exclaimed. "Tom, why didn't you tell me?"

He put his arm around her, and she rested her head in the hollow of his shoulder. "I've only had a moment with them, sweet. I don't have your talent for shaking facts out of people so quickly."

Bess spread her hands. "Shall we sit, then, and I'll see what else I can shake from him?"

The table cleared at her approach. I sat between Robin and Seb, with Tom, Bess, and Ned across from us. More ale was poured, and I watched Robin take a healthy swallow before he turned to Bess. "When did you return?"

"About ten years ago." Although there was plenty of space, she leaned against Tom as she spoke. "Ewan died, and his lord asked us to stay, but we decided it was time to come home. The younger children never knew England, and Harry was only a boy when we left."

"How did you end up here?" Ned gestured with his cup. "From minstrels to innkeepers."

"I learned brewing in Wales," Tom said. "It seemed a useful skill—you can't feed a family playing and singing, unless you're with the court." He nodded toward a young man coming through the back door with a barrel on his shoulder. "That's our Harry. He runs the place with us."

"That's Harry?" Robin blinked. "The day you left, he was looking forward to an adventure."

"He's coming on thirty," Bess said. "Go ahead and feel your age. I do."

Ned drained his ale and reached for the pitcher, refilling every cup within reach. "I don't mean to be ungracious," he said, "but do the landlords plan to entertain us again, or are they just going to sit about, gabbing with customers?"

Tom and Bess rose together. "How could we not?"

A few notes on the lute, and Bess began to sing. Her rich soprano befitted a mature woman, but there was an almost childlike purity about it. I reached for Robin's hand under the table; he clasped it firmly.

They performed for over an hour. Their son brought a small harp from the back room, and Bess played a few Welsh airs, unaccompanied, singing in that impenetrable language. I understood not a word, and it didn't matter; I still had tears on my face. I was not the only one.

I leaned against Robin's shoulder. "Have they always been this good?"

"Always," he said. "I've known them since I was twelve." There was a strange energy about him. He was reacting to the music, as we all were, but I'd never seen him pay this kind of attention to the queen's musicians.

Tom resumed his position next to Bess, and struck up a lively tune. She beckoned to the crowd. "Come on, dance!" she called. "Work up a thirst—drink more of our ale!"

They were familiar country dances; I'd done them myself, at Winterset, this past Christmas. I tapped my feet beneath my skirts, wanting to join in, but Robin's gaze was faraway, and he showed no signs of moving.

Ned offered a hand. "May I have this dance, Mistress Margaery, since your husband neglects you so dreadfully?"

"Robin?" I glanced to my left.

He barely looked away from the stage. "Dance with Ned, there's a good girl."

I followed Ned to the floor, fuming, but my ill temper soon faded. For all his bulk, he was a good dancer, and the crowd fell back to watch as we executed a quick-footed galliard in the middle of the room. Encouraged, Tom played on, and we quickly drew others in to join us.

When at last I dropped back beside Robin, I was breathing hard and my hair had come loose. I reached beneath my coif to anchor my pins.

He shifted to make room. "You enjoyed yourself?"

"Isn't it obvious?" I put my hand over his. "Why won't you dance?"

"Have you ever seen me dance?" He turned his cup in his fingers, making wet rings on the table. "In all the time you've known me?"

We stayed seated, watching the remaining dancers—of whom Ned was one, having tempted the serving maid into a round—and listening to the music. I couldn't imagine the time; it felt as if we'd been there forever, or only minutes.

Robin leaned behind me to speak quietly to Seb. His servant made his way over to Tom, who nodded and directed a word to Bess. The music ceased, and she stepped forward. "We'll be ending directly," she said, "but first, as a treat, a wedding dance for our old friend, Robin Lewis, and his bride."

I turned to Robin. Was this his doing?

"May I have this dance, wife?"

Tom began a slow, stately melody and we walked, side by side, to the center of the floor. Robin held out his hand and I placed mine lightly on top. We began the simple sequence of the pavane: forward with the left foot, the right foot coming to meet it, then a step with the right. A double—four steps—and up on the balls of our feet. A second sequence, and we turned, me moving forward and Robin back.

It was a formal, courtly dance, with few steps, and could be done in almost no space at all. Depending on the partner, it could be stultifyingly boring or intensely romantic. I had danced it countless times, with countless gentlemen, but never like this. There was no contact beyond my fingertips on the back of Robin's hand, but as we turned, our eyes met and held.

The crowd clustered around, watching the unfamiliar movements. It must have seemed plodding, after the livelier dances, but I held my breath with excitement.

Robin dropped to one knee, as required, but because of his injury, he went down on the wrong side. I kept my hand on his and promenaded around him, my green skirts brushing his legs. I returned to his right, and he got to his feet with a pained indrawn breath, covered by the music.

When we moved forward, Robin turned his hand over. We circled, looking over our shoulders, our eyes locked. I could feel his pulse through our joined palms; it was strangely intimate.

His gaze, filled with something beyond his normal absent curiosity, held me upright, as my legs weakened with desire. He looked at me as if he saw me—saw the woman whose heart beat in time with his through our linked hands. We continued the steps until the time came for him to kneel again.

"I can't do it," he murmured. "Not and be able to walk out of here."

The lute was plaintive, its plangent notes the only sounds in the world besides the beat of our pulses.

I broke the thread that held us together and knelt, taking the gentleman's moves as Robin slowly circled me. When we returned to our places, I made certain our palms connected again. "A full partnership," I said beneath the crowd's applause. "What one cannot do, the other must."

His eyes widened and he gave me a most un-Robin-like smile.

One last set of steps, forward and back, and Tom's lute fell silent. Our hands parted as I sunk into a curtsy deep enough to please the queen. Robin bowed, his lips barely brushing my fingers, yet somehow scorching my flesh.

Chapter 23

IT WAS VERY LATE. Seb immediately set to preparing his pallet in the antechamber and we retreated to our room, where I got a good look at what I'd done to Alice's kirtle. I inspected the mud-encrusted hem and a few spots on the skirt which might have been ale.

"Did you enjoy yourself?" Robin dealt rapidly with his own clothes and reached for my laces. They moved smoothly through the eyelets; he had grown practiced in assisting me.

"Yes." Bess's voice still sang in my head. "Did you?"

"It's been years since I've heard such music."

"I can't imagine hearing that every day."

"I did, every day for years." He pushed the kirtle off my shoulders. "There you are."

Wriggling free, I spread it over a chest to dry and untied my petticoat. Hopefully I would be able to brush off the worst of the mud before Alice saw, else I would have to give her my nightdress. I turned and leaned full length against Robin, wearing nothing but shift and stockings, and put my arms around his neck. "Thank you for the dance. It was lovely."

"It was only right." He removed my pins, and my hair fell to my waist. "We did not dance at our wedding."

I looked up at him. "We did not kiss at our wedding, either." The amount of ale I'd drunk made me bold. "Will you not remedy that?"

His fingers coiled in my hair, drawing me close. "That is not the relationship we have."

I stared into his eyes. His pupils were large; I was not the only one to have overindulged. "It is the relationship I want," I said, and kissed him.

For a moment he held back, and then his lips parted and he returned the kiss. My dizziness dropped from my head to my belly, then lower.

He tore himself away. "That was a lovely end to the evening. Shall we go to bed?"

I was not being put off again. I knew from our dance—from his kiss—that he felt something. Catching his hands, I brought them to my breasts. "Only if you don't plan to sleep."

His hands were warm through the linen. "Enough, Margaery."

"No." I kept hold of his hands and walked backward to the bed. "Not enough. This marriage is not enough, Robin. You—as you choose to be—are not enough." He followed unwillingly. "You will either make me your wife, tonight, or tomorrow I will go to Mistress Ashley and tell her I'm returning to Yorkshire."

Was I threatening to leave Robin if he didn't consummate our marriage? I thought of what my stepfather had said, that unmarried women were lusty, and needed to be wed else they would bring shame on themselves. Perhaps it was true; I certainly felt ashamed.

Robin considered my words. "You would do that?"

I blinked away tears. "I'm tired of always making way for others. I want a place in your life where they are not."

He caressed my cheek with the backs of his fingers. "I care for you very much."

"Then show me." I tugged my shift over my head and lay back against the pillows, naked but for my red knitted stockings. "Show me, Robin, or watch me leave you. I can get an annulment."

Non-consummation was considered a just cause for dissolving a marriage. I would be free, and could go home to Winterset and consider my options. Grand-mère would not approve, but she thought me a properly bedded wife.

A charge of non-consummation would make Robin a laughingstock among his peers. I watched that realization sink in, along with something else.

He sat on the bed, keeping a safe distance. "I do not keep away to hurt you," he said. "I am unlikely to please a young wife."

I rested my hand lightly on his bare knee. "We'll never know until you try."

A flicker of pain crossed his face. "What we have isn't perfect, but it's good." His voice was soft. "What if we ruin everything?"

"Look at me." I put my hand on my pounding heart, trying not to think of how I looked, with my breasts exposed in the candlelight. "I swear if we do not take pleasure in this, we will go back to the way we were. Good companions. Friends. Will you swear the same?"

"I will." His hand was likewise on his heart. "Oh, Margaery, it's not that I haven't wanted—"

"Then trust me." I drew him down beside me. "Trust us."

I was giddy from lack of sleep when I reached the presence chamber the next morning, but there was such a commotion I was able to ease into my duties without anyone noticing the circles under my eyes or the smile that came, unbidden, to my lips.

Marriage was a revelation. The first time wasn't entirely pleasurable—there was a moment where it was indeed quite uncomfortable—but being close to Robin, our skins touching, made up for that brief flare of pain. He held me afterward, the two of us wrapped in my hair. When I moved to retrieve the covers, I saw the marks of tears on his face.

"What is it, husband? Did I not please you?"

He smiled crookedly. "You please me by existing, darling girl. This was…more than I could have hoped."

I drew up the coverlet and cuddled against him. "I didn't know what to expect," I said. "The queen's ladies are indiscreet, but not explicit."

He stroked my breast. "Do ladies talk about such things?"

His touch made me think about what we had just done, and when we might do it again. "Lady Clinton talks about what she does with Sir John Tyrell, but I don't understand all of it."

"They had best be careful," Robin said. "Her husband will soon be back from France, and while the man is stupid, he can count."

"I think that's what she's talking about." I repeated what she said, that she let him touch her with his hands, and with his mouth, but he must spill his seed elsewhere.

"Well, at least one of them is thinking." He slid down onto the pillow, ready for sleep.

"But I don't understand," I said. "What we've just done—is there more to it than that?"

"There's quite a bit more," he said, "which need not be explained all at once. If you are pleased with this night's endeavors, we can try further tomorrow."

"Or tonight." My curiosity was piqued.

He kissed me. "Have pity. I'm not as young as I once was."

"All right," I huffed, making him laugh. "Leave me with questions. I thought a husband's duty was to school his wife in these matters."

His hand slipped between my legs. "This is part of what she was talking about." His voice held a hint of laughter as I squirmed beneath his fingers. "And this."

The candle guttered but I did not see it, only the blackness of the insides of my eyelids as my husband made the stars come out.

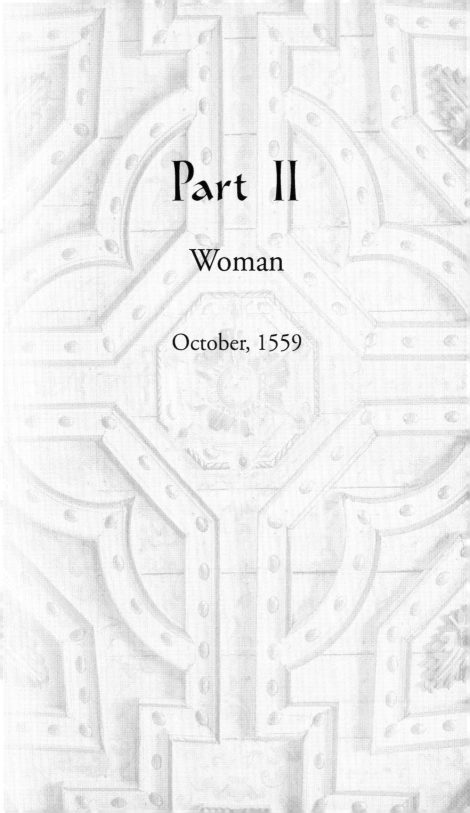

Part II

Woman

October, 1559

Chapter 24

THE QUEEN CHOSE TO walk in the privy gardens and take advantage of the bright October afternoon. Her ladies followed in small groups, talking and keeping an eye on Elizabeth for a change of mood or direction. Nell bounced along beside me, swinging her new red mitts. "You're different, Margaery. Something has changed."

"I don't know what you mean."

Her blue eyes crinkled. "Don't you? I think you are in love—you were singing today while counting pins."

"I must do something while counting pins, otherwise I will run mad."

"Is it"—she looked around—"Master Morven?"

"No!" I did not want her to think the spell I was under had anything to do with Edmund Morven.

"You were in love with him this summer," she persisted. "I know you parted, but who else could it be?"

"I was not in love." I walked faster.

"You're right, this is different." She rubbed her hands and stuck them into her mitts. "You're happy."

"Perhaps that's it." I *was* happy.

"I'm always in love, but it never lasts." She brushed her hand over the top of the clipped privet hedge. "What is it like?"

Did I love Robin, or was I just enchanted by what we did together? "Love is love, Nell," I said. "You love your brother, your father. It's the same, but...different."

She giggled. "Well, I would hope so! You've never met my father."

In spite of Robin's description, I still imagined an older version of Will, thickset, with gray in his brown hair. "Is he like your brother?"

"Heavens, no!" Her eyes widened. "Father is very dark, and a bit severe. Never with me, but if I'd been a boy, I would be frightened of him. He is stern with my brothers, especially Will."

"What about your mother?" I listened while keeping an ear cocked to the conversation ahead of us; it never hurt to know what the other women were talking about.

"She died a few years ago. I am like her," she said, "only taller."

Taller! Nell was no bigger than a poppet; how tiny had her mother been?

The queen turned abruptly; the breeze was sharp and her head ached. Once indoors, she lay down in her chamber, and thoughts of love were put aside as I was asked to read to her until supper.

The months leading up to Christmas were peaceful but for the usual turmoil over whether—and whom—the queen would marry, but I ignored it as best I could and tried to settle into this strange new world Robin and I had created between us.

I had been afraid, after our first lovemaking, that he would pretend it never happened and we would go back to our sterile existence, but instead he awakened me each day with kisses and sweet words—not love words, such as Edmund had used—but words that showed his caring.

As the weather grew colder, we spent many of our evenings in bed, though not all our time was spent in lovemaking. Robin was not always able, and when that happened, he would smile wryly and say, "This is why you should have married a younger man."

I thought exhaustion was as likely a cause as age, and was happy just to be with him inside the curtained cave of our bed, endlessly talking. He told me of his travels, which fascinated me, and in turn, I related stories of my life with my grandparents, and what I remembered of my childhood at Winterset.

He also explained to me, in words and actions, some of what the queen's ladies talked about.

"Goodness," I said breathlessly the first time he demonstrated that a mouth had purposes beyond eating and kissing. "Does everyone do that?"

Robin shifted up to lie beside me. "I don't know. It's not something men talk about."

I snickered, imagining such a conversation between Robin and Ned. "It might be interesting."

"I think not." He reached for my hand, placing it on his body. "This is interesting enough."

Closing my eyes, I duplicated the movements he had taught me.

It was a powerful feeling, knowing I could reduce my focused, intellectual husband to a handful of hot, unthinking flesh. "Robin?"

"Hmm?"

I stopped moving. "Do ladies do such things?"

His voice was thick. "Some do."

I released my grip and moved down the bed until I knelt between his legs. "Then I shall be one of them." I wet my lips. "You will have to tell me if I do it correctly."

At my first touch, he let out a sound which was neither gasp nor laugh. "You'll do fine, wife."

The year before, uncertain of our relationship and myself, I had embroidered my hopes onto a nightdress and called it a gift. It had been worn—and cast aside—many times since, but this Christmas, I wanted to give Robin something which truly suited him.

"It must be a book," I said to Nell. "That is what he loves, more than anything."

"Except you, of course," she countered. "He could not wish to hold a leather binding more closely than his wife."

I planned the errand for a day when we were both free of duties to the queen. Because he would not allow his sister to go into London unescorted, Will Hawkins accompanied us. I offered no protest, for fear of Nell's teasing; I had never told her of Will's attempt to destroy my marriage.

According to Sebastian, not all bookshops would be welcoming to a female customer. He recommended the stalls on Paternoster Row, near St. Paul's, where one could find nearly everything. "I'm sorry I can't be there," he said. "Hawkins will keep you safe, but do not listen to his recommendations."

I promised I would not. "I wish you could come along. I'm afraid I'll find the perfect book only to discover he has a copy at Winterset."

"Even I don't know his entire collection," Seb admitted with a laugh. After some thought, he suggested I look for volumes published in the last several years. "We bought almost nothing in our last year in Venice, and he's had little time to acquire books since coming to court."

With that in mind, I rode with Will, Nell, and a groom down the Strand and along Fleet Street until it turned into St. Paul's church-yard.

"Let's stop here," I said. "Paternoster Row is just to the north, and there will be plenty of occupation for you if my errand becomes overlong."

The groom settled himself with the horses, and we picked our way across the churchyard. It was crowded with all manner of people, buying and selling, waiting for someone to preach, or just taking it all in, as I was.

"Have you been here on a Sunday?" Will asked, gesturing toward the stone cross where worshippers met for public sermons. "I came two weeks ago. It was fascinating, but a little puritanical for my tastes."

It had been more than a month, though it was on Robin's agenda before the cold set in. Being seen at an occasional public sermon was advisable, if not particularly enjoyable. Like my husband, I preferred my religion indoors, and with comforts attached.

The booksellers had everything I could possibly want. The only problem was choosing the perfect book. I darted from stall to stall, wishing I had the coin to buy everything that caught my eye.

"I didn't know so many books existed. Surely you've found some-thing." Nell leaned against a stall. "My feet are freezing."

My hands clenched inside fur-lined mitts. "You asked to come along."

She stared blankly at me. "I thought it would be fun."

"It's been hours," Will pronounced, "and you've purchased nothing. We should return to Whitehall before Nell takes a chill."

According to the bells, it had not been two hours, and while I'd made no purchases, I had found several books which would please Robin. It remained only to make my selection, but their whining made me want to linger until the light was completely gone.

"I'm almost done. Why don't you take Nell to that cookshop"—I pointed across the street—"and I will join you in a few minutes."

Grumbling about the impropriety of an unmarried girl, a maid of honor to the queen, being seen in such a place, Will was eventually convinced by his sister giving a credible imitation of a three-year-old child.

The nearest bookseller had two of the best candidates, and I determined to choose between them before I was driven to distraction. Next time, I would come with Alice, or wait until Sebastian was free.

When I returned to the stall, the elderly merchant came around to the street, his rusty black gown flapping in the wind. "You saw something you liked, mistress?" Though his voice was high and piping as a boy's, his eyes were keen.

"Yes," I said. "I would buy a gift for my husband. I am torn between the *Historia Animalium* and *Les Regrets.*"

Unkempt eyebrows raised as he reevaluated me. "Natural history or du Bellay? He reads both languages?"

"Fluently," I said. "He works for the court."

"Hmm. I have but one volume of the *Historia Animalium* at present." His expression was exaggeratedly sad. "If you are interested in the full four volumes, I could procure the others."

The encyclopedia of animals, with its lavish descriptions and illustrations of creatures both real and fantastical, made my heart beat faster, but it would be as much a gift for me as Robin. Those creatures would find their way very quickly into my embroidery, but would he truly enjoy them?

"Perhaps later," I said. "I suppose it will be the poems, then."

The bookseller paused. "I do have something else. It is a recent arrival, and not for every customer." He disappeared and returned cradling a cloth-wrapped package. "Has your husband read *The Decameron*?"

"I believe so." If I had heard of it, Robin must surely have read it.

"Behold." He untied the tapes and exposed a thick volume, bound in gray calf with gold stamping on the cover. "This is of similar structure to the Bocaccio, but in French."

I opened it to the title page. *L'Heptameron, ou Histoires des Amans Fortunez*—stories of fortunate lovers! Unable to quell the smile that spread across my face, I said, "This is the one."

We held our gifts until bedtime, when we were free of all

obligations save those to each other. I released the servants early: Sebastian wanted to go to mass, and Alice, curiously, decided to accompany him. I'd never known her to be particularly religious, but Christmas was a special time.

Dressed only in our night things, we sat before the fire and toasted each other with a bottle of exceptional Italian wine, Robin's contribution to our feast. I had sent out for sugared almonds and raisins and a half-dozen Seville oranges, the remains of which lingered in pewter bowls on the table.

"Tired?" Robin's eyes were heavy-lidded; I did not want him to fall asleep before he unwrapped his book.

"A bit," he said. "Mostly thinking how wonderful it is to have peace and quiet."

He didn't just mean the lack of company, Ned having gone home for Christmas. The constant busyness of working with Cecil wore on him, as did missing his library and Anselm, as I missed Grand-mère. Our life was far from the Yorkshire idyll we had planned.

"Let's go to bed," I suggested. "We can leave the rest for Seb and Alice. They might like a little something when they come in from the cold."

He stood and stretched, his spine crackling. "You don't have to ask me twice." Catching up our glasses, he followed me into the bedchamber.

The shutters were latched against the wind, but a slight draft stirred the wall hanging and bent the flames of the bedside candles. The room was otherwise in darkness.

"Do you want your gift now?" I kissed him lightly.

Robin caught me to him in a brief, tight embrace. "I am grateful for the gifts I already have."

In the golden light, the lines around his eyes were more noticeable. He slept too little and worked too hard. If I said as much, he would agree, but he would not change.

"You must be grateful for one more, then." I retrieved the book from beneath my pillow. It was wrapped now in a white linen kerchief embellished with his interlocked initials.

He undid the wrapping, admiring my handwork before even

looking at the book. "It's like an extra gift," he said, "knowing how much work goes into these pieces." Robin folded it neatly and brought the book closer to the light.

"*Heptaméron*," he murmured. "I haven't seen this one yet."

A heady flush of victory made me clap my hands. "It's in French," I said. "I thought we might read it together, in the evenings when Ned is absent."

He skimmed the pages, turning them quickly, reading a few words aloud. "It's stories, like *The Decameron*," he said, pleased. "I read that with Bianca, years ago. How wonderful to have something similar to share with you."

His words were better than a gift. I had begun to feel, ever since my return from Hampton, that he valued my thoughts and listened to me with as much attention as he would to any man of his acquaintance. It was not just that my opinions were useful to his work; his appraising eyes made me feel seen.

"And now it's your turn." He produced a small box and pressed it into my hand. "I had this made for you. Sebastian helped with the design."

The inlaid rosewood box was a work of art on its own. I stroked the satin finish and looked up to find him watching me with a strange combination of anticipation and fear. Did my reaction matter so much?

When I raised the lid, my eyes were dazzled by the scarlet velvet lining, but then I turned it over and tipped the contents into my palm.

"It's beautiful." My voice caught.

His gift was a pendant jewel of the kind ladies wore on their bodices, usually in combination with a long strand of pearls like the ones Grand-mère had given me. Made of gold, it was an intricately-wrought M, with a square-cut black jewel in the center and three pearls dangling from the bottom.

"I know jet isn't fashionable." Robin clasped his long-fingered hands. "But it's from Whitby, and I thought it would remind you of home."

"I love it." I held it up, turning the pendant so the candles reflected in the gold. The opaque jewel was like a drop of ink. "Aren't these usually made with two initials, intertwined?"

His face altered. "I did not want to presume."

Chapter 25

Our lives returned to their settled rhythms, but a scarlet thread of passion ran through everything now. Life was the same, yet very different.

Shortly after the new year, the Grey sisters were restored as ladies of the bedchamber. Since no one had left or been demoted, there was constant jostling for position and consequent bad tempers all around.

"It seems to have been done on a whim." I was exhausted by the drama of my day.

Robin quirked an eyebrow. "Do you think so?" he asked. "Is it a privilege to be constantly under Elizabeth's eye?"

Put that way, it could also be a form of protective custody. The queen's gaze could be nerve-wracking when you had nothing to hide; how could Katherine continue her love affair under such close supervision?

"I hadn't thought of that." I dropped into my chair.

"Did anything interesting happen today?" He stared through his wine at the flames.

A chill crawled up the back of my neck; Robin's questions were never idle. "Such as?"

He shrugged. "Perhaps you have overheard the queen voice an opinion on Cecil's latest candidate?"

The queen's every word, every gesture, was open to the judgment and interpretation of all—including my husband. I blinked at him. "She did say one thing…"

"What?" He straightened. "You can tell me."

"*Video et taceo.*" It was such elementary Latin even I understood it. *I see, and say nothing.*

Nell spoke in my ear under the music. "Edmund Morven is watching you."

"He can't miss me." Among the maids, I stood out like a blot of ink on a white page.

"He hasn't gotten over you, Margaery, for all that he's paying court to Frances. Look at him."

I risked a sideways glance: so beautiful, and yet he conjured no feelings in me at all but a faint mortification. How had I allowed myself to desire such a man, a vessel filled with pretty words, who understood me no better than I understood the Greek texts on Robin's shelves?

Her fingers curled around my wrist. "He's coming over!"

Edmund threaded his way through the crowd and bowed to the assembled women. His eyes raked my face. "May I have the honor of this dance, Mistress Lewis?"

The gossip would be worse if I refused. "Certainly."

He held out his hand, palm up, his mouth curving into the smile that had tempted me all summer. I turned his hand over and placed mine atop his. *I have decided to be a wife*, the gesture said clearly. I hoped Will Hawkins was watching.

For the first minutes we executed the steps in silence, but as we turned and faced the musicians, Edmund spoke. "You may not wish to hear this, Margaery, but you are glowing."

"Thank you." I removed my hand, turning. His smile still made me quiver, just a bit, and I lowered my eyes to his jeweled buttons. "Your opinion is most important to me."

"You are more desirable now than you were in September. Your husband is a fortunate man."

"I am fortunate in my husband."

Edmund circled me, letting his blue velvet sleeve brush my shoulder. "I'd appreciate it if you called off your dog." He nodded toward Will, standing at the side of the room. "He's cost me a few opportunities lately."

I looked up and found his long-lashed hazel eyes sincere. "Master Hawkins does not take direction from me."

"From your husband, then, who is no doubt behind his actions." His tone was light, but the accusation was serious.

Robin was not the type to hold a grudge over something that never happened, and even if he did, thwarting Edmund's chances was hardly worth his effort. Will, on the other hand...

"I'll do what I can." I gave him an impersonal smile. "Perhaps if you paid attention to his sister, he would think more kindly of you."

"Good God, no," he said. "She is a beautiful creature, but a little too willing to be wed and bred for my liking."

The music came to an end and I dipped a curtsy, eager to get away. "Was that my attraction? Being already wed, you had no pressure to make an honest woman of me."

A tiny shake of his head as he backed away. "It was more than that, as well you know. I am glad to see you happy."

Katherine's return to her former status did not alter her behavior. She still spoke rashly, and once again had been sent from the presence chamber. Not having duties of my own, I accompanied her on a walk along the river.

"Why do you provoke her?" I wound my arm through hers to keep her from wandering away. "You are your own worst enemy."

She tilted her head to look at the pale winter sky. A tear slipped from down her cheek. "This is not the life I was meant for. I could have been Countess of Pembroke."

"You could also have been imprisoned," I reminded her. "You are fortunate Queen Mary did not blame you for the actions of your family."

Her lip came out. "Your father was also executed for treason."

Katherine's words often concealed knives. Was her unhappiness so deep she did not see their effect, or did she not care? Swallowing my hurt, I said, "But not for putting his own daughter on the throne."

She drifted toward the rail. A group of young men were jumping from an incoming barge, with much shouting and laughter. Eventually, one fell in and the merriment increased. Edward Seymour was among them. Katherine waited, white-knuckled, until he acknowledged her, then turned away.

"My mother and grandmother married men who gave them their own power," she said. "That will not be my path."

I didn't understand how she could be so obtuse. "Katherine, you will make a marriage in time—a better one than the Earl of Pembroke."

"I will not," she said doggedly, "if *she* has anything to do with it."

Elizabeth did not hide her disdain for Katherine, but how much of her feelings were caused by my friend's own behavior? "You could try a bit harder. You treat her like an enemy."

"The crown must go to someone." There was venom in her light voice. "If I marry and prove I can breed, she would hate me even more."

She was not wrong, but she was wrong-headed. "Be careful, Katherine."

"A blessed new year to you, Mistress Margaery. You were much missed this evening." Ned was in the corridor outside our apartments, and I hid a smile of relief at his early departure.

"We have missed you, as well." I wondered if Robin had warned him off, or if he understood we wished to be alone. Either way, his less frequent presence at our fireside made me appreciate his company— just not on this particular evening. "Is your family well?"

A wide smile split his face. "They are, indeed. Perhaps together we can convince Rob to make a visit in the spring."

"I'm sure we would enjoy that." I wanted to visit Grand-mère— her letters of late had been short and unsatisfying—but Yorkshire was a longer journey and it would be difficult to convince Robin to take the time. Ned's home in Surrey was a more practical suggestion.

"Did you see Ned?" Robin turned from the bookshelf, pulling me in for a brief embrace.

I nodded. "He invited us to visit him in the spring."

"He knows how difficult that is." Releasing me, he put a volume back into its proper place.

"And yet he manages," I said. "Why don't you ever take time away?"

He needed a day—a week, a month—away from court. Somewhere with books, and wine, and a large bed, and no demands on his time but mine.

"Because it takes only one day for it to fall apart," he said wearily. "Not just the queen's marriage, you understand. But Parliament, and convincing the Catholics—ours and those in Europe—to accept her."

"I still don't see why she must marry outside England." Elizabeth had met with the council that morning and spent the rest of the day in a rage. No one was safe: she shouted at Mistress Ashley, threw a book at Elizabeth Howard, and called Philadelphia Carey a fool when she broke a lute string. Katherine was lucky not to have been there; she would have surely been a target. "Would it not be wiser for her to marry an Englishman, after what happened with Mary?"

"It must be done," Robin said. "And soon. Who is next in the line of succession?"

"Katherine." She would be unbearable in a position of power.

"Elizabeth will never allow that, no matter how much Cecil promotes her. Who else?"

"Margaret Douglas?" I guessed.

"Very good. Who else?" Robin unbuttoned his doublet and shed the rest of his clothes as I mulled my answer.

"The Scottish queen." I remembered Elizabeth's reaction each time Mary's name was mentioned. "Is she the problem?"

"The problem," he said, coming to stand behind me, "is Elizabeth's refusal to marry and provide her own heir. When Mary was the dauphine, she was but a thorn in Cecil's paw. Now that she has the auld alliance with France behind her, she is infinitely more dangerous."

I reached behind and brought his hands to my breasts. "Is her claim so strong?"

"Look at you," he said. "Asking a question and then distracting me."

"I have an exceptional husband." I leaned back against him. "You'll manage."

He slipped one hand inside the neck of my gown. "She is the granddaughter of Henry's older sister, Margaret, who was married to the Scottish king."

I listened to his recitation of Mary Stuart's bloodline as his thumb circled my nipple. "Her religion is also a problem, yes?" My breath caught, and I wondered how the touch of one finger could sound through my body like a bell.

"Yes." He removed his hand, but only to finish my interrupted laces. "The old Catholic families who can't bring themselves to support Elizabeth would flock to her if she made a play for England."

Robin eased into his chair and pulled me onto his lap. "Do you really want to hear all this?"

I settled in, squirming until I had his full attention. "I want to know what you know."

He swallowed hard. "What I know is you're making it difficult for me to think clearly."

"Try." I nibbled at his neck. "The old Catholic families…?"

"God, woman." He tucked his chin to make me stop. "The old Catholic families would undoubtedly prefer Mary on the throne. That is why Cecil tries so hard to get the queen to choose a husband. Not all of the princes of Europe are inbred Habsburgs. There are some virile young men on Cecil's list."

"Ah, I want to hear about them." I wriggled to pull my petticoat from beneath me. "Tell me about the virile young men."

Robin's eyes were closed, his breathing uneven. His desire was evident through the thin shirt which was his only covering. "What do you want to know, Margaery?"

I clasped him beneath the shirt. "Tell me about the men who want to marry Elizabeth."

"There's Philip of Spain." He gasped as I threw one leg over the chair, and him, wrapping us in my bunched skirts. "And Erik of Sweden."

"Mmm." Raising myself up, I slid down his length, my body tensing for a moment, then opening to welcome him. "Erik," I repeated, rocking my hips. "Prince of Sweden?"

"Yes." Robin's eyes were open now, locked on mine, as we were locked into the same rhythm. His hands caught my shoulders, bearing me down upon him. "He is a very good candidate."

My response came out as a moan. "If she can't have Dudley, she might refuse to marry anyone. That could bring war."

"You're"—he began to thrust, and the chair rocked beneath us—"learning."

"I have an excellent teacher." Closing my eyes, I let the stars scatter across my vision and within seconds his groan told me he'd completed his own journey. I sagged forward against him, energy and curiosity temporarily sapped.

"Shall we go to bed?"

We parted stickily, and I brought my leg back over his lap. "I miss riding astride."

"You must be content with the fine gallop you've had tonight." He got up and lurched to one side, his hand going to his knee.

"Are you all right?" I didn't want to be the cause of a new injury.

"It was worth it." He straightened and kissed me. "Let's get you out of the rest of your clothes. I may have had my wife, but I didn't get to see all of her."

Chapter 26

"ARE YOU FEELING WELL?" Alice tied my farthingale and reached for my kirtle.

"Yes, why?" I winced as she did up my laces. "You've pulled them too tight again."

She adjusted them until I could take a full breath. "I did them the same as always," she said. "They're worn from going through the holes."

"That's impossible. It feels like I'm being squeezed to pieces."

Alice stood back and regarded me, then reached to tug at my square neckline, which also didn't fit properly. "Your courses are late," she said. "I haven't washed any linens in at least six weeks."

"Is it that long?" I tried to remember the last time I'd bled. "I can't be—"

She burst into delighted laughter. "You are! Lady Margaret will be so happy!"

I sat on my dressing stool, my recent nausea suddenly making sense. It was more than my old friend, worry; more than the stress of dealing with Elizabeth's demands or the meals at all hours; more than the late nights with Robin—though those nights certainly led to my condition.

"She will be," I said. "But what about my husband?"

Alice smiled broadly. "He won't be surprised."

I wasn't so sure. I was surprised enough for both of us, and paid no attention as she did my hair, chattering all the while.

A baby. I had thought of babies, in an abstract sense, since I was a child myself, vowing that if I ever had children, I would give them the kind of love and upbringing that had been mine for my first five years.

Was I capable of that? Was Robin? Could he even love a child? He showed physical affection easily enough now, but he'd still never said he loved me.

A final pat told me Alice was satisfied. I looked down at my intricate black and white forepart, and wondered how long my gowns would fit. Mary Sidney stayed at court until just a few weeks before her confinement for her third child. She'd been cumbersome and slow-moving, her wrists and ankles swelling even as her black hair grew lustrous. Her gowns laced at the sides, for comfort, and she seemed unbothered by the changes in her body, being more concerned with the queen's grumbling over her imminent departure.

Elizabeth would not be distressed at my confinement. She liked me well enough, but I was interchangeable with any one of a dozen others.

The passage to the royal apartments was longer than usual, as I pondered my predicament. Would I give birth at Winterset? I wanted my grandmother with me, and she could not come to London. Robin would most likely escort me home, but could I convince him to stay for the birth, or would he be like Ned, kissing my cheek and fleeing back to the only world that mattered, his dark rooms filled with intrigue and diplomacy?

The guards greeted me and swung open the doors. The heat and noise rose in a wave to greet me. I took a deep breath, willing my stomach into submission. The queen would soon be ready to face the day.

I held my secret close for two weeks, waiting to see if Alice was wrong, expecting at any moment the dull ache across my low back that heralded the arrival of my courses. They remained stubbornly absent, and instead I became sensitive to everything, my breasts tender, the smell of meat and ale causing my stomach to rebel. I was both starving and unable to eat, and I ran to the jakes so often Mistress Parry asked if I was quite well.

"Just an upset stomach." I smiled brightly and squeezed my legs together as the urge to urinate struck again.

She patted my shoulder. "I'll let Kat know you're poorly. Go on, now."

Our rooms were deserted, Sebastian and Alice having finished their duties and gone elsewhere. I put a spill to the ready-laid fire before fetching my embroidery basket, and settled in to work until I felt better.

"Margaery?"

The voice was far away, and I struggled to hear it over the booming footsteps. When I opened my eyes, Robin's face was so close I could count his freckles.

"Are you all right?" he asked. "You're back early."

I blinked, the last of the dream fading. "I returned at noon. What time is it?"

"Nearly six." He pulled his chair close. "Have you had dinner?"

Had I? No—the queen's dinner was being delivered as I left. I'd slept the day away. "I *am* a bit hungry."

"I'm not surprised. Shall we eat in the hall?" He picked up my silks from the floor; I must have fallen asleep almost immediately.

"Bread and cheese will do." My head was still hazy; the noise in the hall would set it to pounding. "Something light."

Robin took my hands. "That's not enough. You've been looking a bit wan these last days."

"That's because I'm pregnant." I flinched as his grip tightened, then fell away as he sat back, stunned.

"Are you sure?"

I mustered up a smile. "We've done all the right things." Was he upset? Angry?

He called Sebastian from the antechamber. "Mistress Margaery needs bread and cheese, Seb. And bring wine."

His mind turned to what—to him—would be most important. "Should you continue to work?"

"Women have been bearing children since Eve. I'll manage, once these early days are over." I explained my exhaustion and distaste for certain smells. "And my skin is very sensitive," I said. "I can feel every thread in my shift."

"Then I shall keep well away." He smiled faintly from across the table. "It's not recommended when you're with child, anyway."

"What isn't?" I looked at the cloth I had been embroidering when I drifted off. It was meant to be a new forepart for my day gown, and I was already bored with it.

"Relations," he said, swallowing the word.

"We had relations three days ago, and I was pregnant then."

I could make baby gowns now, and swaddling bands. Something cheerful to stitch all my hopes into. "It can't hurt this early."

Robin held his hands toward the fire. "It's best to be careful."

After much negotiation, it was decided Robin would escort me to Winterset and stay until I was safely delivered, so long as the babe appeared promptly.

"There's so much to be done," he said, forestalling my protests. "I am fortunate Cecil has granted me leave to make the journey at all."

Fortunate was not the word I would have chosen. Cecil did not own my husband, any more than the queen owned me. When I told Mistress Ashley of my condition, she congratulated me, but her next words were as I expected. "Her Majesty does not like her ladies to be too long away. Will you be confined in London?"

"Yorkshire," I said. "My grandmother is already making plans."

"Then you should ask her to arrange for a wet nurse."

"Why?"

Mistress Ashley looked surprised. "You cannot serve the queen and nurse a babe. He will stay behind with his nurse, and you will return to court knowing he is well cared for."

Other women managed it. Mary Sidney returned within a month, leaving her infant behind, but I wanted that no more than confinement. At what point did our own lives take precedence? One person understood. When I told her of the impending baby, Nell squealed and cried and embraced me, all at once. "May I stand godmother?" she asked. "I love babies. I want lots of them."

"You need to acquire a husband first," I said dryly. "Once that is accomplished, I'm sure you'll produce them as regularly as bread loaves."

She giggled, all dimples and wide eyes. "Well, my mother did. She caught my oldest brother almost immediately."

Though our first year had been unusual, I was grateful I'd had time with Robin as his wife, not just as the mother of his children. I wondered if our relationship ever be the same.

"Do you want a boy or a girl?" Nell answered herself. "A boy, of course, so Master Lewis has his heir. Then you can have as many girls as you want. Oh, Margaery"—she clasped my hands—"it will be such fun!"

What little I knew of childbirth didn't sound like fun. All my life, I'd heard tales of pain and complications; my mother said bearing me had nearly killed her. Childbed fever, a common complaint, took Jane Seymour after the birth of Prince Edward, and Kathryn Parr, the old king's last wife, died a scant week after bearing a babe to Thomas Seymour.

I was not afraid of pain, but I didn't want to have a child only to leave it—and leave Robin a widower. He would have to remarry, or else turn the child over to Grand-mère; he would have no more idea what to do with a baby than with a rhinoceros.

Admitting this to Nell sobered her for a moment, but nothing kept her unsmiling for long. "That will not happen," she said. "You are young and strong. It is only sad, weak women who die in childbed."

My mother was neither sad nor weak, and had everything to live for, but nothing would change Nell's mind. In truth, it did no good to dwell on my fears, and I did my best to put them aside.

There were interesting aspects to being pregnant, once the nausea and sleepiness subsided. For several weeks, I had the energy of two women, and until Robin heard about it, I continued to ride with the queen.

"How could you be so irresponsible?" he asked, when I returned to change out of my riding clothes. "It's bad for the child."

He'd never been angry with me before. "I cannot see why."

"You don't need to see why." Robin folded his arms. "I would prefer you stay off Artemis until you are well again."

Pregnancy caused my husband to withdraw from me as surely as he had in the early days of our marriage, staying on his side of the bed and putting me off when I rolled against him. His conversation consisted of queries about my health and warnings of the dire things that could happen if I lived a normal life. The only time he showed any emotion was the night I took his hand and placed it, palm down, on my rounding belly.

"Feel it." My nightdress was a fragile barrier between him and my flesh.

"You've had a long day, Margaery." He tried to pull away. "You must be tired."

I was the furthest thing from tired. When I was small, my father took me to visit a beehive and held my hand on the side so I could feel the tiny insects humming within. I felt like that: like I was full of bees, thousands of tiny pulses of energy surging around with no outlet.

I couldn't make Robin understand, but perhaps he would feel what I'd felt this afternoon, in the royal bedchamber.

There. A tiny flicker, almost imperceptible—except to me. And, apparently, to Robin. He stayed there, unmoving, his fingers spread wide, until it happened again. "What is it?"

"The baby's quickened."

Chapter 27

A TENDRIL OF PAIN curled through my low belly and I sat up straight, my embroidery dropping to my lap.

"Are you all right?" Nell was at my side in an instant.

"Just a twinge." It faded quickly, and I felt silly for making a fuss.

"You've gone all white." She cocked her head. "Mistress Parry," she called. "Mistress Lewis is unwell."

Blanche Parry bustled over, and I wanted to crawl under my chair from embarrassment. "What's the problem, dear?"

"Nothing." Another thread of discomfort unfurled between my hip bones. "I'm fine."

Nell leaned forward. "She's near five months gone with child," she said softly. "And she's having pains."

The older woman considered me. "It may be nothing, but I would rather be over careful. Fetch a groom to escort Mistress Lewis to her rooms. You may accompany her."

In the middle of the day, the journey should have only taken fifteen minutes, but the increasing frequency of the cramps meant we stopped several times. Nell was surprisingly stoic, letting me lean on her while the groom looked on in consternation.

"Should I carry her?" His eyes flickered from me to Nell.

"No." I felt a sudden wetness, like the abrupt arrival of my courses. Except I hadn't had my courses in months. "I can walk."

Apparently I could not, because we were at my door and I was in the groom's arms, with no recollection of being picked up.

"Get her inside." Alice ordered the queen's man about as if he were a page. "Put her there and go find a midwife—or a physician. Whichever can get here first."

The groom set me gently down on the bed. "I will pray for your recovery." He bowed and ducked past the women.

"How do you feel?" Alice swiftly removed my outer garments. I sighed with relief as she took out my pins; everything felt tender, and my hair dragged at my scalp.

"I think I'm bleeding." I raised my hips so she could pull my petticoats free.

"You are, a bit," she confirmed, shoving a towel under me. "It can happen, in the early months. Don't fret yourself."

Nell fluttered about, trying to be useful. It would be terrible if she got blood on her white gown, I thought hazily. "You should go back to the queen."

Her eyes widened at my suggestion. "Mistress Parry gave me leave to stay, and so I shall." She took a breath. "At least until the physician arrives."

The feather bed felt no better than straw, lumpy and poking me everywhere. I shifted irritably, trying to find a comfortable position. "Could I have a drink?"

Nell scurried to fulfill my request, and Alice came close, placing a cool hand on my forehead. I brought my knees up, the thread pulling tight. "Shall I send for Master Lewis?"

"No."

Nell reappeared with a cup. The ale quenched my thirst, but did nothing to quell the growing fear that I was losing my child.

"But—"

I shook my head. "He does not need to see this."

He did not need to see *me* this way, brought low, unable to bend my weak body to my will.

One thread became many, and when the real pain began, I did what I had learned to do as a child—I stepped aside and watched the woman on the bed, watched the red blossom beneath her, gules on argent.

I watched the lamentations of her women.

I watched the physician as he packed a wad of cloth between her legs and shook his head.

I watched her husband as he knelt by the bedside, held her hand, and cried.

The candle near the door offered only a dim, flickering light. I let my eyes adjust and tried to remember what had happened, why I was in the bed with Robin asleep in a chair nearby. Why I was so sore. When I moved, he sat up.

"How do you feel?" His eyes were puffy.

I reached down, felt the wadding between my thighs. "I lost the baby?"

He nodded, his face tight. "The physician says you will recover. That is what matters."

Who was the physician, or Robin, to say what mattered? I was empty. My mind and body echoed with loss. "Was it a boy or a girl?"

"I didn't think to ask him."

It didn't matter. I knew it had been a boy. Those tiny flutters had been my son, and now he was gone. I closed my eyes. "I'm tired."

"Of course." Robin kissed my forehead. "I'll sleep in the outer chamber, but I'll leave the door open." He straightened my pillow. "Call if you need me."

"Where is Alice?" She had been with me through it all.

"In the withdrawing room," he said. "She was exhausted."

"I want her," I said. "She can sleep with me."

My maid shared my bed, but Robin was with me every other moment of the day. Ned stayed away, and even Sebastian kept to the outer chamber. Robin looked devastated, but I couldn't think about that. I tried very hard not to think about anything.

He tried to tempt me from my lassitude. "What about pears in wine?" He knew they were a favorite. "I could send Sebastian for them—or perhaps some other treat?"

"I'm not hungry." I might never be hungry again.

"You must eat, darling girl." He took my lifeless hand. "How else will you regain your strength?"

His earnest gaze made my skin prickle. "My strength ran out of me with my child," I said. "Doesn't Cecil need you?"

Robin blanched. "I would rather stay with you."

"And I would rather be alone." I folded my hands over my deflated stomach. "Please."

When the door closed and Alice did not appear, I understood I was alone. I had been told to rest, but if I stayed in bed much longer, I would go mad. I got up slowly, the floor cool beneath my bare feet. Moving slowly, I kept close to the bed in case of weakness. When it appeared my legs would bear my weight, I put a loose gown over my nightdress and ventured into the outer chamber.

Two days ago, it had been the center of our existence, but now it was unfamiliar. The room hadn't changed; I had. Nothing would be the same after this. I lowered myself into a chair and closed my eyes.

Alice lectured me for getting up, but when I proved I could manage, she subsided, slightly mollified. "I do not want the master to shout at me, should you fall."

"When has Master Lewis ever shouted at anyone?" I wasn't certain Robin had that kind of passion in him.

She crossed her arms. "He would have my head if you were hurt."

I flinched.

"Oh, mistress," she said, realizing her mistake, "I am sorry. I only meant the master loves you so much—"

I held up a hand to stanch the flow of words. "Just because I am Master Lewis's wife does not mean there is any great love between us."

She pushed me lightly into my chair. "And just because it was not a love match doesn't mean love cannot grow between two people." Leaving me with my thoughts, she went in to set the bedchamber to rights.

Robin returned for supper, bearing a clutch of heart's ease and forget-me-nots. "The queen will never miss them."

I forgot myself enough to smile. "You picked them from the palace gardens?"

"Only the best for you." He touched my hair lightly.

Alice put them in a jug, while Robin joined me at the table and poured two glasses of wine. "I'm glad to see you up."

"I can't stay in bed forever," I said. "The queen will want me back soon."

The glass stopped halfway to his lips. "Surely not?"

"Katherine Grey was sent to inquire about my health," I informed him. "Her Majesty has little patience with malingerers."

He leaned back so Sebastian could shift our supper from the tray to the table. "You are hardly malingering. You've been ill."

"I'm not ill now." I gazed down at my supper. "Just very, very tired."

"Then you should rest. I'll speak to Mistress Ashley." Robin ate and I picked at my food. The silence grew, but it wasn't our usual comfortable silence.

Before Katherine's visit, I'd spent an hour reading, remembering when I had tried to tempt Robin with my intelligence. It was restful, alone in our rooms, and I understood why he came back during the day.

"Were you missed?"

"Cecil has ten of me," he said. "I am not special."

I didn't believe him for an instant. Ned told me Robin's long history with the court, as well as his insights, were highly valued by the principal secretary. "What did he need today?"

Robin sobered. "He had one request, but I turned him down."

"Why?" My husband hadn't refused an assignment since Cromwell.

He took my hand. "Because he wants me to accompany him to Edinburgh."

I let my hand remain in his. How had he become a stranger in such a short time? "When?"

"Friday." His fingers curled around mine. "He's going to negotiate the treaty to remove the French presence from Scotland. I refused, of course."

"Why would you?" Talking was exhausting.

"Because I can't leave you like this."

Would it be better or worse if he stayed? "How long would you be gone?"

"It doesn't matter." His tone was sharp. "I'm not leaving you in this state."

"Am I in a state?" Where had those words come from? "I thought I'd lost a child."

"Margaery—"

I cut him off. "I think you should go."

"It could be months." His grip tightened.

"Perhaps that would be for the best," I said, pulling free.

His face closed, his feelings—whatever they were—put away. "And why would that be?" It was his logical tone, the one he used when Ned was being recalcitrant. "Can you tell me?"

I pushed my chair away from the table. "Because I don't know if I can be your wife right now."

Chapter 28

CECIL LEFT FOR SCOTLAND, and Robin went with him, for however long it took to convince the French of the rightness of the English cause. He tried once more to change my mind, but I would not hear of it.

"Cecil needs you."

"I'd prefer *you* need me." He was tall and thin and angular, dressed in his finest doublet and gown, having just come from a meeting of the council.

"I'll be fine." If I said it often enough, perhaps someone would believe me.

He opened his mouth to argue, then shook his head. "If it makes you happy, I'll go, but Seb will stay behind to look after you."

"I can—"

It was his turn to cut me off. "I'm sure you can, but this is *sine qua non.*" He gathered me to him, his arms resting lightly around my back. "Please."

"You and your Latin." I did not dare lean into his embrace, having almost mastered my tears. Such a relaxation of my vigilance would be fatal. "Absolutely necessary? I think not—but I'll be nice to him."

"Please do." He kissed my forehead and looked searchingly into my face. "You know I would rather stay with you."

"You cannot refuse Cecil," I said brightly. "It could ruin your chances—and what if the French overran Scotland while you were here, holding my hand? How would you feel then?"

"You are as serpentine with your words as he is." He smiled briefly. "What a mind, to be wasted on a woman."

For a moment I heard Edmund Morven, damning my French with his faint praise, and I was furious at the unfairness of it all—not with Robin, who had not meant it as an insult, but with the world at large. It didn't matter how many books I read or languages I spoke, only rare individuals would take me seriously. Even the queen treated female intelligence—other than her own—as an aberration.

My strength returned, but the space which had swelled with the baby now roiled with anger: at Cecil and the queen for sending my husband to Scotland, at Robin for leaving. At myself, for not insisting he stay behind, and most of all, for failing at that most basic of womanly duties—to produce a living child.

After Robin's departure, my days were filled with women. They visited in twos and threes, twittering with sympathy at my loss and subsequent abandonment until I feigned exhaustion. Nell came later, on her own, and played cards with me. Occupied with her daydreams, she paid no attention and I won every game.

I listened to the gossip, said all the right words, and knew, in my bones, that I had reached my limit. When Sebastian brought supper, I met his eyes. "I can do this no more."

"Would you like me to keep them away, until you feel stronger?" he asked, sliding the plate in front of me.

It wasn't the well-meaning women that bothered me, or not entirely. "I can't stay here."

Sebastian rested his hands on the back of Robin's empty chair. "What can I do, mistress?"

I poked the meat with my knife. "I want to go home."

"To Winterset?" He'd expected a simple request: a trip to the shops, or some tempting delicacy. "The master did not say you could travel."

The miscarriage cured my nausea, but my appetite had not returned. I pushed the plate aside, the food almost untouched. "I want my grandmother." My voice shook, and I cleared my throat. "Please, Sebastian."

He spread his hands, with their surprising pink palms. "Then it shall be done. You will require a coach?"

"Yes." Riding would be faster, but I was still bleeding. "But we'll bring Artemis, for when I am better."

That was what I needed, as much as my grandmother's arms: to gallop across the moors until my troubles blew away like so much smoke. Maybe then, I would begin to heal.

"Her Majesty does not like her ladies to come and go," Mistress

Ashley said. "I heard you were much improved."

"I am better," I said, "but I am of no use to the queen as I am." I smiled to soften my words. "And she will require fewer ladies when the court goes on progress."

She fixed me with a keen eye. "Your husband is still in Scotland?" I agreed that he was.

"If it is companionship you require," she said, reluctant to grant permission, "you could sleep with the other women."

Such companionship would not improve my state of mind. "I have not seen my grandmother in over a year." When she did not speak, I added a small lie, "My husband thought I would recover best in her care."

Ned insisted on lending us his coach and driver, and as the weather was dry, the trip took but four long days. The journey made so little impression I might as well have been packed in straw, like the precious and fragile object Sebastian deemed me to be.

We stayed each night at a roadside inn, Alice and I sharing a narrow bed, while Sebastian slept on a pallet, barring the door. I was touched at how easily his care transferred from Robin to me. How wrong I had been about him.

We arrived at Winterset just after noon. Seb rode ahead, and by the time the coach rumbled through the gate, Grand-mère, Anselm, and Fowler were waiting in the courtyard.

I was lifted down and handed into my grandmother's embrace. "My poor duckling," she crooned. "Sebastian told me of your sorrow."

That was what I needed. Voluble, encompassing sympathy. I leaned on her arm, and we went in, Seb at our heels.

Mistress Dunham greeted me in the hall. "Do you want dinner, little mistress? I could bring it to your chamber."

"Yes, please." I wanted to lie in that green curtained bed, listen to the sea, and figure out how everything had gone so wrong.

For a few days, I indulged myself, sleeping late and spending my afternoons with Grand-mère. She cosseted me in a most satisfying manner, and I could go most of the day without thinking about Robin. I never stopped thinking about the baby.

One afternoon, after she had dozed off, I went up to the attics. Among the unused furnishings, hidden under canvas, was the cradle my father had made. I'd looked forward to having it brought down to our chamber, so we could rock our son as we sat together before bed.

Farewell to that dream, and to all the other fancies I'd had while the baby grew inside me. My legs folded and I sat on a crate, as bereft as the child Margaery who had hidden in this attic after her father's death.

Fingers of light stretched across the floor from the open shutters. The day was fine, with a cloudless sky and a light breeze. I was suddenly sick of self-pity. It was a perfect day to ride.

Artemis nickered when I approached. I rubbed her velvet nose and let her nibble a carrot from my fingers while I waited for Dickon to saddle her. "Not that one," I said as he staggered up with the sidesaddle. "Use the other one."

"But—"

"Do as your mistress says." Seb stood in the doorway.

Had he followed me? Fowler had kept him busy since we arrived, but I was never out of his sight, so he could report to Robin on my progress.

"May I ride with you?" He stroked Artemis's neck.

"I'd rather be alone." His care was sweet, but I needed to get away from Winterset in the same way I'd needed to get away from court.

"I'll stay well back," he said with a tiny shake of the head. "You're only just feeling better."

"Fine." It was like having a nursemaid. "Make sure you do."

As I'd hoped, being on horseback cleared my head. Seb kept his promised distance, trotting only when I got too far ahead of him. I rode up to the tower and slid carefully down, looping Artemis's reins over a branch.

This had always been a special place. My father brought me here at least once a week; he liked to sit on these same tumbled stones and look at the estate spread out below, green and brown and tan, as clearly marked as a tapestry. "The world at your feet," he said, making me giggle.

He was right: it was my world. London was not. No one there—

save Robin and Nell—truly cared, and I spent too much energy trying to fit into a place not shaped for me. Being home made me realize how much a part of me this place truly was.

Could I even go back to court? And what would it mean for my marriage, if I did not? Many courtiers had wives in the country, but Robin and I hadn't wanted that.

I wiped an errant tear and focused on Winterset's tiled roof. This was where I belonged. If Robin wanted me back, he would have to come and get me.

Chapter 29

THERE WERE A HUNDRED reasons why Seb should not leave Winterset, but the only one that mattered was how Robin would respond if he appeared in Edinburgh without being summoned. "He bade me watch over you."

"Am I not safe here?" My wave encompassed the house, and the land beyond. "And am I not much improved?"

"You are," he agreed, "for which I thank God. But the master does not want you to be alone."

"Lady Margaret and Anselm are here," I said. "Not to mention Alice and Fowler, Mistress Dunham and the maids. How many people are required?"

His lower lip came out while he mulled his objections. "But the master said—"

"I'm as happy here as I will be anywhere." Sebastian's chief concern would always be Robin, and I leaned hard on it. "Master Lewis is alone, and his need is greater than mine—he can barely dress himself without you. Think of the harm that can befall a man who walks around with his head in the clouds."

Seb's mind immediately flew to footpads and thieves and murderers, and he agreed to leave at first light. If all men could be so easily manipulated, women's lives would be much easier.

Robin's letters were forwarded from Whitehall, and once Seb joined him, they came direct to Winterset, bland missives inquiring after my health and that of my grandmother, telling me of the climate in Scotland and how much he thought I would like it.

"Edinburgh is a beautiful town, with the hills rising up behind in shades of green never imagined in Yorkshire. I ride in the early mornings and think of you."

I rode in the early mornings and thought of him. Each day I missed him more: our nightly conversations; the slow picking-over of our day; the minutiae of Cecil's plans to lead the queen in the direction he wished her to go; the queen's determination to thwart him. I missed him in my bed, though I could not bring myself to think about that at any length.

Losing the baby had shaken me in a way I didn't completely understand. While many of the queen's women tried to avoid pregnancy and fretted when they got in that state, I hadn't feared it. I was young and healthy; I trusted my body, and it had betrayed me.

Grand-mère attempted to console me. "I lost a child for nearly every one I birthed," she said. "We stopped trying after Walter."

"How did you survive it?" It came out as a whisper. I did not want to die, but I could not remember how to live as I had before.

"You speak as if there was a choice." She raised her rounded shoulders, not quite a shrug. "I couldn't give up with your father still at the breast. Then I stayed for Ellen, then Sybil, and finally Walter." Her chin trembled. "And for your grandfather. I couldn't leave him, no matter how much I wanted to die."

Did I feel that way about Robin? I loved him, I knew that now. I had been fond of him from the beginning, but over time, a new part of me had opened because of him, a Margaery who didn't worry herself into knots, who spoke without anticipating every response. Who could relax enough to care for someone else.

Was that marriage—becoming the person I always wanted to be? Robin gave me that, and more. He gave me my baby.

Our baby. His loss was as great as mine, but being Robin, he couldn't bring himself to speak of it. He could only take care of me, and I hadn't allowed him to do that.

"I've made such a mess of things."

"Messes can be cleaned up." Grand-mère patted my hand. "I want to rest. Send Alice to me, dear."

I relayed her message before walking in the orchard. It was the second time she'd forgotten the girl's name, but Alice had been with her for years, and sturdy, red-cheeked Susan for less than two. Change was difficult at her age.

Anselm too had aged since we left for London. His hair was completely white, and his hands, always knotted, were gnarled and painful-looking. He had difficulty holding his knife at dinner, but the few times I'd ventured into the library, he was scratching away with his quill, albeit holding it at an odd angle.

Robin had been his student at the monastery school, but no one had yet explained Anselm's journey from monk to faux-uncle residing in the bedchamber next to ours. One day, I asked, straight out, "How did you come to be here?"

"Margaery, mind your manners. Brother Anselm is a guest in this house."

"I'm sorry." A reprimand from my grandmother still made me feel like a child.

He looked up. "Has Robin never told you?"

"No." I dabbed my mouth with a linen napkin. "I've asked, but…"

"I did my best." His smile was rueful. "Logic and poetry, literature and rhetoric. The man can't communicate, no matter how many words he's consumed."

As those were my own thoughts, I had to laugh. "You don't mind my asking?"

"Not at all." He pushed his pottage away, half-eaten. "Hatton was one of the last houses in the north to close. Some of us held on, though I'm not sure why. We knew the end was coming." He shook his head. "Robin came with Cromwell's men, to evict us."

I gasped.

"He didn't know, of course, that anyone was there." Anselm's eyes were far away. "One of our elders was dying, and Robin gave us the time he needed to die in his bed."

This must be what Robin meant with his cryptic remark about forgiveness. "You forgave him?"

"Not then," he said. "Not for a long time. I prayed, but my anger was too great. We raised him, and he came back to destroy not just us, but our way of life. How does one forgive that?"

Grand-mère spoke up. "This is all in the past. Let us speak of pleasant things. Margaery, did you ride this morning?"

My husband's secret history was about to be exposed; I would not be distracted. "But you did forgive him."

Anselm inclined his head. "Eventually. He saved some of my brethren from harm. To him, it was penance, but I saw a man who regretted his past actions, and tried to remedy them. The others left, but I stayed on. For him."

June became July. There was so little rain Anselm took to petitioning the Almighty before each meal, to keep Fowler from fretting over the crops.

I continued my morning rides, and filled the hours before dinner by stitching in my grandmother's chamber. It preserved Anselm's solitude, and I enjoyed our time together. Enthroned in her chair, her feet propped on a stool, she told me of coming to Winterset as a bride, and the changes my grandfather made when he inherited the estate from his father. I had an interest in estate matters, but she discouraged me from asking questions, or interfering with Fowler's management.

One morning I returned late from my ride, and spent too long with Alice afterward. I hurried to Grand-mère's chamber, expecting a lecture on punctuality, but instead found her in a gray quilted loose gown, with her hair as yet undressed.

"Are you unwell?" I gestured at the thin braid that hung over her shoulder. "I can come back later if you'd rather sleep."

"I've gotten into bad habits," she said. "With no one about, Alice sometimes does not dress me until dinner."

My current handwork was a pair of white linen bands ornamented with black thread. I started with a traditional design, but in a moment of mischief, I added a small tortoise onto each. It would be invisible to a casual observer, but I looked forward to Robin's reaction when he saw his emblem hidden in the design of his new cuffs.

"Those are very pretty." She leaned forward to examine my stitching. "You've always had a good hand."

With her guidance, I had completed my first piece of embroidery before we left for France. Embroidery had so occupied my time in exile that most surfaces in both our chambers were ornamented with it: pillows, hangings, even a velvet cover for her prayer book.

She handed the cuff to me and asked, "Will your father be home soon?"

"My father? You mean my husband?"

"No, your father." She flapped her hand irritably. "He's been away—I don't even remember how long he's been gone. I miss my boy."

In my despair, I'd made excuses for the changes in her, but this was more than forgetting the name of her maid. "He's dead. Don't you remember?"

She obviously did not; the sound that burst from her throat was as fresh as the pain of my own loss. "Not my Ralph!" She buried her face in her hands.

What had I unleashed? I knelt and put my arms around her. "It will be all right, Grand-mère."

"What has happened?" Anselm appeared at my side, bending over her. "Lady Margaret, how may I be of service?"

"My son," she wailed, turning her face to his shoulder. "This girl tells me my son is dead."

Over her head, Anselm met my eyes. From his somber expression, I understood this was not the first time she had forgotten herself.

He took one of her tear-wet hands. "I grieve to hear it, my lady, him being such a fine young man. But he is with God now, and later, once you have rested, I will say a mass for his soul."

"Is he in heaven, do you think?"

He marked a blessing on her forehead. "How could he be anywhere else? Such a good man, with a mother who prays for him so faithfully." Anselm took her hand and murmured a prayer in the old, familiar Latin. After a moment, she joined in.

I stumbled over the words, my racing thoughts interfering with my memory. What was wrong with her? And how had I not noticed?

Praying soothed her, and she leaned back in the chair again, her eyelids drooping.

"I have poppy syrup for days like this," Anselm said quietly. "I'll show you the dosage, so you can care for her yourself."

She took the poppy from him like a child, and once she slept, we ventured downstairs. "How long has she been like this?"

He passed a hand over his eyes. "I'm not certain, having known her such a short time. Leon says there were changes soon after you left for London." Clearing his throat, he continued, "She would be herself, bright and cheerful, and then she would forget a word."

"That happens to us all." What ailed my grandmother was more than the forgetfulness of age.

"It does, indeed." His shaggy eyebrows raised; he was her contemporary. "But forgetting upset her far more than was appropriate, and made it worse. There are days when she is quite herself, as you have seen."

"I didn't notice any difference when we first arrived." I was so sunk in misery we might have gone to the wrong house and I wouldn't have noticed.

"Perhaps your need called her back to herself," he speculated. "She sees you are better now, and begins to think of her son again."

"How can you say I am better?" My voice shook. "I have lost a child."

Unlike my husband, Anselm was trained to minister to others. He did not leave me alone to deal with this latest worry, but took my arm and brought me into the library. "I do not make light of your pain. It is a loss which comes to many women."

I settled on the window seat, where I had watched my grandfather bury himself in work or simply sit, his rosary loose in his fingers. His adult grief—so much more controlled than my noisy tears— frightened me, but I clung to him.

Learning of Grand-mère's losses made me look differently at my own sorrow. I had lost a wanted child, but I had not known him; once born, he would have been someone entirely different. "How did she survive losing her son as a grown man?"

"Women are stronger than they know," Anselm told me. "That is why they are given the most pain in this world. It's not fair, and I've had words with God over it, but it's not likely to change now."

"I hurt her." She was everything to me, and I had failed to see the changes in her. "How could I be so blind?"

"You'll know next time." He smoothed his hair. "I tell her he's away on estate business, that we're expecting a letter any day."

"I saw my father die. I'm not certain I can resurrect him, even for her." I clapped my hand over my mouth.

Anselm was silent. He got up from the desk and joined me on the window seat. "You witnessed the execution?"

"Yes." My heart was pounding so hard I could almost hear it. "Yes."

"Do you want to tell me?"

The scent of rosemary wafted through the open casement. Robin said it was an *aide-memoire*, something I had never required. "I've never told anyone."

He waited quietly, as patient as the very stones of Winterset. "Unburden your heart, if it will give you peace."

I shook my head. "I don't care for myself, but I pray my father has found peace."

"Your father died for his faith," Anselm said with perfect belief. He still followed the old religion, the religion I gave up because believing in it had killed Ralph Preston. "I did not lie to Lady Margaret when I said he was in heaven."

Chapter 30

I WAS PLAYING AT the gate, my nurse off on some errand, when clouds of dust appeared on the coast road. Dust meant riders, and riders meant horses. I loved horses. I clambered up on the limestone blocks to see more clearly.

A half dozen men, taking their time. They turned into the lane, and flowed smoothly through the gate and into the courtyard. Then they dismounted, all their leisure gone, and rushed the house, pounding with the bronze dolphin until the door opened.

With no one to stop me, I slid down, rubbing the horses' smooth flanks and letting them mouth my fingers. Visitors were rare and horses not often left where I could get at them; I wasn't allowed in the stables alone because I was small enough to walk under the horses' bellies, and my father worried I would be kicked.

The door banged open and the men spilled into the courtyard, laughing. Two men had my father in their grasp. He hung limp, his head lolling, his fingers trailing over the cobbles. There was blood on his face.

"Let him go!" My grandfather bolted from the stables and struck at the largest man, who wore a mail shirt over a plain brown jerkin. "Let him go! You've no right to take him."

The horses shied, and I spun away from their dangerous hooves, throwing myself instead at the men who held my father. "Papa!"

The man with the mail shirt turned to my grandfather. "Get the brat out of here," he said harshly, "or we'll take her, too."

Grandfather swept me into his arms. "My son has done nothing wrong."

"Tell that to the magistrates." They slung my father over a gray horse and bound him securely. "Lord Cromwell finds all traitors."

I didn't understand, knowing only that my father was being taken away by these awful men. Squirming until my grandfather put me down, I ran at the man in the mail shirt and kicked him in the shins. He swore and swung at me, and I grabbed his hand and bit down, tasting blood.

"Little bitch!" His fist flashed out and the world went dark.

I awoke cradled in my grandfather's arms, my mother and grandmother peering anxiously at me. "Where's Papa? Why did they hurt him?" They had hurt me, but I only remembered the blood on his face.

Mama wailed and my grandmother shushed her. "Be still, Frances, you're scaring the child."

"They're going to kill him!" My pretty mother was wild-eyed, her smooth dark hair in hanks around her face. "I can't raise her alone—you must get him back!"

"He tried," I told Anselm. "He went to Whitby, and then to York, to speak with the magistrates. They drove him off."

My grandfather never recovered from his failure to save his son, and my mother and grandmother refused ever after to speak of it.

"The rebellion was over by then," Anselm said, "but when Robin came to Hatton in 1539, there was still much unrest in the north."

I chewed my thumbnail, picturing a young Robin displacing Anselm from his monastery. "What would the charge have been?"

"Robin looked into it, when he first came here."

My thumb was bleeding and I sucked at it discreetly. "Into what?"

"What happened to your father." He sighed. "His opinion was that he was swept up in a final round of retributory arrests."

"Retribution?" It made no sense. "For what?"

"I've no idea, child. He said it was a sham trial, over before it was begun."

I begged my grandfather to let me go with him to York for the trial, but I was told to stay with the women.

"You'll see your papa when we bring him home." Grandfather believed the charges would be dismissed, and my father, and a score of other men scooped up at the same time, would be set free.

When Fowler brought the cart around, I ran up to pet the horses. "Why don't you ride?"

He tweaked my coif over my eyes. "Because then, little mistress, we'd have to lead a third horse for your papa and that would slow us down."

Later, I understood they were afraid he wouldn't be able to walk, but then, I just saw an opportunity. Fowler went in to fetch my grandfather, and I squeezed under the seat, covering myself thoroughly with blankets and sacks.

The ride was long and the men were quiet, other than the clicking of my grandfather's rosary. I dozed amid the dog-scented blankets, imagining how surprised Papa would be to see me.

We stopped, and Fowler jumped down, causing the cart to groan. "Do you want me with you, sir, or should I wait?"

"Come with me." My grandfather's voice was thick, and he got down more slowly than Fowler. "In case we're both needed."

As their voices faded, I emerged from my hiding place. The square around me was unfamiliar, the buildings taller and grander than those in Whitby. People, more than I'd ever seen, milled around as if it were a fair, but I saw no mummers, heard no musicians.

After carefully marking the location of the cart, I climbed down and merged with the crowd. It was early afternoon, and the air was sticky. I retreated to the shade of an overhanging roof. The building where my grandfather had gone was across from me, and I fixed my eyes on the door and prepared to wait.

"Are you lost, little one?" The woman had several children hanging on her skirts, their eyes wide with excitement.

"I'm waiting for my papa." I straightened my head covering and tried to look grown up.

"Stay well back." She handed me an apple and rejoined her family.

It must be a fair, I decided, looking at the platform in the center of the square. There would be music soon, or a play. I munched on the apple and tried to remember the play we'd seen at the Whitby fair the previous summer.

Hot and bored, I played a game, counting the number of boards in the platform, then the number of children in the crowd. Those weren't too hard—Papa had recently taught me to count to twenty. Ladies were next, but I lost count after using both hands three times. Of men there were even more, dressed in everything from rough country garb to fur-trimmed gentlemen's gowns.

A murmur ran through the gathering. It sounded like waves breaking on the shingle below Winterset. For a moment there was nothing but the immense crowd, everyone taller than me and packed close together. Then a man climbed up onto the platform, raised his hands for silence, and began to speak.

His words were drowned out by the crowd. Standing near the edge, he continued to talk, and was soon joined by ten men, slow-moving and awkward because they were chained together.

My father was one of them.

I threw myself between the nearest bodies and began to shove my way toward the front. Some moved to let me through, but most clung to their spots and ignored the frantic child burrowing between them.

There was more speech from the platform, nearly drowned out by shouts and catcalls from the onlookers. A moment of inhaled silence, then a thud, as if something heavy had fallen onto the boards.

It happened twice more as I pushed my way through the mass of people. After each thud, they fell silent, then bellowed anew, and louder. When I reached the front, I was directly under the platform and I could see nothing but the black cloth roughly nailed around the edges.

I tugged at the nearest hand. "Could you lift me up? Please?" Winding my way between one pair of legs after another, I tugged and begged until someone heard me.

"You don't want to see this, girlie," the man said, but he hauled me obligingly onto his shoulder. From there, I was above the boards I'd counted so carefully, and almost level with a large wooden block.

The block was set in straw, but the straw was red. It looked like harvest time, when Fowler's men slaughtered the pigs, but who would kill livestock in front of a crowd? What sort of fair was this?

My father was unshackled from the man beside him. He stumbled forward, unsteady on his feet. His face was bruised, and the gash over his eye hadn't healed. His brown coat was filthy and torn, one sleeve hanging ragged about his wrist.

He stepped up to the block and began to speak. I strained to hear him, but his voice was halting, and the crowd's jeers grew louder. "I say only that I am a true subject and I pray for the life of King Henry." He crossed himself. "May God have mercy on my soul."

At a word from the man, my father knelt in the mucky straw,

his hands still clasped. Mama would be angry at him for praying in public when we had a perfectly good chapel at home which we weren't supposed to mention. Perhaps he was so glad to be free he forgot.

"That's enough," my bearer said. "You don't need to see what comes next."

I had to get to the cart before my grandfather and Fowler arrived with Papa, so I made no protest. Turning for one last look, I saw the man come up behind him with an ax.

"When I screamed, he turned. The ax struck his neck and knocked him over. They had to haul him back up to finish it."

It took two more strokes, but I couldn't bring myself to tell him that.

"You've borne this alone, all this time?" Anselm's face was filled with sympathy, and tears brimmed his gray eyes.

I shrugged, my throat aching with the cries I'd swallowed for the past twenty years. "I could tell no one."

"Robin said you were exceptional," he said wonderingly. "Now I see it for myself."

"I've dreamed about it, always."

"Because you've kept it inside," Anselm said and kissed my forehead. "The truth will get out, in whatever way it can. See if the dreams stop now."

Wrapped in a shawl, I pushed my way through brush and tall grasses until I reached the cliff. The sea was gray and choppy, with frills of foam on the waves. A tiny ship was visible to the northeast, heading for Hull or Scotland.

The wind dragged my skirts against my legs and tore strands of hair loose from my cap, but its salt-scent cleared my head. I stayed there for an hour, hollowed out by confession.

Before I left the house, Anselm took my shoulders in his hands. "One thing," he said, regarding me with a love so deep it gave me chills.

"Yes?" My husband was so lucky to have this man.

"Tell Robin, when you see him. Trust him with your heart."

Chapter 31

How COULD I TELL Robin, after complaining about his tendency to withhold? All marriages had secrets; this would have to be mine.

After speaking with Anselm, I did not dream of my father. Instead I felt strangely weightless, my only worry the fragile state of my grandmother's health.

My days were spent with her. If I rode, it was at daybreak, or while she napped. Most days she was alert and knew all around her, but there were mornings when she awoke disoriented, asking for my father or grandfather, and had to be distracted with fibs, like a child. Riding was most necessary on those days. I did not like lying to her, but there was no point in upsetting her when she would forget her question soon enough.

She developed a fascination with time and the weather, although her grasp of the seasons had slipped. At the beginning of August, as everyone was sweating and working in the fields, she asked if preparations for Advent had begun.

"Not yet, Grand-mère."

A letter had come from Robin only that morning, telling me of his arrival in London. He had written earlier, offering to leave Cecil's party at York on their return journey, but I wrote back and said I wasn't ready to leave, and Robin had passed us by.

"But it's been snowing for days," she said. "It must be December."

It was blazing hot, and the harvest had begun early due to lack of rain. I'd gone out myself the last two days to help the women flay dried peas and beans from the snarled vines beyond the kitchen, shelling them into great sacks after Grand-mère had gone to bed.

"The sky is blue today. I think it will not snow again for a while."

Momentarily content, she subsided before asking, "Where is your husband? It has been some time since we've seen him."

She asked about Robin every day. "He is in Scotland," I lied. "Perhaps he will visit on his way to London."

Her lips pursed. "I did not give you over to that boy so he could neglect you."

Two decades younger than my grandmother, Robin was still a boy in her eyes. "You know how young men are, Grand-mère."

"And why must you call me that?" she asked. "It sounds ridiculous. We are not in France."

"But we were." My desperation showed in my voice. "I grew up calling you Grand-mère."

Her eyes narrowed; she did not like being contradicted. "You may call me Grandmother."

I looked down at my lap. "Yes, Grandmother."

Where had she gone, my sweet Grand-mère? The woman who would have done anything for me, who had chivvied my grandfather back to life, was nowhere to be found in this angry woman, whose memories—always negative—were so different from the life she'd lived. Lady Margaret Preston was a happy woman, fond of almost everyone, and willing to excuse the rest. This new incarnation distrusted all, assuming they were there to do her harm.

That distrust extended even to me, and it hurt. Being berated for something I hadn't done was bad enough; when she criticized me for marrying a man too old to give me a child, or too disinterested to fetch me back when I ran away, I retreated to my chamber in tears.

"She's not herself." Alice followed as I fled the room. "If she was in her right mind, she would never say such things."

I sniffed. "It doesn't make it easier to hear." I expected to lose her someday, but losing her bit by bit was agonizing.

Alice nodded. "I know. She just accused me of stealing her son." Her lips curled. "I only wish I had."

I retreated to my parlor with a windfall apple and a second letter, this one from Nell. She wrote infrequently, but her letters were always entertaining. This time, instead of distracting me, she added to my dilemma.

"Margaery," she wrote, "you will never believe my news. I am engaged! Richard has but recently come to court, but his family is known to mine, and my father has granted permission for us to wed. He is the handsomest young man in the world, as well as the kindest. I have never felt like this before. It is true love at last."

She continued thus for half a page, describing her intended's hair and eyes and manners, and ending with a financial summary to assure me of her future comfort. "He is his father's eldest son, and so will inherit all upon his sire's death, and become Viscount Curtis. I say this not from greed, but so you know my head has not been completely turned by his pretty green eyes."

I laughed, and hoped this young man was worthy of her.

My heart sank as I turned the page and saw the inevitable request. "My father and sister will come to London at the end of August to assist in the preparations for my wedding. I have already written to Father, explaining I cannot marry without my dearest friend in attendance. I beg you, Margaery, please travel to London under his care."

It was tempting to throw the letter into the kitchen fire and claim ignorance, but I forced myself to read to the end.

"My wedding is but an excuse. I have seen Master Lewis in the presence chamber, and he looks tired and sad and thin. Please return, my dear friend, for all our sakes."

I dropped my head into my hands. I wanted to see Nell married. I wanted to see Robin—oh, how I wanted that—but I couldn't leave Grand-mère now. If something happened in my absence, I would never forgive myself.

When Alice came for me, I was still composing my reply. "Mistress Dunham has laid supper," she said. "It looks like a storm is coming."

"Just when we don't need rain." I held up the letter. "A storm has come up already, for me."

She squinted at the page. "Is it from the master?"

"From Mistress Hawkins." I forgot Alice couldn't read. "She is to be married in September, and asks me to return for the wedding."

"I am glad for her," she said. "Mistress Hawkins is a sweet lady."

"I can't go."

"Because of Lady Margaret?"

"She is too much for Anselm alone, and Susan can't be trusted with her care." I pushed the unfinished letter aside. "I cannot think on this anymore."

The table was filled, all the men freshly washed at the trough by the kitchen door. They rose and bowed, holding their hats to their chests. "Good evening, my lady."

Only two seats were unoccupied. Since Grand-mère no longer took supper downstairs, I reluctantly took her place at the foot of the table, while Robin's chair remained empty.

Alice glared at the nearest man, and he slid down the bench until space was made for her. "I would stay with Lady Margaret," she said quietly. "There is time to train young Susan to care for you."

I choked on my ale. "You would do that?"

"Lady Margaret is not who she was, and neither am I." Alice shrugged. "Your friend needs you, and you need your husband."

"I don't like this chamber." Grand-mère folded her arms. "I'm not happy, Margaery."

My heart sank. "What's wrong?"

"You had no right to move my things in here without asking." Her eyes filled. "How could you?"

I looked around: her great bed, the throne-like carved chair, an abundance of embroidered cushions. The chamber was unchanged since our return from France.

"I'm sorry, I should have asked." Anselm's advice not to challenge her worked, but it was exhausting, as was learning to accept this new grandmother. "We'll move it all back tomorrow."

She set her cup down and looked at me with hard eyes. "It's that husband of yours, I've no doubt."

It would be easy to let Robin take the blame. "He hasn't been here."

"No one has been here." She snatched the napkin from her shoulder and wiped her eyes. "I see no one. Day after day, I'm alone."

Panic surged. I clasped my hands to keep my fingers away from my mouth. "You have me, and Alice and Anselm. Isn't that enough?"

She threw her napkin on the floor. "A child, a servant, and a monk," she spat. "I want people. Where are my children? My daughters haven't visited me in weeks."

It was no surprise she couldn't remember my aunts' last visits. I didn't remember either of them. Walter had said Sybil visited soon after my father's death, but Ellen separated herself from her disgraced family, and we had received no letters in France; if they were alive, it was unlikely they would visit now.

"And where is your husband?" she continued. "The jumped-up Master Lewis, who thinks he can take my house and my granddaughter."

Her evil words made me rise to Robin's defense. "My husband is in London, on the queen's business, and here you sit, in your house, with your granddaughter. If he's taken those from you, he's done a bad job of work."

"I'm sorry, Margaery." Her trembling hands reached for me. "Don't send me away."

"I would never send you away." I dropped to my knees and wrapped my arms around her waist, choking back the tears that threatened to steal my voice. When would I learn to accept her disordered mind? "This is your home."

"Well, I know that," she said pettishly. "You're not an infant. Get up off the floor before you ruin your gown."

I wrote to Nell, but I did not write to Robin. Lord Kelton sent a messenger, thanking me for increasing his daughter's happiness and giving instructions on where and when to meet him for the journey. It concluded with the words of a man who understood women. "Please bring whatever baggage you require, as there will be a cart traveling with the coach."

Alice took Susan in hand, breaking her of the bad habits brought about by Grand-mère's inattention. She quickly learned to do my hair to my liking, and seemed pleasant, if none too bright. "She will do," I said to Alice, "but it won't be the same."

"Lady Margaret will do better in my care," she said. "I can give her the answers she needs. Poor Susan is lost." A faint smile touched her lips. "And to think, you were afraid to take me to London because of my loyalty to your grandmother."

I drew in a breath. "How did you know?"

She put my pins in the rosewood box which had contained my pendant jewel. "I would have felt the same, in your place."

"You've been a good friend." I caught her hand. "Susan will do, but I will miss you."

Flushing, she said, "You'll manage. And I'll be here when you come back."

I would see Nell married and effect some kind of rapprochement with my husband. Then I would return to Winterset.

Robin would understand. I was not so sure about the queen.

Chapter 32

My last full day in Yorkshire was a gift.

Grand-mère's mind was clear at breakfast, her conversation ordered, if a bit incurious about my upcoming departure. Leaving her was the hardest thing I had done since choosing to abandon my marriage. I had been up most of the night, anticipating every possible reaction to the news except the one I received.

"Tell your husband I am disappointed," she said. "Very disappointed."

"What has he done?"

Her expression told me it was a stupid question. "No gentleman should allow his wife to be escorted by a man she has never met. It's scandalous."

"But he knows Lord Kelton," I said. "And his daughter will be there, as chaperone."

When we finished eating, she settled into her chair with her prayer book. "I know you want to ride," she said. "Be off with you. We'll have dinner later."

I didn't need encouraging: I already had my breeches under my kirtle. Dickon was walking Artemis in the courtyard when I came out. "You'll miss this in London, m'lady,"

"I certainly will."

The weather was kind, with a brilliant sky streaked with clouds, but there was an edge to the breeze. Summer would soon be over.

The men were still in the fields, and I waved my hat as I passed. They were startled at first to see me ride astride, but they had come to accept their unusual mistress. It did not hurt my cause that I worked with the women on several occasions, and once even helped to bring the horses in after a long day.

A meandering ride led me to the tower. I looped Artemis's reins over a branch before settling on the stones to look back at the house. It seemed all I ever did was leave Winterset.

As much as my home and my responsibility to Grand-mère drew me, Robin's draw was equally powerful. Nell was my excuse, but

Robin was the true reason for my departure. I wanted to be with my husband again, even if I returned to Yorkshire immediately after the wedding.

When had I come to love him so? There was affection from the first, and attraction, and even passion. But what I was deprived of now was his simple presence and the comfort it brought. I was cold without the warmth he kindled in my heart.

I had never expected to fall in love with my very odd husband, while at the same time being too fearful of losing another child to put myself in a situation where he could touch me. By right of marriage, my body was his, and though he had not availed himself of it in the beginning, we had made up for that lost time. But now, no matter what my body said, my heart was not prepared for another loss.

Would he understand? If he tried to make love to me, I would have a hard time resisting. Even now, I awoke from dreams of his hands on my body, the feeling of completion when he pushed himself inside me, as if we were not fully whole until fitted together.

Could I give that up, from fear?

Fowler drove us to York at daybreak. While Susan drowsed beside me, I tried not to think about an identical journey, in this same cart, twenty years earlier. I hoped our meeting place was nowhere near the minster.

It was not, and when we stopped in front of the Queen's Bells, a black coach was already there, its doors bearing the hawk emblem which marked all Nell's kerchiefs. Will Hawkins was also there, leaning on the door and talking to someone inside. He saw us and a smile broke across his face.

"Mistress Lewis, I am glad you are able to join us." He helped me down, his hand lingering. "My sister will be very happy."

I questioned him while Fowler and Susan dealt with the baggage. "Have you met her Richard?"

"I have," he acknowledged. "He is almost worthy of her."

Before we could speak further, his father stepped out of the coach, and all the light which touched his son transferred itself to him. Though Lord Kelton was past sixty, with curling black hair gone to gray and warm, penetrating brown eyes, he had the demeanor of a younger man. He kissed my hand and murmured a greeting. His voice was low, velvety, and I reacted to its power.

Poor Will, to have such a father.

"My daughter insisted she could not marry without your presence." He took my arm and led me away from his son. "I was instructed to carry you off, if you refused."

He was old enough to be my grandfather, but something in his tone made me think of a candlelit bedchamber, and the things I did there with Robin. *Used to do.*

"I would not put you to such inconvenience, Lord Kelton." His touch made my heart beat faster.

"It would have been no inconvenience at all." He helped me into the coach, settling me onto the seat across from him. A young woman was already seated there. She looked like Nell, but with her father's dark hair. "My daughter, Elizabeth Fremantle," he said. "She shares your unwillingness to miss the ceremony."

"Oh, Father." Her voice was as honeyed as his. "You just don't want to lose your darling."

He protested, but it was obvious she spoke the truth. Nell was the youngest, and from what she and Robin said, the one who most resembled her mother.

Will peered in the window. "Your things are loaded, Mistress Lewis. Do you require anything else?"

I looked at him questioningly. "Aren't you coming with us?"

"I shall ride alongside," he said. "Someone must lead Artemis."

"That isn't necessary. She will follow the baggage cart."

"There isn't room," Lord Kelton said shortly, and drew a curtain over the window.

After several hours, we came to an inn. When the coach stopped, Will opened the door. "I hope you have had a pleasant journey."

"Of course, we have," his father drawled, springing down. "Go in and tell them we're coming."

Will scurried off, and I looked at Elizabeth. "They've always been this way," she said, shrugging. "Mother kept them civil."

But Will wasn't totally cowed by his father. Once we were at the table, he said, "I hadn't realized you were acquainted with Mistress Lewis's husband."

Lord Kelton glanced up. "I knew many people in my years at court."

"Master Lewis made it sound as though you were on more intimate terms."

"As I said, I knew many people." Lord Kelton put his knife down hard, causing ale to slosh from our cups. He turned to me, his expression smoothing. "And how long have you been Mistress Lewis?"

His gaze made me warm. "Almost two years, sir," I said. "We met in France, while my husband was in exile."

He raised an imperious hand for the maid. "Yes, during the reign of the old queen. Shame some people felt they had to leave."

Will's knife stopped halfway to his mouth. "Perhaps he should have married a Catholic heiress and kept himself safe." He winked at me. "No disrespect meant, Mistress Lewis."

It was going to be a long trip if they kept this up all the way to London. "None taken, Master Hawkins."

Apparently Will knew how much his father would tolerate, because he then turned and asked after his sister's children. "Nell will be disappointed you didn't bring them."

Elizabeth ate quietly through the theatrics of her menfolk. "The nurse can manage for a few weeks," she said. "I'm looking forward to spending time with my husband. They would be a distraction."

Her husband was Thomas Fremantle, Will told me. It was a name I recognized from my service with the queen, though I could not remember his face. I hoped he wasn't one of those gentlemen whose wives lived in the country while he preyed on the maids of honor.

Probably not, I decided. Lord Kelton was not the sort of father to abide such disrespect of his daughter—or of himself.

We traveled well into the evening, the light dying around us. At the inn, Elizabeth and I shared a small chamber with our maids. It was cramped, but I didn't care; it was a relief to be out of the coach.

"Do your other brothers get along with your father?"

"There's only Harry, the eldest," she said. "I came second, then

Will. My sister, Agatha, was next, then Barbara, and finally Nell. There was a boy before Will, but he died." She got into bed. "Do you have children, Mistress Lewis?"

"Please, call me Margaery." I tied off my braid and climbed in beside her. "I lost a babe in May."

Susan closed the shutters and blew out the candle, drenching the room in darkness.

"I lost one, early on." Elizabeth's voice was steady. "It's hard, but the next babe takes away much of the pain." She rolled over and said into her pillow, "I hope your husband was not too troublesome."

I wriggled down so the sheet was up to my nose. "He was there when it happened," I said, "but he left a few days later, and knowing he would be gone for some months, I returned home. I stayed on to care for my grandmother."

Said that way, it sounded like an excuse to avoid my husband.

"Sometimes it's for the best," she said, surprising me. "Men don't always understand."

She slept quickly, but I lay awake for some time, listening to the voices and music drifting up from the room below.

The trip continued much the same for the next several days. We stopped to change horses in Hertfordshire; Lord Kelton said the team was too slow. I thought we were making excellent time, but Elizabeth said her father had very high standards regarding horseflesh.

"He has high standards regarding everything." Will looked at me with an odd smile, watching me watch his father. "As you may have noticed."

"I have," I said. "And I understand you better the more I see you together."

Chapter 33

I KNEW WE WERE close when the road stopped being bumpy; close to Whitehall, it was kept sanded, to ease the passage of the queen's coach.

Lord Kelton escorted me to the entrance, dealing brusquely with the guards. "Your things will be delivered in the morning, Mistress Lewis, if you are certain you will not need them tonight."

"You are too kind, sir."

He brought my hand to his lips, his warm breath sending a frisson down my spine. "It has been entirely my pleasure."

Susan stared up at the palace, her mouth gaping. I remembered my own first impression, and forgave her, despite my exhaustion and heightened nerves.

"Lord, mistress, how do you ever know where you are?" She looked around in a panic as I led her through the great hall and up the stairs to the network of corridors which led to the conjugal quarters.

"You'll learn," I assured her. "Sebastian will make you a map."

When Seb opened our door, he broke into a grin and forgot himself so much as to hug me. Susan's squeak of surprise made him step back, his words tumbling over themselves. "Mistress, you've returned—the master did not tell me—I would have had something—do you need food? Wine?"

"I need to come in." I laughed at his excitement. "And I did not tell Master Lewis I was coming. Is he here?"

Sebastian's face fell. "No, but I will send for him. Whatever he's doing, he'll drop it right down."

"Don't do that." I sank into my chair. All looked the same, other than that the books seemed to have multiplied again. "He'll be back tonight?"

"He will," Seb confirmed. "May I get you some wine?"

"Please." I slipped my shoes off and wiggled my toes in pleasure. "Would you get poor Susan some ale, while you're at it?"

He looked at my maid, who was far less self-assured here than she was at Winterset. "Where is Alice?"

I explained about Grand-mère. "Alice will stay with her, and Susan will get to see London."

He smiled encouragingly at her. "Don't worry, you'll learn the place in no time."

While he fetched the drinks, I showed Susan the bedchamber and we proceeded with my undressing. My traveling clothes were stiff with dust, and I did not wish to greet Robin in such a state. I washed and took down my hair, scratching luxuriously where the pins had pressed.

I had taken very little with me when I bolted, and my embroidered silk nightdress was folded in the chest. Susan shook it out, smoothing the stitching with stubby fingers. "The queen can't have better than this."

"The queen sleeps in velvet," I said as she dropped the gown over my head. "With fur trim in cold weather."

When I was settled with a drink, Seb showed Susan where she would sleep, and left me to my thoughts—which were many.

I had returned, unannounced, to the husband who had not requested my return. At least I hadn't walked in and found him with someone else. That had never been a worry with Robin. I did not fear infidelity so much as I feared indifference.

An hour passed, painfully slow. Seb's pen scratched away in the antechamber, but he left me alone.

When the bells struck midnight, I pushed my glass away. "I'm going to sleep," I called. "Goodnight, Sebastian."

The bed seemed larger and softer, especially when compared to the beds I'd recently shared with Elizabeth Fremantle. Best of all, it neither rocked nor swayed nor threw me from side to side. Although I tried to stay awake, I fell asleep almost immediately.

A thud, followed by quiet swearing, woke me. When the door opened, I could make out Robin's silhouette in the faint glow from the outer chamber. His shoulders were slumped, and he moved as if his knee pained him. He sat down to undress, yawning so widely his jaw cracked.

"Good evening, husband."

He bounded off the bed in surprise. "Christ! Margaery, is it you?"

"Yes, you blasphemer, it's me."

Robin sat again, reached for me, and drew back. "I don't know how to greet you."

"You may embrace me," I said, throwing back the covers, "for I have missed you."

With a strangled sound, he pulled me close, holding me so tight it was difficult to draw breath. His heart beat strongly beneath my cheek, and something loosened inside me. It wasn't right yet, but we were together, and we would figure out how to make it right.

"May I kiss you?" His voice was strained. "Why didn't you tell me you were coming?"

I cupped his face, feeling the roughness of several days' growth of beard. "Because you might have shaved."

He laughed, and hugged me to him again. "I thought you weren't coming back."

Lacing my fingers through his, I said, "I'm not sure how long I can stay. Grand-mère isn't well."

"But you're returning for her, not leaving because of me?"

My eyes filled with tears: he had been afraid I wouldn't come back. "I didn't leave because of you. I left because I couldn't be here without you." He deserved my honesty. "I might have gone anyway. I don't know. I wasn't right, after the baby."

"I shouldn't have left you alone," he said bitterly.

"I pushed you away." I began to undress him by feel, my touch impersonal. I didn't want him to make love to me, but I still wanted him in my bed. "Is this a new doublet?"

"Just new buttons." He took over, shedding his clothes efficiently and climbing into bed in his shirt. "Ned brought them back from France."

"What was he doing in France?" His hip was a hand's breadth away.

"Carrying letters, carrying tales." He stretched, and his shoulder brushed mine. "He went to see the Scottish queen."

I was curious about Mary Stuart, but I didn't want Robin to talk about the Scottish queen, or even the English queen, at this hour. "Yes."

"Yes?" he asked.

"You asked if you could kiss me. You may, and then you may go to sleep and tell me everything I've missed in the morning."

He bridged the distance between us, his mouth warm and achingly familiar. I went to sleep with the touch of his lips on mine.

Over breakfast, I filled him in on Grand-mère's condition, and the reason for my return. "Nell wants me at the wedding."

"Was I not reason enough?"

I hesitated. "She gave me the excuse," I said. "Otherwise, I'm not sure when I would have come back."

He reached through the detritus that littered the table and took my hand. "Is it still difficult?"

Difficult. A man's word, a word to represent feelings for which he had no words. I took a breath. He was who he was.

"I'm still sad," I told him. "But I won't die from sadness."

His grip tightened momentarily as he understood the depth of my misery. His thumb caressed the back of my hand. "Now that you're here, we can face things together."

Seb had laid a small fire and I watched as the kindling sparked like firecrackers. "I pushed you to leave because I wasn't sure how to share the pain."

He bowed his head. "I didn't want to pressure you. And I didn't expect to be gone as long as I was."

I looked at him from the corner of my eye. "Diplomacy takes time."

"Cecil takes even more time," he said. "There is not a word spoken that man does not examine from every angle."

How could such an intelligent man be so obtuse? "You're describing yourself."

"No wonder people lose patience, then." He ventured a tentative smile. "It was important work, Margaery. Necessary work. A French foothold in Scotland is something England cannot afford."

He would never be completely mine, so long as he worked for the court. Even after, I thought, because his mind was always occupied with issues more important than domestic matters. "I am glad Cecil accomplished his aim. Perhaps now he can return to worrying about Elizabeth's marriage."

Robin made a face. "I don't think even Cecil can make that happen."

It was tantamount to treason, to be skeptical of Cecil's plans. "I told you."

"And I believe you are correct." He drained his ale. "You understand her better than we do."

I appreciated his acknowledgment that I was right. "Anselm sends greetings."

His expression softened. "I miss him."

"He misses you, though he is very happy in your library." I told him of Anselm's gentle handling of Grand-mère.

"You do not mind that he lives at Winterset?"

"No," I said. "Especially now he that has told me why he is there, and what you did for his brothers."

Robin actually blushed. "I am far less brave now."

"Perhaps what is required now is patience with your disappearing wife."

"I will be patient," he said, meeting my eyes, "but I hope she does not disappear too often."

Sebastian returned; he had gone out shortly after serving our breakfast. "Lord Cecil says you are to spend the day with Mistress Lewis, with his compliments." He looked as happy as I felt. "Shall I clear?"

"Please. Has Susan recovered from the shock of her new surroundings? Could you send her to me?"

He scooped dishes onto the tray. "She's in the antechamber." He raised a brow. "She's still muddle-headed."

Robin read while I dressed, and when Susan left, blushing and smiling, he joined me in the bedchamber. "Alice was much…calmer." He pulled his shirt over his head and washed briskly. "What do you wish to do with our day of freedom?"

"My things should be delivered soon," I said. "And Will Hawkins stabled Artemis last night."

"Will?" He turned from the basin, and I looked away from his naked body. "I hadn't thought to ask. How did you get here?"

"Lord Kelton brought me in his coach." I added a few more pins to my bodice; Susan wasn't as careful as Alice, either. "He and his daughter came for Nell's wedding and she asked him to bring me along."

Robin's face turned an odd shade, and I realized he was holding back laughter.

"What is it?"

He let it out, throwing his head back. When he was able to speak, he said, "How is Will's relationship with his father these days?"

"Prickly." Robin's involvement with the Hawkins family was another thing which required investigation. "Will said something about you knowing Lord Kelton before, and it irritated him."

Robin's head emerged from the open neck of a fresh shirt. "Will and I spoke of his father several times on our journey together."

He meant their abortive trip to the Tower. "Why?"

"We spoke of many things," he said with a shrug. "Fathers were only part of it. But Hawkins—Kelton—and I had some business in the time of the old king. We haven't spoken for perhaps twenty years."

I let it go, one more detail I would learn over time. "I'd like to give a small dinner for Nell. Do you think Ned would let me use his house?"

"As long as you invite him." He grinned. "He'll want to flirt with the maids."

I would see Nell later and fix a date, and Ned would undoubtedly be around in the evening. I could settle the arrangements then.

"I've missed riding with you," I said. "Could we?"

Robin put aside the black doublet he'd selected and retrieved an older gray one from the chest. "Of course. I've missed it as well."

"Have you missed me?" I removed my hanging sleeves and covered my hair with a caul, anchoring the whole affair with extra pins.

"Margaery, how can you ask?" He pulled me against his chest. My head fit just under his chin. "Every day, dear girl. Every day."

The queen was elsewhere, and we rode for an hour across the

hunting park. Speech was unnecessary; riding, and being together again, was sufficient.

After dinner in the hall, where only Robin's presence kept the queen's women at bay, he turned to me. "What next?"

I took his arm. "You choose."

He paused, then his face lit up. "I would like to hire a boat."

It was a perfect day to be on the river, with a light breeze that blew away the worst of the smells. The boat was a surprise—larger than I expected, it had a small canopy where we could sit in seclusion and watch the city flow by.

"We're coming on to Chelsea." When a large house—almost a small palace—came into view, Robin pointed and said, "Thomas More lived there."

"The More who wrote *Utopia?*"

He looked at me in surprise. "You've read it?"

"I finished it in the coach." Laughing, I added, "Anselm made a note, in case I failed to bring it back."

More's house disappeared, and after a short stretch of orchard, we came upon another house. Smaller, built of timber and brick, it had a welcoming aspect.

"I know this place, too." His expression was softer.

"Who lived here?" He had missed me, if we were talking about his past.

"Bianca."

The Italian woman. "I wish I'd known her."

His arm tightened around my shoulders. "You would have been good for each other." He shifted, calling up to the boatman, "Tie up here. We will walk for a while."

We climbed out on the bank across from Bianca's house. It was a beautiful stretch of meadow bordered with trees, as peaceful a spot as could be found this close to London. Had he visited it with her, or observed it from her house? From her bedchamber window, perhaps?

Robin tossed a coin to the boatman. "Wait for us."

It was wonderfully silent. Even the river traffic faded as we got closer to the trees. "I missed you so much," I said. "But I wasn't sure if I could return."

He brought my hand to his lips. "I worked late every night. It didn't feel right, coming back to an empty room."

"You had Ned." I sidestepped a rock buried in the high grass.

"Ned is my friend, not my wife." He stopped, and looked down at me. "You are the one I want in my bed."

I bit my lip. "About that, Robin."

"About what?" He paused, then drew me by the hand into the forest. We were soon surrounded by thick-trunked, ancient trees, as unlike Yorkshire as could be imagined. The air was cooler from the dense canopy overhead.

"Bed." My voice cracked. "I don't know if I can go through it again."

Robin walked me toward a fallen tree. "Given the choice, I would rather live with you than bed you. You needn't worry."

My relief was so great my legs trembled, and I sat on the log. "Thank you."

"Did you think I would be angry?" He sat, and I leaned against him. "I won't lie—I have missed your body, as well as your mind, but I would rather have you with me, in any capacity, than away from me."

My hands were curled, my bitten nails concealed from his gaze, which missed nothing. "There are other ways," I said, mortified by my boldness. "We spoke of them once."

Chuckling, he said, "And we've done most of them." He sobered. "Those acts keep you from catching a child, but they do give a desire for…more." Robin kissed my temple. "I don't mind doing without."

I covered my face with my hands. "I've been afraid to tell you."

He kissed me again, his lips lingering at my hairline. "Never be afraid to tell me anything."

It was the opportunity I needed. Anselm's words echoed in my brain. *Trust him with your heart.*

I told him.

I told him everything I'd told Anselm, and more. I told him about the look in my father's eyes when he realized I was there. I told him about the headsman's oath when he missed the first strike. I told him about my grandfather, weeping like a child all the way from

York, while I pretended not to see.

When I finished, the only sounds were the birds in the branches overhead, and the faint lapping of the river. "Good God," he said finally.

I looked up; his eyes were full of tears. "You've witnessed executions."

"I was a grown man, and they weren't my family." He gathered me close. "When I saw you for the first time, you seemed like such a happy child."

His appearance had been a welcome distraction; we'd only just learned we were leaving. Walter had raged; my mother had cried; Grand-mère hid her feelings and took care of the rest of us.

"I never told them." I gave way to the safety of his embrace, the birds, the river, the rustling of the forest disappearing when he put his arms around me. "I didn't want them to know how bad I was."

"What do you mean?"

"Sneaking out. Going with them." I pressed my fingers to my temples; a headache was settling like an iron band. "When I realized it was my fault…there was a period when I didn't speak at all."

"It wasn't your fault." He took my cold hands in his. "You weren't to blame for any of it, darling girl."

"If I hadn't cried out, they might have done it in one blow." He would have died having commended his soul to God. Instead, his final thoughts were of his disobedient daughter.

"You were a child," he said. "You shouldn't still be punishing yourself all these years later." He stroked my cheek with the sides of his fingers. "When I came to Winterset, I looked into what happened."

"Anselm told me. Why?"

"Winterset was more than a house," he said. "You were forced out, and I felt guilty, even though I had nothing to do with it."

"What did you find?"

"Nothing official." He shook his head. "It may have been a local grudge, and they used Cromwell's name."

"Why do you think that?" My head throbbed.

"The manner of his death." His gaze was inward, remembering. "Traitors were hanged, and if their treason was vile enough, they were drawn and quartered."

My husband had worked with those men, willingly, for years. "Did you know what they were capable of?"

"Not in the beginning." His expression was pained. "And I tried to stay away from the dissolution. I couldn't stop it, but I didn't want to be part of it. I sympathized with those who petitioned the king."

"Sympathy doesn't help much."

"No, it does not." He rubbed at the permanent ink stain on his right forefinger. "I broke with Cromwell after that."

The silence grew around us, broken only by a rustling deep in the trees: a squirrel, perhaps, or a vole.

"Anselm told me to tell you." I picked at the bark, unwilling to look at him.

"He was right."

"You carry things without sharing, all the time."

"It is a hard habit to break." His fingers twitched toward me and then dropped to his leg instead. "I will try to do better."

"If we are to start again, there should be no secrets between us." I put my hand over his, a reminder he could touch me, and changed the subject; I'd had enough sadness. "I thought we could hire your friends—Bess and Tom—to perform at Nell's party."

Robin took a deep breath. "I don't think that's a good idea. Not this time."

"Why not? I'd love to hear them again."

"That business I had with Kelton," he said, scuffing leaves with his boot. "He helped me get them out of London."

I peered into his face. "Then why would he not want to see them again?"

"Because Bess was his mistress, in the days before she and Tom were married. It would be…difficult."

I had liked Bess's Tom, very much, but having spent several days in his company, I thought I understood what she had found attractive in Lord Kelton. For her sake, I was glad she had chosen her blue-eyed musician; I didn't believe Will's father capable of the sort of devotion shown by her husband.

"This is why I should not be kept in the dark." I imagined how

Lord Kelton would react, confronted with his former mistress. "I could have hired them as a surprise, and it would have been a disaster."

A laugh escaped him. "One person would have enjoyed it, anyway."

"Who?" Lord Kelton would storm out; Nell would cry; Robin and Ned would, no doubt, laugh themselves sick.

"The only way you could please Will Hawkins more would be to present yourself to him on a platter."

Chapter 34

"You're happy today," Seb observed the next morning, spooning more pottage into my bowl. "So was the master."

It smelled divine—there was bacon flavoring the usual peas and oats—and I reached for more bread to make sure I got every scrap.

"It is good to be back." Robin had left a note of apology, and promised to be home early. "I'm seeing Mistress Ashley later, so I need all my strength."

The buzzing presence chamber was another world after three months in Yorkshire, and while I waited for the chief gentlewoman, I was greeted by a surprising number of women and maids, all of whom claimed to have missed me.

Cressida embraced me. "I was hoping to see you again. I'm leaving Saturday."

"Why?" Her rough tongue was a balance to the honeyed voices around the queen, a reminder that not everyone thought our rarefied existence was ideal.

"This place doesn't suit me," she said bluntly. "It never has. My father placed me here, but I need my family."

Mistress Ashley eventually found time for me, and assured me I was still a member of the royal household, though my grip on the position was tenuous due to my undependability. I swallowed the reprimand and gave her the thanks she expected, all the while thinking it didn't matter—none of it mattered, because I was finally free.

Nell's wedding was a triumph, beginning with our party—which Ned attended, flirting shamelessly with all the maids—to her father's similar gathering the next day, and finally the ceremony in St. Margaret's church. She wore an ivory satin gown with silver ornaments, given to her by the queen, and looked like an angel.

My dear friend and her Richard started their life together surrounded by love and people who wanted nothing but their happiness. It was very different from my own nuptials, but I wouldn't have switched places. Nell's handsome, unchallenging husband would bore me to tears.

Robin and I stayed overnight at Ned's house before traveling to Windsor, where the court had relocated. I was immediately drawn back into my old existence of pins and sleeves and gossip—and gossip there was, for soon after I returned, Robert Dudley's neglected wife was found dead. The queen's Master of Horse was a widower.

"He's gone to his house at Kew." Ned looked up as I came in. Quarters at Windsor were cramped, and he moved his chair so I could get past. "Would that he'd gone there more often."

I witnessed his departure from the queen's bedchamber, his eyes blazing, a letter crumpled in his fist. He looked neither left nor right as he passed, and as soon as the doors closed, the murmur of gossip began.

When news of his wife's death was made public, there was speculation on how long he and Elizabeth would wait before marrying. I remembered Mistress Ashley's protestations of the summer and thought the opposite. "She'll never marry him now," I said to Robin and Ned. "Will she?"

Robin shook his head. "I don't see how she could." He lowered his voice; we didn't know our neighbors in this place. "There will be an inquiry, undoubtedly. According to Cecil, she had sent all the servants away—"

"Even if her death was an accident—" Ned attempted to finish his sentence.

"It would be too much." I dropped into the chair he'd vacated for me. "No one would trust him."

"Exactly." Robin dragged his fingers through his hair. "In the spring, de Quadra wrote to his master that he believed Dudley would divorce his wife."

"How do you know that?" I filled his glass, then my own.

Ned pushed his own glass forward hopefully. "We read his letters."

Similar tales abounded in the privy apartments: Elizabeth had put off her foreign suitors until Dudley divorced Amy, or she conveniently died. She had been ill—was it poison, and if so, was it administered by her husband? It would have been better for all if Dudley had gone to live with his wife, even for a while, but the queen would not have him out of her sight.

Now Amy was dead, and there was no way they could ever be together that would not bring about war from without or rebellion from within.

Katherine and I visited Nell when the court returned to London. Being married, she was no longer a maid of honor. She took the loss lightly, consumed with her new role and certain of her eventual elevation to lady-in-waiting.

Curtis House was far grander than anyplace I'd visited that did not belong to the queen. Walking in with Katherine, our horses taken from us by liveried grooms in the courtyard, I admired the wide hall with its vivid tapestries and elaborate furnishings. It was more than I would be comfortable with, but Katherine looked about with an approving gaze. "Nell has done well."

I looked up at the painted ceiling, thinking of Winterset's hall and how I would someday like to have it painted. My thoughts were interrupted when Nell flew down the stairs and hurled herself at us.

No longer white-clad and virginal, she had become a noble matron in a matter of days. Her hair was covered—Richard preferred a more modest appearance, she told us over dinner—and her gown was a deep blue that made her eyes glow like sapphires.

"I am the happiest woman in Christendom," she declared as the servants brought out a parade of dishes for our selection. "My husband is a prince. I still cannot believe my good fortune."

"Not a prince," Katherine corrected, dipping a sliver of pheasant into a puddle of rich saffron-and-wine sauce. "But you have married well, and must be congratulated."

Nell sucked in her lower lip, not liking the slight to her husband. "How is Lord Hertford, Katherine?"

I hid a smile as Katherine blanched. Relationships were never as simple as they appeared, especially marriages.

"If only you would talk to my sister." Mary Grey followed me as I returned several books to the queen's library. She picked up a volume, examining its embossed leather cover. "Please, Mistress Lewis."

"What good would it do?" I removed the book from her hand, returning it to its proper place. "She listens to no one but herself."

"The only one who ever listened to me was Jane." Mary's plain little face was earnest. "Please try."

"What would you have me say?" It was painful how matter-of-fact she was about her family's lack of regard.

"I don't know, but I am fearful she will do something impetuous." She smoothed back a tendril of dark red hair. "She may not treat me well, but I have little enough family left."

That I understood. "I will try."

I suspected what Mary feared. In the spring, Edward Seymour withdrew from Katherine, but upon my return, the situation had changed. He now paid public court to her—when the queen's back was turned—and they dined together in the hall, their shoulders touching.

Katherine would not be so stupid as to admit him to her bed, but it would take less than that to draw the queen's ire. Restored to his father's title of Lord Hertford, Seymour would soon be nudged in the direction of some marriageable maid, and that maid would not be Katherine Grey.

Robert Dudley, restored to the queen's favor, strode through the presence chamber, high leather boots gleaming on his fine legs. "Ready yourselves!"

Within the hour, the queen's hunting party would ride to Eltham. Despite the December cold, I looked forward to time on horseback; though never entirely warm, the palace was stuffy. "Katherine, are you not coming with us?"

"Not today." She reclined on the window cushions, her cheek propped in her hand. "Toothache," she explained. "I couldn't bear the cold on my face."

"You should rest, once we're away." Elizabeth suffered from toothache, but she had little sympathy when others claimed her maladies.

"I might visit Jane." She pushed herself up, and despite her languid air, there was a strange energy about her. "She is always diverting."

Several hours later, when our party came back, Katherine was at the window again.

"Are you better?" I was windblown and chilled through, my fingers numb inside my gloves. I caught up an apple from a nearby bowl. The queen's dinner would be carried in soon, but I was too hungry to wait.

"Better?" Her color was high, and I wondered if Jane had given her something for her pain.

"Your toothache?" I prompted. "You were in such distress earlier."

Katherine's face cleared. "Yes, I am much restored."

I bit into the apple, its tart juices flooding my mouth. "Did you see Mistress Jane?"

Her smile bloomed before being quickly tucked away. "Yes. And Edward."

Of course. "Did you know he would be there when you decided to visit his sister?"

Katherine slid from the cushions and took my arm, pulling me into the corner. "We went together to see him in Cannon Street."

"Good God, Katherine, the risks you take." Covered dishes passed into the privy chamber, and I followed them with my eyes. "What if you were seen?"

"I don't care." She bubbled with contained excitement. "Margaery, we are married!"

"You're mad." I threw the apple aside before I choked.

Her eyes turned flinty. "You could try to be happy for me."

"I am happy for you." What I was not was surprised.

Katherine drew me closer. "I shouldn't have told you, not with your husband. You cannot tell Master Lewis—if he knows, all will be lost."

Even as I opened my mouth to object, I knew she was right; Robin couldn't keep such a secret from Cecil, and I did not want my friend separated from her husband, no matter how ill-conceived the marriage.

"I will not tell him," I said reluctantly. "But you will be found out, eventually. It will damage your standing with the queen beyond repair."

"I know." She was almost dancing in place. "We have agreed to keep quiet until the right time."

As the queen's permission was needed for Katherine to marry, it would never be the right time to confess such a transgression. Lord Hertford's penalty would be equally harsh: interfering with a royal virgin was no small crime.

"You will not live together, then," I said.

"Not now." She glanced at her sister, sitting quietly with the maids. Poor Mary, who had not been able to stop the match. "I will live at court, and pretend to be what I am not."

What I am not. "What do you mean?"

"I am a married woman, Margaery." Her lip trembled. "Wedded and bedded and happy."

Her words echoed as I returned to our apartments that evening. Not long ago, I could have used the same words to describe my life—but I would not; I was no Katherine Grey, bleating my happiness to all and sundry.

What words would I use now? I was still wedded; I shared a bed with my husband; I was happy. In some ways, we were closer than ever. Most days, Robin made sure Ned was gone before I came in, and we spent the time before bed in reading and conversation. On my days off, we met for dinner in the hall, and he often found time to go riding with me.

In the early days of our marriage, it would have been enough, but now I knew what was missing. I had imagined making a family with him, and that hope was gone.

And now, after promising there would be no more secrets between us, there was another. The things I'd held back before, because of my oath, were small things. This was different.

Chapter 35

REGULAR LETTERS ARRIVED FROM Anselm. There had been very few episodes of forgetting since I left, he said, which made me wonder if, somehow, I was a catalyst for them. Certainly I was a reminder of everything she'd lost. "Alice is very good with her, and Lady Margaret is content, knowing you are living the life she wished for you."

My original plan had been to return by Christmas, but I put off my departure, unable to bear the thought of leaving Robin. I wrote to Anselm, telling him we would come together in the spring.

The holidays passed in a blur. In early December, we learned the young French king was dead. Mary Stuart was no longer queen of France; instead, she was the most eligible widow in Europe. I watched as my husband worked himself into a shadow, trying, with Cecil and the others, to anticipate her next moves. It was a chess game, writ large, with the fate of England in the balance.

"Cecil thinks the Douglases are plotting," he told me, late one night, as we lay chastely in our curtained bed.

"Aren't they always?"

His laugh rumbled in his chest. "But their son is old enough to be a danger, as well."

I did not see how a boy of fifteen could be a danger. While Robin persisted in worrying about the young Lord Darnley, I fretted over Katherine Grey, rejoiced at Nell's pregnancy, and stifled the desire I felt when I curled against my husband's body each night.

Nell bloomed, her girlish softness transformed into the roundness of impending motherhood. I tried not to envy her, but it was hard: nothing in her life had ever given a moment's trouble. Pregnancy, it seemed, would be no different.

In February, the queen's business again interfered with my personal life. At day's end, when I found Robin lingering outside the doors instead of Sebastian, I suspected something had happened. Our routine was well-established, and any change was concerning.

"What's wrong?" I turned up the collar of my fur-trimmed cloak against the chill in the corridor.

"Why must something be wrong?" He offered his arm. "I just wanted to see you."

I sighed. "You've never had time before, and you have even less now." We hadn't passed at the breakfast table in a week, and three nights in a row I'd fallen asleep before he came in.

"I don't know why I try to soften things." He shook his head. "You'll have it out of me anyway."

"You know me well enough." I curled my fingers through his. "What is it?"

It was another diplomatic journey, leaving in just a few days. An embassy to France this time, with condolences for Mary Stuart; Darnley had been added to the party, and Robin's assistance was required, both with the embassy and to keep an eye on Margaret Douglas's son.

"I don't see how I can refuse."

My grandmother was without me because I wouldn't leave Robin. I bit my tongue and said what must be said. "You cannot refuse."

He stopped, drawing me back when I would continue walking. "I don't want to go," he said. "You do know that?"

"Of course." My words were crisp, hiding the hurt. He had to go, but I didn't have to like it.

We ate a late supper before the fire, talking little. When I finished, I pushed my chair back. "I'm off to bed. I'm sure you have work to do."

Robin put down his glass. "I always have work, but I don't always think my wife needs me." His gaze was probing. "Would you like my company, or have you had enough of me today?"

"I would like your company," I said. "Very much."

The night before Robin left, I tried to make him love me, in one of the ways which would not result in a baby. He refused, giving his early departure as an excuse, but I feared I'd put him off for so long he'd lost interest.

It appeared my mind still interested him; his frequent letters were warm and filled with details of the French court which he thought would interest me. "The women wear their hair in cauls such as you do, but of gold net, with pearls. I will try to obtain one for you before my return."

His trip to France coincided with a period of vile weather, and he was gone for longer than anticipated. Fearing my demons would return with too much solitude, I visited Nell on my days off. As her pregnancy progressed, it grew harder to be in her company and I made my excuses and took my ugly thoughts home, glad for the first time that I had no witnesses to my tears. Sebastian had been convinced to travel with Robin, and Susan would never dare to comfort me, or try to shake me from my mood, as Alice would have done.

My evenings were frequently spent with the Grey sisters. Katherine had little opportunity to be with her husband, and her already-sharp nerves were frayed. Listening to her complain that she missed being in his arms was both frustrating and comforting; neither of us had what we wanted.

We were in the royal bedchamber, readying Elizabeth for the day, when I was given another worry. Multiple layers of splendor had already been laced and pinned, and the queen was awaiting the final touches. Mary Sidney brought her jewels, and Katherine pulled the stopper from a tiny glass bottle of musk and rosewater scent. She took a quick sniff before adorning her mistress, and an expression of surprised nausea flickered across her face.

I recognized that sudden revulsion at a familiar scent. Katherine was pregnant.

It was one more layer in the veil keeping separating me from Robin. How long could I keep silent?

The French delegation returned in mid-March. As promised, Robin brought a beautiful gold net caul studded with pearls. It cost far too much, and it made me feel like a queen.

When he commented that I looked tired, I blamed Elizabeth. I would keep Katherine's secrets, for now, because her life had gone from bad to worse. Jane Seymour, whose health was always fragile, had begun to fail.

I spent my free days with Katherine at her bedside, watching the twenty-year-old girl cough her life away. Katherine held her hand

and sobbed, and Lord Hertford, stiff and careful in my presence, sat on Jane's other side.

She died soon after, and I went with Katherine to the funeral. It was a grand affair, due to Jane's complicated bloodline. The abbey choir sang her to rest in St. Edmund's Chapel, and I held tight to my friend's hand as she watched her husband stand chief mourner for his sister, his handsome face ravaged by grief.

At the end of the service, we lingered in the Westminster courtyard for a moment of privacy. Katherine was pale, her eyes swollen from crying, but she held herself like a lily. Mary Grey clung to us, equally upset, but no one paid much attention to her.

"How do you feel?" I looked closely at Katherine, trying to ascertain if my suspicions were correct.

"Betrayed." She kicked at the paving stones.

"Jane did not wish to die, sister," Mary said. "For shame."

Katherine turned on her. "Don't be a saddle-goose. Jane is an angel. I speak of my husband."

"How has Lord Hertford betrayed you?" I hoped she would not name another of the queen's gentlewomen.

"He has planned a trip abroad—to France, and beyond," she said with a trembling breath. "Jane told me, because he was too cowardly to do it himself."

That was one question answered. "Then you are not…?"

Her composure cracked, and two fat tears rolled down her cheeks. "I don't know," she whispered. "I've never had a baby before. Edward keeps asking—he says he won't leave, if only I can confirm it, but I cannot."

Mary's indrawn breath showed she, at least, was ignorant of her sister's secret. "Sister, if the queen finds out you are with child, you will follow Jane's path."

Katherine looked at her with narrowed eyes. "Jane my sister, or Jane my friend? Either way, I will be dead."

I mentioned Lord Hertford to Robin, to see if he was aware of the plan. He knew everything, of course—except for the secret I harbored.

"Cecil suggested it," he said. "What boy his age would not agree to a tour of Europe? He's too close to Katherine Grey for Cecil's liking."

I shook my head at the maneuverings of men. "Elizabeth and Dudley, Katherine and Hertford," I said. "The principal secretary spends more time worrying about lovers than he does about the policies of England."

"That's where you're wrong," Robin said. "Those lovers *are* England. Katherine must stay as virgin as the queen, in the event she is needed in the marriage game, if not as Elizabeth's heir. Francis was no sooner cold than Spain made their interest known to Mary Stuart."

Sliding into bed, I nudged the warming pan with my toes and found it cold. "Alice never forgot." I moved closer to Robin. "I'm going to beat that girl, I swear."

"Don't put your cold feet on me, or you'll be next." Despite his threat, he put his arm around me. "Why are you so interested in Katherine Grey?"

"She's my friend. And Spain was interested in her, too, this past summer." I burrowed against him, placing one icy foot on his leg. "Is Mary a better candidate because she's queen?"

He yelped and flinched away, then put his leg back where I could reach it. "They are interested in whoever they can get. Hertford will be gone for months, and by the time he returns, Cecil will have lined up an heiress for him, and your friend will no longer be a problem."

The bed warmed slowly. I lay awake, wondering if Katherine's husband had told her how long he would be gone, or how involved he was in the planning of this journey which would leave her so completely alone.

Elizabeth continued to make Cecil's life difficult. In April, she caused an uproar at Whitehall by giving Robert Dudley the apartments next to her own. Her women were shifted, with much grumbling, and their rooms turned into lodgings nearly as luxurious as the privy chambers.

The following month, almost nine months to the day from her

wedding, Nell gave birth to a son, named Nicholas after her father. I visited during her confinement and after the birth, and found tiny Nick to be the most beautiful baby I had ever seen, with Nell's fair hair and his father's eyes. He was swaddled, and thus difficult to hold, but the nurse propped him by the bed where we could admire him.

"Katherine was here," Nell said. "Have you seen her recently?"

I knew what she was too tactful to ask. Katherine had begun to affect loose gowns over her kirtle, beautiful garments which in no way clashed with our wardrobe requirements, but went some way to disguising her widening girth. "I believe she is."

Nell shook her head in disbelief. "How could Lord Hertford have gone to France?" she asked. "He is not even here to stand by her."

"She wasn't certain of her condition when he left." Katherine claimed to be uncertain yet, but her change in dress gave her away. "I only hope he returns before the queen notices."

"What a fool, to give way before he offered marriage," Nell said. "Her Majesty will never let them marry now."

I ran my finger over the baby's cheek and gave it to him to suck, trying to ignore thoughts of my own loss, almost a year ago. "Is he a strong feeder?" I was tired of talking about Katherine.

"Lizzy says so." Nell stretched prettily and leaned against a mountain of goosedown pillows. "I can't bear to watch."

"You don't feed him?" Wellborn women often did not, but I had thought baby-mad Nell would be an exception.

Her eyes widened. "Of course not. Relations are not permitted when a woman is nursing, and Richard and I want another baby as soon as possible."

I interpreted this to mean she and Richard wanted to get back to having relations as soon as possible, and changed the subject again, since relations were absolutely the last thing I wanted to discuss.

Chapter 36

THE DOOR OPENED PARTWAY, and when Ned's voice entered ahead of him, I dashed to the bedchamber to attire myself for visitors. It was nearly eleven; Robin should know better.

As Susan laced me back into my kirtle—they would get that, and no more, at this hour—their voices became contentious. Something was wrong.

"Good evening, husband." I emerged, kissing Robin briefly and making a curtsy to Ned. "You're very late."

Seb poured, and I almost laughed to see how quickly they snatched up the glasses.

"There was a bit of a crisis," Robin said after he'd downed half his drink.

"It's your friend," Ned volunteered, holding his glass out for more. "Do you know that addle-brained girl has gotten herself with child?"

Blood drained from my head so quickly I had to sit. "Where did you hear that?" I tried to keep my voice steady. Most people seemed blind to the fact that the queen's prettiest gentlewoman grown quite stout.

"She wrote to Hertford." Robin made an exasperated noise and rubbed his temples. "The letter came through our offices, and when Cecil read it, there was an explosion."

"I imagine." Katherine would have no idea her letter had been intercepted, and would be unprepared for whatever William Cecil and my husband were planning. Could I get word to her without Robin seeing?

Ned rose abruptly. "I'm sorry, Mistress Margaery, I had no idea of the time. I'll impose no more on your hospitality."

After he was gone, Robin folded his hands over his midsection and leaned back. "Now, why don't you tell me what you know about Lady Katherine's condition?"

Of course he would suspect. There was no getting around Robin's instincts. "It won't be a bastard." I spoke around the edge of my thumb, which had found its way between my teeth. "Her baby, I mean."

"Married?" he sputtered. "When? Why did you not tell me?"

It would come out now, Katherine's secret, and my part in the deception. My next words would doom our fragile reconciliation. "Because you would tell Cecil." Why had I thought her secret worth keeping, when it would destroy Robin's trust in me? "She only wanted to be happy."

Robin sighed impatiently. "That is what most of us want, Margaery, only it is not always possible." He drew the bottle across the table, filling only one glass. "Tell me everything you know of this, and leave nothing out."

His stern voice frightened me into truthfulness. "They were wed around the time of the French king's death, in December. His sister arranged for it to take place at Hertford House."

"What else?"

Pain flared in my thumb, and I tasted blood. "That is all."

Robin closed his eyes. "I am sorry we disturbed your rest. You should go to bed now."

"But I—"

"Go to bed, Margaery."

I woke before dawn to find myself alone, and padded barefoot to the outer chamber. Robin was asleep in his chair, the empty bottle beside him. The best course seemed to be to go back to bed, and hope things would be better in the morning.

"I'm sorry," I said when we met at breakfast. "I didn't mean to interfere."

There was a flicker of warmth in his eyes, quickly hidden. "I know. But you've left me with a mess to clean up." He glanced at my black skirts. "You can change your clothes. You're not going to the privy chambers today."

"But it's Tuesday." Was I to be locked in our apartment?

"I've sent word to Ned—you'll be leaving within the hour to spend some time with Lady Joan." Susan came in with my embroidery basket, and he raised a hand to stop her. "Pack your mistress's things.

She'll be making a visit to the country."

"Yes, sir." She bobbed, still nervous with Robin. "To Yorkshire, sir?"

"Not that far."

A trip to Yorkshire could not be arranged quickly, but he would get me away so I could do no more damage.

"But I don't want to visit Lady Joan," I protested. "The queen—"

"The queen will go on progress soon," Robin said. "You missed it last summer, and you shall miss it again this year."

I wound my arms around his neck. "But I don't want to leave."

He gripped my wrists in strong hands. "Your wishes do not enter into it. I must make a full report to Cecil this morning, and you need to be out of London before he decides to question you about that damnable woman."

"Will he be upset?" I hadn't thought about the harm I might do to Robin's standing with Cecil.

He regarded me dispassionately. "He will undoubtedly feel as I do. Disappointed."

Ned's coach carried us—me, Susan, and Sebastian—through the Surrey countryside, stopping only once for supper and to rest the horses. Lush orchards and fields of grain spread on either side of the road, and the air smelled of wildflowers. It was lovely, and I hated it.

Pickering House was a graceful timber-and-brick prison with well-planned gardens, and pretty Lady Joan was my jailor, with Seb standing deputy. She read the note he gave her, and looked me up and down as I stood in the hall, steaming with anger.

"Keeping secrets." She clicked her tongue. "Haven't you learned yet what it is to be married to one of them?"

"One of what?" I was sulky, bruised by the jouncing coach.

Lady Joan assumed the role of hostess and ushered me to the table, where food and drink were set out by quick-footed servants. "A man who works for the good of England." She spoke as if the words left a bad taste in her mouth. "Whose first loyalty is to something that cannot be seen or tasted or touched, only known." Raising her cup, she added, "And now you understand why we've met so rarely. I love my husband much more when we are apart."

I remained at Pickering House for three long weeks. It was not unpleasant, when I was able to forget I had been banished. Lady Joan was kindness itself, and her daughters were charming.

Far too much of my time was spent with baby Thomas, who was a round, cooing child with his father's bright eyes. My heart squeezed every time he raised his chubby hands.

Such occupations were necessary because Artemis had been left behind at Whitehall. I was not permitted to ride, nor walk beyond the park. I received no visitors, and no letters came from London.

I had not thought Robin would cut me off so entirely.

At first I worried what would become of Katherine when Cecil told the queen, and how she would react when she found her letters had been read.

Then I wondered at Robin's silence. Was it just disappointment that kept him from writing, or was there another reason for his lack of communication? Had he been blamed? Was he perhaps constrained so he could not write to me?

I knew my behavior to be foolish, now; the kind of marriage I wanted did not include secrets, and what I'd kept from Robin had consequences beyond the two of us. Katherine was heir to the throne of England, and could not do as she pleased.

She should have stayed away from Edward Seymour and built a relationship with the queen. A match would have been arranged for her, eventually, but Katherine had no patience for such a long game. She wanted her happiness when and with whom she chose.

If I had told Robin, as I should have, her second marriage would have been annulled more quickly than her first. But she trusted me; she knew the strength of her hold, and I'd kept secrets from the one person who most deserved my honesty.

The more I thought, the more miserable I became. Our marriage wasn't perfect, but I had risked Robin's trust—which I valued far more than Katherine's erratic friendship—for something both dangerous and wrong.

Sebastian, never content when he was apart from Robin, was equally unhappy. He knew I was the cause of our exile, and kept his distance, but he was always there when I left the house—as if I would scamper across the fields and try to reach London on my own.

I wrote again and again to Robin, to Nell, and even to Katherine, but received nothing in return. "No letters?" I asked Lady Joan at dinner each day, and she would shake her head, which made it all the more startling when Sebastian spoke up.

"We return tomorrow," he said. "Susan has already begun to pack."

"Why?"

Seb folded his napkin and stood. "Because the master said we could return."

After three weeks of silence, Robin had written to Seb? "When did you hear from him?"

"Every week."

Desolation spread through me. "Why didn't you tell me?" My dinner lay like a stone in my belly. "Sebastian?"

He gave me a look full of pity. "Because the master did not wish you to know."

When the coach drew up in front of Whitehall, I opened the door before Seb jumped down. "You and Susan can manage," I said peremptorily. "I'm going inside."

The great hall was deserted. As I made my way to our apartments, I saw fewer people at every turn, and those I did see were servants turning the place out for a good cleaning while Elizabeth was away.

Our chamber was empty. I hadn't expected Robin to be waiting, but I thought perhaps—since he knew Seb would obey his summons immediately—there would be a note of welcome.

Seb came in with my box on his shoulder and put it by the bed. "Is that all, mistress?"

"Yes," I said. "What time is Master Lewis due back?"

He raised a shoulder. "I'm not certain. He is at New Hall in Essex."

I stared at him. "Whatever for?"

"He is on progress with the queen."

Robin did not return for several days, during which time I had nothing to do but examine my conscience and wonder how long it would take him to forgive me. I had no distractions from this onerous task: Nell was in Hertfordshire, and Katherine, unexpectedly, was also with the queen.

I read and walked in the gardens, wishing I had Alice for company rather than the block-headed Susan. When Robin walked in, just as I was about to take myself off to the Strand, I cast myself at him, burying my face in his doublet. My legs were shaking, and it was all I could do not to sob aloud.

"What is all this?"

I drew back to look into his face. "I'm just glad to see you," I said. "It's been some time."

He looked uncomfortable. "Yes, about that—"

"I'm so sorry, Robin. I never meant to cause trouble." All the tears I had held back when I was angry began to flow down my cheeks. "I was flattered Katherine confided in me."

"You don't need flattery," he said. "You know your value."

Wiping my streaming eyes, I shook my head. "I think sometimes I do not, or I wouldn't get so turned around."

With a sigh, Robin brought me close to him again, rubbing my back with one hand. "Dry your tears," he said quietly. "I've come all the way from Felix Hall today, and I'm half-starved. Would you like to find a pie shop and eat by the river?"

It was an odd suggestion, but I grasped it, thrilled he wanted to spend time with me after what I'd done. "That's a fine idea." I wiped my eyes with my kerchief and hoped I didn't look too blotchy. "I truly am—"

Robin stopped the flow of words with a finger to my lips. "Speak no more about it."

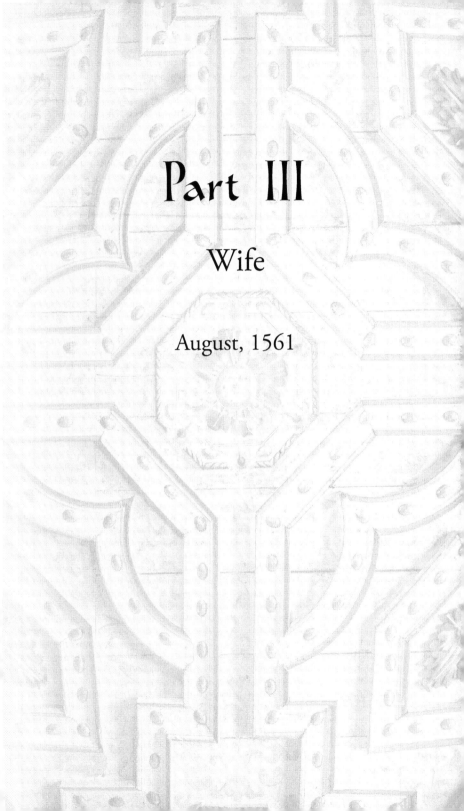

Part III

Wife

August, 1561

Chapter 37

"Has Master Lewis mentioned anything about Scotland?"

Nell and I sat at ease in the gardens of Curtis House, young Master Nicholas propped on his board between us. A silken canopy the color of the sky filtered the afternoon sun.

"No." He'd been speculating with Ned about when Mary Stuart would return, now the French had no more use for her. "What about it?"

She paused to blow a kiss at her son, who watched with large, attentive eyes. "Will is going. According to him, our ambassador will take a party to Edinburgh to welcome the Scottish queen. He doesn't expect to be back before Christmas."

Going to Scotland would be good for her brother; he would learn to stand on his own feet, and not count on Robert Dudley or my husband for his accomplishments.

"He said Master Lewis is also going."

My heart sank. "Are you sure?"

"Will seemed to be." Nell's hands rested on her skirts, which were the same shade as her hair. Her sleeves and bodice were the color of a ripe peach, making her an altogether delicious morsel. It surprised me she had lasted at court until she laid eyes on Richard Curtis.

If Robin were being considered for such a mission, his conversation with Ned should have been full of it. They discussed Ambassador Randolph, but there had been no mention of accompanying him. Despite his decades of travel, Robin grew excited as a child at the opportunity to go anywhere; he would have said something.

"If he is, it'll be a surprise to both of us," I told her. "I wouldn't mind."

Her smile was impish; motherhood hadn't changed my darling in the slightest. "You wouldn't mind if he went, or if you went along?"

The last time Robin went to Scotland had been the start of the breach between us. I was a different person now. I would not fall apart without him, though I might go home to visit Grand-mère. I did not wish to be parted, but wives were not a part of diplomatic missions.

A groom escorted me to Whitehall and handed me off to a palace servant. As I dismounted, brushing dust from my skirts, I saw a familiar figure near the doors. Cecil was speaking with two young men in livery, his long brown beard wagging; within moments they sprinted off to do his bidding. Once they were gone, he turned his face to the sun for a moment.

A thought occurred to me, and I acted before I could think again, and more clearly. "Master Cecil!"

His reverie broken, he turned to me. It shocked me that he was younger than Robin; perhaps dealing with kings and queens was prematurely aging.

"Yes?"

"I would speak with you, sir."

He focused on me, locating my face in his memory. "What can I do for you, Mistress Lewis?"

Now that I had his attention, I wasn't certain what to say. I made a fool of myself by blurting out, "I would first apologize, sir, for my behavior with regard to Lady Katherine Grey—I should have known better than to keep such a matter secret from my husband."

Reaching up to adjust his chain of office, which must be heavy in the heat of summer, he said, "That is between you and your husband, Mistress Lewis. Good day to you."

"Wait, sir!" I plunged after him. "I have heard the Scottish queen returns to Edinburgh. If my husband is sent with the ambassador, I would like to accompany him."

"That is another matter to take up with your husband." He smiled politely. "I must be going."

I followed, not caring how silly he thought me. "Master Cecil, I was raised in France. I grew up speaking French." I appealed to the lack of trust which Robin claimed was Cecil's best quality. "I am content to be Her Majesty's chamberer, but perhaps I might be of more use elsewhere."

Two days later, I received a call to the principal secretary's offices. When the page brought me in, I looked around, but Robin and Ned were nowhere to be seen. The young man knocked on a partly open door. "Mistress Lewis is here, sir."

William Cecil was seated behind a broad wooden desk covered

with tidy piles of documents, each ornamented with some colorful seal or ribbon. The windows were closed tight against the smell of the Thames. He must have been very uncomfortable, buttoned as he was into a woolen doublet, with an old-fashioned bonnet on his head.

He glanced up, ascertaining his minion had brought the right woman, and looked back at his papers. "Your family fled England after your father's execution." He bypassed courteous preliminaries. "Eighteen years you were there, before you wed Master Lewis. Your uncle and grandfather died, your mother remarried a Frenchman. You returned to England with your grandmother, a Catholic."

"That is correct, sir." Was Robin the source of this information, or did Cecil have other means at his disposal?

"Were you at the French court?"

"Briefly." Uninvited, I sank down on a stool before his desk. "When I was sixteen."

Cecil put down his quill. "Did you know the Scottish princess?"

I shook my head. "We met, but we did not speak."

He smoothed his beard with fingers as ink-stained as my husband's. "What do you remember of her?"

I could not have been summoned because William Cecil had questions about the French queen's appearance; there were ambassadors and informants for such details.

"She was tall, for a girl." I twisted my hands together. "Taller than the prince, but boys often grow more slowly. Her hair was red, but darker than Her Majesty's." I barely remembered the nine-year-old princess, having spent my time being paraded before prospective husbands, to my outrage. "She was very lively."

"Did you know her ladies?" His fingers drummed on a sheet of vellum. If he had hoped to fill that with information obtained from me, he would be disappointed. "The ones they call the Maries?"

Mary took four girls with her to France, and they grew up to be her ladies-in-waiting. Inconveniently for those around them, all four were named Mary.

"I knew Mary Livingston, slightly," I said. "There is a distant family connection my mother rooted out, in the hopes of furthering herself."

"It seems it did not work." Cecil's brows raised. "Else you would still be there."

"Perhaps not," I said. "I was…difficult."

My stepfather sent me home in disgust, and I was very glad to escape the attentions of my unappealing suitors. Uncle Walter sickened not long after, and it would have been devastating not to have been with my grandparents when he died.

"Would she remember you, do you think?" His eyes were keen. "Mary Livingston."

"I don't know," I said honestly. "We spoke several times—I remember, she said she had little occasion to speak English—but she had her duties with the princess, and they were much younger than I was."

Cecil nodded once, decisively. "Thank you, Mistress Lewis. That will be all."

Having no duties, I made my way to the gardens and found a secluded spot where I could watch the river. When the bells chimed eight and my stomach began to rumble, I made my way inside, hoping Robin would be home.

He was there with Ned, and I greeted them pleasantly. "Again? It's like having two husbands."

My husband kissed me on both cheeks, inquiring if I had eaten. "Not since dinner."

He called for Sebastian, who appeared as if he'd been waiting for the sound of my husband's voice—which he probably had been. "Your mistress is near starved," he said. "What can you find for her?"

"Anything." Seb smiled at me. "I know my mistress's tastes. I will return shortly."

Settling into my chair at Robin's side, I reached for the swaddling bands I was working on as a gift for Nell. Garlands of minute blue flowers already edged the cloth; I threaded my needle and selected an emerald silk for the leaves.

A glass of wine and some handwork was what I needed to drive away my lurking headache. While I stitched, I listened idly to the conversation flowing around me. Ned mentioned a letter from someone named Lord James which made Cecil swear and take himself out for a walk in the gardens. I appreciated Cecil's cure for a stressful situation was similar to my own.

"Who is Lord James?" I pushed my glass toward Robin.

"James Stewart, the current lord protector—at least until his half-sister returns." Our fingertips touched when he handed me the glass. "Appointed by the council of lords who overthrew her mother."

Goodness. How did the Scottish queen feel about that? "What does Her Majesty think about the Scottish queen's plan to return?" I had witnessed my share of tantrums centering around Mary Stuart.

Ned grinned. "She's in quite a bother."

"Not as bothered as Cecil." Robin's tone was somber as Ned's was ebullient.

"Why?" The queen's upset was easy to comprehend: Mary was a threat to her throne and her vanity.

"She's Catholic."

"And not averse to another marriage," Ned added. "Nineteen, and queen of two countries already. She's an attractive catch, and Cecil is afraid she will be caught by a prince with an eye toward returning England to Rome. Again."

There were still Catholics in England, of course—Grand-mère being one of them, as Cecil pointed out—but if Mary took a Catholic husband, no matter his country of origin, it would be dangerous for Elizabeth.

"Would they try to overthrow her?"

Robin stared at the clean-swept hearth. "They might," he said. "Look at Queen Mary. Look at Jane Grey. Men do stupid things for their God, and they usually end up involving a woman."

I didn't understand him when he spoke this way, and even Ned rolled his eyes. "But would the people accept her? Does she really have a right to the English throne?"

Ned poured wine straight down his throat, an impressive trick. "As much right as good Queen Bess, I'd say, though I'd not say it loudly."

My husband put a hand on his arm. "You shouldn't even say it softly."

I thought no more of Scotland until a week later, when Robin came in late, and alone. "What would you say to a journey?" he asked, kissing the top of my head. "I've been asked to go to Edinburgh with Randolph, and I thought you might like the distraction."

I resisted clapping my hands, and said calmly, "I would enjoy that very much."

"We are to convey the queen's best wishes on Mary's return, but also to feel out her thoughts on marriage."

Men could not leave a woman to manage her own life. For all that Elizabeth might believe she was directing this mission, Cecil had it thoroughly planned, with the assistance of my husband, Ned Pickering, and a score of helpful gentlemen.

"Do you truly think she will tell you her plans?" I focused on young Nicholas's swaddling bands, which were nearly completed. I would like to give them to Nell before we left.

Robin sighed. His life seemed to exhaust and invigorate him in equal measure. "I do not know," he said. "She is young and impetuous, and her half-brother does not like to share authority. Their views are very different, but if she can get him on her side, she will be very powerful."

The Scottish queen was not yet twenty, while Lord James was in his thirties, seasoned by war and statecraft. They differed in age, sex, and religion; why would their opinions as to the young queen's marriage not differ, as well?

Mary Sidney handed me several pins and slowly drew the sleeve from the queen's arm. It was a heavy piece, with strapwork and pearls, and I was certain more pins were used in the morning than were just removed.

"Get the other one off," Elizabeth urged. "You're not paid to linger, Mary!"

Robert Dudley's sister rolled her eyes discreetly; we weren't paid at all, as the queen well knew. The honor of our positions lost its luster when the queen was ill-tempered.

The second sleeve followed the first, and I was given another clutch of pins. Eight, this time. Two more than the first sleeve. Where had they gone?

"Mistress Margaery," the queen said as I knelt to remove her forepart, "Cecil tells us you will accompany your husband to Scotland."

I straightened up and received another handful of pins. Twelve, the correct number. "It was very kind of the master secretary to make room in the party for me."

Elizabeth snorted. "He asked our permission for you to accompany Master Lewis."

"Then it is Your Majesty I must thank." I curtsied, snatching a pin from beneath her foot.

"Hmm." She pivoted, and we followed. "You would do well to keep your eyes open in Scotland, Mistress Margaery. We would be very interested to hear your opinions on our cousin."

I had expected as much. "I would be honored to tell Your Majesty of my experiences upon my return."

"Good." She swung back, causing us to move again. "Do not leave when we are finished. We would speak to you further."

Chapter 38

THE *SWIFT* EASED INTO port at dusk. Edinburgh displayed itself against the fading sky, all sharp roofs and spires, its hilltop castle crouched like a beast overlooking the town. It looked very different from England. By the time we disembarked, it was raining steadily, and we were drenched before sufficient coaches were assembled to carry us to Holyrood.

Word of our arrival spread quickly. Ambassador Randolph was whisked off on horseback before we were all off the ship. He would meet with his counterpart while the rest of us settled into our quarters and found our way into dry clothes. Crammed into a carriage with Nell and three other women, I peered through the window at the unfamiliar streets and felt the first stirring of exhilaration, understanding at last Robin's desire for new places.

The voyage had not been long, but Robin was occupied and Nell seasick, so I spent much of it alone. I came to a decision during those solitary hours, and now that we were at the palace, I was determined to put it into action. The Scots had no idea I was a mere chamberer, barely worthy of notice, nor did they know I was easily cowed, unwilling to speak my mind in public for fear of being put in my place.

They knew none of these things, and my determination was they never should. I would enter the court of Mary Stuart as a vivacious Englishwoman, wife to one of Cecil's men, companion to the queen, and deserving of any and all attention that came my way. It was a way of beginning again, to find the person I'd started to become before the situation at court and my lost child made me shrink into myself.

What would Robin think of this new wife? Would he recognize her as the girl he'd married in France, or would he try to rein her in?

Let him try, I thought, closing my eyes and listening to the murmur of his voice as he spoke to Sebastian. Just let him try.

We were admitted into the royal presence the next evening.

I wore a new gown of Coventry blue and a small blue velvet beret pinned at the back of my head, my hair bundled into Robin's gold net caul. I liked this new fashion; I could show my hair, but Susan did not have to attempt curls or other improbable styles, which did not suit my face or her talents.

Thomas Randolph bowed over the queen's hand, and began to introduce his fellows, who included Robin and Will Hawkins. As they conversed in French, I examined Mary Stuart, who had been a child when I'd last seen her.

She was taller than Elizabeth, with hair more auburn than gold, and she had lovely pale skin that showed no hint of cosmetics. Her gown was deep red, the color of good wine, and her cloth-of-gold sleeves were heavily trimmed with jewels. She was youthful—nineteen to my twenty-six—but she appeared every inch a queen.

At last Robin beckoned me forward. "Your Majesty, may I present my wife, Margaery Lewis."

I curtsied over her hand, and looked up into lively amber eyes. "It is an honor to meet you, Your Majesty." I slipped back into French, as fluent as my diplomat husband. "I saw you in France, when I was young."

Her plucked eyebrows lifted. "You were in France?" She gestured for me to come closer.

"Yes, Your Majesty." I ducked from beneath Robin's restraining hand. "My family moved to Lisieux when I was five. I was brought to court for a season." I scanned the women behind her, looking for a familiar face. "I was not fortunate enough to be presented, but I did know one of your ladies—Marie Livingston."

Her face lit up. "Marie!" She called the lady over. "Do you remember Madame Lewis?"

Mary Livingston looked much the same: a snub-nosed, sandy-haired young woman with a faint dusting of freckles across her nose. "*Oui, ma reine.* I remember—though your name was different then, was it not?"

"I was Margaery Preston then," I said. "That was years before I met my most excellent husband." I glanced at Robin, who goggled at me like a hooked fish. "He's had a long journey—he is generally far more entertaining."

A wave of female laughter rolled over me, and I broke into gooseflesh. This was what I wanted: appreciation, acceptance.

I curtsied again. "May I approach, Your Majesty?"

The Scottish queen nodded. "*Bien sur.*"

I reached into my sleeve and produced the letter given to me before my departure. "This is from the queen, whom I serve. You will hear much from her gentlemen in the next days, but this is from the hand of Elizabeth herself. From one sister queen to another, she bade me tell you."

Taking it from my hand, she kissed it and tucked it away. "Then we honor it, and shall read it before our prayers tonight, so we may include her in them, more so than we already do." She gave me a genuine smile. "You are very welcome in this place, Madame Lewis. We hope your visit is a long one."

I backed slowly away. Placing my hand on Robin's arm, I closed my eyes to better relish my success. I had done it! I had spoken to the queen, given her Elizabeth's letter, and made her see me as something more than an extension of my more interesting husband.

"What was that?" Robin asked, none-too-quietly, looking from me to Randolph.

"Nothing." I turned my face away.

His fingers caught my chin. "Margaery?"

"It was a letter from the queen." I tried not to sound defensive. "She asked me to give it directly to Queen Mary."

Robin's face, never expressive, closed off entirely. "We'll speak about this when we are alone."

"If you can find the time." I joined Nell, who had been presented by her brother. "You look like you're about to drop!"

She giggled, and clasped her hands at her waist. She wore a gown of rose velvet, heavily worked with pearls, and looked like a rose herself. "What has upset Master Lewis?"

"I have." I shrugged. "It's no matter—the music's beginning. Let's see if any of these Scotsmen will dance with us."

Despite tales of Mary's court being Protestant and dour, the music was gay indeed, and there were more than enough dancers, including Will Hawkins, who partnered me with sure hands for a leaping volta. When I rejoined Robin at the end of the evening, my chemise was pasted to my ribs as thoroughly as it had been from the rain the day before. I felt marvelous.

"What's come over you?" he asked, as we made our way back to the rooms set aside for the English delegation.

"Nothing." I hummed a snatch of song as we walked; I was wide awake, even if my feet hurt like blazes.

"Margaery."

I stopped. "Can I not have a bit of fun without it being a matter for discussion?" I pitched my voice low so the others couldn't hear me. "I came to Scotland to enjoy myself."

He looked at me slantwise. "And so you have."

Once inside, he dismissed the waiting Sebastian. "Please tell Susan her attentions will not be required."

Stifling a sigh, I moved past him into the bedchamber. It had taken Susan over an hour to get me into full court garb, and I did not relish reversing the process on my own. I untied my ruff, rubbing my neck where the tape had chafed. Alice had trained Susan to smooth balm on the red marks; I wondered if the girl had left the stuff where I could find it.

Dealing with my sleeves and the upper portion of my gown was easy enough—under its pinned-on placard, it was front laced. I shrugged out of it and left it on the chest. "Robin." I turned and caught him watching me. "Can you help? I can't get out of this on my own."

My voice seemed to bring him back from far away. "Of course," he said. "It was stupid of me to dismiss them." He whipped my laces through their holes. When the pieces were separated, I bent over and he tugged the whole construction over my head, staggering back with the heft of it.

"Don't bother," I said as he reached for the ties at my waist. "I can do the rest."

He retreated, removing the new high-collared black velvet doublet of which he was vain, and the black padded hose which made his legs look spider-like. Even formal dress was less complicated for men—he left his sleeves attached for Seb to deal with, and his ruff was likewise strewn on the floor. Before I had removed my petticoat, he was seated on the bed in his shirt, rubbing at his knee.

"Is that why you refrained?" I wondered why he hung back; it seemed he would want to show himself to his best advantage in a new place.

"My wife was otherwise occupied." He poured wine. "Let me help you with the last of it, so we can sit."

A flurry of petticoats joined his ruff on the floor, and I ducked behind a screen to change. It was a relief to put my finery aside and sit with Robin wearing nothing but my nightdress and stockings. "Should I brace for a lecture?" I accepted a brimming cup.

"No, you were excellent," he said. "Anyone who was watching would have believed you carried that message without my knowledge."

"Who do you think was watching?" The wine wasn't as good as what we drank at home. Robin favored Italian wine; this must be French.

"Quite possibly no one." Robin stroked his beard, which he had grown back when Seb was with me and unable to shave him. "But it does no harm for you to be known as a woman who acts independently of her husband."

I didn't quite understand what Cecil and Robin had come up with, but I was a willing participant; it was my penance for Katherine, and it added a bit of extra excitement to the Scottish trip.

Despite the warmth outdoors, a chill radiated from the stone walls, and I settled the collar of my quilted satin night robe under my ears. "I don't remember the last time I felt like myself—until tonight."

Robin was silent for a long time, turning his cup slowly in his fingers. "It hasn't been good for you, has it?" he asked, finally. "This marriage."

I closed my eyes. "It hasn't been what I expected."

"You should be married to someone your own age, someone with more energy, who can give you the life you deserve."

My husband had the energy of ten men when it was directed at something that interested him. I nearly said so, but contented myself with, "You have this ridiculous notion that your age prevents you from being a proper husband."

"I think I've been husband enough to disprove that." He pressed his lips together. "And look what happened."

"The baby?" My eyes filled, but the pain was not as sharp. "That had nothing to do with your age."

"No, but it happened because I was your husband." He took my hand, bringing it to his lips. "If I'd been able to control myself, to keep you only as a companion, you wouldn't have suffered."

"I suffer worse every day when I am treated as less by the one person who should know who I am." I breathed through my nose, trying to hold my temper. "Rob, I will never stop mourning our baby, but this is harder to bear than when you refused to touch me."

Silence again. When it stretched, I turned and saw tears on his face. "Robin?"

"I wanted the child, too," he said, his voice strangled. "God help me, but I wanted it. And then…seeing your pain. I don't want that for you, ever again."

"What about what I want?"

Robin looked up. "You can't possibly—"

This moment would make or break our marriage; I knew it as surely as I had known marrying him was the answer to my childish wish for security. I knelt before his chair. "I want to try again. I'd like a child—of course, I would—but I want *us* to try again. I miss you in my bed."

"I am there." His hands rested lightly on my shoulders.

"We sleep alone," I said, "no matter that we are in the same bed." I rested my hands on his knees. "I never expected marriage to be so lonely."

"Oh, Margaery." He tilted my face up. "It frightens me how much I have come to care for you, when this was intended as a convenience for us both." He stood, and raised me with him. "I love you, don't you know that?"

"How could I?" Robin had finally said the words I wanted most to hear. I gazed into his light eyes, trying to see what other secrets lurked in that complicated brain. "You don't show it."

"I only know one way to show you," he said with a laugh.

He not only loved me, but he wanted me? "My flow is due any day now." I spoke quickly to quell my embarrassment. "The ladies say that is when it is most difficult to catch a child." This miracle of timing no doubt prevented untold numbers of inconvenient offspring. "We should be safe."

"You are certain? You're willing to risk it?"

I leaned in and kissed him, tasting Scottish Mary's French wine on his lips. Robin drew me close, and I pressed myself to him and felt the stir of his response. "You do want me?"

"I want you." It was almost a groan. "I have wanted you since we met. I've fought against it, I've talked myself out of it, I've worn out my right hand trying to rid myself of desire for you." He pressed his lips to my neck. "It's no good."

"I want you, too, husband." I fumbled a hand between us. "Where you belong."

"Yes, wife." And he picked me up and carried me to the bed, and gave me what I asked for, and more.

We were awakened by Susan, tutting over the mess we'd left for her. "It's near eight." She opened the shutters, admitting a glare of light. "Shouldn't you be with your gentlemen, Master Lewis?"

Robin sat up, realized he was naked, and pulled up the coverlet. "Call for Sebastian, please. I'll be gone in a few minutes, and then you can tend to Mistress Lewis."

She nodded, scooping up our crumpled linen on her way out.

I turned my head, so close to his on the pillow. "Where must you be this morning, when I want you in my bed?"

He kissed me lightly. "With Randolph, of course." Sliding out of bed, he headed for the basin. "And wishing, more importantly, that I was still here, with you."

Within minutes, he was washed and dressed. It wasn't fair how quickly men could be presentable. Before leaving, he kissed me again, and over his shoulder I saw Sebastian's broad smile.

Chapter 39

DESPITE HAVING ONLY BEEN in Scotland a few weeks, a progress was organized shortly after our arrival. The vivacious young queen wanted to see her country—and be seen by her people. She invited the English party to accompany her.

"You don't look excited." Did I need to take my entire Scottish wardrobe? "You love to travel."

Robin rolled his eyes. "This isn't traveling. It's rain and bad roads and being trapped in a coach for hours on end."

"Oh." I would enjoy it less knowing he was miserable.

"But you will ride with the queen, and enjoy her confidences." He buried his face in the crook of my neck. "I will be happy, knowing that."

Linlithgow, our first destination, was an easy ride from Edinburgh. As we trotted along the well-maintained road, Mary chatted with us, keeping none of Elizabeth's distance. She was a queen in her bones; no one would ever mistake her for one of her ladies.

I liked Linlithgow as I had liked the queen: wholly, and at first meeting. It was a proper country palace, overlooking a small lake, which Mary Seton said the Scots called a "loch." The landscape reminded me of Yorkshire, with its broad expanses and windswept skies, and I preferred it to the clamorous city.

We spent two days there, during which I learned Mary was not only a tireless rider, but a daring one. When she was with her ladies, she rode astride, and I was amused to see she wore serge breeches under her skirts.

As we lay in bed, a sudden rainstorm lashing the shutters, I related Mary's conversations to Robin, and told him of her breeches. "The French queen dowager started the fashion, apparently."

He laughed, snugging me against him. "Catherine de Medici could not look as good in breeches as my lady wife." He hesitated, adding, "I reserve judgment about Queen Mary."

I lifted my head slightly. "Mary is very tall, with bony knees."

"I myself am tall, with bony knees," Robin said. "I have no need of one like me."

Our next destination was Stirling, where Mary had been kept safe from the English until she was sent to France. It should have been an uneventful stay, but two things happened which made it memorable for both the English and Scottish members of the party.

The first was when Mary nearly burned to death in her bed, having fallen asleep with a lit taper too near the curtains. By the time her women smelled smoke, the curtains were alight and the queen had to be dragged, choking, from her bedchamber. She bore up well, and rode the next day to prove she was unaffected, but she was unusually silent, and her marble skin was dull, with shadows beneath her eyes.

The second disturbance was religious in nature. When Mary returned to Scotland, she upset the Catholics in her party by not ejecting Protestants from the council. One of them, her half-brother—the man whose letter made Cecil swear—was made chief advisor, and she kept the council balanced. In exchange, Mary was allowed to hear mass in her private chapel at Holyrood.

But Stirling was not Holyrood, and when her priest attempted the mass, he was set upon by Lord James himself, along with Lord Argyll, and a commotion raised that was heard all over the castle grounds. Robin told me later two of the clerks had bloody heads, and the queen shed public tears at her brother's disaffection.

Whatever emotions swelled in her, Mary concealed them better than Elizabeth. She did not shout or throw things—not ever, that I saw. Instead, she drew herself up, made an alabaster mask of her beautiful face, and carried on dancing. It infuriated those who tried to force her hand, and it was exhausting for all involved.

Scottish summers were shorter even than Yorkshire summers. A week later, we awoke in Dundee to crisp, clear air and the scent of autumn. Inside the damp palace, fires roared, and there was talk already of Christmas.

Robin began to look uneasy. I thought the chill had aggravated his knee, but when questioned, he felt we had overstayed our visit. "Cecil sent us here for a reason," he said, "and it has been accomplished. We have greeted the queen, gone on progress with her, observed her. I need to return home."

Whatever their plan had been, my own visit had no such circumscribed purpose, and I was enjoying myself mightily. I revered Elizabeth, but I liked Mary. Her court was not so serious, and I basked in my special status as a guest who could speak French with the queen and her ladies.

"May we wait until the progress is ended?" There would be no changing his mind. "The queen wishes to hunt at St. Andrews, and it would be easiest to leave from Edinburgh."

"The longer we wait," he said, "the more unpleasant the journey."

The North Sea was bothersome in the winter months, and the less said about the roads, the better, especially after the rains commenced. We would have to depart soon.

I bit my lip. "Just until the end of September? Then I will leave, as obedient as you could wish."

Robin's mouth turned up at one corner. "When have I ever asked for obedience?" He framed my face in his hands and kissed me lightly. "You could stay on."

"Without you?"

"I am needed in London, but you have found favor with the queen." He put a hand on my arm. "If you chose to remain, no one would question it."

"You want me to stay here, and carry tales?" Was it Cecil's idea, or Robin's, to leave me behind?

"Nothing so obvious." It was clear he understood my reluctance. "But she likes you, and might come to confide in you over time. Cecil would undoubtedly benefit from a better understanding of her mind, and you could give him that."

Mary being as unpredictable as Elizabeth, I understood Cecil's desire. "I could," I said carefully, "but I will not repeat everything I hear."

An eyebrow raised. "You have sworn no oath to Mary."

How to explain it? "Even a queen is but a woman at the mercy of men. I will tell you what I can."

"That is fair."

I looked down at my hands. "Will you miss me?"

"Of course." He gazed at me with the affection he found so

difficult to put into words. "But this isn't the same as our previous separation, is it?"

I shook my head.

"Then we will manage." He dropped a kiss on my hair. "It won't be forever."

"No." My voice was soft; we'd only just reconciled, and he was willing to leave me.

Robin sat, drawing me onto his lap. "You've changed, darling girl. I think you need time away from court, and possibly from me."

In England, I had two choices: remain small, and in his shadow, or be trodden on by the queen and her ladies. I had been afraid, in one way or another, ever since we married; my fears were groundless, but no less real for being so. I could not finish growing up in such a place.

I must be brave, for both our sakes.

"What if I change too much?" I spoke against his chest. "What if you don't like me?"

His arm tightened. "There is no chance of that."

Mary was overjoyed when I announced I would stay on after Robin left for England. "Master Lewis, we will take the utmost care of your precious jewel." She dimpled and fluttered as if my husband were the most attractive man in Scotland.

He bowed. "I thank you for your care, Your Majesty. She is most dear to me."

Sebastian would not allow Robin to travel the length of the kingdom alone, but I would not be left entirely unattended. Will Hawkins was deputed to watch over me.

I objected to Robin's choice of watchdog. "I thought you did not ask for obedience?"

"In this instance, I do." Robin's face was grave. "I will not leave you in a strange place without someone I trust to look after you. He is staying on, so it makes sense."

"Nell will keep him busy." The queen's ladies had adopted her as a pet, refusing to accept she was eighteen, and a wife and mother.

"She returns with the rest of our party."

Did I want so badly to stay in Edinburgh that I would stay with no one but Will Hawkins for company? I did, even at such a cost. I liked who I was here, and I wasn't certain I could maintain this new assurance if I returned to Whitehall too quickly.

There was plenty to keep me occupied after Robin's departure. Not wanting to be alone with my thoughts—or the desires rekindled by our three weeks' reunion—I moved into a chamber with several other women. They were pleasant companions, and I did not regret my decision.

The rains persisted, and we spent more time at indoor pursuits. Mary Stuart was a kindred spirit in her appreciation of the art of embroidery. I was seated at my frame when a shadow fell over my work. Mary leaned down, her fingernail stroking the black silk pattern I had stitched on the linen.

"You are skilled."

I looked up at her. "Your Majesty's own work is very beautiful."

The queen gestured for me to move closer to her canopied chair of state. "I began with plain sewing, as all girls do." She snapped her fingers and her spaniels closed around her in a wave, diving beneath the skirts of her purple satin day gown. "Being a princess did not save me from that."

"My grandmother taught me," I said. "She believed it more suitable than riding, which was the only other occupation I enjoyed."

Mary laughed, and one of the dogs shot from under her skirt, nearly upending a passing Marie. "In weather such as this, at least." She peered again at my embroidery. "Is that Florentine or Venetian?"

It was a design from the book of emblems Robin had given me, reworked to my own satisfaction. "A bit of both," I said. "And some of my own making."

"We would like this pattern," she said. "If you would agree, one of our Maries would give you one of our silk chemises to work upon."

"Of course, Your Majesty." No matter where I went, some royal woman coveted my stitching. "I would be only too happy."

Due to Ambassador Randolph's continued presence at Holyrood,

I heard from Robin on a weekly basis. No sterile missives this time: his letters were warm and fond, imparting news and gossip in equal measure; describing his days without me; his current reading; and the activities of my friends in London.

"I am sorry to tell you," he wrote in October, "matters do not bode well for your friend. She has been sent to the Tower after the queen learned of her marriage from Robert Dudley, to whom she had gone for advice. This last week, she gave birth to a fine son."

Katherine's labors began during her examination on the validity of her marriage. Summoned from France, Lord Hertford was also imprisoned, although not with his wife.

"They are very miserable," Robin continued. "I cannot help but sympathize, even though their distress was brought about by their own careless actions."

I could do nothing to ease my friend's situation, but I wanted to know why the queen found out from Dudley, when Cecil had at least suspected since July. No matter how secure the mails, it was not a question I could put in a letter.

Nell's letter, arriving in the next pouch, covered the same topic, but with more drama. She closed with a brief mention of her son. "I hardly recognized him, he has grown so much in my absence."

Considering he and his nurse had been sent to the country before we left for Scotland, I was surprised Nell recognized him at all.

Perhaps when I returned, Robin and I could try for a baby. I no longer feared he was unable to love a child; he would make his feelings known, even if he could not say them outright.

Chapter 40

THE QUEEN PROPOSED TO ride into the town to mingle with her subjects—as one of them. And not as a female subject, I soon learned. Mary Stuart stood as tall as any man, and she had a man's suit of clothes, with hose and breeches to aid in her deception. To this was added a short cloak, and a broad-brimmed hat to hide her face, as no man would have skin like hers.

"Would you come with us, Madame Lewis?" She turned before the mirror to admire her trim figure in its dark blue doublet. "It is a merry time."

I looked to the Maries for advice.

"We went out once before," Mary Livingston whispered, "not long after our return. A few gentlemen accompanied us, because our speech would give us away."

It sounded like too merry a time to miss. When I agreed, I was offered a selection of clothing, and chose a costume similar to the queen's. Mary Beaton was thrilled, as my taking part meant she could wear a plain gown with the other Maries. The queen and I swaggered about in our high boots, laughing at our dashing appearance.

An escort waited in the stables. When I saw Will Hawkins among them, I paused. He held my horse, and looked me up and down with a disapproving line between his brows. "What would Master Lewis say?"

"He would approve," I said pertly. "Why are you here, if you do not?"

The horse shied, picking up on his mood. "Because I am sworn to watch over you. If you leave the palace, I must be there."

I touched the horse lightly with my heels and moved ahead to join Mary. Will could escort me if he must, but I would not allow him to spoil my fun.

"Where are we bound, Your Majesty?" The night air was cold on my cheeks, and I was glad of the woolen scarf included with my ensemble.

"To a tavern, *Monsieur* Lewis," she said. "Where else?"

The grooms were sleepy-eyed when we handed over the horses, and the rest of the palace was quiet as we made our way back to the royal apartments. Though the queen's spirits were still high, she yawned behind her hand. I quickly resumed my own clothes and bade them good night.

Will waited outside the door. "It's past curfew."

"So?" I was too tired for politeness. The corridor was dark between widely-spaced torches, and I kept one hand on his arm, hoping he was more sure-footed than I was.

"I can't believe you did that."

How tiresome he was being. "The queen may do as she wishes, and she requested my company."

A flare of light showed his disapproving expression. "But to dress as men—"

I stopped. "Did we shock you? Are you so delicate?"

"I am not shocked," Will said stiffly. "Surprised, perhaps, that women can behave in such a manner." His mouth worked as he tried to express his outrage without offending. "You rode astride."

"And have done, since I was a child." I walked on. "Robin sees no harm in it."

He caught up. "It is unfeminine."

I laughed, and spun so my skirts brushed against his legs. "Am I unfeminine?"

"No," he said. "You are not."

My spinning, and the amount of ale I had consumed at the tavern, unbalanced me, and I tripped over a raised flagstone.

Will caught me before I fell. For a moment, he held my arm, then he drew me to the side of the hall, until my back was up against the softness of an unseen tapestry. "Margaery," he said thickly. "I never meant to do this, but—"

He pulled me close, and his mouth came down over mine. It was pleasant, but when he tried to deepen the kiss, I twisted away.

"I'm sorry." He still held my upper arm. "I've thought about that for so long."

I pulled free, cursing the darkness that kept me from seeing his face. "I'm Robin's wife."

"I know." Will's voice was muffled, but full of miserable awareness. "I'm sorry."

"We won't speak of it." I moved away. If I had to find my chamber alone, then I would.

"But Margaery—" He caught at my shoulder again, and without thinking, I swung. My hand connected with some portion of his face. He gasped, and I took the opportunity to run.

When Will appeared the following day, he had a stunning black eye.

I hadn't meant to hit him so hard. It was dark, and he'd startled me, and the exhilaration from my ride made me react more strongly than I otherwise would have.

Considering the state I was in, it was as likely I could have responded to his kiss until we were discovered or he worked up the nerve to carry it further. Then what would I have done? Will had always seen my behavior as suspect, and he took my new, strange confidence as encouragement; I would have to apologize.

"*Monsieur* Hawkins, your poor face!" It was pretty Mary Beaton, fluttering around Will in a way that would make Ambassador Randolph quite jealous. "Marie, look at poor *Monsieur* Hawkins, he is injured."

He looked miserable, both with himself and with the unwanted female attention.

"Didn't you see?" I got between the Maries and my admirer. "There was a man making lewd comments when we left the tavern. Master Hawkins defended our honor."

That explained his black eye, but it gave them even more reason to coo over him.

After that, he kept his distance, but when I attended Mary's evening entertainments, he was always there. I danced, and he watched. I sang to Marie Fleming's lute, and he watched. I practiced archery with the queen, and Will Hawkins watched.

"Really, *Madame* Lewis, he is quite pathetic," the queen said. "You should kiss him, and end his misery."

The Maries laughed, a ripple of merriment that spread from one to the other.

I made a French gesture. "I have a husband, Your Majesty, with whom I am content."

"But he is in London. *Monsieur* Hawkins is attractive—in an English way." Smiling impishly, she added, "I prefer a taller man, myself, and more handsome."

Mary Stuart wouldn't have an easy time finding a man to look up to, and she did not have a William Cecil to locate suitable candidates.

Mary was occupied with her council, and I had gone to the gardens with her ladies to enjoy the last of the good weather. Will stood off to one side, looking across at the castle looming on its hill.

"I need a word with Master Hawkins," I said to the Maries. "I'll be back."

"Kiss him for me!" one said and the others erupted in giggles.

"No, for me!"

I joined him at the wall. "May we speak?"

He turned, startled by my quiet approach. "If you like."

I seated myself on the rough stones, and waited until he'd done likewise. "I said I would not mention it, but—"

"Then please don't." His ears reddened. "I dishonored you, and myself."

I took a deep breath; he wasn't making this easy. "I think we were both overcome by the events of the evening. I bear you no ill will."

His face cleared, but he would not forgive himself so easily. "I took advantage. Master Lewis is a good friend. You'd be within your rights to tell him what I did. Perhaps you've written to him already."

I tried to imagine Robin's expression upon receiving such a letter, and remembered my first summer at court. "This is not worthy of bringing to my husband's attention."

Will's hands curled into fists. "I was tasked with watching over you," he said bitterly. "And what do I do but treat you like some common—"

"Don't say things you'll regret." Sympathy would make him believe I pitied him, and any display of kindness would work against the outrage I'd shown when I pushed him away.

"I should return to London," he said. "Ambassador Randolph can look after you well enough."

"If you go, they'll expect me to leave, too." I chewed my lip, and told Will Hawkins the truth. "I'm not ready to go back there. I never feel anything but small and stupid and childish at court. I wouldn't go back at all, except for Robin."

His blue eyes regarded me with curiosity. "But you're none of those things. You're everything Master Lewis said you were, when we rode to London together."

The women watched us from across the gardens, bright-eyed as a flock of birds.

"I wouldn't mention that ride, if I were you." I angled myself so they couldn't see my face. "I've not entirely forgiven you for that."

"Then you'll not forgive this either." He stared at the ground, his fists pressed against his thighs. "During our journey, Master Lewis asked me if I had a wife. When I said I did not, he suggested I ride north—after his death—and offer myself to you."

"He did what?" As unbelievable as it was, I could imagine Robin making the suggestion. He told me their relationship had evolved from antagonistic to something else; this seemed like something he would have said in its earlier days.

"He combined it with a request to escort Sebastian home to offer his services."

"Goodness," I said. "All these men rushing to throw themselves at my feet. Grand-mère and I wouldn't have known what to do with you."

"You speak as if we were an army, appearing on your doorstep."

I couldn't resist a smile. "That's how it must have seemed to him. If you'd come for me with an armed escort, you'd have gotten a different reception."

"What would you have done?" he scoffed. "Poured boiling oil from the roof, or is there a moat at Winterset of which I am unaware?"

"Neither." I reached under my skirt, producing from my garter the small blade Walter had given me, after I'd run away the first time. "I'd have welcomed you, plied you with ale, and slit your throat when you passed out on the hearth."

The blood drained from his face. I flipped the knife into the air and caught it by the hilt before making it disappear again.

"You are a most unusual woman." The words were dragged unwillingly from his throat. "Truly."

Chapter 41

SUSAN HAD NEVER BEEN as careful as Alice; for the first few days, I blamed her for my discomfort. Today, as my breasts also protested compression by my kirtle, I realized she was not the culprit.

"You look better in colors instead of all that black." She approached, her arms filled with my blue gown.

I wriggled, trying to find a fraction more breathing room. "We'll go back eventually," I said. "And back into mourning clothes."

"That's a right shame." She dropped the gown over my head. "Not the going back—I miss home—but that Her Majesty is afraid you ladies will outshine her. She's the queen, it don't matter how pretty you are."

"Fetch my jewelry." I dealt with my ruff, still missing Alice's light touch with the starch after all these months.

A pounding on the door made me drop my pins. I bent down, then stopped, remembering I had a maid for such things.

Susan opened the door and Leon fell into the chamber, catching himself before he sprawled on the floor. He bowed, and held out a letter. "I got here as quickly as I could, *madame*."

I drew in a sharp breath. "What has happened?"

Susan handed him a cup of ale, and he threw it back. "It's Lady Margaret."

Anselm's beautiful script was at odds with his news. "My dearest Margaery," he wrote, "if it is within your power to come home, you should do so immediately. Lady Margaret has had an attack which I believe to be her heart. She is somewhat recovered, but I think it will not last. I have sent for Master Lewis."

"I must go to Winterset," I said to anyone and no one. "Susan, send a page for Master Hawkins."

While she was gone, I questioned Leon.

"I didn't see it. I was out with Fowler." He looked as distraught as I felt. "Alice said she complained of a pain in her chest. They— Brother Anselm and Alice—got her to bed, where she has been since."

"How long ago was that?" I couldn't bear not being with her—

no matter that she had been better off without me to remind her of those she'd lost. How could I have stayed away for so long?

"Four days," he said. "I left before dawn the next morning."

Anselm said she was improved, but he would not have asked me to return if Grand-mère weren't likely to die.

"Master Hawkins is with Ambassador Randolph," Susan said, skidding through the door. "He will be here within the hour."

"That will do," I said. "I will be leaving for Winterset as soon as he is able. You will pack my things and follow along with Leon."

"Everything, mistress?" she asked. "Are we coming back?"

"Bring it all." If she recovered, I still couldn't imagine returning. I caught sight of my reflection in the glass: pale, but composed. "I must see the queen. When Master Hawkins arrives, keep him here."

Mary was more understanding of my need to depart than her cousin would have been. "You will take horses from our stables"— she beckoned to a Marie—"and a royal warrant to change as needed on your way. Do you require anything else?"

It had occurred to me, while I waited for my audience, what would be most helpful. "Your Majesty, I must reach Yorkshire in all haste. May I have the suit of clothes I wore when we went into the town?"

"Of course," she said, understanding immediately. "How are you accompanied?"

"Master Hawkins will escort me." At her questioning glance, I added, "With my servants, of course."

"Will that be sufficient? We could send several of our own men."

"Your offer is very gracious," I said, "but I believe a small party will make better time."

Susan had torn apart the chamber in preparation for packing, and Will was seated by the fire with a cup of ale, keeping well out of her way. "I am sorry to hear about your grandmother," he said. "What can I do?"

"I need to go home." I put my jewels into their casket. "I would ask that you ride with me."

"Whatever you require." Susan ran past with an armload of petticoats, and his eyes followed her. "How long until your people are ready to leave?"

"Not soon enough." I looked at the small clock on the mantel. It was Robin's; I would have to remind her to pack it. "How long will it take you to get your things?"

"You would travel alone?"

I put the clock on the table and grabbed a few books from the chest. "No," I said. "I would travel with you."

"We must at least have your servants."

I fixed him with a glare. "So we are slowed by a cart? My grandmother may be dying." My voice shook with the effort of not screaming at him. "I don't care how it looks."

"This is not what Master Lewis—"

"He asked you to watch over me. If you will not, then I will accept the queen's offer of an armed escort. I told her they were unnecessary because I thought you capable of the task."

He blanched. "I will do it, but I don't believe this is what your husband had in mind."

"I believe that is for me to interpret." I removed my cuffs and threw them on the table, threatening to undress in lieu of pitching him out. "I will meet you at the stables in half an hour."

Despite Susan's shock at my change of costume, I reached the stables before him. I carried nothing but a pack containing food and a spare shift, small enough to be tied onto the back of my saddle.

Will hurried around the corner. If I'd had it in me to laugh, his expression would have been amusing. He took in the sight of a young gentlewoman dressed in boots, gray trunk hose and doublet, with cloak over all. "You can't possibly—"

"If you're going to bleat about impropriety, I will go alone." I put my foot in the stirrup. "Explain that to my husband."

He wet his lips. "Whatever you do, see that he understands this was your idea, not mine."

I smiled thinly. "I can promise you that much."

We kept up a swift pace along the rocky coast road, stopping twice to change horses. The light was gone before five, but I insisted we continue. Every hour brought me nearer to Grand-mère.

"Where will we stay?" My legs and seat hurt from hours in the saddle, and I tried not to think about how sore I would be in the morning. Another thought I tried to push away was Will providing a similar escort to my husband three years before. How had Robin managed so many days on horseback, and then turned around and rode to Winterset to meet me?

"This is what I feared," he said. "I've no familiarity with this area. We'll have to find an inn."

"Then we will find an inn. We can manage at least another hour."

He urged his horse on, as if to accomplish the extra distance all at once. When I caught up, he said, "We'll be lucky if they have one room, much less two."

I hadn't thought that far ahead. "We can sleep in the main room, on the floor." He opened his mouth, and I added, "If you say the word 'improper' one more time, I will leave and tell my husband you abandoned me because you were afraid for your reputation."

"It is too much to ask," he said through gritted teeth, "that I be forced to sleep alongside you."

"At the risk of sounding even more heartless, this is not about you." My own grief was all my mind could encompass.

We rode in silence until finally on the track ahead I glimpsed the pendulum swing of a hanging lantern. "That looks to be an inn," I said. "Will you ask for a room, or shall I?"

"I'll do it." A boy ran out to take the horses. My thighs and back protested as I dismounted and tried to straighten up. "Rub them down and feed them well," I said. "They've had a hard ride."

"As have you, by the look of it." The boy grinned as I limped toward the door.

The main room was near-empty, a few figures slumped on benches or on the floor by the hearth. I stood near the fire, holding out my cold hands, while Will inquired about a bed for the night.

"No luck," he said, joining me. "There is food and drink, but all the rooms are taken. He won't charge extra if we sleep down here."

I was tired and hungry, and wanted nothing more than sleep. "Whatever it is, I will eat it gladly."

For all the innkeeper's apologies, the stew was flavorful and not too scant of mutton, and we had a loaf of grainy bread to split between us. As I wiped my bowl with the last of it, Will squatted beside the man nearest the fire. I could not hear their words, but after a moment, the fellow got up and moved.

"You sleep there," Will said. "I'll sleep facing the room."

I finished chewing. "You didn't tell him, did you?"

"I said you were my young brother, and prone to catarrh." He shrugged. "That and a coin bought his cooperation."

Will made a pad out of his cloak, and I stretched out, using mine as a cover. "Won't you be cold?"

"I'll manage," he said brusquely. "I'll not sleep, anyway."

"You'd better." The fire had burned down, but the embers still gave off more warmth than I'd felt in twelve hours. "You'll do me no good if you drop from exhaustion."

We left before it was light, dried meat and another loaf tucked into my pack, while Will carried a large flask of ale. "With all this, we shouldn't have to stop until evening," I said, "except to change horses."

"At least you have pity for them."

I gave him a sideways glance, but refrained from speaking. He was right, but all I could think of was getting to Grand-mère in time. When she died, I would have no family left.

I would have Robin, of course, and if I did not cause myself to miscarry by riding like an Amazon, there would soon be a child. I could not think of that now. I'd lost my little boy after doing everything right: no relations, no riding, no dancing. Now, I was frightened, which everyone knew affected a babe in the womb, and would ride hard for at least two days more before reaching Winterset.

Closing my eyes, I said a prayer that this loss would not be as devastating, and fixed my eyes on the road.

The rain began in the late afternoon, lightly at first, spattering the ground and pelting the brims of our hats. Before too long, the ditches on either side of the road ran with water, and fading sunlight reflected off puddles in the deep wheel-ruts. Wary of the soft ground, my horse stepped daintily, up to his fetlocks in muck.

"We should stop," Will shouted. "Let the storm pass."

The fields on either side were autumn-barren, with no buildings in sight. I shook my head, unwilling to go back. "It's not so bad."

"It will be," he said shortly. "If we don't turn back, we could be stuck out here."

A gust of wind struck us like a blow, and I caught my hat with one hand as I juggled the reins with the other. "No."

The horses became nervous and difficult to handle, picking their way carefully, avoiding stones and hidden obstructions, slipping and righting themselves again and again. We would never get there at this pace.

The rain redoubled, sluicing down from a sky gone the color of slate. My cloak and the suit underneath were soaked through, swaddling me in layers of cold, wet wool. Visibility was reduced to almost nothing.

"This is foolhardy." Will's face was obscured by the rain pouring from his hat. "We can't go on like this."

I was about to agree when he abruptly vanished, his horse sliding over the grassy verge and into the ditch below. "Will!"

I leaped down, nearly falling myself as the mud sucked at my boots. His horse scrambled up onto the road, spattering filth everywhere, and I grabbed its reins. "Stand," I said hopefully and jumped down to look for Will, who had not risen with his horse.

A muffled groan reached my ears, and I inched through the wet brush until it flattened beneath his body. Squatting down, I patted the air until I found him.

"Are you all right?" What if he'd broken a leg? What if the horse was lame? It was pitch dark, I could see nothing, and the man who was supposed to be guiding me was lying in a ditch—all because of my reckless insistence on riding through a storm.

We wouldn't be found before morning. The fields around us were stripped bare. No one with any sense would be out in this weather. Having no sense, I had possibly killed Will Hawkins from sheer stubbornness.

"Will…" I shifted, trying to get closer. "Can you move?"

"No," he said, winded. "You're standing on my arm."

I stepped backward, slipped, and fell on my rump. If there had been a part of me that wasn't wet, it was now. "You're alive." Tears spilled over, tracking through the dirt on my face.

"Apparently so." He thrashed, spattering more mud. "Pull me up."

For the next two hours, we led the horses to avoid any more mishaps. My clothes stiffened in the cold, and my teeth chattered. I tried not to let Will see.

The storm passed, but we did not find a stopping place until after midnight. Sitting on the bench, my head resting on my folded arms, I anticipated another night on the floor.

Will put a cup in front of me. "There's no food left, but they have a room."

I drained the ale in one swallow, and lurched to my feet. "Does it have a bed?"

"I would assume so."

Climbing the uneven stairs, we found an open door. There was indeed a bed, narrow and lumpy, but better than floorboards and wet wool. As I dropped, exhausted, onto the mattress, Will raised his candle. "I'll come for you at dawn."

I took off my hat, and the coif underneath, letting my braids fall to my shoulders. "Don't be silly. Stay here."

"I couldn't." The light wavered.

Too tired for manners, I said frankly, "I'm not asking you to share my bed, but it's ridiculous for you to suffer more discomfort on my behalf than necessary."

He leaned against the door. "I would suffer more here than downstairs."

"It is your place to guard me." I removed my knife from its sheath and eased off my boots. "I'm going to sleep, and I would feel better if you did the same."

"If you insist." Will removed his cloak, folding it before the threshold. He blew out the candle and the room dimmed, a rectangle of light still visible around the badly hung door.

The blanket was scratchy, but blessedly dry. I pulled it up to my chin. "I don't mean to be difficult." There was no response from the darkness. "If you care for me, you must accept me as I am."

His breathing had not altered; he was awake. "It's the caring I can't accept."

"We can't help who we love."

"And you love him, don't you?" Will's voice was tight, waiting for the answer he knew would come.

"I do." I rolled onto my side, so I could speak in his direction. "If I were unmarried, it might be different."

There was a sound of rending cloth as he threw the cloak aside. "This is unbearable."

"Wait." I sat up, struggling against clothing which clung to the blanket. What was there to say to this good man I could not love? "I'm sorry."

The faint light was blotted out as he came closer. "I should not put my feelings on you."

"I'm grateful to you." It was as dark as the road, but again I found his hand. "I should have said so already." He went still as a statue, except for his hand, which trembled. "We said this before, but after tonight, let us never speak of this again."

"I would be happy to remain mute on the subject for the rest of my life." He sounded on the verge of either laughter or tears.

"Would it be better or worse if you kissed me?" In his place, I would feel worse, but it might balance his misguided kiss at Holyrood. If it relieved some of the pressure he'd put on himself, I would manage it. I'd managed worse.

He exhaled, almost laughing. "It would make it so much worse. Please kiss me, Margaery, and I will be your devoted, silent slave forever."

"I don't want a slave," I said, "silent or otherwise."

Will knelt on the rushes. I reached out with my free hand until I found his chest, and leaned forward. Our noses bumped, and he shifted so our lips touched. He tasted of ale, and seemed barely to breathe as we kissed.

"That's enough, now." I drew back, more regretful than he would ever know.

Stumbling to his feet, he opened the door to a wave of voices from below. "I'll come for you in the morning."

Chapter 42

"IF THE ROADS CONTINUE this easy, we should reach Whitby by dark." Will smiled, more relaxed than I'd ever seen him.

"That's good." I had lain awake until I heard the maids get up to do the fires in the predawn darkness. My head rang with exhaustion, worry, and guilt.

I'd never considered being unfaithful—not even with Edmund Morven, though he had tempted me sorely. Why now, when I loved Robin and was carrying his child, did I encourage a man I thought of as my husband's puppy? Worse still, why did my body respond?

My eyes burned, and I rubbed them with the back of my hand. It wasn't Will or even my own behavior that upset me, but the thought of losing my grandmother. I had used Will to steady myself. It wasn't fair to him, or to Robin. I cleared my throat. "Will… I know we said we would never mention this."

"And so I shall not."

"Well, I shall, just once more." I wound the reins around my hand. "I didn't mean to encourage you. I would never be unfaithful to Robin."

His smile was sad, but genuine. "I know."

He wasn't as interesting as Robin, nor as handsome as Morven or Dudley, but he was kinder than I had given him credit for being. I made a note to be nicer in the future.

The landscape became more familiar, the rugged hills smoothing into the moors of my childhood. A stiff wind kept conversation to a minimum, but the bright sky raised my spirits. At an inn outside of Hartlepool, we changed horses one last time. "It's not far now," I said. "If you want to turn back, I can make it from here."

"There's hours to go." He brought his mount close. "I'll see you home, but I think I will go back. I quite like Scotland."

I smiled at him. "And I won't be there to complicate things."

"There's that, as well." He stifled a yawn. "I'll escort you to Winterset, and spend the night, but that's all."

"Stay as long as you like." He would need more than one night to recover from this ride. "You've earned a rest, and Robin will arrive soon. I'm sure he'll want to thank you."

We rode along the coast until Winterset came into sight. If thoughts of Grand-mère hadn't pulled me forward, I would have stopped for a moment to take it in: the weathered gray stone, which made it look part of the cliff upon which it was set; the smoke drifting from the chimneys at either end. It was an isolated house: if anyone was looking, they would see us coming.

I rode through the gate with only the faintest thought of my father. He'd been gone more than two decades, and Grand-mère had been with me nearly every moment of those same twenty years. Right now, her life was more important than my father's memory.

Dickon ran from the stables at the sound of our horses, his freckled face showing no reaction at my attire. "Welcome, mistress!" He caught the reins and helped me down, steadying me when I almost fell.

"Has Master Lewis returned?"

"Not yet," he said. "But Fowler's man rode for him the same day as Leon, so he is expected."

Brushing dust from my breeches, I turned to Will. "Can you fend for yourself?"

"Of course. I'll help this young man with the horses, then come in."

"I can manage, sir." Dickon drew himself up.

"I'm sure you can," Will said genially. "But your mistress has had me on horseback for the last fourteen hours and I need to remember how to stand on my feet."

The door was unbarred, the hall deserted. A wooden bowl had been abandoned on the table, the crusted remains of pottage inside. Mouth dry with panic, I sprinted for the stairs.

"You came." Anselm was framed in the library door. "She'll be glad."

Only the thought of being too late had kept me in the saddle the last few hours. "How—?"

"She lives," he said, "but I think it will not be long before she is with God." He told me of the attacks she'd suffered—another since

Leon departed—and his certainty that it was her heart. "I've been giving her poppy syrup. It slows her heartbeat and keeps her calm."

My throat closed. "Can you keep giving it to her, if it makes her well?"

Anselm took my hand. "It doesn't make her well, child. It only keeps her alive. Do you want her like that indefinitely?"

Pain clawed at my innards. Yes, I wanted her alive indefinitely, because I didn't know how to be without her. I was a selfish, terrible woman who was willing to let my grandmother suffer because I was afraid.

Anselm could not know how terrible I was. I lifted my chin and forced the pain down, the way she had taught me.

"Of course not," I said, my voice even.

"I'll go up and prepare her. The surprise might…" His voice trailed off.

As he made his way upstairs, I went into the chapel. It was damp and dusky as a barn, no light striking the colored glass. The cold didn't matter, because it was a godly place, and I could settle my mind before facing what awaited me in the bedchamber above.

The stone floor was uneven. I missed my skirts, which could be rolled into a pad for my knees. Lowering my head, I let my mind drift until the door opened.

"Mistress!"

"Alice!" I embraced her, my tears overflowing as they could not with Anselm. "How is she? How are you?"

Her face was drawn, but she mustered a smile. "She's waiting for you." As we stepped into the candlelit hall, her eyes widened. "Did you ride all the way dressed like that?"

I looked down at my mud-encrusted boots. "If I'd dressed any other way, I would still be on the road."

"Lady Margaret can wait a moment more." She took my arm in a forceful grip. "Seeing you like this will give her another attack."

Her distaste was visible as she peeled off my filthy clothes, dropping them on the floor. It grew worse when she saw the state of my shift. "You stink," she said plainly, and left me naked and shivering while she went for water.

Ten minutes later, I again resembled Lady Margaret's dutiful granddaughter: mostly clean, dressed in a plain gray kirtle, my hair combed and pinned in a knot. I hesitated at her door, a tightness in my chest which made it difficult to breathe.

Beneath her habitual faint rose scent, the room held a musty odor of sickness, a smell that had nothing to do with Grand-mère. She had never been ill. Between us, we'd nursed my grandfather and Walter several times, but neither of us ever got sick. This wasn't an illness, of course. If Anselm was correct, her body had just caught up with her fading mind.

A branched candleholder stood on a chest inside the door, but her great bed was shadowed by its heavy curtains. Anselm sat on a stool at the bedside, a rosary dangling from his fingers. He stood at my approach. "She's asleep, but she knows you're here."

I kissed his cheek. "I'll sit with her now. What do I need to know?"

"There was another episode at dinner time." His voice was low. "She's weak, but her mind is in good order."

I looked up at him through a wash of tears. Alice said he'd barely left the chamber since Grand-mère was stricken. "Thank you."

His fingertips brushed my forehead. "Would you like to be alone?"

"For a while, yes."

A mass of embroidered cushions supported a body which had grown frail in my absence. Her skin was like parchment, her plump cheeks sunken and scored with lines of pain. A thin gray braid had escaped her ruffled bed cap and I tucked it in. She never liked people seeing her hair.

"Grand-mère?" I leaned close to her ear. "I'm here."

There was a slight change in her breathing. I perched on the edge of the bed, her hand in mine, and told her how much I'd missed her. When her eyes remained closed, I continued on, telling her of my journey with Will, and of a tall, red-haired queen who rode like a man. I told her of Scotland, and described royal palaces and entertainments until exhaustion claimed me.

When I awoke, the fire had been stirred up and there was a blanket around my shoulders, but the room was empty. I shook away the cobwebs of sleep and saw Grand-mère's eyes were open.

"My little one. You came."

"How do you feel?" It was enough that she recognized me.

A down-turning smile. "Like a fool. Everyone waiting on me."

"You've taken care of us, your whole life." I blinked hard. "It's your turn."

Her eyelids fluttered, and I thought she had fallen asleep again. "Are you happy, my child?" she asked, almost inaudibly.

That her first waking thoughts were of my happiness was no surprise; she had always been my champion, even as she pushed me to do better. "Yes, Grand-mère."

She patted my hand. "And your husband, he is good to you?"

"I couldn't ask for better." I wanted Robin to come; she wasn't going to last long, and I needed him with me.

"He's a good man." Her voice was no more than a whisper. "He cares for this place." She held out a hand; of her jewels, only the marriage band remained, loose on her finger. "I wish I had your grandfather's ring for him."

"What ring?"

She was silent, building up the strength to speak. "You were too young to remember." Tears spilled down her soft cheeks. "It should have gone to your father, but…"

But my father was killed. "Did Grandfather sell it?"

"It was lost." She squeezed my fingers. "Did Anselm leave the poppy syrup?"

I kissed her knuckles. "It's right here." I stirred a dose into a cup of watered wine and held it to her lips.

She drank, and sagged against the cushions. "Will you be all right without me?"

If only I could will her back to health! "You need rest, that's all."

One eye opened. "I'm not leaving this room again. I've accepted it. You need to."

"I've lost everyone else." I took a breath, shoved my panic further down. "I can't lose you, too."

"You've got Master Lewis." She pleated the bedcovers between her fingers. "Lean on him."

I rested my head in my hands. "I don't know if I can. I've been a disappointment."

"Any woman can lose a baby." Her palm stroked my hair, light as an angel's wing. "Do not blame yourself."

Anselm had said her faculties were in order; mention of the baby confirmed they were, at least for the moment. "I did, for a long time," I said. "But I know better now."

"Good." Pain flickered across her face. "Blaming yourself never helps. I blamed myself for Ralph's death, and he was a man grown. If a wife and child couldn't keep him from joining that mob and getting himself killed, there was nothing I could have done."

I raised my head. "I thought you supported the pilgrimage?"

"As a Catholic, I supported it." She choked, and reached again for the cup. "Not as a mother. When you have a child, you can see both sides."

I understood how much I took after her: observing others to give them what they needed. After my father's death, she had been a balm for our broken family, keeping my grandfather upright; tempering my mother's loud grief; preventing Walter from following in his brother's footsteps. I needed nothing from her but comfort, which she gave in abundance.

It was Robin who made me see that in anticipating the needs of others, I never gave myself the chance to realize my own feelings.

"You've done so much for me," I said. "Without you, we wouldn't have survived. And if you hadn't stood up for me, I'd be married to some awful Frenchman."

"You would have managed." She touched my chin with cold fingers. "We always manage."

"But you gave me the chance for real happiness."

"You've been separated for some time." My surprise must have shown, for she continued, "I do remember things, I just can't always find my way back."

I took her unresisting hand. "I love you no matter who you are, Grand-mère."

She sighed heavily. "It feels as though clouds are gathering in my head."

I kissed her fingers. "We've been apart for months now, you're right." I was unable to explain my reasons for staying—if they even mattered.

"But you're here," she whispered. "If your man comes, do you go with him?"

The pain of missing Robin was suddenly as sharp as the pain that had drawn me to Yorkshire. "Yes."

"That is enough."

"There is one more thing," I said. "I'm pregnant again."

She gasped. It turned into a cough and I held her as she wheezed, feeling the sharp bones of her shoulder blades. "I am happy for you," she said when she was able. "I pray for you always, but now I will pray for the child." Her fingers waved, and I passed her the rosary from the bedside table.

"Pray later," I suggested. "You should rest."

She laced the beads through her fingers. "I'll be resting for all eternity, soon enough."

Chapter 43

A LANTERN BURNED IN the front window, casting a faint glow over a pile of rags on the hearth. As I approached, the pile snorted and rolled over, one arm emerging from beneath its cloak: Will. There were any number of places he could have chosen to sleep; by trying to make no fuss, he would be in the way as soon as the maids attempted to kindle the morning fire.

The kitchen was warmer and marginally brighter, as its fire was never permitted to go out. I slipped past Mistress Dunham and the maids on their sleeping mats, and snatched a loaf from the table. There was usually cheese under a cloth, but the platter was empty.

Retreating with the bread, I ducked into the hall and walked straight into Robin.

I caught myself before I cried out. Robin pulled me into my parlor and closed the door behind us.

"Seb is in the library." He tossed the bread aside and gathered me close. "When did you get here?"

I rested my cheek against his shoulder. "Just past seven. What about you?"

"Not ten minutes ago. Lady Margaret?"

"She's dying." I took a shaky breath. "I'm glad you're here."

His arms tightened. "My God, I've missed you."

I leaned against him, willing for the moment that he should bear my burdens. "I've missed you, too."

He struck a flint. When the candles were lit, he led me to my seat. "I'll be right back," he said, passing a hand over my hair.

I slumped down, so tired I was boneless, and yet overwhelmingly happy to see him. If only we could stay in my snug parlor until everything was better. We could not, but we could stay for a little while.

Robin returned with two glasses of wine, handing one to me. "You look as if you need it."

"It was a long ride." I drank deeply.

"I saw the horses. Whose are they?"

"Queen Mary gave us horses from her stables." I covered a yawn.

"We changed several times a day to get here as quickly as we did."

Robin put his glass aside. "That snoring bundle on the hearth is Will Hawkins, I assume?"

I nodded. "Poor man, you did ask him to look after me."

His indrawn breath turned into a laugh, and he responded in a credible imitation of Will. "But that's not proper."

"Not in the slightest." I reached for his hand. "Especially when he saw my riding clothes."

"You do realize he's in love with you?" His voice was rough, as it often was. It had been damaged by a fever in his youth, and showed his weariness even when he did not.

"It's your fault." Will didn't have the imagination to fall in love with me without Robin having first suggested it.

"How is it my fault when another man falls in love with my wife?"

I shifted from the chair to his lap, leaning against him and letting his breathing soothe me. "Because you told him if you were executed, he should marry me."

"I only half meant it." Robin linked his arms around me. "Can't he find his own woman?"

"There were a few volunteers in Edinburgh, but he saw none of them." I ran my fingertips over his forearm, across the light, rusty hair, and the faint spattering of freckles.

"I wouldn't have looked at them either." He drew me closer.

I welcomed the familiar bony contours of his body. "You're biased."

He pressed his lips to my temple. "I am indeed."

Alice found us there, sound asleep, dawn leaking in around the shutters. "Welcome home, Master Lewis," she said. "If you'll come to the hall, Mistress Dunham has laid breakfast."

"How is she?" I stifled a groan; my hips and thighs ached, and there was a sharp pain in my tailbone.

"Much the same. She was sleeping when I left her."

Robin winced as he maneuvered himself out of the chair. I turned to help; if the ride caused me pain, he must feel far worse. "I'm fine." He lurched to one side, obviously not fine.

"Be quiet and lean on me." I put my arm around him, but was relieved by the sudden appearance of Sebastian, whose sense of Robin's needs was uncanny.

The table was full, a welcome sight after its barren appearance upon my arrival. Anselm and Fowler were talking quietly. Will was alone, and Robin slid in beside him. I sat with Alice, and tried not to listen to Robin's conversation while Seb caught me up on the gossip.

"Sir Edward's wife is in London," he said. "She sends her greetings."

"I hope to see her soon." It was not her fault she had been given custody of me.

Seb cut a hunk of bread for me, and one for Alice. "I'm not sure how long she will be there. She invited the master to live with Sir Edward, rather than alone at court."

Lady Joan's criticism stung. "He's not alone. He has you."

Sebastian could make me feel like an utter ninny with just a glance. "I'm not the same as a wife."

The day passed, and still she lived. There was another attack at midday, her whole body rigid with pain, and afterward, she was unable to speak. I held her hand and talked to her, Robin beside me. Occasionally I prayed—more for her sake than my own; if she could hear, she would be pleased. Robin followed along. I'd never heard him pray before.

"I feel as though she's waiting for permission."

"Will you tell her, or are you not ready to let her go?" His hand on my shoulder was a comfort.

I tilted my head back against his arm, his linen sleeve rough against my cheek. "I'll never be ready, but I can't bear to see her like this."

"Should I stay?"

Having a witness would only inhibit words that were already impossible to say. "Could you wait outside?"

"Of course." He kissed my hair and was gone.

"It's time, Grand-mère." I sat on the edge of the bed, stroking her cheek. "I'll be all right, you've made sure of that." A tear rolled down my cheek, as I contemplated life without her. "And I have Robin. He'll help me be strong." She would never see me as a mother; never get to hold her great-grandchild. "If it's a boy, I'm going to name him Ralph."

Her fingers were icy, her chest barely rising with the breath that kept her alive. Bending close to her ear, I whispered, "You have my permission, Grand-mère. Go with God, and remember I love you."

I closed my eyes, seeing her as she had been over the years: the sturdy, red-cheeked grandmother of my childhood; the great lady she had become in France; the ghost who had appeared in her place after Walter and Grandfather died. And this last incarnation, back at her beloved Winterset, happier and stronger than I had seen her in years—until her mind failed, and then her heart.

"You loved so hard," I whispered. "You broke your heart from loving so much."

Her breathing grew shallower.

"Robin!" I wanted him here when she left, so that my care, such as it was, would pass from her to him.

He was at my side in an instant. "Is she...?"

"Very soon, I think." I drew him down beside me. "I told her it would be all right."

Anselm and the others entered quietly, gathering at the foot of the bed. Their murmured prayers filled the air.

"And so it will." Robin took her hand. "Lady Margaret, I swear I will care for Margaery for the rest of my life, and make sure she is safe beyond that. I thank you every day for entrusting her to me."

Her breath hitched, then stopped. The room was suddenly very empty.

I kissed her forehead, then moved to open the shutters. The moon, waxing gibbous, flooded through the casement, so bright I could see the pansies stitched on the cushion behind her head.

Robin wrapped his arms around me. "Are you all right, darling girl?"

"I am," I said. "I will be."

There were fresh linens on the bed, and a jug of rosemary and dried flowers on the mantel, the scent sharp as grief. A small fire burned, enough to take the chill from the corners of the room.

"Do you want wine?"

"No." I rolled my neck and the small bones popped. "Has Will gone?"

"Not yet." Robin's fingers dug into my shoulders, eliciting a sigh of relief. "He will stay to pay his respects to Lady Margaret. And to you."

Fowler would ride into Whitby in the morning to make arrangements with the priest. "It may be a few days."

"He'll wait." There was a smile in Robin's voice, but he would not tease me, not now. "What can I do?"

"Just be here." I undid the knots at the top of my kirtle. "If I don't get out of this, I will scream."

"Let me." He helped me to undress, then combed my hair. "Are you tired?"

I sat on the edge of the bed and dropped backward like a felled tree. "Exhausted, and wide awake. You?"

"The same." He shed his own clothes. "Get under the covers. You'll catch a chill."

"I will, if you open the shutters. I want to hear the sea."

He did as I asked, then blew out the candle. The moon had moved and the window was no more than a lighter square in the darkness, but I could hear the rush of the waves and something shifted inside me. I was home.

"Come." He fluffed the pillow. "Lie back."

"No." I turned to him. "The antidote to death is life. It's love. I would like to be loved by my husband, to remind me I'm alive."

He put his arm around me. "I heard what you said to Lady Margaret."

"Mmm?" I burrowed against his neck, inhaling the scent of soap; he'd found time, at some point, to wash.

"You're with child?" He played with my braid. "Is it true, or were you just telling her what she wanted to hear?"

"There wasn't time to tell you." I turned and kissed him. "Until now."

He returned the kiss, but his hand remained on my hair. "Then we'd best not. Look what happened last time."

I heard his words, and I heard something clearer, inside myself. *He was wrong to be afraid.* "Robin, I rode all the way from Edinburgh, and I feel fine—or I will, in a few days. I didn't ride at all last time, and still lost the baby."

"We were so careful," he said. "There must be more we can do."

He felt the same guilt; I hadn't understood.

"I want this baby," I said, "but I will not live in fear. When it becomes uncomfortable, I'll stop riding." Throwing the covers back, I knelt beside him on the feather mattress. "And I'll not be deprived of my husband, now that I've got him back."

"I've missed you." He caressed my face.

"In your bed, and out?" I tucked two fingers into the front of his shirt. "Is that what you meant to say?"

"In a manner of speaking, yes."

"I won't be ruled by fear," I told him, drawing my shift over my head. "I need this—I need you."

He reached for me. "Then we shall sink or swim together."

Chapter 44

ANSELM AND FOWLER SETTLED matters with the priest. "He asked if she's to be put in the family tomb," Fowler said, red-eyed with grief and fury. "He dared to say she kept to the old faith in her heart, the heretic bastard."

"Many people keep to the old faith," Robin said. "I'll ride in and speak to him after dinner."

"There is no need," Anselm said placidly. "He saw sense, in the end."

I did not inquire as to how the priest's mind had been changed. Anselm was religious, but he was a man, and men had ways I did not care to investigate. Still numb, but feeling more like myself since I'd risen from our bed, I leaned against Robin's shoulder while they discussed arrangements for the funeral.

The estate carpenter delivered the coffin, stopping to pay his respects. It was a beautiful object of smooth and shining oak, but I could barely bring myself to look at it, or thank him. The coffin—and Grand-mère—would rest in the hall until her final journey to the church.

"Do you want to ride?" Robin was at my shoulder; he had been there constantly since we got up.

My hips and back still hurt; I did not think I could mount, much less ride. "I'd rather walk."

Now that the leaves had fallen, Winterset was clearly visible from Bowman's Hill. I hitched myself up onto the stones, my legs suddenly unwilling to bear my weight.

"Once everything is…settled, will you come back to London?" Robin's gaze was fixed on the house.

"Yes." I had no wish to remain in Yorkshire without my grandmother. "Will Anselm be all right on his own?"

"He is rarely lonely," Robin said, "but I'll ask if he'd like to come with us."

The scent of smoke carried up from the cottages; it made me think of what might be cooking over all those fires, and my stomach rumbled. "If he did, we wouldn't have space at court."

Robin nodded. "Lady Joan suggested we share Ned's house."

"Would we have our own rooms?" It would be unbearable if we had no private space. "I have no objection, so long as I have a chamber where Ned is not."

Laughing, he said, "I think that can be arranged." He sobered. "And it's not a far ride from Whitehall, should you decide to return to court."

Did I want to go back to the queen's service? It might be different, after Edinburgh. Perhaps I wouldn't feel so squashed and insignificant among the other ladies—after all, I'd ridden the streets with the queen of Scotland. In breeches. That had to count for something.

Word had spread, and a surprising number of people came, from Whitby and the houses hidden away on the moors, to pay their final respects to Lady Margaret Preston. I stayed close to Robin, allowing him to speak for me.

The squat church tower seemed out of proportion to its location, but perhaps it was just that the dramatic ruins of Whitby Abbey loomed almost directly overhead, dwarfing the living church into insignificance.

St. Mary's churchyard went right to the cliff's edge, but here, unlike at Winterset, the cliff meandered toward the town along several steep paths. It was dizzying, standing there and seeing the tiled roofs of the houses so close below, while the autumn sky met the sea in an almost invisible line.

Inside, the church was dim, light filtering in through narrow lancet windows. I walked without plan to the Preston memorial in the transept, resting my palms against the white marble. The names stretched up to the ceiling, the carving faint with age. My father was the most recent addition, the dates 1512-1539 beneath his name.

I pressed my fingers to the carved letters and said a prayer for his peaceful rest, and his forgiveness.

Throughout the service, my thoughts strayed again and again to my father, as I realized I was as old now as he had been at the time of his death. He hadn't been so clearly in my mind since the day I told Robin about the execution. Closing my eyes, I saw him before me—not that last day, but as the towering figure of my childhood, the man who made everything right. His hair was like mine: dark brown and straight. His eyes were dark, too, but there was a joyous light in them. He smiled easily, and made my mother laugh when no one else could.

When he died, everyone wept; the tenants and estate workers had crowded the hall when his body was brought home. I remembered little of it—not knowing I'd seen him die, my grandparents thought to keep the worst of it from me. I crept downstairs, determined to say my own farewell, and found Walter asleep by the coffin, worn out from crying.

Grandfather had been hard on Walter; he wanted to keep his younger son from going astray, as my father had, but all it did was drive a wedge between them. I watched the distance grow between them, helpless to stop it, loving them both so fiercely.

I was fortunate in my family. While they were mine, they were everything, and even when lost—

It was lost.

Grand-mère's words came back to me, and I suddenly remembered the ring. It had always been on Grandfather's finger, a thick band with a jet stone. The only time he took it off was when he was working in the stables, so it wouldn't get caught in the harness.

Memory jolted me upright, and Robin looked at me, concern in his eyes. I shook my head—*I'm all right*—and he returned his judgmental gaze to the priest, who was maundering on about hellfire, a topic wholly inappropriate for a woman as devout as my grandmother.

He had been in the stables the day my father was taken. I could see him, coming across the yard to reason with the men. After they rode off, he'd gone inside, and while my mother and grandmother were wailing, I ran to the stables to hide.

Will Hawkins left the next morning. I thanked him for his trouble on my behalf, and he shrugged it off, lighter, somehow, since that fraught moment at the inn. He and Robin shared one of those odd, manly embraces which consisted mostly of pounding each other on the back, and then he rode away.

I thought Robin would ask me to ride with him, but he said he needed to go into Whitby. Once he was gone, I ventured up the twisting stairs to the attic. When I first came home, being there had bothered me, but I didn't understand why and had disregarded it in my nervousness over seeing my husband again.

Now, crossing the space, I knew what it was. I stooped as the ceiling slanted down, the rough floorboards creaking. In the corner was a board that could be raised by a little girl's fingers. Mine were too large now, so I had to use my knife to pry it up. Thrusting my hand into the dark, I retrieved a packet wrapped in a grubby kerchief. I had no recollection of leaving it there; perhaps I had locked the memory away, as I had so many others.

Unfolded, the square of linen revealed a cache of small Margaery's treasures: two long curls of birch bark, which shattered at my touch; a coil of embroidery silk, faded rusty-brown; a tiny carved bird; and my grandfather's ring.

My fingers closed around the heavy gold band, and I remembered the furor of its disappearance. The men who took my father were blamed, but no accusation could be made for fear of making things worse.

Grandfather had left it on a nail in the stable, and I had taken it. I didn't know why. My childhood behavior was unfathomable now, as the world had been unfathomable then. It was his; I was afraid; I took it.

Robin shook himself like a dog, water spraying everywhere. "Why do I love this place so much when it never stops raining?"

"It doesn't rain all the time," I protested, though it often did.

"Just when I want to go somewhere."

I lifted off his wet cloak. "Perhaps it's trying to keep you here."

"You may be right." He touched my cheek with chilly fingers. "Someday, hundreds of years from now, they'll find me encased in Yorkshire mud and think me a superior example of my kind."

Throwing the cloak over a bench by the fire, I stretched to kiss him. "Maybe not a superior example."

"A fine example, then," he said. "Is that better?"

"But a superior husband." I looked at him. "Where were you this morning?"

"I went to see the priest." He peeled off his damp doublet. "He needed further instruction about the tomb."

How hard was it to have a name carved onto the marble slab? "What else is there?"

Robin put his arm around me. "I told him to add your grandfather's and uncle's names and dates. So they're all together."

Because of my grandfather, I could list my Preston ancestors back to the time of King John, while Robin didn't even know his parents' names. Nevertheless, he understood how important the tomb at St. Mary the Virgin was to me.

Chapter 45

NED'S HOUSE ON LOTHBURY Street was larger than I remembered, but his unusual neighbors were not so easily forgotten. The street was home to several small foundries, and the din, as we brought our caravan to a stop in front of the house, was alarming.

"Why would he choose to live here?" I asked Robin, flinching at a particularly loud clang.

"It's close to Austin Friars," he explained. "I'm not sure if it's sentimentality or laziness."

Ned was there to welcome us, throwing open the door and ushering us inside. As our things were brought in, I looked around the hall. "If you have all this space, why did you spend so much time with us?"

"This is just a house without my family." He shrugged. "You made a home at court."

I glanced over my shoulder. The servants were ranged behind me, waiting to be released. "It'll be a home soon enough."

The possessions of the Pickering family were spread throughout the house, but with Ned's permission, Leon and Sebastian shifted them all to rooms on the two lower floors. Robin and I, along with our people, would share the top floor, under the attics.

We would have a private parlor, with a spacious bedchamber beyond. On the other side of the central hall were several smaller rooms. I chose one for the nursery, and Robin rightly insisted Sebastian have a chamber of his own where he could sleep and work on his maps.

"Susan and I can bed down in the nursery," Alice said. "The cradle fits perfectly, mistress."

I hesitated when Leon asked if he should bring it down from the attic. It felt almost unlucky, when I'd wanted so badly to use it the first time. "Superstitious nonsense," I heard Grand-mère declare. "Your father would want it to be used."

Alice stowed my nightdresses and shifts in a chest, sprinkling lavender between the layers of folded linens. "Mistress, did Susan get up to anything in Scotland?"

"What do you mean?" I looked up from my jewel case.

"Have you looked at her? She runs from the room at the scent of meat, and she's on the jordan more than she's not."

"Oh, lord." Susan had been taken in by some of the Scottish servants—very kindly, I had thought. "Call her in."

Looking at the girl, I didn't even have to ask. Her laces strained, her red cheeks were rounder than ever, and the brown hair at the front of her coif was as glossy as Artemis's flank. "Did you leave anyone special behind in Scotland, Susan? I never thought to ask."

She clasped her hands under her apron. "Not especially, mistress."

"Not even the man"—I nodded at her belly—"who put that there?"

"Is it noticeable, mistress?" she asked, looking down at herself.

"It is," I said. "Does the man know?"

Cornered, she looked around. Alice stared back at her, hard-eyed. "I'm not certain."

"You're not certain he knows?" My maid was being sterner with Susan than I was.

"I'm not certain who he is," she confessed, and put her apron over her face.

Sitting her down before the cold fireplace, I asked, "Were you attacked?"

The apron fell. "Attacked, mistress?"

I took a deep breath. "Did some man have his way with you?"

"Well, yes." A tremulous smile touched her lips. "But not without me inviting him, if that's your meaning."

"You daft wench!" Alice slapped her so hard she fell over. "You were to serve Mistress Margaery while I stayed to care for Lady Margaret, and you're off getting into trouble instead of doing your work."

Susan rubbed her cheek. "I did it on my own time."

Alice's hand twitched. I shook my head; we needed to deal with this situation, not make it worse. "Was it just the one time?"

She shook her head, her eyes gleaming. "Those Scotsmen are a bonny lot."

The extent of my obliviousness spread before me. "Was there… more than one?"

Her grin widened. "Four. Or was it five?" She ticked them on her fingers. "Jack, from the stables. Jamie, he worked for Lady Mary Beaton. Matty was one of the guards who stood in the hall, all handsome in his tunic…"

"Stop now," Alice said. "Unless you want a proper beating."

I rose. "That's enough from both of you." My thoughts were in as much disarray as the chamber. "Alice, I'm going down. Please get this together before Master Lewis returns."

She nodded, turning from Susan without another glance. Susan looked at me. "What's to be done with me, mistress?"

It came to me, then: the solution to our problem. "You will be my baby's wet nurse," I said. "In the meantime, stay inside and keep away from anyone in breeches. Do you understand?"

Susan curtsied, stammering, "Yes, mistress, even the handsome ones."

I glared at her. "*Especially* the handsome ones."

Robin laughed far too hard when I told him we had acquired a wet nurse before our baby was halfway to being born. "It will make your life easier, should you decide to go back to Elizabeth."

"But I want to feed our baby myself."

"Then why did you ask her?" He put his feet up and closed his eyes, a sure sign another glass of wine was required.

I reached for the bottle. "I felt guilty—she's young, and none too bright. I should have kept a closer eye on her."

He took a long swallow. "It sounds as if she enjoyed her time in Edinburgh as much as you did."

According to Alice, who had continued her questioning after I'd gone downstairs, my baby would be born only a few weeks before Susan's. I put my hand over his. "We wouldn't be in the same state if we hadn't had some of the same pleasures."

After we were settled and Robin was satisfied the journey had not been too much for me, I accompanied him to Whitehall and presented myself to Mistress Ashley.

The presence chamber was packed with courtiers awaiting the queen's appearance. It being before ten of the clock, they had a considerable wait ahead of them, especially if she decided to walk or ride before showing herself. Nell, dazzling in black satin, was in a knot with the maids of honor, their clear voices rising to accompany a tune on the lute.

"So you've returned from bonny Scotland at last?"

I explained my attendance upon my grandmother. "We are now returned to London, though we lodge in Sir Edward Pickering's house." I looked down at my still-flat front. "Our household will increase in the spring, and it seemed practical to move before the weather grew worse."

Mistress Ashley's face creased with pleasure, though she was not ready to give in. "You are to be congratulated." Looking over her shoulder at the doors to the inner chamber, she said, "There is no place for you at the moment. We couldn't keep your position open all these months, and then to have you go into confinement…"

'All these months' was but three, and I'd gone to Scotland with the queen's own blessing. "I do not intend to go into confinement," I said. "If a position becomes available, please let me know."

She shook her head regretfully. "You are, of course, welcome in the presence chamber at any time."

It wasn't so bad, being dismissed from the queen's service; I could visit whenever I liked, see my friends, and be a part of the court without actually being at the center. It might be an improvement.

Nell flew to me when Mistress Ashley departed for the bedchamber, responding to a muffled summons. "Are you back?"

"I am in London," I told her, "but not in the privy chambers."

"Aren't you the lucky one?" She touched her hair, done this day in tiny ringlets around her face. "Every time Her Majesty hears Queen Mary spoken of, she goes into a rage."

Elizabeth appeared moments later in a gold brocade gown thickly embroidered with roses, a gauzy lace ruff, and a ransom of pearls. She took two steps into the privy chamber, saw me, and looked away.

Had I been snubbed? I bit the inside of my cheek until it hurt. "How is your family?"

Her eyes lit up. "He is wonderful, Margaery. He is the best man ever born, and I am lucky to have him."

That raised an eyebrow; it was more the other way round, in my view, and I had been inquiring after her son. "What about Nicholas? Did he miss you?"

"He did!" She clasped her hands under her chin. "I would not have left you behind, but for them." She caught my hand. "What of my brother? I've not had a letter from him in weeks."

"I believe he is content." I told her of his escort, neglecting to mention anything about mud or breeches or kissing. "He stayed for my grandmother's burial, then returned to Edinburgh. It suits him."

Nell pouted. "I miss him—but I missed you more. Is that wrong of me?"

"Perhaps." Nell was unserious, entirely too pretty, and apparently forgetful of her child, but she had a good heart, and I'd missed her confidences.

"Were you not friends with the Maries by the time of your departure?" She waggled her fingers at Philadelphia Carey, stuck talking to an over-attentive older man.

I cast a sympathetic glance at the trapped maid of honor. I had not entirely missed the presence chamber. "Not really. The Maries belong to the queen."

The call came as I gathered myself to leave. Dorothy Bradbelt, who had just carried in the queen's dinner, came out and looked around. "Mistress Margaery," she called, "Her Majesty asks for your company."

"Now?" Elizabeth did not like people to watch her eat.

"Yes. She wishes to hear about your Scottish trip."

I passed into the privy chamber, where the queen sat at a table holding enough food to feed my entire household. She would eat little of it; she saved her appetite for sweets.

I curtsied and waited to be recognized.

Elizabeth speared a slice of duck and put it into her mouth, chewing with gusto, and reaching for the napkin held by one of the maids. She patted her lips. "So, Mistress Margaery, you have returned."

"Yes, Your Majesty."

She stabbed at another piece of meat, pausing long enough to say, "We were told of your grandmother, and are very sorry."

"Thank you. Losing her was a shock."

The queen reached a jeweled hand for an equally sparkling goblet. "She was quite elderly, was she not?"

"She was." I swallowed my hurt. "But she was my only remaining family."

The queen digested this as she continued to eat. I stood before her, my stomach quivering at the scent of so much rich food, and the knowledge that I would need a chamber pot sooner rather than later.

At last she tossed the napkin aside. While her women cleared, Elizabeth fixed her dark eyes on me. "We would hear about our cousin, and her court," she said. "Your husband returned without you."

"Queen Mary requested I stay on, and Master Lewis consented."

A nearly invisible eyebrow arched toward her plucked hairline. "Did Master Lewis not want his wife with him?"

"Master Lewis is a creature of the courts." I looked past her to the window, wondering how much to reveal about her cousin. "He understood it might be beneficial for me to remain."

"And was it *beneficial?*" Her voice was as pointed as her fingernails.

"It was." I recalled the light and frivolous atmosphere of Holyrood, so different from the Elizabethan court. Perhaps to an insider it was just as cutthroat, but I had never felt that. "I would be happy to answer any questions Your Majesty has."

She nodded curtly. "We will sit."

The women were ahead of us, arranging a low stool before Elizabeth's chair. I would look like a supplicant huddled at her feet, which was no doubt the intention.

"What of our cousin?" The queen's white hands lay motionless in her lap, but I knew well the amount of effort it took to attain such repose. "Tell us of her."

"She is quite beautiful." The royal eyes narrowed, and I continued. "Her hair is darker than Your Majesty's and she wears it in the French style."

Her mouth pursed. "What about her skin? Is it good?"

"It is very good, Your Majesty." Mary had the skin of a marble statue, but it would be worth my head to say as much. "But she is very pale."

"Unhealthy, then." She sounded satisfied. "We have heard she suffers with stomach pains."

"And frequent headaches." I could not let Mary sound delicate. "But she is not all unhealthy. She likes to ride as much as Your Majesty."

Elizabeth smiled. "Are her hunters equal to mine?"

"They are not," I said truthfully. "They are very good, but not of the same quality as those in the royal stables. And she does not wear out as many horses in a hunt as Your Majesty does." I did not mention Mary's habit of riding astride; if word spread south, through ambassadors or visitors, I would confirm it then.

"How tall is our cousin?"

Mary's height was much talked about; she had to know. "As tall as any man."

"Then she is too tall," the queen pronounced. "For we are the correct height for a woman, do you not agree?"

"Of course." I had another thought. "I believe Queen Mary asked me to stay because of my ability to speak French." I allowed myself a smile. "She does not have Your Majesty's facility with languages—she speaks Latin and Greek, and she can communicate with her ministers in Scots, but she has no English at all."

"The queen of an English-speaking country, unable to make herself understood," she cackled, clapping her hands. "Perhaps you should have stayed and become her tutor."

I put no little effort into turning the house into a place of celebration at Christmastide. Grand-mère's spirit was with me as I directed that swathes of greenery be put up in the hall. "We will need a Yorkshire pie," I told the cook, having convinced Mistress Dunham to tell me how hers was made. "In addition to whatever Sir Edward normally has."

His Christmas pie was a complicated matter involving a turkey, a goose, a chicken, a partridge, and a pigeon, all spiced and stuffed, one within the other, encased in a pastry shaped like a coffin. I had seen such dishes at court, but preferred Mistress Dunham's simpler version with mutton, pork, and game birds to such a fantastical construction.

On the day, however, served with a large slice of five roasted meats with their pastry shell, a rich sauce poured over all, I had to admit it was delicious. As was the Yorkshire pie; the bacon-fortified pottage we had to start; the salads; the vegetables; and the sugared dates and almonds which ended the meal.

I was almost always hungry, and as I grew rounder, I let the baby have what he craved. Robin watched as I ate and drank, smiling when he thought himself unobserved.

The revels lasted until everyone was near dropping—Ned had taken to the Winterset custom of combining feasts, and all the servants were at the table with us, making merry. I finally whispered to Sebastian that I was ready to retire, and by some miracle, he made everyone understand the party was over.

"Are you tired?" Robin asked, when we were finally alone.

"A bit." I ducked into the bedroom before joining him before the fire. "But I wanted some time with you before we slept."

"As did I." He produced an enameled box at the same time I retrieved a small embroidered bag from my sleeve. "What is this?"

"My gift to you," I said. "By way of Grand-mère, and my grandfather before her." I waited for him to open it before looking at my own present.

He put it on the table. "You first, Margaery. Please."

It *was* a most intriguing box. I opened the cunning latch to find a necklace—certainly far beyond Robin's means—coiled on a scrap of black velvet. Made of pearls alternating with small gold discs, at its center was a pendant whose stones reflected the firelight. "Robin!"

He smiled. "I hoped you would like it."

There were two stones: a small, rectangular one of mossy green, and a larger red one. A garnet, I thought. They were set unbacked, to touch my skin, and held in golden scrolls with a teardrop pearl suspended at the bottom. Where my jet pendant was specific to me, this was a necklace any lady would be proud to wear.

"It's the most beautiful thing I've ever seen," I said honestly. "Can we afford it?"

He settled it around my neck and fastened it. "We can," he said. "And you deserve it."

I put a hand to my throat, feeling the unfamiliar textures, knowing I would wear it every chance I got. "Now yours."

Robin loosened the ties of the pouch and shook its contents into his palm. The thick gold band glinted in the light, while the jet stone seemed to absorb it. "What is this?"

"It belonged to my grandfather," I explained, "and two generations before him. Grand-mère wanted you to have it."

"But it belongs to your family."

I slid the ring on his left forefinger, where it fit as if it had been made for him. "It belongs to the master of Winterset."

He looked uncomfortable. "Perhaps it should be kept for our son."

"Our son—if he is not our daughter—has yet to be born." I bridged the distance between us and kissed him. "The master of Winterset is a grown man, and he is mine. That is enough."

Chapter 46

Katherine Grey had been in the Tower for nearly six months. I had put off visiting her long enough. When I told Robin, he looked at me quizzically. "I'm not sure if she's allowed visitors."

"Why not? Marrying without permission isn't treason."

He put a hand to his neck, and I moved behind him to rub his shoulders. "For someone like her, it's close enough. Not to mention the damage she did to the Scottish alliance."

"What damage?" I slid my hands inside his doublet.

"There were plans," he said, "to marry her to the Earl of Arran."

"She is not an object to be given away as others see fit." I took my anger out on his stiff muscles, digging into the knots in his flesh. "Elizabeth would never allow herself to be treated in such a way."

He reached up and caught my hands. "It's not about Elizabeth. It's about her perception of what Katherine has done."

"Nonetheless." I was determined to visit my friend. "Can you apply for me? They will listen to you."

Robin patted my hand. *Go easier this time.* "I'll talk to Cecil," he said. "But Sebastian will escort you."

Even on a bright day, the Tower was awe-inspiring in its age and the sprawl of its many buildings, intimidating in its purpose. Palace and prison, it showed both faces plainly. Looking up at the White Tower, I shivered; Robin told me it was over six hundred years old.

Sebastian and I applied at the gatehouse, where my husband's letter, with its impressive seals, gained us admittance to the Lieutenant's mansion. We stood back as the guard unlocked the door to Katherine's rooms. Seb would undoubtedly cultivate the man in my absence, and draw from him a wealth of information useful to Robin.

I had worried my friend was languishing in some dank cell, but her lodgings were pleasant and well-kept. The barred windows allowed abundant winter light to fall upon the tapestries. The furniture was comfortable, if a bit worn; the equivalent of what Robin and I had in our Whitehall apartment. Katherine was seated before a crackling fire, her back to the door. Two small dogs were curled at her feet.

"What is it?" She did not turn.

"It's me."

"Margaery! You finally came!" Katherine tossed her embroidery aside. "I've only seen Mary, in all this time."

Her embrace was a bit too tight, her face thinner than I remembered. "My husband managed it," I said. "How are you?"

"As you see." She gestured at the snug chamber. "Locked in a place fit only for servants, with just two women, a wet nurse and a nursery maid."

There was no sign of the child. "May I see your son?"

"When he wakes." She collapsed back into her seat. "Which will be soon enough, to scream and feed and scream again." She scooped up one of the dogs, absently fondling its silken ears. "I would like to scream as he does, and have someone take care of me."

Katherine was imprisoned with as many servants at her command as Robin and I had in our entire household, but logic only made her more determined in her unhappiness.

"I'm having a baby."

She didn't look up. "Your pains will not begin in a room full of men asking intimate questions about your relations with your husband."

Sharing my own good fortune would not bring out the best in her, so I changed topics. "Are you allowed letters from Lord Hertford?"

"My jailors—and probably Cecil—read my letters before I receive them, but yes, we are permitted to write." She looked down at her folded hands and smiled.

"What is it, Katherine?"

"Sir Edward is a sympathetic man," she said. "He has been known to leave doors unlatched."

Was she planning an escape? "How far do you think you will get, on your own? They would only bring you back."

Her laugh was like glass shattering. "Mark me, Margaery, I would do almost anything to obtain my freedom, but what the Lord Lieutenant gives me is just as valuable. He gives me access to my husband."

If they were discovered, it would be as bad as actually plotting an escape. "What are you playing at?"

"Marriage," she said, "in the only way I am permitted. Do you know, I have been married for over a year, and I have never spent a single night with my husband."

I sympathized, but what Katherine chose not to see was her situation could be far worse. She could be deprived of her inadequate servants, her nursery maid, her son. Her dogs, and that ridiculous monkey, nibbling quietly on a tapestry, could be given to the sympathetic lieutenant's children or flung into the Thames.

A howl issued from an inner chamber. "My little prince is awake," she said. "Come and see him, before he sleeps again."

The bedchamber was equally well appointed, with a curtained bed, several chests, and an elaborate cradle for young Edward Seymour, Lord Beauchamp.

His crying had already stopped, because the wet nurse had clapped him to her breast. Pacing back and forth, she jiggled the feeding boy, so all I saw was a blanket and a quiff of peach-colored hair which bobbed as he suckled.

"Give him to me, Sarah," Katherine said. "Mistress Lewis wishes to see him."

The nurse looked up. "But he's not done—"

"There will be time for him to finish." She held out her hands. "What do we have, but time?"

Katherine took the stiffly swaddled infant and put him on the bed to be admired. His small mouth worked, searching for the nipple. There would be little time to praise him before he started to cry again.

"What a handsome fellow." I touched his satin cheek with a fingertip. "He looks like you."

She cupped the baby's head, a gesture more maternal than her nonchalant words. "A proper Tudor," she said. "I hoped he would look like Edward, but perhaps the next one will."

"Katherine, you aren't—?"

Her catlike smile reappeared, and she turned away from the baby. "Not yet. But it did not take long the first time."

Seeing her mistress's attention was elsewhere, the nurse swept the baby up and resumed his feeding.

"What will the queen say, if you bear another child?"

Leading me back to the outer chamber, Katherine spun around, her green-and-gold skirts billowing out around her. "Let her think on her cousin, fertile and locked away, able at any time to take her place and provide a clutch of heirs."

This was treason, her words as dangerous for the listener as the speaker. "I cannot hear this," I said. "You endanger both of us."

"Let them listen," she said. "What else can they do to me?"

My nails dug into my palms. "It is not just you," I said. "I have no wish to give birth in the Tower."

"No one would believe it," she said coyly, dimpling at me; I was supposed to forgive her now. "You are safe by reason of your husband's position."

How long until the guard returned? "And what of your position?" I asked. "Blood relative to the queen, and no more sense than that babe in the other chamber. Honestly, you should know better."

She took up her embroidery again. It was the Seymour arms, and she was picking out a line of azure around the royal lions to match the fleurs-de-lis. "You sound like Mary. She is forever telling me to mind my words."

No doubt she was. Without her sister's companionship, Mary had moved in with the queen's other maids, and was most likely both safer and happier.

"You should listen to her."

"Did you come to visit or lecture me?" Her tone was cross. "I heard you were in Scotland."

"I was, and then I was called home to my grandmother's sickbed. We returned to London after her funeral, but we no longer live at Whitehall."

Her eyes widened. "Did Elizabeth force you to leave? Was it because of me?"

In the end, everything came back to Katherine. "We're sharing a house with Sir Edward Pickering. We will need more room when the child comes."

"It took you long enough to catch a baby." She blinked. "How long have you been married? I believe I conceived on my wedding day."

"Three years," I said. "But I lost a child, if you remember."

The embroidery dropped again. "Of course. I get so caught up in my own troubles, I forget other people have them, as well."

This was the danger of Katherine Grey. Her sympathy was convincing, but if I let myself believe it, it would only hurt worse the next time she failed to remember.

"Well, you have your share of troubles." I folded my hands and wished again for the guard. No doubt he and Sebastian were drinking ale with no concern for my suffering.

"It lightens them, to know you are willing to visit me. I hope you will come often; Mary is such a sour-faced little thing." She giggled with sisterly malice. "If they forget to retrieve her, I could hide her in a cupboard, and no one would be the wiser."

Mary was very close to being a dwarf, but how unkind for her sister—so fortunate in her beauty—to say so.

"She cannot help her height." I should have brought my own embroidery, or some knitting to occupy my hands. I had brought only Sebastian, and he was not here to protect me from the bitterness that dripped like poison from Katherine's lips.

She snipped the thread and held out her work to be admired. "You are too kind." Rubbing her thumb over the raised threadwork, she added, "I would make one for you, if your husband had a crest, but he is not a gentleman."

"He has not been knighted." I stood. "But he is more of a gentleman than many born to the title." I pounded on the door, hoping the guard was not too far away. "I can't stay. I'm expected at court this afternoon."

Her mouth opened in surprise. "Give Her Majesty my regards."

I would not. I valued my head, and if I mentioned Katherine, the queen would likely throw a cup at it. "I will try to come again."

She rose to embrace me again, and I caught a whiff of something that reminded me of dark rooms and tangled sheets: she'd been with Hertford recently.

"Please. It is lonely here, with only my thoughts." She picked at her jeweled sleeve. "They say there will be another commission next month, this time headed by Archbishop Parker."

It did not bode well for Katherine that the queen had not given up, and she would not be able to disrupt the proceedings this time by giving birth.

"What do they ask of you?" On the other side of the door came heavy footsteps.

"Facts," she said airily. "The date of our marriage, the name of the clergyman who married us. Even the letter Edward gave me when he went to France with Tom Cecil."

A key ground in the lock. "Does the letter not prove everything?"

Katherine's veneer cracked, for just a moment. "It would," she said, "if I hadn't lost it."

I lied; I had no duties. Sebastian escorted me home in silence, took my cloak, and settled me before the fire. "Should I send for the master?"

"I'll be fine." I looked into his worried eyes. "I just need to be alone."

When he left, I closed my eyes, exhausted by both pregnancy and my friend's situation. How was it possible she could not see the reason for her imprisonment? It would have gone badly enough had they confessed their marriage early on, but waiting until just before her child was born was an affront the queen could not forgive—and filtering the news through Robert Dudley made it worse.

Beyond her insult to the queen, Katherine's only crime was her blood, and a young woman's natural desire for love.

Elizabeth's situation was not so different. She might be queen, but she could not love where she chose; even if Dudley's wife had never existed, his family history and his own unpopularity would have doomed any chance of their marrying. Now, with suspicion still hovering over him, he could never be more to Elizabeth than her Master of Horse.

Cecil yet believed he could convince her to marry, for the good of the country. I thought not, and Robin agreed with me, though he publicly supported Cecil's policies. "I do not think she will give in," he said. "She and her sister are two sides of the same coin."

"How is that?" They were night and day, as far as I could tell.

"They were both blighted by their parents' marriages," he explained. "In Mary's case, it made her crave acceptance, and desire a husband above all things."

"And with Elizabeth, it's the opposite." I blew out a breath. "She will cede power to no man."

Those were my thoughts as I drifted off to sleep. When Robin returned, I had just roused myself and sent Sebastian to see what we were having for supper.

"Seb said you did not stay overlong." He spun his hat across the room, and removed the fitted cap beneath, running long fingers through his hair. "Was it so bad?"

"Her accommodations are comfortable, though she will not admit it." I shifted in my chair, my low back aching. "It was not the Tower so much as Katherine herself."

"Ah." He brought my fingers to his lips. "It is not always pleasant, being the friend of a powerful person."

"Especially a powerful person who refuses to understand why she is imprisoned." I did not have the strength to tell him, and sat in silence as Robin told me bits and pieces of his day. The slamming of a door below alerted us to Ned's arrival. "He is like a boy," I said. "He will not walk when he can run, he will not speak when he can yell, and he never closes a door but to bang it."

Robin shook his head ruefully. "It has been ever thus, my love."

Over supper, Ned, who was frightfully well-informed, asked me pointed questions about Katherine, most of which I refused to answer.

"She says there is to be another investigation into her marriage." I tried my own line of inquiry. "What do they hope to find?"

Ned tried to speak, but was defeated by the sheer amount of food he had shoveled into his mouth. Cheeks bulging like a squirrel's, he chewed until he could say, "They hope one of them will deny the marriage."

"She would never." For all that she paid less attention to him than her monkey, Katherine's son was proof of her fertility, a bargaining chip with those who would support her over the queen. She would not de-legitimize him.

"Well, then, Hertford will do it."

"Not now." He might have, before Katherine had borne his son; though I had no high opinion of Edward Seymour, I thought he would not abandon his first-born.

"We shall see." Ned jerked his head for more ale. "The queen will have what the queen will have, else Katherine and young Hertford will not see daylight again but through a barred window."

Robin had no role in the second investigation, but he brought home what information he was able to glean. "They cannot seem to help themselves," he said exasperatedly. "He wrote the letter, and kept no copy. She had the letter, but lost it. Who knows if it even existed?"

I was silent for too long, and looked up to find his eyes upon me. "Margaery?"

"I never saw it," I said. "She said he made her his heir, should anything happen before he could publicly declare the marriage."

"Jesus." The color drained from Robin's face. "I will not have you go before the commission."

"Would it help?" Katherine would have had me summoned by now, if it would.

"I don't know, but I will not risk you—risk our child—for the Greys or the Seymours."

It was as if he only saw their families, not this new generation whose lives were to be destroyed because of their forebears' actions.

"What would become of them if their marriage is declared illegitimate?" I no more wanted to go in front of the commission than Robin wanted me to, but nor did I wish my friend—no matter my current feelings for her—to stay imprisoned any longer than necessary.

"It will be, do you not understand? Their guilt is as foregone as Anne Boleyn's. The queen will have it no other way."

I racked my brain. "What if she swore an oath, removing herself from the succession?"

"Easier said than done." Robin withdrew some papers from his satchel. "You know her better than I—even if it were possible, do you believe she would? She is attached to the idea of being Elizabeth's heir."

"And her sister would be next in line."

He groaned aloud. "The council would never agree. Imagine trying to peddle Mary Grey to a foreign prince."

"She is not so unattractive." I pitied the young woman whom everyone discounted.

His forehead wrinkled. "Perhaps not, but Elizabeth is considered to be aging out of the marriage market at thirty-two. No one would take kindly to the offer of a small, hunchbacked replacement, despite her youth."

He was correct. The world was unkind, and while Katherine was tough enough for that world, Mary was not.

"Could I write a statement?" I asked. "It's not as if I know anything other than that the letter existed."

"That is more than enough to have you called in for questioning." He ran his fingers through his hair again. "I don't want you involved. If it means so much, I'll speak to Ned in the morning. He may know things of which I am unaware." He caught my hand and held it, hard. "Will you be guided by me in this, Margaery? Even if you disagree?"

I chewed my lip. He asked me to trust his judgment over my own desires, but was that not what marriage was about—occasionally giving way for the greater good? "I will be guided," I said. "But I will ask for your reasons."

"I would expect nothing else." His tone was relieved, and I understood how worried he was on my behalf. That, too, was marriage.

Chapter 47

ROBIN FOUND TWO MIDWIVES, and I chose the one who gave me the most comfort. We spoke about the birth and my fears, because of the miscarriage. Rebecca Trott was satisfyingly matter-of-fact.

"Just because you lost one doesn't mean this one is at any risk." She eyed me. "If you were going to lose it, it would have happened by now."

I appreciated her bluntness. "My grandmother said she lost one between every child who lived."

Mistress Trott's face puckered around her toothless mouth. "'Tis unlucky, but it doesn't mean you'll do the same."

We had a cup of ale and then she said she needed to look at me. "Just to see for myself."

"See what?" I asked, as we climbed the stairs.

"The width of your hips, how the child is positioned."

When we reached the bedchamber, Alice was waiting. She shared Sebastian's sense of when she would be needed. "Should I undress her?"

Mistress Trott shook her head. "No need. A woman can catch a baby by raising her skirts, I can look at her purse easily enough by doing the same."

Blood rushed to my face. I had heard coarse words from Elizabeth's ladies, but it was embarrassing to hear them in the presence of my maid.

At the midwife's request, Alice fetched the basin and Mistress Trott washed thoroughly, making profligate use of my scented soap.

I lay back against the pillows and closed my eyes as my skirts were bunched up around my hips. It was difficult not to remember the physician's rough hands, but Mistress Trott's touch was different. Impersonal yet respectful, she spanned my hip bones and made approving noises.

"Narrow, but not too," she said to herself. "They've widened a bit."

"All of me has widened."

Her head appeared over the voluminous fabric. "The bones

spread as the baby starts to drop down."

I sat up. "Does that mean he's coming soon?"

She pushed on my knees until I subsided. "Not yet. But there are stages for these things."

"Really?" There was a world of knowledge of which I was ignorant, and it involved my own body. "Tell me."

"There are five stages," she said equably. "Conception, that's the first stage. The waiting, that's where you are now."

"It's the longest period of my life."

She hooted with laughter. "When your labor begins, that's the longest period of your life."

"That's the third stage? And then the birth is four." What was the fifth stage?

"Not so, my lady." Pressing on my knees, she said, "I'm going to examine you now." She looked at Alice. "Why don't you hold your mistress's hand?"

The midwife produced a pottery jar from her pocket. A sharp herbal scent reached my nostrils as she rubbed grease onto her hands. Alice put her arm around my shoulders. "Breathe," she said softly. "Let her rummage around, and just breathe."

That was hard advice to take when a finger was suddenly inserted into my body. It was so different from Robin I jumped.

"Relax your parts," Mistress Trott said. "I need more than the one finger, and if you clamp down like that again, you're like to snap it off."

I laughed, and it became easier. "Tell me about the stages again," I said to distract myself. "I'm in the second."

"The third," she said, "comes before your pains begin. You'll think it's labor, but it's just your body getting ready. Cramps, the kind you had when your courses first started. Some blood, perhaps."

"Blood?" I hated that my voice wobbled. Alice squeezed my fingers. "How much?"

"Not enough to frighten. Just wear your linen as if you were expecting your flow." Mistress Trott wiped her hand on her apron. "Everything as it should be down there."

My sigh came all the way from my bare knees. "Thank you."

"Do you want to know the rest?" She looked at the chair and I nodded permission, as I resumed my skirts and my dignity. "The fourth is your true labor. You'll know the difference."

"What if I don't?" It would be so easy for me to get it wrong.

"You will." Her tone was so certain I believed her. "Trust me, you won't mistake it."

I nodded. "All right. What's the final stage, if it's not labor?"

Her lips spread in a smile. "The turning point, I call it. Labor can go for a long time—I once delivered a babe after three full days, the poor mother near dead of exhaustion—but there's a point where you'll know it's almost over."

Queen Jane Seymour had labored three days to produce her prince, and it nearly killed her. "How will I know?"

"You just will." Her grin was filled with the wisdom of decades. "You'll think you can't bear another moment, and that's when he'll come."

Our business was concluded with another cup of ale, and Mistress Trott told me she thought the baby was due in mid-May. That meant he was likely conceived that night in Scotland when I put my fear aside.

"How many babies have you delivered?" I'd wanted to ask before, but not while she was examining me.

"Three hundred and twelve," she said proudly. "As of yesterday."

"Three hundred and twelve?" My mind could not encompass that many babies.

She slurped the last of her ale. "I've been doing this for nigh on forty years, Mistress Lewis. It's your first, but to me, it's just one more."

I could not bring myself to visit Katherine again, worrying that her misery would affect my own pregnancy. Perhaps it was a silly fancy, but I allowed it; what good was it, being a pregnant woman, without a few fancies?

The Archbishop of Canterbury made his ruling. Her marriage was declared invalid and her baby—little Lord Beauchamp—a bastard. I was not strong enough to face Katherine after such news.

How would it be for the child, growing up in a place like the Tower, with parents who were not only separated, but never legally wed? I wondered at the effects of these adult actions on him, considering my own life and how it had been changed by things beyond my control.

Who would I be if my father hadn't been killed? It was something I tried not to think about, but now, with motherhood so close, it was impossible to avoid. If he had lived, I would have grown up with two parents, and possibly siblings. Without the heartbreak of his death, my mother would have loved me, and I would have a far better idea how to be a mother myself.

My grandparents would have remained at Winterset until their deaths. Walter would have lived, might even have married Alice, despite his mother's misgivings.

Even with brothers, I would have been an heiress. I would have come to court, or married some Yorkshire noble—perhaps even Will Hawkins.

If my father had lived, Robin Lewis would have never leased my home. He might still have gone to France, but I wouldn't have been there to meet him.

The thought of never knowing Robin was impossible.

I had convinced Robin that confinement was unnecessary, promising to be sensible, and as my time approached, it felt natural to curtail my activities. As fate would have it, though, my pains began while I was on a rare visit to the presence chamber. This time, it was no tendril, but a punch to my low back. I stood upright, and my body said it would rather I not do that.

This was what Mistress Trott meant. I *did* know the difference. I called the nearest woman. "Get a page, please. I need to return home at once."

She looked at my face and understood. "Wait right here."

Within minutes, two grooms of the chamber were there to escort me down to a coach. They were joined by a handful of women. "Send word as soon as you're delivered," Nell pleaded.

"I will. Go back, before Her Majesty misses you."

As I climbed into the coach, Sebastian sprinted from the palace, dodging men and horses in the courtyard until he reached me. "I've sent word to Master Lewis by way of Sir Edward," he gasped. "I'll accompany you home."

"Perhaps you can go for the midwife once we get there?" I suggested, overwhelmed with gratitude. "Alice will bar you from the room anyway."

He sat across from me, ignoring the groom's curious stare. "How do you feel?"

I leaned back, clutching the edge of the seat. "About as you'd expect."

He ducked his head, an oddly boyish gesture. "I wouldn't have a clue what to expect, mistress."

"It's damned uncomfortable, that's what it is." I pressed my lips together as another contraction curved my body like a bow. "Oww."

The seat creaked as he sat beside me. "Squeeze my hand, if it will help."

By the time we reached the house I had come close to breaking the small bones of Seb's hands, but he nevertheless swept me up and carried me to the door.

"Mistress, are you—" Gibbon's mouth hung open.

"Send for the midwife," Sebastian ordered, taking the stairs two at a time. "The lady is near her time."

"I don't think I am," I confessed, my face against his neck. He smelled of sweat and, oddly, my own fear. "I think it just hurts."

"That is enough." He stepped back as Alice took over. Susan, eyes wide in anticipation of her own impending birth, stood with her hands bunched in her apron.

"Go downstairs and wait for the midwife," Alice said. "You've been a great help."

"But I'd like to—" He looked from me to Alice, who folded her arms and stared at him. "I'll go downstairs and wait for the midwife."

She shut the door behind him, chivvying Susan before her like a lost chick. "Help your mistress get out of all that while I ready the bed."

Susan began to undress me, her movements as slow and fumbling as my own. We had only reached my kirtle by the time Alice returned, having stopped for a contraction and because Susan got a stitch in her side.

"If that's all the help you'll be, you may leave, too." She finished my undressing, letting my kirtle and petticoats drop to the floor in a manner most unlike her. "Go, Susan."

I looked at Alice. "She's just nervous."

Alice held out her arm and I leaned on her. "You don't need her nerves on top of your own." She lowered me to the edge of the bed. "Nightdress?" she asked, almost to herself. "No, let's leave your shift. It's not your best—if it gets spoiled, you have others."

Mistress Trott arrived in under an hour, and after poking about between my legs, declared I was not yet ready. "It's true labor, but you've got hours to go, my lady." She straightened. "I'll wait in the kitchen. Is there any chance of some ale, and mayhap a bite to eat?"

In the absence of midwife and maid, I hauled myself off the bed. It felt better to stand, and I could hold the bedpost when a pain struck. Between contractions, I walked back and forth across the chamber, trying to breathe normally and keep panic at bay.

"She's settled downstairs." Alice shut the door.

"Sit with me?"

She retrieved her knitting and moved a stool beside the bed. "He's almost here, Mistress Margaery. Are you excited?"

My back had ached for three solid months, and I could no longer put on my own stockings. I looked forward to meeting my baby, but I was also excited to be done with pregnancy. "Have you ever wanted children, Alice?"

"Of course." She sounded surprised. "What woman doesn't? But when Walter gave me up…" She shrugged. "There was no one else."

I sucked in a breath and held it for a moment, to see if it helped the pain. It didn't. "I always wondered if you and Leon—"

"No." She dropped her needles. "He's a good man, but no. He's not for me." Looking down at the stocking in her lap, she said, "There was a time when I thought…but I was mistaken. Sebastian is as oblivious as the master."

Laughter was better than holding my breath. "Do you like him, Alice?"

She knelt to stir the fire, though the room, with its covered windows, was already unbearably hot. "I did," she said, "but I'm too old to break my heart over a man who doesn't know how to love me back."

I was sorry to hear it. Sebastian was a worthy match. "Are you sure? I can ask Robin—"

"Please don't." She looked alarmed. "I think the monks spoiled him for looking at women." Resuming her seat, she added, "And maybe it's that I'm not like him."

"Black, you mean?" There were black women in London, but they were not so common in the areas frequented by court servants, and Robin kept him busy. "Do you think it matters to him?"

"I don't know." Alice brushed a stray hair from her eyes. "I suppose if I was different, I might want someone like myself." She fixed her gaze on me. "That's enough about Sebastian. Shall we have Mistress Trott back for Susan?"

I shrugged. "Assuming all goes well, I see no reason why not." I looked at her. "Unless *you* want to deliver the baby?"

She shook her head so hard her coif slipped. "No, I would not."

Her disapproval of Susan was amusing, except when it was not. "She's not so bad, you know."

"I know." Alice puffed out a breath. "But she's not so good, either. Imagine, coming back from Scotland not even knowing the father of your child." She busied herself tying the bed curtains out of the way. "She was there to take care of you, not herself."

"She managed both, as far as I can tell."

The midwife was correct. As the day wore on, my pains faded and I grew bored. Alice brought my embroidery, but I could not bring myself to work on it. She tried books, but I could no more focus on the letters than I could the intricate needlework. I paced, trying to convince the baby it was time to come.

A knock heralded Robin's arrival. Mistress Trott would not allow him in the chamber when I was being delivered, but that appeared to be some time in the future. Let him distract me, if he could. "Come in."

He entered, closing the door behind him. "What's happening? The midwife is asleep in the kitchen."

"Let her sleep," I said. "Alice, you may leave us. I'll call when I have need."

"Very good." She curtsied and left us alone.

"Are you well?" He looked unsettled. "You seem perfectly normal."

I laughed. "I am perfectly normal, as is what I'm going through. Mistress Trott said there might be a pause, and I should just wait until it started again." I sat back in my chair, the mound of my belly rising before me like a sea creature. "I'm glad you're here."

"Can I do anything?"

"Rub my back?" I plodded to the bed, my thighs wider apart than before. It was the baby's head, pressing down, I realized. What a strange thought, to know our child was so close. I wrapped my arms around the bedpost and presented him with my low back.

His touch was tentative, but my muscles had been screaming for so long anything was an improvement. When I did not object, he pressed harder, and the tightness at the base of my spine began to loosen.

My eyes closed and I drifted along on the pleasure of his touch and the lack of pain when there was a disconcerting *pop!* Wetness gushed down my legs and onto the floor. I jumped back, startled. "It's my waters," I said at his alarmed expression. "Call for Alice."

Opening the door, he shouted her name over the rail, and I returned to my chair, putting a thick towel on the seat. Something had changed; the pains were back now, a definite contraction that made me want to bring my knees to my chest, if only that were possible.

Alice and Mistress Trott arrived. The midwife looked at the mess on the floor, and then at me. "Now, can you feel the difference?"

I nodded.

Robin hovered. "What should I do?"

The midwife looked at him. "It's bad luck for a man to see his child brought forth." Lowering her voice, she said to me, "And a man will never look at his wife the same again, once he's seen her in her extremity."

"I'm not ready yet." I reached out my hand. "Sit with me a few minutes longer, and then you can stay with Ned and Sebastian."

We lingered by the fire for another half hour, until my pains came closer together. "You can go now," I said. "I am in good hands."

He leaned over and kissed me, a lingering touching of our lips that made me—absurd thought!—want him very badly. "I pray it goes easy," he said. "I never thought to have this in my life, and I am grateful every day for you."

Alice and Mistress Trott moved me to the bed and my body got down to the business at hand. My grandmother had borne this, at least four times. My mother had survived birthing me. Every person living had been born of woman, and the women had—for the most part—survived it. I could do this.

I twisted the sheet in my hand, feeling the fibers separate, and did as Mistress Trott instructed: breathing when she said to breathe, pushing when she said to push, and resting in the spaces between.

"Why do women do this more than once?" It occurred to me that a very large baby was working his way through a very small opening.

Mistress Trott's head appeared between my knees. "Because we enjoy the thing that gets us in this state," she said. "I can see the head already. No risk your husband won't claim this child, his hair's red as fire."

I fell back and let the final contractions roll over me. A little red-haired baby! Love welled up in me so I could barely breathe, and the baby slid out in a rush of wetness. Alice put him on my breast, not caring about the damage to my shift.

"Rub his back, now," Mistress Trott said, still busy at her end of the proceedings. "Buff him up until he yells."

The small red face crumpled almost immediately and wailed straight into mine. I laughed with exhaustion and joy and kissed his sticky face.

Robin appeared before the baby's cries had finished echoing through the house. Mistress Trott checked me one last time, told me the afterbirth was safely delivered, and said, "I'll go down and have myself another cup, if you don't mind, while you show the master his son."

She smiled widely at Robin as he tried to enter the door around her. "Thank you," he said distractedly, and rushed to the bedside. "How are you?"

I nodded toward the loosely-wrapped bundle in my arms, not yet swaddled so his father could see him in his perfection. "You have a son."

His face emptied of all expression and he sat, gulping air. His hands, resting on his black-clad thighs, were trembling. "Do I?"

"Do you want to hold him?"

That broke the spell. "I might drop him." He raised his hands. "You hold him—I can admire him from here."

"As you wish, husband." It would take time for him to become accustomed to his new role. "Is he not beautiful?"

"He has my hair," he said. "Poor boy."

It seemed funny now, Mistress Trott watching that flaming head emerge from my body. "I hope he's as smart as you."

Robin stroked the baby's cheek with one finger. "And as kind as his mother." Growing bolder, he ran the finger under his chin and along his shoulder. The baby's arm waved, tiny fingers opening and closing until they found something to grab onto. "Oh."

He tried to suckle Robin's finger, and my milk rose to the demand. "He wants me." I untied the strings of my shift. and picked him up, and it took but a moment for him to find the nipple.

"It's the strangest feeling," I said in wonder. "Like I've always known this."

He took my hand. "I know you've worried," he said, "but you're already a good mother."

"I'd like to name him after my father." Was it his suckling that made me sleepy or the hours of labor? I wanted to lie back and rest, with the baby still attached. "Would you mind?"

"I had always assumed he would be called Ralph."

I couldn't imagine I had more love left, but another wave submerged me. "Thank you."

"Could he have a second name?" he asked. "One for me?"

My eyelids were growing heavy. "Of course."

"Antony," he said. "Ralph Antony Lewis."

Chapter 48

"*MADAME,* MAY I SPEAK with you?" Leon stood tentatively in the doorway.

"Of course." After my grandmother's funeral, we offered to send him back to France, but he refused. Had he changed his mind?

"It is about Susan." He turned his cap in his hands. "Do you plan to keep her on once the young master is weaned?"

It was odd to hear my son called the young master, as odd as thinking of Susan as a mother, but she had produced her own child, a girl, not ten days after Ralph was born. "I suppose so," I said. "She's a better nurse than lady's maid."

"I was not certain you would keep her," he said. "Because she had no husband."

"She does not need a husband to be a wet nurse."

He looked at the floor. "But she has a bastard child. You could be fined for harboring her."

It hadn't occurred to me, and I could only think how ridiculous it was that my maid's fornication mattered to anyone but her. "It would not be so much."

"You can afford it," he conceded. "But what if we return to Yorkshire?"

I looked at him closely. "Two babies, two women, and one husband? Do you think anyone would care?"

"I thought I might marry her." He wiped his palms on his tunic. "In order to give the babe a name."

"Goodness," I said. "That is very kind of you, Leon, but do you really want to marry Susan just to give the child a name?"

His sallow cheeks became ruddy. "Well, *madame,* it could be mine."

I swallowed my laughter. "The child is not yours. She is a sweet girl—the babe, I mean—but is this what you want?"

Recovered, he nodded. "*Oui, madame.* Susan will make a wife, over time. Her tendencies will improve, with a husband of her own."

I picked up my needle. "Then you have my permission. Master

Lewis will not object."

He bowed. "*Merci, madame.*"

"I do wonder," I said as he turned to go, "you did not wish to marry Alice."

His eyes widened. "Alice is *une bonne femme*," he said, "but she does not want me. And I would not dare to cross Sebastian."

Was Alice wrong, or was Leon? Seb certainly hadn't confided in his fellow servant. He would tell Robin, if anyone, but I doubted he would even do that, being as private as my husband. It was as if they had a door inside which could be closed, to keep out the world and its prying eyes.

And men wondered why women talked. How else were we to understand the world, when they told us so little?

Mistress Ashley invited me to rejoin the court while they were at Hampton. The queen's current chamberer was on a visit to her family, and her position was mine, if I wanted it, for the month of October.

I had no desire to return to Hampton on my own. I didn't fear a recurrence of that first summer—Edmund Morven was no longer at court, having been caught in his own net and helped into a hasty marriage by the father of a young widow—but I would not be without my son, or, for that matter, my husband. Let Elizabeth think what she would.

After Ralph was born, I decided I would not return to court, but the prospect of a brief visit was enticing. When Robin said lodgings could be arranged, including space for Susan and Ralph, I sent word to Mistress Ashley that I would come.

We arrived in the afternoon, and while the rest of us settled in, Robin went immediately to the Paradise Chamber to speak with William Cecil, who had traveled down earlier in the day.

He returned an hour later, bursting through the door and leaning against a chair back, his face flushed with effort. "You have to leave."

I was on the floor with Ralph on my lap, and looked up. "What do you mean? We've just unpacked."

"You have to leave," he repeated, and tossed back the ale Alice handed to him. "There's sickness in the privy chambers."

"There is always sickness in the summer." I pressed my lips to Ralph's downy head. "I'm sure it will be fine."

He put a hand on my shoulder. "Margaery, it's the queen."

There were no barges for London until the morning. While Sebastian made inquiries throughout the palace, Robin received visitors in our chamber throughout the evening. With each conversation, his expression grew graver. I went to bed near midnight, when he left to meet someone in the hall.

Ralph fussed all night, and Robin never came to bed. When Alice drew the curtains, my eyes were open but I was tired to my bones. "What news?"

She shook her head. "The master is waiting. He does not look happy."

He never looked particularly happy. I shrugged into a loose gown and joined him at the table, which was littered with cups and empty plates. Sebastian drowsed in a corner.

"It's worrisome," he said. "I won't have you in this place if there is a risk to your health."

I sat across from him. "Tell me."

"Cecil spoke to Mary Sidney yesterday," he said. "Elizabeth was unwell two days ago. She took a hot bath and walked in the gardens, but woke the next day with a fever."

The queen was often unwell. Even fever was not uncommon. The contents of the royal medicine chest would put an apothecary to shame.

I said as much, but Robin shook his head. "She is not herself."

"She will be better soon." I toyed with a piece of stale bread, wondering if it would be unkind to wake Sebastian and ask him to fetch breakfast. "Lady Mary is a skilled nurse."

He put his hand over mine, stilling my restless movements. "I don't care."

"But I'm needed here." I didn't want to lose my place—temporary though it was—because my husband had a morbid fear of sickness. "You're overreacting. It's just a summer fever."

"In October." Robin's gaze was serious. "Do you not understand I am afraid? For you, and for Ralph." He reached for my hand, but I pulled away. "Do you want him to grow up with one parent?"

My heart constricted at the thought of our sunny little boy deprived of anything. "Mistress Ashley will never allow me back."

Robin was gentle in his victory. "If the queen wishes something embroidered, doubtless she will find a way to retrieve you."

While I fretted at home and spent too much time—in Susan's view—playing with my son, Robin traveled between Hampton and Whitehall and reported on the queen's condition. Two days after my return, he came back early, his expression somber. "Dr. Burcot has been with the queen."

Burcot was a German physician who had treated the Duchess of Bedford before her recent death. "She is not improved?"

Robin took my hand. "Let us walk while it is still light."

I understood this to mean he wanted to talk without the servants overhearing, but it turned out he needed movement to distract himself. "This is the crisis Cecil has dreaded," he said as we walked through St. Margaret's gate and into the churchyard. "If anything happens to her, there is no heir."

Stillness surrounded us; the clangor of Lothbury Street faded as we passed beyond the stone walls of the church.

"Is she so seriously ill?" It was difficult to believe Elizabeth would allow an illness to take up residence in her person; her other maladies—headaches, pains in her stomach, toothache—were all brought on by her bad diet or used as excuses to avoid things she did not wish to do.

"Burcot was ejected from the chamber for daring to say the word 'smallpox' in her presence." Robin was too shaken to smile. "Her fever has not broken, but neither has she developed any pustules."

Smallpox did not always kill its victims, but its survivors rarely escaped unscathed. How would Elizabeth face her courtiers, play her flirtatious games, with a scarred face?

I thought of the obvious heir, tucked away in her comfortable prison. "What of Katherine?"

Robin stopped. "Cecil will not propose her to the council, at least not until he is sure the queen will die."

The fate of England hung by a thread, and the news from the privy apartments continued dire: Elizabeth's fever did not break for four days; she lapsed into unconsciousness; death appeared imminent.

Cecil called a meeting of the privy council to discuss the succession. Robin returned late that night, limping, his face drawn with pain.

"They are like children, bragging over their toys," he said disgustedly. "Each has the best—some want Henry's will followed to the letter, no matter the danger of Katherine Grey. Others believe the Scottish queen is the best choice, despite her Catholicism. Some even mention Margaret Douglas, though everyone knows Henry wanted her as far from the succession as she could be thrown. They rage and they shout and they cry tears of great pain over Elizabeth's health, but they cannot choose her successor."

I handed him a brimming glass and moved behind him to rub his shoulders. "Who does Dudley want?" As the queen's favorite, he would have an opinion, and I thought it would not be Katherine— not after she had gone to him to save her from Elizabeth's wrath the year before.

"Henry Hastings." Robin shook his head.

I didn't see how the Earl of Huntingdon had any connection to the queen. "Why?"

Robin put the wine aside, bringing me around to sit with him. "He has an obscure claim through Edward III," he said. "And he is married to Dudley's sister, Kate. I don't believe he would be accepted—and Dudley's support does him no favors. But he is Protestant, and a man."

The next day, the queen regained consciousness to find her councilors clustered around her bed. She asked them to appoint Dudley as Protector of the Realm, should she die of her illness— which she still refused to admit was smallpox. The thought of Dudley as Protector forced the council into action. Two men were sent to retrieve the banished Dr. Burcot, and when he refused to come, he was forcibly conveyed to the palace.

He was almost too late. Delirious and raving, Elizabeth was wrapped in scarlet flannel until only her face and one hand were exposed. She was kept near the fire and forced to drink, and her hand soon developed spots. Once they became pustules, the fever broke.

The worst was over; the queen would not die. The council withdrew, and Cecil subsided to work on new plans for a royal marriage once she was recovered. It was obvious that Elizabeth could no longer put the welfare of the country at risk because of her personal distaste for to marriage.

Because of my abrupt withdrawal—"during the queen's hour of most violent need," according to Mistress Ashley—I was not invited to return to the privy chambers. New women were sought, not just to replace me, but to replace Lady Mary Sidney, who through her devoted nursing had contracted the smallpox herself and nearly died. Grievously scarred, she retired from court life.

Chapter 49

THE QUEEN REGAINED HER strength, only to take to her bed again when she learned Katherine had been delivered of a second healthy son. Since husband and wife were imprisoned separately, there were ribald jokes about an immaculate conception, which made Elizabeth even more ill-tempered.

Cecil intensified his campaign, his logic being if the queen would not accept her fertile cousin, she must then provide her own heir, for he would never accept the Scottish queen.

Robin and Ned's conversations on this topic were less interesting now, my attention taken up with the fire-thatched mite in the nursery upstairs. I continually marveled that such a small person could make me feel so much just by existing.

Ralph walked early, defeating Susan's attempts to keep him swaddled. He would work a hand or a foot loose, or clench himself so tightly the bands loosened when he relaxed. I understood her distress—babies were supposed to be swaddled through their ninth month, to promote straight growth—but I was also proud of his refusal to be restrained.

When he was with me in the afternoons, I unwrapped him and let him crawl around in his linen gown and pull himself up on the furniture. His impatience was visible, and he kept up a babbling, incoherent commentary all the while.

"He never stops," Susan said, coming for him and sighing at the mess of swaddling bands on the floor.

"Young Master Ralph will be quite the orator, once he learns to use his words." Seb had come with a delivery for Robin, which he put down in exchange for lifting up my son and whirling him over his head.

"Sebby, Sebby!" Ralph crowed with joy, his mangling of Sebastian's name one of the few clear sounds he managed. "Up!"

Sebastian played with Ralph in a way Robin could not. Watching him look hungrily at his son, while not knowing how to speak to or play with him, made me want to lay hands on the people who had blighted his ability to show affection.

"Time to go, Master Ralph." Seb turned the twisting boy over so his head hung down. Ralph's tiny hands flailed, and his laughter floated back as he was carried off.

Robin was sent back to Scotland, and we traveled with him as far as York. I tried not to show my unhappiness at this latest separation. To me, marriage was being together, not at opposite ends of the country for weeks on end.

None of this was what I wanted for us. I wanted to live in our home, and sleep in a bed where the only intrusions were our son's voice and the sounds of the sea. I could not ask Robin to give up his life at court, but those were my thoughts as our small coach turned east, toward Whitby, and I watched him ride away with Randolph's men.

"Spend some time with Anselm," Robin urged. "Ride up to the tower and look down on Winterset, and imagine a day when we can be there together."

I did that, nearly every day, and with Fowler's assistance I found a way to strap Ralph to my back so he could come with me. He loved it from the first, crowing every time we left the house and wailing when he was taken from the stables. Dickon adored him, and there were afternoons when I left Ralph in his capable hands and rode alone, coming back to find my child asleep, dirty and smiling, in a pile of straw.

It was the childhood I wanted for him.

The idyll lasted less than two months. Late one evening, Robin and Sebastian arrived with Will Hawkins, having separated from the rest of their party. They would spend a few days at Winterset before we all returned to London.

"Can't you delay?" My head rested on Robin's bare shoulder. "You look exhausted."

"I am," he said. "I must admit, working for Elizabeth has taken the joy from travel." He sighed, and his thin frame shifted beneath me. "We were there to propose a new alliance. Can you guess what it was?"

There was a storm coming; the sea was rough, and the sound of waves filled the chamber. I wanted to lie back with my husband and listen to them, and then sleep until he had the energy to love me properly.

"What?"

"Dudley." He said the name as if he did not believe it himself. "Elizabeth proposes the queen of Scots marry Robert Dudley."

I had thought she could no longer surprise me. "If she cannot have him herself, she will make him a king." I settled my head more firmly. "What has he to say about it?"

"He has not been asked." Robin put his arm around me. "Let us leave Elizabeth and Dudley to their own devices," he said. "I have been thinking about this bed for weeks. I want to lie here, hold my wife, and put the queen out of my mind."

When we returned, Robin was drawn back into negotiations with Scotland; Mary at first refused to marry her cousin's horsekeeper, but wavered when being named heir to the English throne was dangled before her. She would think about it.

Elizabeth's brush with death frightened her, as had the fact that her council would have likely chosen Katherine as her successor; Cecil would have had his way, via threats, persuasion or blackmail. Whether to thwart him, or from her own perverse nature, Elizabeth forgave the Earl and Countess of Lennox, and their son, Darnley, whom Robin had once escorted to France, and released them from prison. They returned to court, giving rise to rumors that Margaret Douglas, Lady Lennox, was being restored to the succession.

It was a tangle, and it was like to drive my husband mad before it was done. I'd never seen him as disturbed as he was during that period, arriving late with Ned and talking long into the night, drinking too much and sleeping too little. He never saw Ralph and barely saw me. When I tried to convince him to keep better hours, he turned bleak eyes on me and left the room.

Sebastian had no better luck, nor did Ned. They came in arguing one evening, and Ned followed him all the way to our parlor. Seb poured ale and stepped back, raising an eyebrow at me.

Their argument ebbed and flowed: Lennox and Dudley, Darnley and Cecil, names which haunted Robin's waking and sleeping hours. Whether, since she had ostensibly forgiven the Lennoxes, the queen could be convinced to release Katherine and Lord Hertford. Whether that couple would willingly retire to the country and keep a low profile, or, alternately, live at court and prove their loyalty.

"We work and we toil and we give them what they ask, only to be told it's no longer what they want." Robin slammed his cup down on the table, ale sloshing on the polished surface.

I reached for a cloth, before the mess could run to his papers, and gave his shoulder a comforting squeeze. Their bickering made my head hurt.

Ned leaned forward. "They've always been this way, Rob. You've dealt with them for over thirty years."

"Mayhap thirty years is too many." There was weariness in every line of his body. "I'm tired, Ned."

His friend took the words literally, and stood to leave. Robin did not stop him.

When the door closed, he said, "I have never truly questioned the value of my life before this." He raised his eyes to mine. "The court is eating away at my strength, and for what?"

I laced my fingers through his. "To build the England you believed possible. Isn't that what you told me?"

"I suppose." He rubbed his eyes. "Given more time, would I have chosen differently? I should have thought first, and not jumped at the queen's invitation without speaking to you."

"And what man would be foolish enough to refuse such a request?" I didn't know what he needed from me. "You wanted to make an England that wouldn't execute a man for his beliefs."

He shoved his chair back. "We are not so far removed from Bloody Mary as I would like. I worry, both about the Catholics who would overthrow Elizabeth, and about Cecil."

"I thought you trusted him?"

"I do." There was a hesitation in his voice. "But he is as strong a Protestant as Edward, or Jane Grey. He would persecute Catholics, if given the opportunity."

I fell silent. One of the few things about Robin of which I was certain was his belief in God, and his disbelief in any particular religion, all of them having betrayed him at one point or another.

Chapter 50

"WHAT ARE YOUR PLANS for the day?" Robin asked, buttoning his black doublet. He had moved from ale to wine after Ned's departure, and finally had been helped to bed by Sebastian. Only a few hours later, he was bright-eyed, if somewhat brittle. "Anything special?"

"No." The light hurt my eyes. Nell had come the day before with her two children, and I was still tired. Our boys had gotten into every corner of the house, their nurses trailing behind, alternatively threatening and pleading for them to behave. "I've got a headache. I think I'll just stay in today."

He left soon after, and I dozed in my chair, having turned it away from the window. I slept until nearly noon, when Alice woke me by coming in suddenly.

"Are you well, mistress?"

"Of course." I didn't feel well, and when I got up, my legs did not seem to work. I fainted before she could reach me.

A wet cloth on my forehead brought me around, and I raised myself up on my elbows. "I'm all right."

Alice squatted beside me. "You are not," she said. "I'm going to send for the master."

"No." I dragged myself upright, holding onto the chair. "I'll be fine," I said. "I just need to rest."

She reached out to steady me. "You're ill. You cannot hide it."

"I'm not hiding anything." Tears filled my eyes, whether from the blinding pain in my head or the sudden, sure knowledge of what ailed me.

Ever since we'd returned from Winterset in June, there had been rumors of deaths, but they were mostly in the poor parishes. Remembering Robin's reaction when the queen contracted smallpox, I tried to keep safe, rarely leaving the house except to visit with Nell or my friends at Whitehall, surely the safest place in the world, and yet—somehow—I was ill.

I looked at Alice. "You should go."

She shook her head. "I will not. Who should care for you, but me?"

A sudden cramp ripped through my belly and I lurched for the basin, vomiting up everything I'd eaten for the last day. I choked and heaved until there was nothing left, and sagged against her.

"Get in the bed now." She put her arm around my waist and half-dragged me there. "I'll go downstairs and get what I need, and then you and I will stay in this chamber until you're well again."

I collapsed on the bed and catalogued my ills, so sudden and severe. Headache, fever, vomiting. They could be any random summer sickness, but like the queen's illness the previous autumn, I knew them for something worse: there were pockets of soreness under my arms, and a similar feeling in my groin.

Plague.

My hand was heavy as I felt the swellings, and a wave of dread, worse than the nausea, rolled over me. Few survived the plague, and those who did were often marked by black streaks on their skin and scars from the lancing of boils. If I lived, what beauty I had would be gone. I thought of Mary Sidney, who still had a good life with her many children, but I did not wish to frighten my son with any disfigurement of the face he knew best.

My mind clung to Ralph. Such a vital, energetic boy, a fascinating combination of the two of us, yet wholly his own small person. I could not bear the thought of him growing up without me. As much as I wanted to lean on Robin's strength, I could not permit him into this death-chamber.

It was too much. I lay back against the pillows, tears leaking from the corners of my eyes. We had done everything last year to keep me safe from smallpox, and now I was sick with something far worse.

The day passed in chills and fever. Alice built up the fire and made me sit as close to the flames as I could bear, all while forcing me to drink cup after cup of ale. "You need to sweat it out," she said.

"How do you know that?" The ale tasted vile.

"Grandmother's tales," she said. "She talked of an outbreak when I was small."

A door banged below and footsteps thundered unevenly up the stairs. Before he reached the landing, Robin was calling my name.

"He can't come in," I said. "Lock the door if you must."

"Yes, mistress."

The door rattled, then jarred in the frame as he pounded on it. "Margaery!"

My head swam, but with Alice's help I got up, leaning against the panel to which he had just applied his fist. "You cannot be here."

"I am here," he said. "I am here, and I will not leave you."

The words I had wanted him to say, said at exactly the wrong time. I held back sobs which might cause him to break down the door. "Listen to me," I said, coming as close as I dared. "You must take Ralph and keep away from here until Alice sends for you. Take Susan and her girl, too."

He was silent, and I imagined him raking his fingers through his hair while he considered my words. "I need to be with you."

I shook my head, though he could not see it. "Get Ralph out of the house, Robin, and stay with him. He needs one of us alive, you said it yourself. Promise me."

There was a long silence. "I promise," he said, his voice ragged. "If anything happens—and I pray God it will not—I will give him everything you would want for him, and more."

"That is all I need." It was becoming difficult to force out words. "Stay well, husband."

"Be strong, my darling girl."

Those were the last words I heard for some time, as the fever overtook me again. Alice bundled me into bed, and kept me swaddled like a babe as I froze and burned, sweated and shook.

The buboes under my arms swelled until I cried with the pain of them. "I can't bear it, Alice. You must cut them."

Alice had a deep notch between her brows. "I'm afraid to. What if I make you worse?"

Could I *be* worse? My head clanged like Ralph banging a kettle, and my fever was so high I felt disconnected from my body. "Do it," I said weakly. "It cannot be worse than this."

She fetched a wad of linens she'd stripped from the bed, and put it under my shoulder. "I'll fetch a knife."

"No." I tried to gesture, but my hand fell back. "My knife...in the chest."

Alice understood, and went to the chest where my things were kept. She found my small blade, drawing it from its sheath and looking at it. "I don't think I can do it."

"You must." I would do it myself, if I could only lift my head from the pillow.

She looked from me to the door, the knife hanging loose in her hand. "It will kill you," she said and burst into tears. "I will not tell the master I've killed you."

"Please…" The darkness closed in again.

I awoke and found myself unable to move. A sickening smell filled the air, and I forced my eyes open. My arms were stretched over my head, my wrists loosely tied to the bedposts. "Alice? What is this?"

She approached, her expression determined. "It's stewed onions. Granny said they drew out the pestilence." Her lower lip protruded. "I will not cut you."

Turning my head slightly, I could see them, masses of slimy brown, their juices running down my bare skin. "The feather bed will be ruined."

Alice passed a wet cloth over my face and neck. "That is the least of your worries. How do you feel?"

I tried to move. "Like a game bird, trussed for roasting."

She loosened the ties, and I brought my arms down, trying not to touch the onions. The pressure was still there, but it was no worse.

"What day is it?"

"I believe it's Tuesday," she said. "It's the fifth day."

Robin must be so worried. How did he explain my absence to Ralph? "Do you know where they are?" My voice was faint.

"He went to court with Sir Edward," she said. "I've been giving word twice a day—he sends a messenger to the hall, and I call down to him."

"Look after them," I said. "Robin swears he will do right by our boy, but he needs guidance. Stay with him, Alice."

"Stop your nonsense," she said brusquely. "You'll be able to guide him yourself, soon enough. They say with the plague it's end or mend, and you've not ended." She smoothed my hair and put another cloth on my forehead. I had never felt anything so soothing.

I thought we continued to speak, but when I looked up again, the light was different and she was across the room, her face in her hands. "What is it? Is it Ralph?"

She looked up, dragging her sleeve across her face. "No, mistress." Her voice was flat. "I was just praying."

I squinted across the chamber. She had been crying. "Don't weep," I said. "I feel better, I swear."

"Well, that is good news, then." She managed a smile, and came over to lay her hand on my forehead. "You are cooler."

I closed my eyes. I felt better, but speech was exhausting. Wondering why she cried was even more so.

Later—and it could have been days, or only hours—I awoke to find Robin beside me, his chair pulled close to the bed. His eyes were closed, and he was snoring.

I watched him, understanding that if Alice had allowed him in, I must be better. I tentatively turned my head, waiting for the sharp pains in my neck. Both the pains and the dizziness were gone, only a deep exhaustion remaining.

Robin looked as weary as I felt. His cheeks were hollow, and there were dull shadows beneath his eyes. He wore nothing but a shirt and hose, and his sleeves were folded back to reveal freckled forearms, surprisingly muscled by decades of writing.

"Husband."

His eyes flew open and an expression crossed his face such that I would never again doubt his love for me. "Margaery," he said, his voice breaking, "are you yourself?"

"I believe so," I said. "Are you?"

"I've been worried about you." He smiled faintly, but there was a deep sorrow within him. "And there has been other sickness in the house."

I sat up and the dizziness returned, slamming me back against the pillows. "Is it Ralph? I thought he was safe?"

His smile then was genuine. "Our boy is well," he said. "I have not left him for an instant, until Alice sent word you were recovered enough to visit."

"Then who?"

Robin raised his eyes to mine. "Sebastian. He is dead, and I could not be with him."

Chapter 51

SEBASTIAN. THAT EXPLAINED ALICE'S tears. They had never, so far as I knew, spoken of their feelings, but there was a well of affection between them nonetheless. She would feel his loss sorely.

It would be worse for Robin. He and Sebastian had been inseparable for a quarter-century, more friends than master-servant. Even discounting their friendship, how would Robin cope without Seb? Dressing, eating, drinking, working. He was there for every moment of my husband's day, short of our time in bed, and even then he was within calling distance. Seb undoubtedly knew as many court secrets as Robin and Ned combined. He would be irreplaceable.

I considered all this from my seat by the fire, where I had moved as soon as Alice judged me strong enough.

"Here is the medicine you need," she said from the door.

I looked up. She held my squirming son, and when I raised my arms, she gave him to me. The tears I was unable to shed for Sebastian streamed down my cheeks at my first contact with Ralph.

At fourteen months, he was more boy than baby, a solid, strong-willed mass of interests and passions. "Mama?" His tone was conversational

I kissed the top of his flaming head. "I'm here, darling."

He stayed with me, quite calmly, until it was time to nurse. When Susan took him away, I made myself get up and walk to the window.

Alice was there immediately. "You should not tax yourself." I looked at her, saw the hidden grief, the second man of her heart lost to sickness.

"*You* should rest," I said gently. "You have worn yourself out."

She shook her head. "I am better busy. I am not ready to think."

I wondered when my husband would allow himself to think of his loss, and that he could not be with Sebastian because I had made him promise to stay with our son.

Robin returned in the afternoon. "The queen has determined to go to Windsor," he said. "The court will begin the move on Friday."

"It's for the best," I said. "The air is no doubt less noxious in the country."

I waited for the inevitable. The conjugal lodgings at Windsor were not set up for families, and the queen, fearing contagion even more since the smallpox, would not allow people to live outside the castle. I resigned myself to months without my husband.

"I shall have to attend her," he said, "but not until after I have delivered you to Winterset."

"Winterset!" If we had to be separated for a significant period, I would rather be in our home than in London. "Ralph will like that." I tried to conceal my own excitement. "Will you stay on, or must you return immediately?"

He cupped my cheek with ink-stained fingers. "We will see." Robin looked at me, unfathomable pain in his eyes. "I will be frank, Margaery. I do not know if I am fit company."

I took his hand. "Then you will stay in your library, and perhaps Anselm can work the same miracle for you as he did for me."

"Perhaps." Robin's eyes filled, and he put his head against my shoulder and sobbed, as artlessly as a child.

Fatigue kept me abed most mornings, and even after I was up, it dragged at my heels. I found myself sitting for long stretches of the day, wondering when I would be able to manage the journey north.

Robin returned early one afternoon, his expression grim. "We will leave tomorrow," he said. "We must get away."

"If you think it best." I did not have the energy to argue.

"It is not what I think," he said. "They are about to impose a forty-day isolation on plague victims. I will not have you and Ralph trapped in London for so long."

There was something else. His expression was more than urgent; there was a sadness—a new sadness—behind it. "What are you not telling me?"

"It's Nell Hawkins." He sighed, looking at the floor. "I just heard today. She and her husband are dead. And their boy."

I gasped. My sweet friend, who had never wanted anything more than her handsome, loving husband, and a house full of children. "What of the baby?"

"Alive," he told me, "but with no one to care for her but a

few servants. A letter has been sent to Kelton, and another to the Fremantles."

The poor mite. Pretty, sweet-tempered Jane was a few months younger than Ralph. "What about his family? Don't they want her?"

"Apparently not." Robin rested his hands on my shoulders. "His brother is the heir now. They must put all their efforts behind him."

"It's not fair." If she had been John Curtis, rather than Jane, there would have been a family brawl over her keeping, but a girl was nothing but an expense. At least she would have a good home with Nell's sister.

It occurred to me that both Elizabeth Fremantle and Lord Kelton lived in Yorkshire. "Could we bring her with us?" I asked. "It would save them the journey, and we are heading north anyway."

"Are you strong enough to handle two children?"

I tilted my head back against his chest. "She should not be left alone with no family to protect her."

Thus it came about that when we departed, Alice, Susan, and I were in the coach with the children, while Robin rode alongside and Leon drove the baggage cart. We felt Sebastian's absence keenly; he had always organized our moves.

Our son missed him, too, asking for "Sebby" in a querulous tone until Robin's eyes filled with tears.

"Sebby went to sea," I told him, finally. "He took ship with Francis Drake to become an explorer."

It would make no sense to him, but I thought it was what Seb would have done, if he hadn't dedicated himself to Robin, and I preferred to think of him thus: aboard ship, the salt wind in his face, smiling into the future.

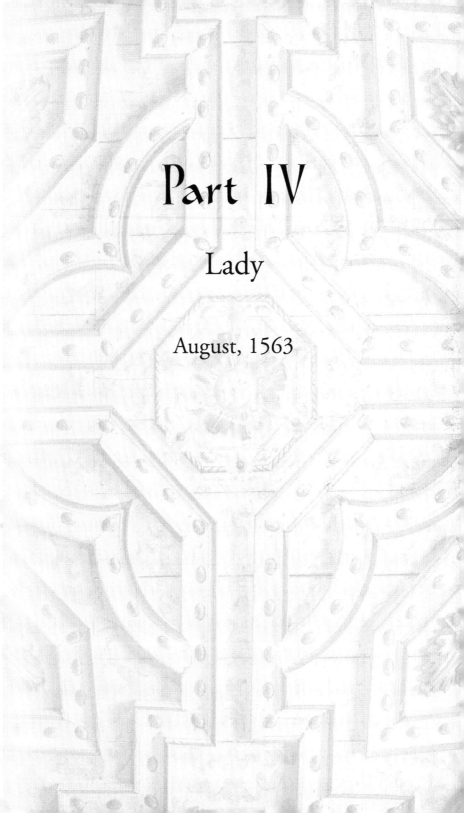

Part IV

Lady

August, 1563

Chapter 52

THREE YEARS AGO, I had been the one to flee our marriage; now it was Robin's turn. The loss of Sebastian had broken something inside him, and that break could not be mended by my will, nor by begging him to remain at Winterset. He needed activity, away from those who loved him most, until he was whole again.

Seb had come to Robin when he was new to the north, and they had grown into their lives together. According to Seb, Robin had saved his life, and taught him how to be a man outside the monasteries.

I could say the same for Sebastian. My husband was a kinder man, a softer man, because of Sebastian Black.

When Robin left, a week after delivering us to Winterset, I let him go without recrimination.

He would return, eventually. Not when he was released by the queen, but when he was able to live with himself again. I could not hold his retreat against him. He had suffered a body blow, and whether I liked it or not, Ralph and I were tied up in that loss.

During the day, I was able to put Robin from my mind and settle into the work of making Winterset a place worthy of our son's inheritance. I found the estate ledgers in the library and brought them into the hall, where I could examine them without disturbing Anselm's reading.

The years of listening to my grandfather stood me in good stead; I had a head for figures, and Fowler's tidy records needed little clarification to bring the estate to vivid life before my eyes. There were some debts, but nothing that could not be covered by sales of wool, grain, and livestock in the coming year, assuming everything went as planned.

I put an evening aside to meet with the steward, to explore what could be done to improve matters. If I was to stay here, without my husband, I would need occupation.

"It's not that it's run down," I said to Fowler. "It just seems to me, things could be done differently."

His craggy face split into a grin. "You have no idea how happy that makes me." Fowler looked down at his hands, splayed on the knees of his breeches. "The master cares about this place, but his care starts in his library and doesn't venture far outside." He glanced at me. "Begging your pardon."

"My husband was not brought up to this," I said. "But he will not gainsay our plans—he knows his strengths. You will have to explain to me how things are done now, and what changes you believe are necessary." I had my own ideas, but I wanted to listen to his first.

Fowler looked as though I had given him a gift. "There are a few things which should be done before any improvements are commenced." He explained some of the workers' cottages had fallen into disrepair. "The men can do the work themselves," he said, "and once they've completed them, you could take on a few more families. It would be helpful, with the harvest."

We decided also to clear a small wood beyond the pastures and expand the grazing. It was not too late for the rams to be let in with the unbred ewes; in early spring, if all went well, we could come close to doubling our flock.

"We should look into a different buyer for the wool," Fowler said. "We've not gotten the best price from Sayre in the past few years."

"Then why do we continue to sell to him?" I had noted the increased wool yield, year after year, and wondered at the infinitesimal increase in profit.

He shrugged. "Habit, and not being able to discuss it proper with Master Lewis, him not being here."

I folded my hands. "Well, you've discussed it with me, and you have my permission to look for another buyer, or to see if Master Sayre would prefer to adjust his offer and not lose out on our excellent wool."

"As you say, mistress." Fowler ducked his head. "Will that be all for the day?"

"Almost." I glanced at the book again. "I would like one of those cottages put aside for Leon and Susan," I said. "I think little Mary will not be their last youngling, and when Master Lewis returns, the presence of his own child in this house will be more than enough."

Being mistress of Winterset took more energy than I had early on, and after I kissed Ralph goodnight and had a final cup of ale with Anselm in the library, I was too exhausted to do more than say a quick prayer for Robin before falling into my own bed. The work was interesting, and I felt my brain stretching to accommodate new ways of thinking, and new methods of running my beloved home.

I had no wish to invade the library, but I could not continue to work in the hall, and my parlor was not set up to run the estate. I made do, stacking ledgers on the floor and piles of notes and receipts on my chair, anchored with my embroidery basket, but it was not a proper solution.

Returning from a morning ride, I saw Leon coming out of my parlor. "Is something wrong?"

"No, mistress. Anselm and I just thought you needed a better way to work." He opened the door, and I saw Grand-mère's writing desk centered at the window, and a straight chair on which to sit while I worked.

Thoughts of Winterset's future were the only things that helped when I ached with loneliness for Robin. Without him, and on his behalf, I threw myself into projects long-planned and unfinished. Mistress Dunham got her enlarged buttery and larder, along with a new brewhouse, set at a safe distance from the main house. A new privy was built and the old one filled in. Glass had come down in price, and I had all the remaining windows glazed, even the small ones in the attic; there was no reason for Winterset to have medieval drafts.

I even tracked down an artist to make new wall hangings, and to complete the painted ceiling I had envisioned when I first came home from France.

If Robin returned—when he returned—I wanted him to be proud of what had been done in his absence.

Harvest time came, without my husband. His brief letters satisfied me he was well enough to hold a pen, but I got no sense of how he truly fared. I wrote separately to Ned and was told only that Robin was working, and when he was fit to travel again, Ned would send him north.

When would that be? I did not want our son to forget his father.

The workers had grown accustomed to seeing me dressed as one of them when on horseback, but I resumed my woman's clothes as soon as I returned to the house. For all that I enjoyed the freedom of breeches, I had no desire to spend my life attired as a man, and I needed the workers to understand my position as mistress in Robin's absence.

Ralph thrived in his new environment. He attached himself to Fowler and followed him everywhere, staggering on chubby legs. Understanding he would now live outdoors, I breeched him early, folding his skirts away in case we were ever fortunate enough to have another child.

He was old enough to enjoy the Christmas festivities this year, and when Dickon was declared Lord of Misrule, my son took to his shoulders like the imp he was and refused to be separated from him for the entire festive night.

I had hoped Robin would come home for Christmas. His dislike of winter travel was plain, but we had been apart for almost five months now, and Ralph had stopped asking for him.

There was much to celebrate. The breeding project had been a success—in early March, the ewes began to bear, and Fowler and his men were in the byre and the sheep pens almost every night. Lambing seemed mostly to happen in the coldest, darkest hours, but if a birth occurred in daylight, I made certain Ralph and I were there.

Bundled against the cold, we watched, fascinated as the ewe, her fleece long and winter-matted, labored with a focus I recognized, producing a spindly-legged lamb which nonetheless staggered direct to the teat. In the older sheep, a second lamb would often follow the first. I swelled with pride at what Fowler and I had achieved.

"What do you think?" I said to Ralph's ear, the only bit of him visible besides his very red nose. "Do you like the lambs?"

He nodded vigorously, rubbing his stomach.

Fowler laughed so hard he had to hold onto the lambing pen, and the ewe bleated annoyance. "We'll leave you to it." I hid my own laughter and carried Ralph back to the warm house.

In May, Elizabeth Fremantle brought little Jane for a visit. She and Ralph remembered each other, and they ran off hand-in-hand toward the stables, followed by Jane's nurse.

"They'll be fine," I said to Elizabeth. "Ralph has the stable boys very well trained."

"I wish Jane was as easy with me," she said. "My boys tease her and she does nothing but cry."

We were seated on the bench near the front door, able to enjoy the air and keep an eye on the children at the same time. I was pleased she could see my fine house, with its gardens just beginning to bloom, and the fragrant rosemary hedge on the other side of the entrance.

"Could one of your sisters take her?" I felt bad for the sweet child who looked so like her mother. "Or your older brother?"

She shook her head. "They've all families of their own—as do I, but because I live closest to Father, I was chosen." Elizabeth pleated the fine blue fabric of her skirt. "She will leave soon. He has decided to bring her up himself."

I tried to imagine the frightening Lord Kelton with such a tiny sprite, and somehow, I could. Her mother had, after all, been his darling. "She may keep him young."

"He wants to have Nell over again." There was a bitter edge to Elizabeth's words. "May he have better luck this time."

Mistress Dunham brought out a small table and a plate of suckets, and we whiled away an hour in the sun. When it came time for Elizabeth to leave, I embraced her and kissed little Jane. "Please," I said to her, "tell your father we would be happy to have her at any time."

"He will be pleased," she said. "He liked you for your care of Nell."

Ralph came to sit on the bench beside me, his face and hands covered with dirt from the stable yard.

"Can you never stay clean?" I asked, rubbing at a smudge on his nose. "You look like you belong in a stall."

"Why clean?" He spiked his fingers through his hair and for a moment I saw his father.

He hopped down and struck out for the stable again, and I snatched his shirt before he could get away. "We're going in."

"More company?"

"No, no more company today." I tweaked a curl over his eye. "But I'm giving you over to Susan, so she can clean you."

Twisting away, he pointed, and I followed his finger until I saw a rider on a gray horse, coming slowly along the coast road.

My heart thudded in my chest. "Alice!"

The door opened. "Yes, mistress?"

I picked Ralph up under his arms and handed him over. "Tell Mistress Dunham. Tell everyone. The master's coming home."

Chapter 53

By the time Robin reached the gate, Anselm and the household servants had gathered in the yard. Remembering our first reunion in this house, and how Grand-mère held me back, I took a deep breath and ran straight toward him.

He swung down from Plato and landed hard, staggering a bit, but then he caught me up and everything was right. "You saw me coming," he said against my neck.

"Your son spotted you." I looked over my shoulder and saw Ralph straining in Susan's arms. I nodded, and she set him on the ground. He took off across the cobbles until he reached us, wrapping his arms around one of Robin's high, dusty boots.

"Papa?" he asked, looking up suspiciously. "You love Mama?"

Robin threw his head back. "I do indeed, young man." He lowered himself until he was eye-level with his son. "I'm sorry I've been away so long, but I've brought you something."

"What?" His eyes were wide. "Where is?"

"In my saddle bag, and you'll have it as soon as I finish kissing your mother." Keeping one hand on Ralph's head, Robin stood slowly and turned to me. "I don't think I've quite finished telling *you* how sorry I am that I've been away so long."

Knowing I would have him to myself later, I helped Mistress Dunham prepare supper while Robin and Anselm retreated to his library. I hoped he would like the surprise I had left for him—an arrangement of Sebastian's maps, pinned to the wall by his desk.

Ralph buzzed about like a bee, demanding to see his father, asking about his gift, until I finally took him aside. "You'll get your gift," I said, "and you'll see your father, but Ralph, there's one thing you must understand."

"What?" He squirmed, seeing Robin's bag by the door.

"When your papa is with Grandfather"—he had taken to calling Anselm by that name on his own—"he mustn't be disturbed. Especially when they're in the library."

"The book room." His lip came out. "Susan says no."

I stroked his cheek. "Not on your own, not yet. But someday your papa will show you the book room."

"Like you and the sheep?" He considered that: an indoor parent, and an outdoor one. It was as good a division as any, I supposed.

"Just like that."

I allowed him to knock at the door and announce that supper was ready, and was surprised to see Robin emerge holding his son in his arms. He looked uncomfortable, but he was trying, and something inside me relaxed at the sight of them.

"Anselm has been telling me you've transformed the place in my absence," he said, depositing Ralph on his high stool near Susan. "I'll have a good look tomorrow, when I can face getting on Plato again."

"You stay?" Ralph asked, his mouth full of pottage. Susan swatted his hand and he narrowed his eyes at her, but finished chewing and put the question again. "You stay, Papa?"

It was the same question I wanted to ask, and I silently thanked my son for his lack of tact, if not his table manners.

"For a while." He turned to me. "Is there anything left for me to do here?"

"Teach your son to be a man?" I offered. "The rest is under control."

Ralph's present was a short wooden sword, which made him happy beyond words. He ran about, poking at the wall hangings until Susan finally dragged him off, hours later than his usual bedtime.

We retired soon after, going up the steps together to the chamber that had been so empty without him. Alice had gone to her own room, but she'd put out my best gown and left a bottle of wine and two glasses on the table.

"As if I'd never left." He looked around. "This much has not changed."

"That's because it's been waiting for you," I said. "As I have."

We sat at the table, getting reacquainted after so many months apart. I felt the same draw as before, but there was an invisible barrier around him that would need to be breached.

"I wasn't certain you would come back." I sipped my wine and watched him.

He exhaled. "Losing Seb…it was like being thrown by a horse. It took my wind and a good bit of my heart. I would have come sooner, but I didn't want to come to you unless I could be fully here."

"I understand." I missed Seb, too. "Have you found someone else? I know he cannot be replaced, but—"

"No," he said. "I've used Ned's man while in London, but I haven't been able to bring myself to look for anyone."

We fell silent, watching the dying fire. "Leon could do it," I suggested. "Or perhaps Dickon could be trained up. He's a bright boy."

"That's a thought." He said no more about it, stretching his feet toward the hearth and closing his eyes. "Would I insult you if I said I wanted to take you to bed now?"

"Not at all."

"Do you want to return to London?" I rested my head on his chest, which was covered, as was mine, with a light coating of sweat from our loving. We had not managed it the night before, but we woke early and made up for the lack.

"Do I want to? No." He combed his fingers through my hair. "Must I? Yes."

It was what I had expected. "Why?"

I could feel his sigh all the way through him. "Things with Scotland are still too unsettled. I'm needed, Margaery. I wish I weren't."

The morning light streamed through the window. I could hear the muffled hush of the waves. "When will you leave?"

His hand stilled. "I'd like you to come with me," he said. "You and Ralph. I know it's not the best place for him, but I don't want to be apart any longer."

I leaned over him, my breasts brushing his chest. "I don't want to be apart, either, and I want Ralph to know his father. He can't, if we stay here."

The worry in his eyes eased. "Thank you." He tweaked my chin in his fingers and I stretched to kiss him. "There is work to be done, but I don't believe I can do it without you there." One corner of his mouth turned up. "I need you."

That was all I needed to hear. "Then you shall have me," I said. "I'll have Alice start packing after breakfast. We can leave by Thursday, if that suits you."

The work I had done with Fowler over the last months had put Winterset on a stronger footing; I did not worry about leaving matters in his hands. He'd acquired a promising young man named Colin to assist him in the management of the estate, and they, along with Anselm, promised regular progress reports.

We left in the early morning. I hadn't expected to see anyone other than Fowler and Anselm, but when we emerged from the house, the servants, the estate workers, and their families lined the courtyard, all the way to the gate—nearly sixty people, the entire Winterset community.

"They've come to say farewell," Fowler said.

I put my hand over my heart and curtsied, showing my gratitude in the only way I knew how. Then Dickon handed me up into the coach, and we left our home again.

Epilogue

July, 1565

THE COUNCIL MEETING CONTINUED all afternoon. Every so often, the privy chamber doors would open and a man would scuttle in or out, averting his eyes from the curious onlookers. Robin had been in there for hours, and had not come out once. Finally, near suppertime, Will Hawkins slipped out and arrowed through the presence chamber without stopping to speak to anyone.

I edged around the room, dodging bored courtiers and sulky maids, and met him at the entry door. "What's going on in there?"

He looked over his shoulder, but the privy chamber doors had closed again. "Come outside."

I followed him into the hall, sidestepping the guard, who also looked bored.

"News from Scotland." He looked exhausted.

More than a year had passed since we'd returned from Winterset. Mary had issued a final refusal of Robert Dudley, simultaneous to his own refusal of the match, and the Scots had been quiet since. Cecil worried about the Scottish queen, but Cecil would worry about the Scottish queen until one or both of them were dead. I'd heard nothing that led me to believe there was any new unrest.

"What is it?"

Will rubbed his hands over his face. "She has married Lord Darnley." He gave me a quick smile. "I'm sorry, Mistress Margaery, I must go."

Henry Stuart, Lord Darnley, was English. I tried to decipher why this union would cause a meeting of such length and contentiousness; Cecil wanted Mary to marry an Englishman, so her husband's loyalties would be known. Then I heard Robin's dry voice, telling me to look at the match from all angles, and I understood why the council still raged.

Darnley was the son of Margaret Douglas, and through her, he was related to both Elizabeth and Mary. While certainly English, he was also obstinately Catholic, and his claim to the English throne was nearly as good as that of his new wife.

If Catholics wanted a reason to overthrow Elizabeth, it had just been given the crown matrimonial over the northern border.

Robin did not arrive until after ten. I had not been far ahead of him. On rainy nights such as this, I missed the convenience of palace lodgings, but when I walked into Ned's house and was greeted by silence, it was worth the journey from Whitehall.

The steward took my wet things. "You're the first one back, Mistress Lewis. Shall I send wine to your chamber?"

I stopped, my hand on the rail. "Thank you, Gibbon, and if there is anything left—cold meat and bread will do—have it sent up when my husband returns."

When the meeting ended, the queen was in a vile temper and refused to eat, and thus the food prepared for her had been set out in the hall instead. None of her women had a chance to snatch a bite before the platters disappeared, and none were willing to sneak out when Elizabeth was in such a state. While I was not an official waiting-woman, on the days when I visited the privy chambers, I behaved as one, and had missed my supper along with the rest.

Mistress Ashley had recently died. Her calming presence was sorely missed, for although Blanche Parry had been with the queen equally long, her attempts to pacify Elizabeth often ended in shouting.

The door to our chamber was open, and when I entered, resting my palm for a moment against the jamb, Alice appeared. "You're late." She hurried to my side. "Is the master back as well?"

"No." I sighed with relief under her capable hands. "He's still there, and so is Sir Edward. It looks to be a long night."

She began to unlace me. "Is there trouble?"

I unpinned my cuffs and fore-sleeves, tossing them onto the chest. Normally I tried to make her job easier, but I was limp with exhaustion, and I wanted to check on Ralph before Robin got in.

"When is there not?" As the pins were drawn from my hair, I massaged my scalp with my fingertips. "The Scottish queen has married, and the English queen is not happy about it."

Alice put my gown aside. "I'm sure there's a crowd of men who aren't happy, either, because it's their job to know what's best for women."

"And I'm sure my husband is one of them." I closed my eyes as she dealt with the rest of my costume, only opening them when she said, "Raise your arms."

I did, and my shift was removed and replaced with a lightweight embroidered nightdress. I shrugged into a loose gown, and with my hair still down, took a candle into the nursery to gaze at my son.

He was asleep in his cot, the cradle my father had made standing sentinel in the corner, too small for him now. Susan and Mary slept in the trundle alongside, and I stepped carefully past them, my hand curled around the flame so as not to wake the three sleepers.

Ralph slept as hard as he played, his fists clenched, his snores surprisingly adult. His eyes weren't just closed, but squeezed shut. He had more energy than I could cope with, and I understood why many ladies kept their offspring in the country—for the sake of their own and their children's sanity. Ralph could not stay penned up in London for much longer, but I was not ready to send him away.

I watched him until I heard Robin's step on the stairs, then I retreated to our chamber and poured the wine.

His face resembled Will's earlier, pale and drawn, worn down by a day of Elizabethan drama.

I handed him the glass before he could even greet me. "You look like you need this."

He downed it in one gulp, then squeezed his eyes shut, looking uncannily like his son. "I don't know who is worse," he said hoarsely, "Cecil or that woman."

Having spent more than twelve hours with that woman, I had my own opinions. I unbuttoned his doublet and pulled it from his shoulders. "They deserve each other."

His smile was faint. "They do. As do Mary and Darnley."

Beneath the rain-wet doublet, his shirt was soaked with sweat. "Go and get out of that," I said. "A cold supper will be up soon."

"That sounds wonderful." He leaned on the table so hard it creaked. "We never got around to eating."

When would he give in and use a stick? It wouldn't make him look any older than limping and propping himself on furniture. Robin tried not to draw attention to his age, but he couldn't conceal he was in pain most of the time.

While he undressed, Leon set up a repast on the table: cold sliced beef, a small meat pie, a half-loaf of manchet with an accompanying wedge of cheese, and a bowl of peaches.

"Thank you, Leon. Has Sir Edward returned?"

"Yes, mistress. The gentlemen came in together."

I looked past him to the bedchamber wall, where Robin's shadow slowly stripped off its clothes. "If Sir Edward asks, we retired early."

He bowed. "Yes, mistress."

The door closed, and we were alone. I went to fetch Robin. He had changed into a fresh shirt but had gotten no further, sitting on the edge of the bed.

I pulled myself up beside him. "What is it?

He shook himself, as if I'd woken him from a dream. "Just worn out," he said. "It's the same thing, day after day. The queen shouts, Cecil placates her, and then he spends the rest of the day trying to concoct a way to get her to do what he wants, while making her think it's her idea."

I put my hand over his. "And she spends the rest of the day raging at her women, and trying to anticipate his plans so she can thwart them."

"They deserve each other." Robin echoed my earlier words. "Unless the Catholics rise against her, she'll never be as Protestant as he wishes, and all her fine words to the contrary, she'll never marry."

Sliding off the bed, I led him to the table. "I'm just glad Mary didn't accept the Earl of Leicester." The idea of Elizabeth without Robert Dudley was not to be borne.

"Dudley was given the earldom to make him worthy of her—he got what he wanted." Robin propped his leg up on a low stool. "He'd not give it back at sword point."

Nor should he; for all his family's misdeeds, and even his own questionable behavior, Dudley had earned his place on the council, as well as his title. "He was too old for Mary, as Darnley is too young."

"Age does not matter with royal marriages." Robin loaded his plate. "It's almost as if she made the match to thwart Cecil's plans."

A rumble of thunder hid the laugh that bubbled up. "You know the Scottish queen." I appealed to him. "Do you think she would marry to please anyone but herself?"

"No." He pinched the bridge of his nose. "No more than Elizabeth would."

"Then why do men keep making plans for women's lives, and being confounded when we don't fall into line?"

He laughed weakly. "I don't know. I'm as guilty of it as Cecil."

I had known Mary Stuart, as much as she allowed herself to be known. "She's in love."

"Do you think so?"

"She understands his usefulness as a dynastic match, but Mary is as romantic as Nell was. I'm sure he wooed her with pretty speeches—in French, since English is a barbarous tongue."

There were no sounds but the rain against the shuttered casements, and the continued faraway rumbling. "Darnley is the barbarian," Robin said. "The lad spent a long stretch of time in France. It was no doubt a selling point to his new wife, but ambassadors gossip, and ours had nothing good to say about him."

Whatever the gossip was, I hoped it was wrong. I liked Mary; she was a kinder woman than Elizabeth, and I would have been happy to stay and serve her, had the situation been different.

"He's a drinker," Robin said. "And not like this." He waved his arm at the bottle on our table. "Darnley drinks as a vocation, and when he is deep in his cups, he's not kind." His lip curled. "He has his mother's temperament."

I'd met Lady Lennox several times, and hoped never to meet her again. She had a core of ice inside her, and looked at everyone as if calculating their potential use. "I hope not," I said. "I would like to think he loves her."

Robin drained his glass. "Another rumor is he was quite the profligate in Paris."

"What does that mean? He's had lovers?" Darnley was only seventeen, but a young man as pretty as he would undoubtedly attract his share of admirers.

"Yes. Both male and female." Robin's eyes were hooded, perhaps thinking of his own past. "It's not the best recommendation for a happy marriage."

"I don't know," I said. "I think we're happy enough."

He ducked his head. "Darnley has bedded more people in his short life than I've even considered in my much longer one. And you were warned—I do not believe Mary was."

I let him eat, and turned over in my mind the idea that had come to me. "I was thinking…when Will told me about the marriage, I looked at it from all sides, like you said. What if the Darnley match was promoted to make certain the Catholics did rise?"

Robin's knife stopped halfway to his mouth. "Did Will say that?"

"He didn't even want to be seen talking to me." I cut a slice of cheese and nibbled the edge. "It just makes sense." I thought of something I'd seen as the council finally left. "You were already gone, but when the others came out of the privy chamber, the Earl of Leicester winked at Master Cecil."

He threw down his knife, and it clattered off the plate and onto the hearth. "I've been wondering about those two—Cecil can't abide Leicester on a good day, and yet they've had much to say to each other lately. Ned told me Leicester was seen coming out of Cecil House early yesterday."

I slid my knife over for him to use. "Do you think the news from Scotland arrived sooner than reported?"

He cut a bit of the beef, brought it to his mouth, chewed reflectively. "That's my guess. At some point the truth will be known, but by then Cecil will have another plot, and another." He sighed, and took another sip of wine. "It makes me tired."

How many nights had we spent like this? Eating and drinking far too late, talking about the lives of our betters as if we hadn't our own lives to live—such as we could in the tiny corners of time allotted to us. Ralph would be grown before we knew it, and would know his parents only as the faces who peered in at him in the mornings before disappearing for the rest of the day. I thought of my own childhood and the vow I had made to my son.

"Robin, what do you think about returning to Winterset?"

His eyes brightened, almost balancing the dark circles beneath. "Nothing would make me happier." His brow furrowed. "There will be no time in the autumn, I'm afraid. And Christmas will be impossible. Winter travel is unpleasant, and even more so with a child."

"So that means?" I folded my hands on the table, waiting.

"Spring?" His smile was crooked. "I know that's not what you want."

I reached for his hand, placing it on my midsection. "There will be another child to transport by then."

It took a moment for the news to sink in, but then he bounded from the chair and swept me into his arms. "Are you sure?" he asked, his face buried in my hair.

"I thought perhaps my husband who never misses anything would have noticed by now."

His hand circled the barely perceptible curve of our second child, which had been well concealed under flowing nightdresses and loose gowns. "You should go, even if I can't. You and Ralph. Alice, Susan, and her girl. I'll try to come for Christmas. Damn, I wish Seb was here."

I sat again, crossing my arms over my swollen breasts. He'd been too busy these last weeks to notice even that difference. "I'm not going without you."

"But I have work to do." His eyes moved to the chest across the room, where a pile of papers from Cecil's offices awaited his attention.

"You've a family, as well." I blinked back tears. "Do you want to be like Ned, seeing your wife once a year, barely acquainted with your children? What happened to the life you promised me?"

"I don't want to be Ned." He passed a hand over his eyes. "You have no idea how much I want that life, Margaery." He curled a lock of my hair around his finger. "What we've made together has been unexpected in every way."

I reached up to clasp his hand. "It was not what I expected either, but it's a good life."

"All the glitter of the court does not hold a candle to it." Twisting my hair into a braid, he said, "I'll speak to Cecil in the morning and tell him I'm taking my wife home to Yorkshire, where I shall become a country gentleman with a large library and a small, but perfect family."

Could it be that easy to leave the court? As it turned out, it could. More families every day clamored to get a sister or daughter into the queen's graces, and I was not reliable, always jaunting off to Yorkshire or Scotland or wanting to spend time with my child.

It was more difficult for Robin, but with Ned's support and pleading his failing health—that nagging injury had never been so useful—Cecil granted his request. Despite his long history with the court, Robin had too many scruples to survive for long in this place, and I believe they both knew it.

The trip north was slower than ever before, loaded down as we were with furnishings, books, children, servants, and extra horses, and without Seb's excellent management. We arrived at Winterset at dusk, the light fading to lavender over the sea. The waves were a murmur as we climbed down from the coach, and from Whitby came the faint sound of bells.

I handed Ralph to Susan and turned to my husband, whose face bore an odd expression. "What is it?"

"Vespers," he said with a bemused smile. "I've always arrived home at vespers."

I shook my head, not understanding, and put my arms around his neck. "Are we home, Robin? Are we really home?"

He drew back, his eyes shining. "We are," he said and kissed me.

Leaning my head against his shoulder, I looked toward the house. Windows bloomed into light as the servants readied chambers for the rest of our lives. "Asking you to marry me was one of my better ideas."

THE POEM MARGAERY QUOTES to Edmund Morven, in
Chapter 20, translates as follows:

> *Within this tomb, which is a harsh, locked cell,*
> *Lies the green lover, the very worthy slave*
> *Whose noble heart, drunk with true, pure love,*
> *Losing its lady, cannot bear to live.*

—Jean LeMaire de Belges, *Épîtres de l'amant vert*

Author's Note

THIS BOOK EXISTS IN part because of the pandemic. I started writing *Lady, in Waiting* almost immediately after finishing *A Wider World*, because I wanted to see what happened next in the unconventional marriage I had created. (The best part of writing is telling yourself the story, and occasionally being surprised.)

My husband and I had planned a trip to Edinburgh for March, 2020. It was either travel or renovate the kitchen, and travel won, as it usually does.

Except this time, it didn't.

Two days before we were scheduled to leave, the world shut down, and British airways canceled our flight. I wasn't exactly upset—who really wanted to travel at that point?—but it had only recently occurred to me that I could do some research for *Lady, in Waiting* while in Edinburgh, and as an only child, I've never liked being thwarted.

The entire Mary Queen of Scots/Scotland plot line was spite-written because of my Covid-canceled vacation, but all in all, I think the book was better for it.

Another subplot which wasn't included in my original draft was Katherine Grey, one of the most tragic stories in an era that was bursting at the seams with tragedy. (It doesn't matter that she brought a lot of it on herself by being hardheaded; that shouldn't be enough to have you imprisoned and separated from your children until you die of tuberculosis while under house arrest). I could feel sympathy for Katherine while not actually liking her—and it turned out to be impossible to write about the early years of Elizabeth's reign from an insider's viewpoint without including her Grey cousins.

Considering I think of these books as a sort of "Tudor court from the point of view of ordinary people," there was a lot of royalty in this one—certainly more than the prior books. But of course many people in the Elizabeth's court was related to her in one way or another, so Margaery and Robin did stand out a bit.

But that brings me to Margaery and Robin. I wrote this book

because I wanted to explore what it was like to be married when you were never expecting to and don't particularly understand the rules. This applies, I think, to both of them, though Robin certainly had a longer time to get used to the idea of being alone. Finding their feet as a married couple would have been difficult to begin with, but throwing them head first into the court situation—in addition to Robin's near-miss at execution—and they aren't the same couple in England as they started out in France, in *A Wider World*. Which just added to the fun for me, and hopefully for you.

There's a personal aspect to this one, as well. I didn't get married until just before my forty-seventh birthday, and even though we'd lived together for a few years before we decided to get married, I wasn't sure what changes to expect, if any. Thankfully my husband is nothing like Robin, so I didn't have to indulge in as much worry as Margaery to get it right. We've figured it out, together. As have Margaery and Robin, in the end.

For anyone who's followed along this far, there will be at least one more book to this series: Will Hawkins is finally going to get his say. And the first thing he'd say is, "About time." But he's being very patient as I finish up the first book in my 1930s series, *My Sister's Child*, which will be out in October, 2022. After that, I can't guarantee his patience much longer, and his book, tentatively titled *The Son in Shadow*, will be out...well, sometime.

About the Author

As an only child, Karen Heenan learned at an early age that boredom was the ultimate enemy. Shortly after, she discovered perpetual motion and since then, she has rarely been seen holding still.

She lives in Lansdowne, PA, just outside Philadelphia, where she grows much of her own food, makes her own clothes, and generally confuses the neighbors. She is accompanied on her quest for self-sufficiency by a very patient husband and an ever-changing number of cats.

One constant: she is always writing her next book.

Other Books by Karen Heenan

The Tudor Court Series
Songbird – Book I
A Wider World – Book II
Lady, in Waiting – Book III

Follow her online:

Twitter: @karen_heenan
Facebook: @karenheenanwriter
Instagram: @karen.heenan

Or sign up for her mailing list on her website:
www.karenheenan.com

Printed in Great Britain
by Amazon

12572293R00217